HEADS YOU LOSE

GRIM & BEAST'S DUET - BOOK TWO

BEA PAIGE

GRITTY. ANGSTY. DANGEROUS ROMANCE

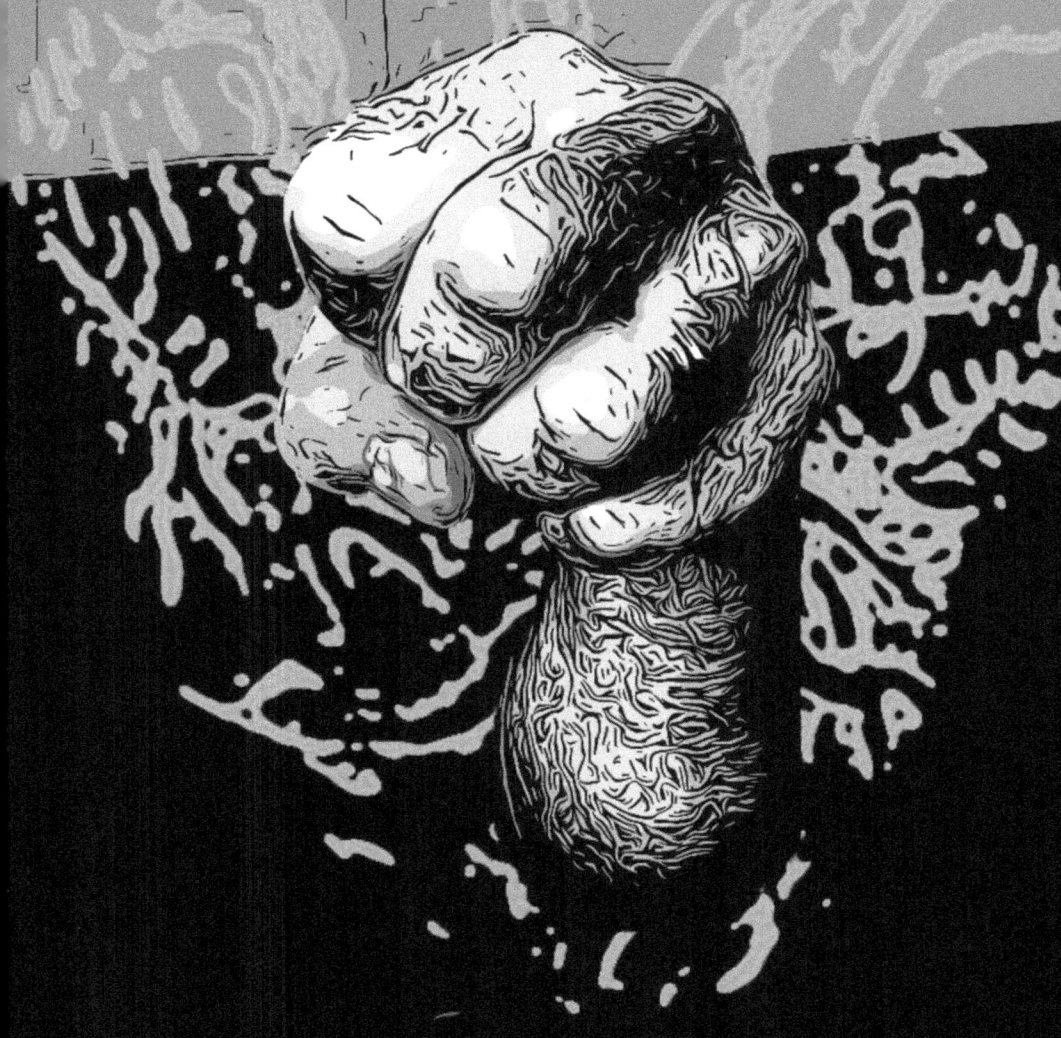

HEADS YOU LOSE

Cover Design by Everly Yours Cover Designs

Interior title page art by @StockeArtworks (find him on IG)

Photographer for image of 'Beast': Michelle Lancaster

Beast chapter model: Chase Cassels

CONTENTS

FOREWARD

Dear Reader,

BEFORE YOU START READING the final book in Grim & Beast's duet I wanted to give you a heads up about possible SPOILERS.

This duet was specifically written by popular demand for my readers who fell in love with Grim & Beast in my bestselling Academy of Stardom series, and for those hardcore readers who met Grim in the Academy of Misfits way back when in 2019!

In truth, I never thought this duet would blow up the way it has and whilst that is absolutely AMAZING because it has brought me new readers. *Hello new readers!* I realise that within the epilogue of this book there are some spoilers for my other series, namely the Academy of Misfits, the Academy of Stardom series and Their Obsession Duet (in particular), so I wanted to highlight that here.

Please note: YOU DO NOT HAVE TO READ THOSE SERIES TO ENJOY THIS DUET.

However, it became apparent when writing the second book of this duet that there was no way around potential spoilers for my other series. I have tried to keep them to an absolute minimum in case new readers wanted to go on to read those stories.

Truthfully, I couldn't write Grim & Beast's happily ever after without including some very popular characters in the epilogue scene. If you've read all my books you'll understand why that is.

All of my contemporary books so far are set in the same world, and Grim & Beast have been a huge part of that world since Academy of Misfits was released in 2019. It would've been an injustice if I didn't write the epilogue the way I did.

This duet has also introduced (to new readers) some characters who already have their own series - or will get their own upcoming series. I have listed them below.

This is also my recommended reading order if you were interested:

- **The Brothers Freed trilogy** (Reverse harem romance) - featuring Hudson Freed (Grim's best friend), Bryce and Max.
- **Academy of Misfits trilogy** (Reverse harem romance) - featuring Ford, Asia and her other 'bad boys'; Eastern, Camden and Sonny, as well as cameos from Grim and Hudson Freed.

- **Beyond the Horizon** (M/F age gap romance) - featuring Malakai and has cameos from Ford, Asia and her other 'bad boys'; Eastern, Camden, Sonny.
- **Finding Their Muse** (Reverse harem romance) - featuring Asia from Academy of Misfits.
- **Academy of Stardom series** (Reverse harem romance) - featuring Pen and her Breakers (mentioned in the epilogue of this book), with cameos of Grim and Beast, Hudson Freed, and Asia (off-page).
- **Their Obsession Duet** (Reverse harem romance) - featuring Christy and her men The Masks. This duet also has cameos from Grim, Beast, Ford and Camden. This duet also introduces The Deana-dhe.
- ** **Grim & Beast's Duet** (M/F romance) - prequel to all of the above stories, and includes cameos of characters from many of the books listed above with the exception of Finding Their Muse series.
- **The Deana-dhe Duet** (Reverse harem romance) This will feature Cyn aka 'Thirteen' who appears in Their Obsession Duet and her love interests, The Deana-Dhe, who cameo in Academy of Stardom and Their Obsession Duet.

I hope, if anything, this duet will make you curious about the other characters mentioned in this duet and you will want to read their love stories. What's better than reading about enduring love, heart-warming romance, knicker-melting sex and incredible friendships, right?

Whatever you choose to read, I hope you enjoy the stories. I write out of passion and love for these characters as well as a desire to give my readers what they want, I hope that shines through.

Much love,

Bea xoxo

CONTENT WARNING

Please note that this book includes the following: abusive parents, child abuse (off-page), murder, violence.

BOOK PLAYLIST

If you're familiar with my books you'll know that I love a book playlist. Each chapter of **Heads You Lose** has a song that I've selected which is specific to that chapter, but if you want the playlist in full, then you can find it on Spotify here: **Heads You Lose**

"He who helped you when you were in trouble ought not afterwards be despised by you."

— **Wilhelm Karl Grimm, Grimm's Fairy Tales**

To my readers. You asked, I delivered.
This duet is for you.
Bea Paige
xoxo

PROLOGUE

Mindfields

GRIM

Dear Iris

If there's one thing that I know with absolute certainty, it's this: love is complicated.

It's like a jigsaw puzzle with constantly moving pieces.

One day everything slots into place and you can see your future with the person you love ahead of you, and the next a piece goes missing and you'll never be whole again.

That's what it felt like the night I put a bullet in your dad.

A piece of me left with him. A bloody, jagged, broken piece.

It hurt.

Actually thinking about that night and the two lonely years that followed still hurts.

It's time we won't ever get back.

Living the life I do, that we do, time is precious.

It's a gift that many take for granted.

Do I regret shooting your dad?

That shouldn't be a difficult question to answer, but it is.

I regret hurting him. I regret not seeing the bigger picture.

In retrospect, it had to happen, and whilst I now know the real reason Beast killed Carter, at the time I didn't. I made a judgement call based on the facts I had, and truthfully no matter which way I look at it—and believe me I've re-lived that night over and over again—I always end up with the same answer.

I had to shoot him.

He killed Carter Davidson, the Ruler of Tales, and it wouldn't have mattered to anyone why he did it, just that he did. Beast broke his loyalty, a pledge that means everything in the world we live in. It didn't matter that he did it for me. It didn't matter that he did it for love.

It only mattered that he did.

And I also knew that if I didn't at least punish your dad, banish him for his actions, then I would've been seen as weak, and I understood the consequences of that.

So that night your dad bled for me, because of me.

But I bled too. God, how I bled.

Every day, for two long years, I mourned your dad as though he were dead, as though that bullet I fired into him had actually killed him.

Of course, it didn't.

And that isn't because I'm a terrible markswoman, it's because my love for him wouldn't allow me to end his life.

Fuck, I'm glad of that.

So, so glad.

Because as it turns out, your dad was always the hero of our story.

He was the hunter who took Snow White into the forest and let her go, carving out the heart of a pig in order to protect her from the real villain.

Your grandfather, Carter Davidson, was the villain.

The King was his accomplice.

But I wouldn't find that out until two years later when the man I still loved came back to tell me the truth.

So, my sweet baby girl, this is the second part to our twisted love story where the foundation of our love was made solid, unbreakable. This is the part when that missing piece of the puzzle was slotted back into place and we were both made whole again.

This is where the fairy tale becomes a reality.

This is where true love lives and ultimately ends up leading to you.

Max

CHAPTER ONE

Coldest Fire

BEAST

"People like you and me don't get to love..."

Those are the words that play on repeat inside my head as I stagger to my feet, blood seeping from the bullet wound just below my right shoulder and mixing with the drying blood already covering my body. I don't feel the pain from it. On the contrary, I'm numb to everything bar Kate's words.

People like you and me...

Don't get to love...

Don't. Get. To. Love...

She's right in a way, but not entirely.

It's true that the likes of us don't get to love *without fear.*

When you mix with the people we do, you gain enemies. Even the friends you think you have can turn against you on a penny if the price is right. Look at the King - he was 'friends' with Carter, but he took the opportunity to take him out the moment it was offered.

I took out my boss without a second thought.

Granted it was to protect the woman I love from her very own dad, but she doesn't know that, and I can't tell her.

Not yet, anyway.

But one thing I do know with absolute certainty is that I *do* get to love.

And I never thought that was possible for me.

Yeah, it's dangerous to love when it can be held against you, but it doesn't make it any less true. If I know anything about myself, it's this: I won't give up on our love. I refuse to, because what the fuck kind of man would I be to turn my back on something so fundamental to my very existence? A fucking pussy, that's what, and if there's one thing I'm not, it's a pussy.

I won't give up on our love. Not now, not ever.

Lifting my head, I meet Kate's hard stare with that promise burning in my veins.

But right now, no matter what I say, I know it won't make a difference.

Kate might love me, but Grim *has* to make a stand.

We both know that.

Shooting me was her only choice given the circumstances. Closing herself off, shutting down, was her only option.

I don't fight it, I can't fight it, but most importantly, I won't.

"Get. Out!" she snarls, the slightest flicker of regret in her eyes the only sign that beneath the pain, betrayal and disappointment, she still cares for me. That Kate is still there inside of Grim, who stands before me now. "I said, get the fuck out!"

I ignore Rodriguez's laugh. I ignore the King's smirk. I ignore Dom asking Kate to reconsider.

Instead, I lower my head in acquiesce. I raise my hand and place it over my heart, over the tattoo of her handprint embedded in my skin and vow to myself that I will find a way to protect her from afar, no matter what.

With one last look at Kate that I hope conveys all the love and affection I feel for her, I twist on my feet and stagger towards the exit, my gaze falling to Dom as I reach the door.

"Take care of her," I bite out through gritted teeth, fighting the darkness that's threatening to drag me under.

He nods. "You can count on me, Beast."

"FUCK ME SIDEWAYS!" Connall exclaims as I blink back the heavy fog of sleep and try to get my bearings.

"Where am I?" I ask, groaning as I try to sit up. Bright white light pricks my eyes like a bullet straight to my brain, and I lift my hand to my head, feeling my scalp where Derby whacked me, hissing when I feel the tender skin and the stitches there.

"Joey's place. He's fixed you up. Got you on a drip as soon as we arrived and gave you a couple pints of blood. There was a moment I thought we'd lose you."

"I'm hard to lose," I reply, giving him a weak smile. "But man, do I feel like shit."

"You look like shit too," Joey says, stepping into his makeshift operating theatre and giving me a toothy grin, antiseptic and the scent of car oil following him into the room. The amount of times I've been in the back of his garage getting fixed up is crazy, though to be fair, he keeps this room spotless. I mean, I haven't died of my injuries or a nasty infection yet. That's got to count for something, right?

"Thanks, old man," I reply, easing myself upright on the gurney. It creaks under my weight, and I feel every single bit of pain now that the adrenaline has worn off. Damn, I could chuck up. Swallowing back the queasiness, I wait for the room to stop spinning.

"What's the damage?" Connall asks, frowning as he stares at me.

I have a vague recollection of calling him for help, but other than that I remember nothing after stepping outside of Tales. He's a good man, one I can count on. *The fucking best.*

"Couple broken ribs, lots of bruising," Joey says, drawing some clear liquid from a vial into a needle. He pulls it free, presses the plunger to get rid of any air bubbles, then stabs me in the bicep with it, dispensing the liquid.

"I fucking hope that's painkillers," I say, trying to laugh but failing.

He nods, pulling the needle free before throwing it in the medical waste bin. "I got you, pal."

"What else?" Connall urges impatiently.

"The gash to his head was pretty fucking deep. I've sewn it up but you'll need to keep an eye on him over the next few days. He was concussed pretty badly, and there's always a danger of bleeding into the skull or swelling on the brain, but I think we're good where that's concerned."

Connall swipes a hand through his hair. "You *think?*"

"Well, short of getting Beast into hospital for a CT scan, I can't say any better than that."

"No hospitals," I say firmly. "Don't need the law on my arse for offing Carter-fucking-Davidson."

"You *what?!*" Connall exclaims, looking from me to Joey. "Did you know about this?"

"First I've heard," Joey says, casting a look my way. He knows I had my suspicions about Carter and his relationship with the King, so I imagine he's putting two and two together and coming up with a pretty good assumption about what went down.

"Jesus fuck, Beast! What the hell happened last night?"

"Last night?" I question. "How long have I been out?"

"Ten hours, but stop avoiding the fucking question. Spill. I need to know so that I can give the family a head's up. If a war is coming, they'll want to back you."

"There'll be no war. We're leaving."

"You and Grim?" Joey asks, even though I'm pretty fucking sure it's a trick question given she ain't here and he's not fucking stupid.

"No." I shake my head, ignoring the pain in my chest that isn't coming from my bullet wound, but is most definitely coming from my heart. I look at Connall. "When I said *we*, I was kind of hoping you'd come with me."

"Me? Go where, exactly? And what about Grim?"

"Kate was the one who shot me," I explain, leaning my head back against the gurney.

Joey whistles and Connall's mouth drops open in shock. "Wait, back the fuck up a minute," he says scraping a hand over his face. "You killed Carter Davidson and Grim shot you for it?"

"Pretty much," I reply.

"But she's in love with you," he counters.

"He's her *dad*, Connall."

"And clearly a prick given you killed him. You don't need to tell me what he's done for me to know you'd only ever off your boss because he's done something unforgivable. So, I'll ask again. Why would Grim shoot you when we all know that girl is head over heels in love with you?"

I heave out a sigh. "I wish I could say that was still true."

"Are you still in love with her?" Joey asks me pointedly.

"Yes."

"Jesus, Mary and Joseph! She shot you, Beast. Are you gone in the head?" Connall yells, shaking his head in frustration. "You know what, don't fucking answer that."

"So you're running?" Joey asks, moving the conversation along.

"It's complicated."

"So UN-complicate it for us because as much as I like Grim, I don't like the fact she nearly killed you and you're leaving like a beat-down dog."

"Number fucking one, I'm not a beat-down dog! Number fucking two, if she wanted me dead, I'd be dead. We were five feet apart, there is no way she would've missed from that distance. No fucking way," I say, pointing to my bandaged shoulder.

"He's right. Even if she wasn't a trained markswoman, which I understand that she is, there'd be no missing. So do you want to tell us *why* you killed Carter?" Joey asks.

"Because the cunt was going to use her to pay off his debts to the King."

"The *fuck* you say?!" Connall yells.

"You heard me. Carter got into a lot of trouble fucking his way around the escorts at The Crib Club, not to mention racking up a substantial gambling debt. I found out about his plans and made the King a better offer." Drawing in a deep breath to fend off the queasiness, I continue, "I would kill Carter if he backed the fuck off from Kate. He agreed, providing I stay quiet about his involvement, and he could remain a silent partner in Tales."

"The conniving bastard. Why didn't you just kill the cunt as well?" Connall asks.

"Because, as you well know, he's powerful. Much more powerful than me on my jack jones and far more powerful than one woman with a dead dad. She needs him... For now."

"And you're okay with that?" Joey asks this time.

"Of course I'm not, but equally she's backed into a corner. The King has a forty-eight percent share in Tales, he has a big army behind him and lots of fucking connections. She can't go up against him. This way she keeps his protection and a share in Tales whilst she establishes herself, and we find her a way out of this mess."

"And you believe he won't go back on his word the minute you're gone, and take her for himself?"

"I know he won't. Kate shooting me *proved* she's tough enough to run Tales. Besides, the King doesn't want a woman who'll fucking shoot him when he tries to raise a hand to her. Kate is too much of a handful, and one he ain't willing to mess with, thank fuck."

"So let me get this straight," Connall tries to rationalise, pacing up and down as he gets all the information straight in his head. "Carter was in debt so he goes to the King for a loan, the payment of which is his own fucking daughter and a share in Tales."

"Yes," I say, the pain in my head, shoulder and ribs easing a little now the medication is doing its job. Doesn't stop the ache in my heart though, or the constant feeling of nausea when I'm reminded of how Kate had looked at me as though I'd broken her heart as surely as her banishing me had broken mine. She had to do it, I don't fucking blame her for it, but it still fucking hurts.

"You find out and cut another deal with the King," Connall continues, "You kill Carter and the King backs off from Grim, acting as what, a silent partner in the club?"

"Precisely, he's also got connections with some of the best clubs in the world. He can bring in the fighters. She's smart, she'll grow the business, and won't throw it down the drain alongside whisky and stripper cum like her dad did."

Connall raises his brow at that. We both know Carter wasn't the type of man who cared about a woman's pleasure over his own.

"Turn of phrase," I mumble.

"So the King gets to sit back and reap the benefits whilst you take the blame for killing Carter, am I close?"

"I don't know about that part. That all depends on what happens now, but I'm not sticking around to find out whether Kate grasses on me. Though I wouldn't fucking blame her if she did."

"She won't," Joey says, sounding far more certain than I feel.

"And you know this how?" Connall asks.

"As you well know, there are rules we all live by,

unspoken ones, but ones we *all* obey. No fucking police. However Grim chooses to deal with this is up to her, but that girl has grown up in this life and she won't be pulling the police in unless they're bent and she's using them to cover her back."

"Fair point," Connall concedes, leaning back against the counter as he regards me. "And your big plan is to slope off with your tail between your legs, heart fucking broken, whilst there are a fuck load of snakes and sharks out there who are more than willing to take a bite out of your woman?"

"I'm not sloping off," I growl, "And I'm not willing to let *anyone* do any such thing. I trust Dom to keep an eye on her, and I believe the King will have her back whilst it suits him. Right now keeping her safe, and more importantly the *business* safe, is in his best interests."

"So what's the plan, and why do you want me tagging along for the ride?" Connall asks.

"For your charm and wit, of course," I reply, deadly fucking serious.

He laughs. I don't.

"Okay spill."

"I'm gonna find her an army of the best men and women money, *charm* and connections can buy, and you're going to help me."

"Well, when you put it like that, how can a man say no?" Connalls replies, grinning.

"And what do you need me to do?" Joey asks.

"Keep your ear to the ground and let me know the second you hear anything about the King that should concern me. Better still, ingratiate yourself with Grim. Get in on the business. She'll need someone to fix up her men after they've been in the cage. Make sure that man is you."

Joey nods. "You got it."

"So where to first?" Connall asks me as my eyes begin to drift shut.

"Italy. Romeo Ricci has some contacts out there I'd like to explore..."

"Italy it is," Connall replies as exhaustion and a heavy dose of painkiller pull me under.

CHAPTER TWO

Dreams

GRIM - TWO YEARS LATER

"You will arrive at your destination in two hundred and fifty yards," the Sat Nav drones as I crawl along the quiet street in Betws-y-Coed, Wales, looking for number thirty-five. It's been a long drive from London, and the picturesque village is a far cry from the hustle and bustle of my hometown. Instead of concrete high-rises, smog and litter, there's pretty cottages, fresh air and greenery. I find myself wondering what living here must feel like.

Peaceful, I imagine.

"You have reached your destination."

I put the car in park and kill the engine, rubbing at the ache in my chest that's a permanent reminder of how *un*peaceful my life is. Being the owner of Tales is a full-time job. Being Grim, a ball and chain.

I both love her and hate her.

Sighing, I pull down the visor and check my reflection in the mirror. Tired eyes stare back at me, but that's no surprise given I haven't really slept since my dad's will was read a couple weeks back. Nothing like finding out you have a younger half-sister to add to your troubles. That and running a business that has only officially become yours since the remains of your dad's body was found, and he was no longer deemed a "missing person".

I laugh at that.

Fucking ridiculous, but it kept the cops and the bastard criminal underbelly off my back long enough to build an army to protect what's mine because, fuck, this life is tough.

I've always known it, but Carter had been a buffer between my reality and the real world. Now I'm in the thick of it, there's no hiding behind a book of fairy tales or romantic notions. Just like the majority of the characters in Grimms' Fairy Tales, I don't get a happily ever after.

I scowl at my reflection, if I look a little too closely there's more than exhaustion swelling in my eyes, there's lingering heartbreak too that no amount of time seems to diminish.

It's been almost two years since I shot Beast.

Two long years and the girl I've tried to bury with the memory of him refuses to fucking leave. She clings onto that man fiercely, and in turn I cling onto her because... If I let Kate go, I let him go, and even after everything that's happened I don't fucking want to.

Not that I'd admit that to anyone, *ever*.

Gripping the steering wheel, I rest my forehead against my curled fists and squeeze my eyes shut, trying to forget how it felt to see the man I loved battered and bleeding on his knees before me.

I could've killed him.

I'd considered it. Had turned the thought over and over in my head as Carter had stared sightlessly up at the ceiling and the King, Rodriguez and Dom had waited for me to act.

But I didn't.

I shot him and banished him instead.

I will never forget the way he looked at me after the bullet ripped through his skin and muscle, knocking him back only for him to right himself again. The way he lifted his hand, not to stem the flow of blood from the bullet wound in his shoulder, but to rest it over my handprint tattooed on his chest.

It broke me.

I've been in pieces ever since.

"I love you, Kate," he'd said, then he turned to Dom and asked him to watch over me before he staggered to his feet and left.

I've thought about him every day since, both hating him and loving him. Truth be known, behind closed doors, in the privacy of my bedroom, he's the one I hunger for. I can't seem to let him go, and because of that I've never allowed another man in my bed despite the offers I've received.

The woman who single-handedly made Tales into the most successful fight club in Europe, making a reputation for herself at the same time, is *still* a virgin.

Fuck, the criminals I rub shoulders with on the daily would have a field day knowing that, because according to every one of those motherfuckers you can't be a badass—not-to-be-fucked-with—bitch who will sooner kneecap you than let you call her by her real name *and* be a virgin. Their small arse brains just can't deal with that.

To them, being a virgin equals purity and purity equals innocence, and that couldn't be further from the truth. Sure I've considered fucking around with a select few, but when it came to the crunch I couldn't bring myself to sleep with them or do anything more than kiss. I just didn't want them like that. I *couldn't* do it because no matter what I told myself, my heart belongs to one man and one man only. Beast.

Despite that, I'm *not* pure. Not in my actions or in my thoughts, and certainly not when I make myself come night after night thinking of the only man I will ever love, a man who'll never be a part of my life again. Not ever.

I won't get to call him Roger and see his eyes flash with warning. I won't get to press my body against his and feel the thump of his heart trying to make an escape through his ribcage. I won't get to joke with him, to provoke him, to talk with him and feel comfortable doing it. I won't get to watch him spar, his muscles flexing, the veins on his arms and hands rippling beneath his skin as he moves. I won't get to kiss him, to feel his tongue lick past my lips and stroke my own with greed. I won't get to feel his possessiveness in the way he stares at me, holds me, and claims me as his. I won't get to lose my virginity to the only man I've ever wanted to give it to.

I won't. I won't. I fucking won't.

Gripping the wheel tightly, I draw in a few deep breaths, telling myself to calm the fuck down. That part of my life, where love had been a possibility, is over.

It's over.

I wasn't wrong when I said that people like us, criminals like us, don't get to love.

There's too much at stake.

Too much to lose.

We fuck and fight. We kill or be killed. We don't love.

"Erm, hello?" a sweet, lyrical voice calls through the window, dragging me away from my thoughts and back into the present. A middle aged woman with a sweet smile waves at me shyly. "Miss Davidson?"

There's a question in her eyes, an openness that I don't see when I meet people for the first time. She's not guarded, there's no expectation that I might shoot her if she pisses me off. She just sees a young woman, not a threat. Not even my edgy clothing and shaved undercut seems to warrant any concern from her. That confirms what I already know to be true, that she's a good woman. Taking care of my half-sister for the past four years since her mum passed is proof enough of that. Grabbing my bag, I step out of the car, closing the door behind me.

"Yes, hey. I'm..."

"You're?" she smiles gently, offering me her hand to shake.

Fuck, what name do I use? Am I Grim or Kate? Chewing on the inside of my cheek I make a split-second decision. "I'm Kate."

"Nice to finally meet you, Kate. I'm Sandy and my husband is Frank. Christy has been looking forward to this day for quite some time."

"She knows about me already?" I ask as she ushers me up the garden path towards the bright red front door, passing through a pretty garden that has a neatly trimmed lawn and wildflowers growing around the edges. Everything about this village, this woman, and this house is so far removed from what I know that it's making me nervous, which is fucking ridiculous really. Apparently you can surround me with a bunch of cussing, weapon-wielding, violent criminals and I'm at ease, but invite me to a pretty house with sweet people and I'm a fucking nervous wreck.

"Oh, yes dear, Christy has known about you for some time now."

"How?"

My question remains unanswered as the front door is pulled open by a man, who I'm assuming is Frank, with salt and pepper hair and an equally warm smile.

"Come in, come in!" he exclaims, his bright blue eyes glinting with happiness as he steps aside. I pass him and step into a brightly lit tiled hallway with fresh flowers sitting in a vase on a console table and paintings of landscapes hanging on the wall opposite. "Christy is in her dance studio at the bottom of the garden."

"Her dance studio?" I ask, casting my gaze about the place and searching for any hidden threats, coming up empty. It's a force of habit and demonstrates just how deeply I'm in the quagmire of the criminal underbelly of London. Back home there's a threat around every corner, and nowhere is truly safe. Here it's... *different.*

I let out a long breath, giving them both a small smile. I've no idea if I should go through to her dance studio and introduce myself or wait for them to bring her to me.

"Should I wait here?" I ask, looking between them both. Frank has his arm around Sandy's shoulder and they're both staring at me with such warmth I don't really know how to handle it.

"My goodness!" Sandy exclaims, grinning a little sheepishly. "We're both terribly nervous and not ourselves. Where are our manners? Frank, go and make us all tea and I'll take Kate here to the studio."

Frank nods. "Yes of course, I'll bring it out to the garden given it's such a nice day out." He winks at me. "*And* I'll crack open the box of biscuits the wife has hidden in the pantry. She thinks I don't know about them."

"Sounds good, thanks," I reply, my cheeks heating at the way the pair interact. I can feel their love for one another, it's heartwarming. Frank gives me one last smile, then disappears through a door off the hallway.

"Do you need a moment?" Sandy asks, sensing my hesitation.

I feel like an interloper, like I have no right to be here in their home, let alone disrupt their lives. Part of me wants to turn on my heels and stride right out of the house, the other part wants to meet my little sister more than anything in the world.

"I can give you a moment, if that's what you need. This must be quite a shock for you. We've had much longer to process this news."

"How come? I only found out about Christy when my dad's will was read a couple weeks ago."

Sandy slides her arm through mine and walks me towards the back door at the end of the hallway. "That's a very good question which we will explain, but first I want you to know how sorry I am for your loss."

"Thank you," I reply, biting back the words I truly want to say.

Witnessing the man I love murder my dad was hard, of course it was, but shooting the man I love and sending him away, harder still. That loss is something I don't think I'll ever get over. Not in this lifetime, anyway.

"Losing a parent is so terribly difficult. Christy knows that better than anyone," Sandy continues as she guides me towards the wooden studio at the bottom of their very large, neatly kept garden. I can hear instrumental music playing, and my stomach flips with nerves.

"I understand her mother died in a fire when she was eight, and that she's been living with you both for the last four years, is that right?" I ask as we stop outside the studio, standing slightly back from the French doors that open out to the garden. I can't see into the space from our position, but right now I'm keen to learn how Christy ended up with Frank and Sandy, and not my dad and I after her mother died.

"That's right. To everyone outside of this house we are her aunt and uncle, but in truth we're not blood related."

"You're not? I thought you were her mother's sister?"

Sandy shakes her head. "No, Christy's mother was my friend."

"So why didn't she come to live with us when her mother died?"

Sandy gives me a small smile. "Because your father didn't want that."

"He didn't?"

"No. He wanted to keep her safe," she says, giving me a

knowing smile. "I understand that your father was a man who lived on the other side of the law to the rest of us."

I nod. "Yes."

"And you?" she asks, but there's no judgement in her question. In fact, if I'm not mistaken there's an edge of sympathy in her tone, like she can see deep inside of me and know that I'm a product of my upbringing.

"I'm my father's daughter," I reply with a shrug. "This life is all I know."

Sandy gives my arm a squeeze before letting it go. "I understand," she says, and for the first time I see some hesitancy in her expression.

"What?"

She sighs. "You are Christy's blood relation. You have every right to make a decision about her life and what happens from this moment on, but I will say this, Kate, we love her as if she's our own flesh and blood. She is a bright star in a world that can be incredibly dark, and she is special in more ways than one. Neither Frank nor I will stop you if you decide that her living with you is best, but before you make that decision there are things you must know about Christy. She isn't like everyone else—"

"Kate!" a delighted voice screeches, interrupting our conversation and drawing my attention from Sandy to a girl with bright red hair and a deep purple birthmark covering the right side of her face.

"Christy?" I gasp, taken aback by this beautiful girl standing before me.

She nods, and with a huge smile spreading across her face, runs into my open arms like this isn't the first time we've met and we're not strangers. For a split second, I stiffen, but when she hugs me closer and leans into my embrace, I hug her back just as fiercely, a well of protectiveness expanding in my chest.

It's sudden and overwhelming, and I know in an instant that I'll protect this girl with my life.

Sandy smiles at us both, tears pricking her eyes as we hug for long minutes. Christy's face is buried in the crook of my neck with my cheek pressed against the top of her head. Eventually I let out a small laugh and lean back, cupping her cheeks in my palms so I can get a good look at her, gasping at her eyes. One is a blue so bright it rivals the cloudless spring sky above us while the other is so brown it verges on black.

"Look at you, you're so pretty!" I exclaim, shaking my head in wonder at the little girl before me. Her colouring is completely different to mine, but I see a likeness in the shape of her eyes and the way her lips tilt upwards when she smiles. Even the small dimple in her left cheek is the same as my own.

"And you're just as beautiful in real life as you are in my visions," she replies happily.

"Your visions?" I question with a small laugh, looking from her sweet face to Sandy's and back again.

"That's right. Come on big sis, show me that musty old fairy tale book you've got in your bag. Those Grimm brothers were kind of messed up, right?" she says, laughing at my shocked expression as she slides her hand in mine and tugs me towards the garden table where Frank is waiting for us with a pot of tea and a plate of biscuits just like he promised.

"How the hell—? I begin, only for the questions to die on my lips when Sandy steps into stride beside us.

"Like I said, Christy isn't like everyone else."

"DO you have to go back to London this morning?" Christy asks me two days later as we sit and eat breakfast in Frank and Sandy's kitchen.

"I'm afraid so. I have a business to run, Christy, and now that I know about you, it's even more important that I make it a success. I gotta take care of my kid sister, haven't I?"

"Oh, you don't need to worry about that," she says flippantly, grinning around a mouthful of buttered toast. "Once you sort your love life out with Roger, there'll be no stopping you."

"What?!" I blurt, choking on a mouthful of tea.

She gives me a slap on the back, laughing in that carefree way of hers. For someone who's been through so much in her short life, I'm amazed by her sweetness. I hadn't known she was burned in the fire that had also killed her mum. When she'd shown me her scars yesterday I'd felt so much guilt for not being there for her, followed by a well of hatred towards Carter for keeping her from me. The moment I realised he'd known she'd been in hospital fighting for her life and hadn't once visited her made me feel physically sick. There's no excuse for abandoning your own flesh and blood.

None.

A part of me, one that's growing with every passing day, is glad he's dead, because a man who is capable of ignoring a child in pain isn't a man I'd want in my life. But right now, I can't think about what could've been or the fact that if Carter was still alive I might never have known about Christy. I have to be grateful that she's alive and well, and *happy*.

"Don't look so shocked," Christy says, pushing her hair back off her face and giving me a knowing look.

"How do you even—?" I begin, then shake my head, because I already know how she seems to know things that no one else possibly could.

According to Sandy and Frank, Christy has a *gift*. She can see things that haven't happened yet. I'd laughed it off at first, but in the short time we've spent together she's proven over and over again that she's special. I can't wrap my head around it, but it's true.

"Roger... *Beast* deserves a second chance," she chatters on.

"You don't know what he did," I say, then chew on the inside of my cheek. Maybe she does? I hope not. "Do you?"

"Not exactly," she admits, and the relief I feel knowing she hadn't seen him murder our dad is huge.

"I do know that he hurt you, and I know that he's sorry for it," she says.

"You've seen something in my future?" I ask, still shocked at how odd this all is, but more so because I believe her.

"Yes, he, erm... He proves to you how sorry he is," she says, looking sheepish.

My eyes widen, my mind running wild with possibilities. "Please don't tell me you've seen things no twelve year old should..."

"No I don't mean *sex*—"

"Oh, thank fuck!" I say, then slam my hand over my mouth, pulling a face. "Sorry."

Christy waves her hand in the air. "Fuck is just another word in the English language," she shrugs.

"Not one of the better ones though."

"*Definitely* one of the better ones," Christy says, rolling her eyes. I hold in a grin. There's a sassiness about her that reminds me of myself. It's weirdly comforting.

"What I meant was, he loves you, and he isn't afraid to prove it," she murmurs, absentmindedly pressing her palm against her birthmarked cheek. It's something she does often, almost like a reflex, a way to comfort herself, or perhaps to cover up.

"I'm not easily impressed," I say with a shrug, not able to get my head around the fact that I'm actually having a discussion with Christy about Beast. I'm not sure what I find more crazy, the fact Christy can see into the future, the fact that I believe her, or the fact Beast and I actually *have* a future.

"You don't believe me, do you?" she asks, rubbing her cheek as though trying to rub away her birthmark and the gift that is probably more of a curse, especially in this unforgiving world.

I take her hand in mine, curling my fingers around her palm.

"I *believe* you," I say, lifting her chin with my finger and giving her a smile that I hope conveys how much I actually do. In the short time I've come to know her, I'm already fiercely protective. She's my family, my flesh and blood, and I will do anything to reassure her that I accept her for who she is, no matter what, no matter how bizarre this all is.

"Thank you."

"You know, you can always be yourself around me, Christy. Don't hide who you are. Not to me."

"And you know that the only person you can be your true self with is *him*," she replies, cocking her head as she looks at me with a sense of knowing that simultaneously chills me to the bone and puts me at ease. She's an enigma.

"Maybe, but that ship has sailed." I sigh, giving her a weak smile.

"Has it though?" She grins. "He won't give up on you. He *hasn't* given up on you."

"He left—"

"You *made* him," she counters, narrowing her eyes at me, her cute button nose wrinkling.

God, lying to this kid is going to be impossible.

"Okay, I made him," I admit.

She nods. "It's okay to want him still. He's a good man."

"You don't know the things he's done... *Do you?*" I ask as an afterthought.

She shakes her head. "No, but I know the things he *will* do, and those things make him a good man."

Now it's my turn to narrow my eyes at her. "Tell me."

She shakes her head, her expression serious as she places her small hand over mine, tears welling in her eyes. "I can't."

Her tears pull me up sharp, and I see her for who she is in this moment: a child who's gone through severe trauma and is different in a world where difference is dissected and ridiculed. Her life won't be an easy one, I don't have to be clairvoyant to know that.

"Hey, it's okay. I don't need to know. I've gotten by so far without looking into my future."

She nods, sniffing as she swipes at her tears. "I would tell you if I could. It's just..."

"It's okay," I repeat.

We sit in silence for a few minutes just holding each other's hands until she picks up the book I brought with me. My dog-eared copy of Grimms' Fairy Tales has become a source of entertainment for the both of us these past couple days. She thinks the twisted stories are hilarious, and the fact that I love to read them even more so.

"You know, your story, yours and Roger's—"

"Beast," I interject. "He hates his real name."

She gives me a small smile, tapping the cover of the book. "Your story is like one of these tales."

"Is that so?"

"Yes. Except *yours* has a happy ending."

"It does?" I find myself whispering, wanting so much for that to be true and then despising myself a little for it. I have so many conflicting emotions when it comes to Beast. I don't really know how to start unravelling them. It's complicated.

"Promise me that when he comes to you, that you'll listen to what he has to say."

"I'll try," I say, climbing to my feet.

"*Promise me*," she insists, pushing back her chair and reaching for me. "It's important."

I nod my head, swallowing past the tightness in my throat as I grasp her hand in mine. "I promise."

"I wish I could come live with you," she says after a beat, throwing herself into my arms as a sob escapes her lips.

"I wish you could too, but you're safe here. Carter was right about that, at least. I will ring you every day, and come visit as often as I can. I promise. You're my sister and that's never going to change. I'll be like a bad smell that you won't be able to get rid of, the black sheep of the family you'll be embarrassed by in a few years."

"Never," she giggles.

"You swear?"

"I swear it," she agrees, swiping at her eyes as she looks up at me. "I'm sorry about your dad, Kate."

"Our dad.".

"*Our* dad," she agrees. Her gaze lifts to my neck and she reaches up and presses her fingers against my skin. "I like the rose tattoo. It's really cool."

"Rose tattoo? But I haven't got a tattoo..."

"Not yet," she says knowingly, and I'm suddenly reminded of that time in the ring with Beast when I'd told him that I wanted a tattoo of a climbing rose, thorns and all, inked into my neck. "You're pretty fucking amazing, you know that?" I say, pulling her in for one last hug, before pressing the book into her hands. "I want you to have this."

"Are you sure?" she asks, tears brimming in her pretty eyes. She swipes at them as they fall, jutting her chin and straightening her spine, just like a Davidson would.

"I'm positive... Speak soon, okay?"

"Yes," she whispers just as Sandy and Frank enter the kitchen from the back door, moving to stand behind her.

I flick my gaze between the three of them, feeling happy with my decision. I'd come here this weekend with the intention of taking Christy home, but witnessing the love and affection between them has soothed my heart and shown me that what she really needs is to stay here with them. Carter kept her a secret for a reason and I'm not willing to risk her safety no matter how much I despise him for keeping her from me.

"You take care of each other."

"Always," Sandy replies, wrapping her arm around Christy's shoulder and pulling her into her side as I grab my holdall and stride towards the door.

"Wait!" Christy calls, and when I glance over my shoulder at her she looks at the book in her hands then back up at me. "It's all going to work out, you'll see."

I can't bring myself to answer. Instead I give her a weak smile.

"Roger was always supposed to be your Beast, and you were always supposed to be his Princess... *Queen*," she adds with conviction.

"Bye for now," I reply, then head out to my car, my heart lighter than it has been in years.

CHAPTER THREE

Ain't No Sunshine

BEAST

It's been almost two years since I left.

Two long motherfucking years where I've watched over Kate from afar.

My Princess. My woman. My heart.

She turns twenty in a week.

And I'm back to tell her the truth, the whole truth and nothing but the truth, so help me fucking God.

I owe her an explanation, my apologies and my love. But more than that, I owe her my life.

Kate isn't a crap shot, and no one misses major organs when they're firing a bullet from a few feet away without purposefully intending to miss. She shot me that night in the cage, banishing me from her life and sending out a message to the criminal underworld.

No one fucks with *Grim*. Not even the ones she loves.

It was her saving grace, because when she pulled the trigger she proved herself a Davidson more than worthy of standing in Carter's shoes, and she's been proving herself ever since, building a business and an army that she can be proud of. Unofficially she's been running Tales from the moment Carter was murdered by yours truly, officially just a few short weeks since his will was read and her name replaced his as the owner of Tales.

Either way, she's gained respect and a reputation. According to Dom, who's been my inside man this whole time, despite the King still having involvement in Tales, he's backed off and allowed her to make a name for herself whilst he reaped the benefits. It won't be long before she buys him out, or better yet kills the cunt, but all in good time.

For now, she's running the most lucrative fight club in all of Europe. Two months after the refurbishment, the old club *mysteriously* burnt to the ground and she moved premises to a larger, more discrete site where Tales has also become more commonly known as Grim's Fight Club.

As it should be.

She's a badass, and I'm so fucking proud of her.

Two weeks ago, Dom called me to let me know that Carter's will had finally been read, after his funeral took place a couple weeks before that. A funeral that, by all accounts, was attended by every fucking lowlife criminal you could think of. None of them were there for Carter, and even less to pay their respects to Kate. Like vultures around a rotting carcass, they wanted to see what they could get out of the situation because up until three months ago, Carter was deemed a missing person.

And a missing person is still a threat, but a dead man? Not so much.

What they hadn't counted on was the woman they met at the funeral. A woman who, according to Dom, single-handedly laid out three men and shot a fourth in the kneecap for even trying to disrespect her. They also hadn't counted on the soldiers she's acquired or the loyalty of mercenaries with a big enough reputation to scare even the most hardened criminal off.

Like I said, she's been building an army.

It's also common knowledge that the remains of Carter's skull was found in a shallow grave in Hampstead Heath, and that he was identified by his teeth. It's not common knowledge that the police were tipped-off with where to find Carter's remains, or the fact that the rest of his body was fed to pigs who have long since been butchered too. Both calculated decisions that were made by Kate herself.

Of course, speculation had been rife in the criminal under-world, and according to Dom, Kate endured weeks of police interrogations, interviews and accusations. But she never wavered from her story, and she never once ratted me out.

Carter's cause of death was deemed suspicious, but given there was very little left of Carter's body and no other evidence to be found given the old club is now nothing but a pile of ash, the case ran cold. Though I'm more than fucking positive that there was a handout to the police chief and a few people higher up the chain of command to nip any further investigations in the bud.

Like I said, Kate has come into her own.

Or should I say *Grim* has come into her own, because there isn't one person now who'll call her Kate. She won't allow it. The last person who tried was beaten by her men so badly that he can't even remember his own name, let alone hers, or so I'm told.

Kate has well and truly shredded her skin and stepped into the role of Grim completely. It's a heavy burden to know that I'm part of the reason for that. That my actions, my half-truths and my lies to keep her safe, forced her into a persona she couldn't escape from.

Honestly, I'm not certain she would even want to now.

But I'm not back to change her in any way, I'm back because I can't stay away a moment longer. There's so much I need to fix and I'm not self-centred enough to believe I'll be successful, but I've got to fucking try.

I blow out a steady breath, swiping at the mist covering the mirror from the shower I've just taken, and stare at my reflection. I look much the same as I did when I left. I'm still a bulky fucker, probably bigger than I was given I've spent a lot of my time training in gyms around the world, but it didn't matter where I was, there was no sunshine without her. My happiness wasn't a focus, her safety was, still is. I haven't been complacent in my time away. I've made alliances, acquaintances and friends with powerful men *and* women.

And I've done it all for Kate, for *Grim*.

I've been standing by her side this whole fucking time we've been apart. I never stopped working to build her army. Never stopped loving her. Never stopped dreaming about her every fucking night, and thinking about her every minute of every day.

I'm surprised my dick hasn't dropped off from the amount of times I've abused it whilst thinking of her. That night in her bedroom where she'd spread herself for me and finger-fucked herself so perfectly has been on repeat in my head for the last two years. Even now, after all this time, thoughts of her make me hard. That won't ever change.

Scraping a hand over my face, I mentally psych myself up, because if I was nervous about telling Kate about my feelings back in my tattoo shop two years ago, that's nothing to how I'm feeling now.

I ain't shitting a brick. I'm shitting a goddamn mountain.

Dom has made it perfectly clear that she's not the same person I left behind, but then again neither am I. Truth be known, being away has changed me. I was never a spiritual man, and I won't pretend that I am now, but a few months back I accompanied Connall on a trip to Ireland to visit his family and met a lad who has this uncanny ability to uncover a man's secrets and capitalise on them. The little fucker got me talking about personal shit that I would *never* share with anyone. I can't even blame my loose mouth on the pints of Guinness I knocked back, given I only had two. Pretty sure he pulled some voodoo shit on me.

All I know is if anyone has the heart of a criminal, the soul of a thief and the mind of a genius, it's Arden Dálaigh, and I have no doubts we'll meet again when he's grown a few more chest hairs.

But that's a concern for another day.

With a shake of my head, my gaze falls to Kate's handprint tattooed on my chest, the outline of which is now completely filled with black ink. From there my eyes track across to the puckered scar that sits just beneath my right collar bone where Kate shot me. Both are a prominent reminder of the woman I love, and I will wear them with pride until the day I fucking die.

"ARE you sure you're ready for this?" Connall asks, the second I slide into the passenger seat beside him.

I give him a look. "Not in the fucking slightest, but it's time."

"She might actually kill you this time."

"She might, but it's a risk I'm willing to take," I reply, drumming my fingers against my knee in agitation.

The fucker of course notices. He's been a good friend to me and I owe him so much more than I could ever repay. Connall has been my right-hand man through all of my travels around the world.

"Listen, mate, I love you, you know that right?"

I laugh. "If you're about to tell me to run away with you—"

"We've been there, done that already," he cuts in with a smirk, breaking sharply and swearing at a kid that suddenly dashes out into the road in front of us. She slams her fist against the bonnet, before giving us the middle finger. Beneath her hood I can see bright blue hair and a scowl that would rival the many Kate has given me in the past.

"Watch where you're going, arsewipe!" she yells, then pelts it across the street chucking a spray can at the car for good measure.

"The little fucker!" Connall exclaims as we both watch her leg it down the street and disappear down an alleyway a little further up. "That one's gonna cause someone a heap of shit in a few years."

"Looks like she's already causing a heap of shit," I remark, as Connall puts the car in drive and moves on. We both laugh, the tension easing a little.

Ten minutes later Connall pulls up outside a gated industrial estate, manned by a security guard who looks very familiar.

Mark.

The last time I saw him, he was in the crowd at Tales whilst I was getting the shit kicked out of me by Derby.

Connall gives me a look. "Is he gonna give us trouble?"

"I guess you'd better roll your window down so we can find out."

Mark steps out of the little hut he's sitting in and strolls over to the car, ducking down to look through the now open window. It takes him less than a second to lock eyes with me.

"Well, fuck! Dom said you were back, but I didn't believe it. Beast, as I live and breathe. How are you, mate?"

Not quite the reception I was expecting, but okay. I grin. "I'm good, you?"

"Head of security here these days," he says with a wink, tapping on the walkie-talkie attached to his chest.

"That uniform looks good on you," Connall says, jerking his chin towards Mark's outfit. He looks like a cross between a copper and a bouncer in his deep blue shirt and trousers. The fact he's got a handgun strapped to his hip and a knife slotted next to it just adds to the whole *don't fuck with me vibe* he's got going on.

"Grim likes her soldiers dressing smart. Things have changed around here since..."

His voice trails off and neither of us fill in the silence. Mark was at the club the night I fought Derby, but he wasn't there when I killed Carter. I found out later he was dragging a fuming Hudson Freed home. Though he couldn't keep him away according to Dom, who's been my inside man this whole time. Hudson came back an hour after I left and is as deep in this pile of shit as the rest of us in attendance that night.

Honestly, I expected to hear that Kate and him had got together after I'd gone, but to my surprise they're still just friends and have remained close. I guess I owe him a thank you for looking out for my girl too, even if it pisses me off that he got to spend time with her and I didn't. I should be grateful, I *am* grateful, but it doesn't stop me from wanting to beat the shit out of him for having her time and attention though. Never thought I'd be a jealous man, but here we are.

"Beast is here to see Grim. Is that gonna be a problem?" Connall asks, before I'm able to even clear my head enough to do the same.

For a beat Mark looks between us, his expression serious. We were friends once, and the thought of having to knock the fucker out so I can get inside the gates doesn't sit well with me, but I'll do it if I have to.

"A few weeks back I would've seen you on your way," he admits with a wry grin.

"And today?" I ask, my stomach churning at the thought that just on the other side of this gate is the woman I love.

"Today you're allowed in."

Connall grins. "Excellent, want to get the gate open then?"

Mark's smile drops. "Sorry, Connall. Beast goes in alone. Orders of the Boss."

Connall looks affronted, glancing at me. "Why is she pissed at me? I ain't done nothing wrong. Surely, she has missed my Irish charm?"

I laugh, and Mark grins. "Couldn't tell you. All I've been told is if Beast turns up he comes in alone."

"Not a problem," I say, unclipping my seat belt.

"Follow me then," Mark replies, bumping fists with a put-out Connall, before striding back to the gate.

"Seriously, Beast, are you sure you wanna do this? We both know that Grim has quite the reputation these days."

"I'm sure. Go home. I'll call you later."

Connall nods, blowing out a breath. "Well, don't let me tell you I told you so when you end up in the coroner's office with a bullet in your brain."

"Pretty sure I'll be incapable of listening *or* responding at that point," I say with a laugh, before jumping out of the car and striding through the open gate.

Two minutes later I'm pushing open the door into the warehouse Mark pointed me towards, and stepping into a cornered off wire cage with wrap around curtains and a locked door opposite. In the corner of the space is a table and a sign that says:

Remove all weapons or entry will be denied.

I grin. Kate is way smarter than her father. Security is clearly a priority, as it should be.

Glancing around the space, my attention is caught by a tiny red light flashing in the top right hand corner of the cage. I stare up at the camera and wait, a smile pulling up my lips.

"Weapons on the table," a familiar female voice barks through the intercom.

It's been a long time since I heard her voice and for a moment I'm taken aback.

Struck fucking dumb, actually, though my dick doesn't seem to have the same problem. It jerks at her voice, standing to fucking attention.

"Jesus fuck," I mutter.

"Weapons on the table, Roger. You'll get them back when you leave."

Roger.

Call me a fool, call me whatever the fuck you like, but the sheer fact she's addressing me by my real name is a good fucking sign. I hear the sass buried deep beneath the coolness, and it fires my fucking blood like nothing else. Maybe there's hope.

"I have no weapons. I come in peace," I reply, grinning, unable to help myself.

For long moments there's just silence, then the intercom makes a clicking noise and her voice follows shortly after. "Prove it. *Strip.*"

"Sure thing, Princess," I reply without hesitation, more than happy to oblige. I hear the sound of the intercom clicking once more and wait, but there's nothing but static. Maybe it's too early to be calling her Princess again so I follow my reply up with a statement that I hope she takes as truthfully as it's meant. "Ain't nothing I wouldn't do for you."

Her scoff comes through the intercom clear as fuck then.

"Just get on with it."

I stare up at the camera and nod. If she wants me naked, then I'll get naked. She can see how my cock is growing for her too. I don't fucking care. She can take her fill.

Removing my jacket and boots first, I throw the former onto

the table and kick the latter across the concrete floor. There isn't one moment when my gaze isn't focussed on the camera, and I'm hoping she can feel the intensity of my stare, because I sure as fuck can feel hers.

Next, my t-shirt, jeans and socks come off and I stand in my boxers with a raging hard on that would rival any of those other fuckers that she might've invited into her bed. I sure hope I get the chance to erase any bastard cock that has had the pleasure of her attention these past couple years. It fucking kills me to know that someone else has taken what was always supposed to be mine, but I can't blame her for it.

I won't do that.

Doesn't mean it doesn't fucking gut me though, or that I won't off the fucker who took it from me. *Just saying.*

"Do you need me to remove my boxers too, because you know I will, Princess," I say unabashedly.

This wasn't exactly how I pictured our reunion, but I get the psychology behind it. She wants to show me who's boss, what she doesn't realise is that I never wanted to be hers. Every action I took came from a place of love, and the need to protect her.

"Is that a gun in your pants or are you just glad to see me?" a familiar *male* voice says, followed by a burst of laughter that has my cock deflating quicker than you can say gonorrhoea.

Across the other side of the space the curtain surrounding the cage is pulled back and Dom is smiling at me. "Fucking hell, Beast, I can see that cock of yours is still a lethal weapon."

I bark out a laugh, shaking my head. "You prick!"

"Nope, you're *definitely* the prick."

"Good to see you, Dom," I reply, my smile fading as I give

him a look that I hope he interprets as gratefulness. Without him keeping an eye on Kate, and letting me know how she's been doing, I would've been even more of a fucking mess.

"Get dressed. Grim's waiting for you in her office," he gives me a knowing look, then punches a number into a keypad on his side of the cage and pulls the door open. He waits for me to put my clothes back on, and with one last glance at the camera, I follow Dom into the lioness's den.

CHAPTER FOUR

Midnight Sky

GRIM

I stare at the screen, at the man who stole my heart and made me an orphan. He looks the same as I remember and different in a way that's difficult to pinpoint. There are lines around his eyes, and a tightness around his mouth that I have the sudden urge to soothe. He's more muscular, if that's even possible. His hair is a little longer on top and he's clean shaven. If I weren't already sitting down, I'd need to.

There's no doubt that he's grown even more handsome, and despite my head telling me not to get drawn in, my foolish heart is beating wildly. Don't even ask me about my pussy because she's already forgiven him and is about ready to throw herself at his cock and beg for oblivion.

"Fuck!" I swear, my gaze roving over every inch of his face as he stares up at the camera. This was a bad fucking idea. I can't be weak for this man, *I can't.*

Flicking my gaze to my phone, I consider calling Mark to come get his arse and chuck him out, but then I remember what Christy had said and I hesitate. My stomach churns with anxiety, and I grab my packet of cigarettes from the table, lighting one and dragging in a deep lungful. The tip sizzles, and when I blow out a stream of blue-grey smoke, some of the anxiety lifts. Narrowing my eyes at him I make a decision, then lean back in my chair and press the intercom button.

"Weapons on the table," I say, keeping my voice steady, cold.

He stiffens, his muscles locking tight as he blinks back up at the camera. He wasn't expecting to hear my voice. Good, let him feel as fucked in the head as I do. I take another drag of my cigarette, enjoying the power shift as he chews on his lip.

There's no doubt that he's nervous. Well that makes two of us.

"Weapons on the table, *Roger.* You'll get them back when you leave." I can't help but grin at the surprise in his eyes when I call him by his real name.

Before, when I used to call him Roger, it was to wind him up, to get a rise out of him. Now, I just want to remind him that I can call him whatever the fuck I want and he can't do a damn thing about it. It takes him a beat to reply, but when he does he gives me a grin that almost makes me forget what he did. *Almost.*

"I have no weapons. I come in peace," he says.

I take another pull of my cigarette. There's nothing about his body language that tells me he's being anything other than truthful, and despite everything, I believe he isn't carrying. Not that it would matter if he was, because my soldiers would have him disarmed and on his knees with a gun cocked at his head before he could even blink. Beast might be the best fighter in the cage, but he's no match for the combined force of the mercenaries I've gathered over the two years since he's been gone. Every single one of them walked into Tales as a fighter and stayed as my soldier, and I took full advantage of the universe bringing them to me.

We eyeball each other through the screen, and deciding that he needs to be knocked down a peg, or five thousand, I test his willingness to follow my orders because there is no way I'll even entertain talking to him if he thinks he can just waltz back in here and pick up where we left off. I don't care how fucking sexy he is, or how much he still makes my legs go weak and my pussy wet.

"Prove it. Strip," I demand, smirking as I lean back in my chair and wait.

I don't have to wait for long.

"Sure thing, *Princess*," he replies then begins to remove his clothes.

I press down on the intercom about ready to tell him to fuck off for calling me Princess, but then he says something else that stills my heart and immediately puts me back in the headspace of the girl who was utterly in love with him.

"Ain't nothing I wouldn't do for you."

I blink at the screen, at his sincerity.

Fuck. Fuck. *Fuck*!

Swallowing hard and pushing those feelings deep down, I scoff, then say; "Just get on with it." Then I click off the intercom so that I don't do something fucking stupid like ask him to do everything I've dreamed of in the privacy of my bedroom these past couple years since he's been gone.

Dragging in another hit of my cigarette, I watch him undress, my mouth dropping open as I stare at the screen, transfixed. He strips right down to his boxers and there's no denying that his almost naked form is as stunningly attractive as it ever was, but it isn't his defined muscles or his broad shoulders and strong thighs that leaves me breathless. It isn't even the intimidating size of his erection. It's my handprint that's completely filled in and resting over his heart in a permanent tattoo that sucks all the oxygen from the room and has my own heart pounding so loud that I barely hear my phone ringing.

"Shit! Fuck!" I exclaim, picking it up. "What?" I snap into the mouthpiece.

"He's about to take his fucking pants off. Are you still convinced he's packing?" Dom asks me, undeniable laughter in his voice.

He's certainly packing, I think, my gaze trailing to his boxers and the bulge there. "Bring him to me," I order.

"Sure thing... And boss?"

"Yes?"

"He's a good guy."

I snort. "Tell that to Carter."

By the time Dom knocks on my door five minutes later, I've shrugged off the girl who was in love with Beast and firmly stepped into the role of Grim. I promised Christy I would listen to him, and I will, but that doesn't mean I'm just going to take him back no matter what she has seen in our future.

"Come in," I call out, arms folded across my chest in defence mode that I quickly uncross because letting him know I'm feeling out of sorts by his sudden appearance today isn't what Grim would do. She is strong, unfazed by anyone, and it's her grit I funnel as Dom opens the door and Beast steps past him into my office. I glance at Beast quickly, willing my heart to stop racing and ignoring the very real need to just go to him, then give a tight smile to Dom.

"Need me to stay?" he asks.

"No. Get home to Nancy. I'll see you back here tomorrow night for Ziggy's fight."

"Sure thing." He nods once, flicks his gaze to the back of Beast's head and smirks, shutting the door behind him.

"I should shoot you dead now," I state, my fingers running over the Glock resting on my desk, internally wincing at the opposing emotions fucking with my head. I just want to go to him, wrap my arms around him, but I can't. I fucking can't.

"I wouldn't stop you," he replies evenly.

"Do you have a death wish?" I ask, genuinely interested, and trying hard to focus on being Grim and not the girl who's still in love with him.

He holds his hands out, palms up. "The only wish I have is for the chance to talk. That's it. That's all."

We stare at each other for long moments, and I'd be a liar if I didn't want to throw caution to the wind and forgive him instantly for everything.

But I can't do that.

I *won't* do that.

"Drink?" I ask instead, if only because I need something to do with my hands.

Without waiting for him to reply, I push back from the table and stride over to the drinks cabinet in the corner of the room, pouring us both a three-fingered shot of bourbon. I take my time, letting him get his fill of my fitted shirt, tight leather skirt, bare legs, and stiletto ankle boots. I know for a fact my knee-length skirt hugs my arse, and the slit at the back gives glimpses of my thighs. He's not the only one who's kept themselves fit these past couple years. I spar three times a week with Dom and Mark and train with Cleveland, one of the mercenaries, twice a week too. I keep up with pole dancing as much as I can with Nancy and Matty as well. Exercise has helped to keep my mind focused, sharp. What no one knows is that on my nights off I indulge in copious amounts of junk food to ease the pain in my chest whilst sitting in my threadbare pyjamas, feeling lonely as fuck.

There has to be balance, right?

With his eyes on me, I grab the drinks and return to my seat, sliding one across the table to him. "Sit."

Beast nods, watching me carefully as he pulls out the chair and takes a seat opposite me. I will my cheeks not to flush at the intense way he stares at me, but rather than looking away I stare right back, *not* willing to let him see how affected I am by him.

Taking a sip of the bourbon, I wait.

"Kate..." Beast begins.

"Grim," I retort firmly.

"Grim," he corrects, leaning forward and clasping his hands together on the table, completely ignoring the glass of bourbon. My gaze trails over his thick fingers and the veins protruding on the back of his hands before I slowly lift my eyes to meet his. I'm pretty sure he was just checking out my tits too. Can't say I blame him, they've filled out some since he left. I guess I'm what you call a late bloomer.

"You've got five minutes. Speak," I demand, so fucking grateful my voice remains steady.

"You look good," he remarks, the sound of lust in his voice like a wet dream come true.

There's no denying the need in his eyes and for a second I allow myself to bask in it. To let his words wash over me like a sweet caress. Then I pull my shit together.

"If you're just here to compliment me on my looks then you can get your arse up out of that chair and fuck right off. I don't need your compliments, Beast. I get enough of them as it is."

His eyes flash with possession, and a whole dose of jealousy, but he shuts both down and nods, clearing his throat. "I'm sure you do."

We fall silent again, and I pick up another cigarette, lighting it. He looks surprised but instead of questioning why I've taken up smoking, he nods towards the cigarette packet. "May I?"

"You may," I say, inwardly smiling at the way he seems to shift uncomfortably in his seat. I wonder if he still has a boner. The sheer fact he got hard because he knew I was watching him strip makes me feel all kinds of ways. Mostly horny, but also wanted, *desired*.

Yeah, I've had plenty men want to fuck me, but the way Beast is looking at me now, it's different. It's more.

As he leans forward and reaches across the table, his loose fitting, v-neck shirt gapes a little, revealing the top of the handprint tattoo. Now it's me who's staring as I remember the day he took me to his tattoo shop and stole my breath with his actions and his promises.

"I like what you've done with the club," he interrupts my reminiscing. I rip my gaze upwards and watch him place a cigarette between his lips before lighting it. "You've been busy building quite an empire since I've been gone."

"You sound surprised."

"No. I never doubted you."

Blue-grey smoke curls up out of his mouth as he speaks and I can't help but notice the note of pride in his voice. I don't need a man's validation, but surprisingly getting this recognition from Beast means more to me than it probably should.

"Yeah, you're right. I have been building an empire since I *banished* you," I reply, forcing all those warm feelings I have no business entertaining deep into the pit of my stomach. Anger is by far a safer emotion right now, and I'm clinging onto it with everything I have.

"I'll rephrase that. You've been building quite an empire since you banished me."

There's a hint of a smile in his eyes that warms a part of me that turned cold a long time ago, and it's that feeling and not his flirty smile that has me reacting the way I do.

I. Can't. Let. Him. In.

I. Can't.

"Get out!" I snap. Stubbing out my cigarette, I push up from my desk and stride towards the door. "Now!"

He twists in his seat, frowning as he watches me yank open the door . "What?"

"I said, get the fuck out!" My voice is low, dripping with fury.

"Woah, Grim," he retorts, stubbing his own cigarette into the ashtray before getting to his feet. "Calm down."

"*Calm down?* Calm-fucking-down! No. You don't get to patronise me."

"I wasn't! Shit! Fuck, that's not what I was doing!"

I bark out a laugh, feeling a lot less Grim and way more Kate than I have in a very long time. Kate is the one who flies off the handle at the drop of a hat, who's *emotional*. Grim is nothing like that and a large part of me resents that he still has the ability to pull her out of me.

"Did you honestly think you could waltz in here, flash me a smile, give me flirty fuck-me eyes and think I would fall at your feet like some lovesick teenager?"

"Well, I—" he smiles again in that infuriating way that makes my heart squeeze.

"Don't you dare!" I hiss, slamming the door shut in anger instead of slamming my fist into his cocky face. "Don't make this into a fucking joke."

"I'm sorry, let me start again," he begins, scraping a hand over his face. "Fuck, I knew I'd balls this up."

"I'm not that girl anymore. I'm not someone you can flirt with and charm, who begs for your attention. I won't just roll over and forgive you for everything just because you're back."

"I don't expect you to do any of that," he replies earnestly as he steps towards me. "I misjudged the situation. I guess I thought—I *hoped*—that because you hadn't already shot me dead that we were on better terms than we actually are. I was wrong. I apologise."

"The only terms we're on is me giving you a chance to shoot

your shot before I decide whether to shoot you dead for good this time!" I bite back.

"That's fair," he replies, holding his hands aloft as he approaches me guardedly. "I'm just asking you to listen to what I have to say. Will you?"

"So now you want my obedience?" I shake my head. "Nothing's changed there then."

"You were *never* obedient," he retorts, moving closer still. "As I recall, you did nothing but cause me shit. I've missed that."

This time his smile isn't flirty, it's pitted with regret and the barely stitched together wounds in my chest rip open at that. He missed me. God, I missed him too. So fucking much. But I don't admit it.

"And you were nothing but a tease and a heartbreaker!" I retort, hating the fact that I'm losing my cool so spectacularly, that somehow I've moved towards him instead of putting more space between us.

"I'm sorry it felt that way."

"Are you?"

"Kate," he says, then slams his mouth shut when I give him a glare that ordinarily would end in someone getting kneecapped. "Grim," he repeats, still stepping towards me. "I never meant to hurt you."

"But you did. And that girl you made an orphan? She's gone now."

"I understand," he acknowledges, stopping a few inches from me.

"You don't understand though," I reply. "You don't understand anything."

"Then explain it to me. What's going on in your head, Princess?"

I look up at him unable, or perhaps unwilling, to drag my gaze away. I don't even pull him up for calling me Princess again because, fuck, I've missed him so much. I ache to step into his arms. It's physically painful to keep this distance between us, but I have a reputation to uphold and letting him back in would ruin mine. No one knows for certain that he killed Carter, but speculation has been rife since his body, or what was left of it, was found. The fact Beast disappeared the same night my dad did but has turned up alive and well two years later is a big fucking red flag.

Not to mention that he did actually kill my dad.

It's just as well I've got the police chief in my pocket, otherwise Beast would've been pulled in for questioning the second he stepped back in town. He knows that just as much as I do.

"You lost the right to ask those kinds of questions two years ago, Beast."

"You're right, I did, and it guts me to know that." He sighs, tracing my features with his gaze. "There's so much I need to say to you, but all I can think about right now is taking you in my arms and loving you until you understand that *I'm sorry.*"

"Beast," I warn, but he ignores me and brushes his knuckles against my cheek, and just for a moment I'm caught in his pull, in the chemistry and the attraction we've always shared. It's as strong as it ever was.

It's intoxicating.

"Fuck, Grim. Fuck," he murmurs, his thumb brushing over my lips.

"Beast," I say, trying and failing not to lean into his hold as his palm presses against my cheek and his fingers massage the shaven hair behind my ear. I can feel myself giving in, feel my heart calling out to his whilst my brain screams at me to stop, to think, to step the fuck away from him.

"We belong together, you and me," he murmurs as I struggle internally, wanting to let him in, knowing that I shouldn't.

He lowers his head slowly towards mine, and in the short time it takes for him to lean closer, Grim comes back fighting. I shove at his chest, taking a step back and putting space between us.

"I don't belong to anyone, Beast. I don't need to be loved by you. I do just fine without that bullshit in my life!" I lie, my chest heaving as we stare at one another.

"We both know that isn't true, because this thing we have, this connection, it ain't going away. We're inevitable, you and me..."

And he's right. We are.

A part of me, a desperately needy, lonely part that has missed him, has yearned for him, wants him to take charge and pull me into his arms and kiss me stupid. The other part sighs in relief when he backs up.

"But right now we can't explore *us* until you know the truth, and I'm here to give it to you."

"And what truth is that?" I ask, feeling the hair on the back of my neck stand. The look in his eyes is enough to make me withdraw emotionally, locking my feelings down, hardening up. Whatever he's about to say isn't going to be good.

"That I killed Carter not because he wanted me dead for loving you, although that's reason enough in my book, but because he drew up a contract with the King selling you to that arsehole in exchange for paying off his debts."

Stunned doesn't even begin to cover what I'm feeling. I'm fucking stupified, a sudden ringing in my ear drowning out every other sound. It takes me a few moments to gather my thoughts and I have to blink back my shock.

"What?" I eventually choke out, the floor tipping beneath my feet as I try to make sense of what he's just said. "That's a fucking lie!"

"I wish it was." Beast blows out a sharp breath, my reaction to the truth hurting him as much as the truth hurts me. "I made a new deal with the King as soon as I found out what your dad had planned. I would kill Carter and the King would back off from you, remaining a silent partner in Tales. I did it so that I could give you time to build an army so that one day, when the time was right, you could take out the motherfucker yourself."

"He was going to sell me to the King?" I ask, disbelief quickly dissolving into rage that fires my blood and makes me wish Carter was still alive so that *I* could drive the mother-fucking knife into his back, just like Beast did that night.

"Yeah, he was," Beast confirms, giving me a look of such deep sorrow that I almost, almost step into his arms.

Instead, I tip up my chin, straighten my spine and funnel some Grim energy. Maybe my dad had a hand in bringing her to life, but it was always Beast who fuelled her strength.

"Tell me why I should believe you?" I ask, not because I don't believe him—the truth is, I do—but because I need a moment to gather my thoughts. To figure out what the fuck I should do now.

"You don't have to believe me, but if you want to corroborate my story you just need to check the accounts at The Crib Club," Beast says.

"And how do you propose I do that?"

"You managed to shut down the case investigating Carter's murder. I'm sure you'll find a way," he says, knowingly.

"Yeah," I retort, already knowing exactly who to go to for help in that department.

"Carter was a bastard, and he deserved to die," he continues, "And what's more, I'd do it all again to keep you safe."

I swallow hard, trying to form the words that just won't come, because even though I believe him, I have to know for sure he's telling the truth.

When I don't respond, he swipes a hand through his hair then says: "The only mistake I made was not telling you everything at the time. You weren't wrong when you said that you didn't need a man to make decisions for you. I can see just how capable you are, have *always* been. I'm proud of you. I'm proud of what you've built and I'm truly sorry for not giving you the respect you deserved and coming to you with what I found out."

My chest swells with conflicting emotions and it takes a great deal of strength not to fucking buckle, but I stand my ground and remain calm on the surface, even though beneath it all I'm struggling to make sense of everything. I stare at him for a long long time, my throat dry, my pulse racing, my stomach churning and my heart trying its very best to punch a hole through my chest. But I have to keep my head. First I need to check out his story, and then I need to decide what I do with that information.

Eventually, I swallow hard and nod. "I appreciate you coming here and telling me."

"It's the least you deserve."

"I have a lot to think about," I admit.

"Yeah, I imagine you do," he acknowledges. "What are you going to do about the King?"

"I don't know yet."

"Well, when you figure that out, I've got your back, no strings attached," he says, giving me a tight smile before heading towards the door and pulling it open.

"Beast!" I call out before I can stop myself, swallowing back the fucking neediness in my voice.

He stills, glancing over his shoulder at me, his eyes flickering with hope. "Yeah?"

"Are you still fighting?"

"Not since I fought against Derby, why?"

"Next weekend I'm holding a contest at Tales to celebrate my birthday. Anyone can fight."

"Is that an invitation?"

"The winner gets to become one of my soldiers. Are you still a beast, *Roger*?" I ask, picking up the glass of bourbon I poured for him and knocking it back in one gulp, relishing the burn. We both know that this is a test, but it's also an olive branch. The question is, will he take it?

"I'll be here," he replies, then steps out into the hallway and leaves.

CHAPTER FIVE

Power Over Me

BEAST

"How are you feeling, mate?" Connall asks a couple nights later whilst we sit in his older brother's pub nursing a few beers.

"Looks like your brother could use a hand," I remark, absentmindedly watching Tom as he serves his regulars here at The Noble Arms. They've been getting more and more inebriated as the night drags on. "Shouldn't you go and help him out?"

"Tom's used to it," he replies, waving my concern off. "Now stop avoiding the question. You've been tighter-lipped than a virgin fucking for the first time. Spit it out."

Downing the last of my pint, I place the glass on the table

and scrape a hand over my face. "It ain't me who that question should be aimed at."

"Grim take what you told her badly then?"

"What do *you* think? I should've stayed to see if she was okay."

"Yeah, I imagine hearing the news was like getting punched in the bollocks."

"Or the tits..."

"What the shit?" I exclaim as we both look up at Nancy, Dom's girl, who's standing by the table with a tray of drinks in her hand. I'm about to ask her how much she knows when Dom pushes through the crowd and pecks her on the cheek.

"Alright?" he asks, looking between us.

Nancy slides the tray onto the table and hands out the drinks, taking a seat opposite us, then says, "Beast was just explaining to Connall about how Grim took the news about Carter and that prick the King."

"You know?" I ask, narrowing my eyes at her.

"Yeah, about that," Dom begins, pulling a face as he sits down next to her.

"What part of *keeping that information to yourself* didn't you understand?" I hiss, pissed off that he broke my trust.

"Easy now," Connall warns, forever the voice of reason. He's got me out of untold scrapes over the past couple years when my head has been all over the place and my fuse short.

Dom meets my hard stare. "You've got a right to be angry, Beast," he says, lowering his voice even though the punters in the pub are far too busy getting merry to give a shit about what we're discussing. "Truth is, Nancy was getting suspicious of all of the secret phone calls and texts that I had no choice but to tell her the truth if I wanted to keep my bollocks intact. Besides, after you left, Grim needed a friend of the female variety. Being surrounded by all those pumped-up men, she needed some female company to balance shit out. Nancy was more than happy to step into that role given the friendship they'd already begun to form before you left."

"Surrounded by *what* men?" I grind out, forgetting about everything else he's just said and honing in on that fucking part.

Connall laughs. "Did that bullet Grim fired into your chest somehow affect your brain or was it the crack to the head from Derby that did the job?"

"Shut the fuck up, " I retort, grabbing the drink Nancy brought over and gulping some back, knowing I'm acting like a possessive prick, but unable to help myself.

"Seriously mate, Grim's the *Queen of Tales*, and spends every day with a fuck-load of men. She's stunning *and* powerful. What man in his right mind wouldn't want to pursue her?" Connall says.

My head snaps around, and I glare at the bastard for speaking the truth. I know Kate's been surrounded by a whole host of eligible men these past two years, and without me as a buffer, to protect her from their greedy motherfucking hands, they've had ample opportunity to try and get into her knickers. It doesn't make it any easier to hear though. Just thinking about it gets me raging, and my fingers twitching to cut out their damn hearts.

"You know you don't have to worry about me," Nancy says, defusing my anger a little with the change of subject. "I'd never do anything to hurt Grim. I *swear* it. I've got her back just as much as you do."

I meet her gaze and nod. Nancy's a good woman, I already know that. "I believe you."

Her shoulders relax and she gives me a warm smile. "Good, because it's the truth."

Next to her Dom takes a long swig of his drink. "Thank fuck, I wasn't looking forward to going at it with you, not after how you finished off Derby."

"Luckily for you I don't fight my friends."

"We're friends?" he asks jokingly.

"You've looked out for my girl since I've been gone, I can't thank you enough and I'll never forget it," I say earnestly.

"Ah shucks, you'll be having us all in tears next," Connall says with a chuckle, earning him another glare.

"I've done what I can. But Nancy has been the one who's had Grim's back in all the ways I wasn't able to. She's been that person Grim could confide in," Dom explains, dropping his arm over Nancy's shoulders and planting a kiss on her temple. I've never seen the man so loved up, he's got it bad. I know how that feels.

"What about Hudson? I thought you said he's been a good friend to her," I ask as casually as I fucking can. None of them are buying it though. They all know I'm a jealous fuck when it comes to his relationship with Kate.

"He has," Dom confirms. "In the early days he was the one she spent the most time with. She stayed over at his place a lot. He took care of her, but after a while she had to pull up her big girl pants and become the woman we all knew she could be. Besides, Hudson's been busy building his business with his brothers. As soon as he thought she was good, he took a step back, giving her the breathing space to grow. Just like you did, I guess."

"Oh yeah?" I snatch up my drink and take another sip, jealousy rearing its ugly head. I swallow it down along with the beer.

Nancy watches me with amusement in her eyes. "It's not like that between them. I know for a fact that Hudson is just a friend."

"I'm not sure that makes me feel any better. He's been there when I haven't. They share the kind of intimacy that I want with her. She trusts him."

"Mate, don't do that," Connall interrupts. "You've been there for Grim every step of the way since we left. When you tell her about what you've been doing for her, she'll see that."

"Doing for her?" Dom asks, sipping on his pint.

"The mercenaries," Connall points out whilst I try not to think about how Hudson has been all the things to her that I should've been, that I *should be*.

"What're you saying?"

Connall rolls his eyes. "Come on, man. You don't think they just turned up at Tales of their own accord, do you? Beast has been working hard to supply Grim with an army large enough to fend off any fucker who tries to take her on."

"Well, fuck me," Dom says, shaking his head, a smile spreading across his face. "You're one sneaky bastard, but I fucking like your style."

"Me too," Nancy agrees, giving Dom a stern look. "Why haven't you sent me an army of mercenaries to watch over me? *That's* the kind of romantic gesture I'm after."

Next to me Connall snorts with laughter. "Fucking hell, there's me thinking a bunch of flowers and a nice meal out is enough to woo the ladies these days. Looks like I need to up my game."

Dom scowls at Connall before returning his attention to a straight-faced Nancy. I've got to hand it to her, she's playing this brilliantly. Nothing like keeping a man on his toes.

"Well?" Nancy persists.

"Because you've got *me*. Why do you need anyone else?"

Nancy raises her brows, holding his stare for as long as possible before she bursts out laughing. "Oh, babe, come here," she says before grasping his cheeks in her hands and planting a kiss on his lips, one that quickly turns X-rated.

"Right then, that's my cue to fuck-off home," I say, pushing back my chair and nudging Connall.

"What?" he asks, focussed on the pair as they make out like a couple of horny teenagers.

"Time to go," I point out.

"Fuck that. This is the kind of entertainment I've been missing since propping up your arse the last couple years."

I shake my head. "Whatever. You've had your fair share of excitement."

"Shh, don't tell them that. They might not take pity on me and let me indulge my voyeuristic urges."

"Not in a million years," Dom says, his mouth and chin covered in Nancy's red lipstick as he pulls back and grins.

Connall huffs out a breath. "Don't spoil my fun!"

"I'm heading out," I say, not in the mood to watch the loved-up couple get it on with my best mate flirting to the max. He's insatiable when it comes to sex, and I'm pretty sure he's open to fucking men as well as women, though he's never come right out and confirmed that. Not that it's any of my business, he can shag whoever he wants. It makes no difference to me. "Catch you at Tales, yeah?"

"You're gonna step back in the cage then, fight for a spot by her side?" Dom asks me, knowing full well that there's no question.

"Of course I am. If Kate—"

"Grim," he corrects me.

"If *Grim* wants me to prove myself to her. I'll do it. I'll do anything she asks."

"He's under her thumb already, and he ain't even won her back yet," Connall remarks, earning him a punch to the bicep. He laughs, grabbing his glass and quietening his smartarse mouth with another glug of beer.

"Have a good night," I say, eyeing the exit, more than ready to get the fuck out of here and drown my sorrows in the privacy of my own home.

"Wait," Nancy says, quickly pulling out her phone.

"What're you doing?"

"Don't tell Grim it was me who gave you her number."

"Then why are you giving me her number if you're worried she'll find out?" I ask as she pulls up Kate's number and shows it to me.

"Because I'm concerned about her, and it's a risk I'm willing to take. Now that you're back I just thought that maybe—"

"Concerned why?" I interrupt.

"This goes no further, right?" she asks.

"It goes without saying," I reply, looking between Dom and Connall who nod in agreement.

"Grim has been out of sorts recently. Preoccupied," Nancy explains in a rush of words.

"Beast is back, makes total sense," Connall points out.

Nancy shakes her head. "No, she's been like this since Carter's will was read. Something happened that day. A couple weeks later she went away for the weekend."

"Shit, yeah. I remember wondering about that. She never spends time away from the club," Dom adds.

"Went where?" I ask.

"That's just it, she didn't say. When she came back she was... *different*."

"Different how?"

"Happy..." Nancy's voice trails off, and she frowns.

"Happy? You mean she has a man?" Connall asks before I can.

"No," Nancy says quickly. "Not that kind of happy."

"What aren't you saying?" I press.

"I can't put my finger on it. She's just not herself. She's worried in a way that isn't like her. It's a weird combination."

"That sounds *exactly* like how a woman behaves when they get a new man," Connall points out unhelpfully.

"No. She's not seeing anyone," Nancy insists.

"I hope to fuck you're right because if she is, I might just have to hunt the bastard down and cut out his heart," I blurt out, earning me a wide-eyed look from Nancy and a chuckle from Dom and Connall.

"You gotta chill, man," Connall says, smirking.

"You've asked her about it?" I ask, scowling. I promised myself I wouldn't act like a murdering psycho and go around killing the men she's been with these past couple years, but fuck it's hard to suppress that urge.

"Every time I ask her whether she wants to talk about what's going on she clams up, saying nothing's wrong. I'm worried. It's not like her."

"You're so close that she tells you everything?"

"No," Nancy sighs. "She doesn't tell me everything. Just call it instinct. Something's up, something big, but she's not talking to me about it."

"What about Hudson? Could he know?"

"Maybe."

"Do you think it's the King or something to do with the club?" Connall asks, shifting forward in his seat.

He's been wanting to off the fucker for months now, and whilst I want to do exactly the same thing I ain't jumping on that until I know we can win. The King is a cunt and deserves to die, but he's also extremely powerful. We have to play the long game. Line up all the ducks in a nice, easily killable, row.

"No, I don't," Nancy says, looking back at me. "Just call her."

"I'm not sure she'll answer," I say, punching the number into my phone and saving it anyway.

"She saw you today, didn't she...?" Nancy points out.

"Yeah, but if something's truly bothering her do you really think she's going to confide in me?"

Nancy's lips press into a line as she considers what I've said. "Honestly, for her sake I hope so because whether she wants to admit it or not, she needs you."

I nod. "Thanks, Nancy, I'll call her."

OF COURSE KATE ignores my fucking calls.

I didn't expect any less. Maybe it's because I have a different number and she doesn't know who the fuck's ringing, or maybe she knows exactly who it is.

Either way it's bullshit.

Drumming my fingers on my knee I stare at the wall, wondering whether I should bite the fucking bullet and head over to her place. I promised myself I'd take it slow, follow her lead, but now that I'm back I can't seem to follow my own advice. Dialling her number once more, I wait for her voicemail to kick in and this time I leave a message.

"Kate... Fuck, *Grim*," I say, correcting myself. "Would you answer, please? I just wanna talk."

Stabbing my finger against the screen, I stand and begin pacing back and forth, trying to find some semblance of control, or at the very least get rid of this excess energy I've been carrying with me ever since I stepped into Kate's office two days ago.

Fuck, she'd been a vision, a fucking queen. It's not that she has changed physically all that much, and apart from the new hairstyle, she's exactly the same, but it's her energy that's different.

Powerful, actually.

Truthfully, I would've been less floored if she'd thrown a left hook. Her clothes, her attitude, her confidence, her power. It was ball-breaking in the best possible way.

Shaking out my hands and rolling my shoulders, I continue to pace my living room, trying to figure out what I should do.

Connall would tell me to drive over to her place and apologise to her with my hands and my tongue and my dick. Joey would tell me to wait, that I've been patient for two years so what's another week? My mum, God rest her soul, would tell me to write her a love letter and pour out my feelings to her.

That thought has me stopping in my tracks and turning to the bookshelf still filled with my mum's books, my gaze falling to her favourite, *Lady Chatterley's Lover*. I pull it free from the shelf, remembering when Kate had done the same thing that night she played with fire, and we both got fucking burned.

Opening the book on a random page, I read a few lines, frowning at the flowery language. My mum ate this shit up. I remember her clutching the book to her chest and sighing like a woman in love, all gooey-eyed and flush-cheeked after reading it for the millionth time. Back then I couldn't understand her reaction to words on a page, but now I realise that she was so lonely, so badly abused by my prick of a dad, that finding escape in a book was her way of coping. She found peace and happiness, just as much as she found love and romance.

As I turn the book over in my hands, my mum's voice sounds in my mind, and it's so clear, so crisp, that I can't help but be stunned by the feelings of grief it evokes.

"Love isn't always a straightforward path, son. For some, it's an easy journey, and for others it's complicated and filled with obstacles. I wish I could stick around to meet the person you'll fall for, and I'm sorry that I won't, but I will impart a little bit of wisdom if you'll humour a dying woman?"

I remember being so choked up that I'd just nodded, squeezing her hand that little bit tighter as she battled to get the words out between raspy breaths.

"Words are your greatest tool when it comes to love. Speak the truth of your heart and you can't go wrong. Be honest, even if it hurts, even if it makes you feel like you've split open your chest and let the world see the most vulnerable part of yourself. Whoever you love will thank you for it. And if you find it hard to speak the words, then write them. There's not a woman in the world who doesn't want to receive a love letter."

Sitting back on the sofa, I pull out my phone and stare at the screen, trying to figure out where to begin. Just as I'm about to punch out a long text to Kate, my mother's voice drifts into my thoughts again and I can almost see her shaking her head, a hint of amusement in her eyes.

A love letter, son. Not a text.

"Alright mum, a love letter it is," I say to the ghost of her memory, then grab a pen and pad of paper and spill the contents of my heart, being honest just like she'd asked me to be.

CHAPTER SIX

Lost Without You

GRIM

Hudson leans forward in his seat and grabs the last slice of garlic bread from the plate situated between us on the table. His cooking skills over the past couple of years have improved, and tonight's spaghetti bolognese is actually quite tasty.

"Thanks for this," I say, leaning back in my chair and popping the top button of my jeans, relaxed in the knowledge that we're at his flat and I can let it all hang out. "I'm so full."

"You're welcome," he replies around a mouthful of garlic bread. "It's just as well Max and Bryce have gone out tonight, otherwise they'd have probably demolished it all before you even got here."

"Out partying again?" I ask, grabbing my glass of red wine and taking a sip.

"*Fucking.* They're out fucking."

"They're getting quite the reputation," I remark, rolling my eyes. "Those two are horny bastards. I'm pretty sure they've shagged half the strippers at Nine Lives."

"Yeah, and the rest."

"It's a miracle they've got enough energy to get up in the morning to go to work with you."

Hudson smirks. "Believe me, those two arseholes get a rude awakening every morning at seven am sharp. I don't care how late they've been up or if they've still got a woman in bed. They know the score. What we're building together will only succeed if they're giving a hundred percent too."

"And are they giving a hundred percent?"

"Yeah, to be fair they are. Once on the job they're all in, so I can't begrudge them their downtime."

"How close are you to finishing?" I ask, referring to the renovation of the two terrace houses they bought just three months ago.

"Almost done. We've got the electrics going in at the end of the week, and then we can plaster the walls, fit the kitchen and bathroom, and decorate. We'll put them up for sale the second the paint has dried."

"And Building Hope?" I ask, referring to the charity he and his brothers set up last year for kids in care.

"Going well," he replies, humble as usual.

Truth is their charity has made a difference for hundreds of kids in care already, and it's a passion he and his brothers are wholly behind. They set it up wanting to help kids who were like them, forgotten, often misunderstood, and I've never been more proud of them than I am right now. Sometimes when I think about how different our lives are, it's hard for me to feel worthy of his friendship. I'm a criminal after all, and he's... He's a really good man. But Hudson has never made me feel less for who I am, and neither have Bryce or Max.

"I'm really proud of you, you know," I say, my heart squeezing as I'm reminded of Beast saying the very same thing to me just two nights ago.

Admittedly, it feels good to have some recognition for all your hard work, and I don't say it often enough to Hudson. Carter might've been wrong about a lot of things, but he was right about my best friend. He's been single-minded in his determination to build an empire, and over the past two years, Hudson, Bryce and Max have been doing exactly that by buying flats and houses no one wants, doing them up and flipping them for a profit. Each time they invest in a new, bigger project, doing most of the work themselves, and not only that, they've funded their own charity with the profits. No three men work harder than the Freed brothers, and I know they're going places. I can feel it.

"Thanks," he replies, his cheeks heating. Hudson takes compliments about as well as I do. Which isn't all that well.

"And what about you? Have you found someone yet?" I ask, changing the subject.

Hudson places the half-eaten garlic bread on his plate and shakes his head. "No."

"Why not? It can't be all work and no play."

"Coming from the woman who never stops working."

I give him a half smile. "You've got a point there..."

My voice trails off as I stare at my empty plate, momentarily distracted by thoughts of Beast, my father, the King and Christy. Beneath the cool exterior I've perfected, I'm a fucking mess. I'm off my game and if I don't sort this shit out soon, people are going to start to notice. There's no place for weakness in my line of work.

"Grim, do you want to talk about the elephant in the room, or are we just going to pretend that you didn't come here tonight to offload about the fact that Beast has returned?"

I snap my gaze back up to meet Hudson's. He saw me at my worst those first few months after I sent Beast away, and despite me not wanting to get him involved, turning back up at the club an hour after I shot Beast meant that he was as complicit in the events of that night as I was. That worries me most of all. If anyone ever found out, all that he and his brothers have built will come crashing down. I'm determined never to let that happen.

"He came to see me at the club a couple days ago," I admit, chewing on the inside of my cheek, a nervous habit that I've taken great lengths to disguise over the years. I've learnt to shut down every emotional tell so that no one ever has a reason to accuse me of being a bleeding heart and use that against me. But in the presence of Hudson, I don't have to pretend to be okay when I'm not. It's a luxury that I don't fucking take for granted.

"And?" Hudson asks, his eyebrows drawing together in a frown.

"He told me some things."

"What things?"

I blow out a long breath, itching for a cigarette, but respecting Hudson's house rules of no smoking inside. "Beast didn't kill my dad because he wouldn't allow us to be together, he killed Carter because he tried to use me to pay off his debts."

"Please tell me you're joking!" Hudson shifts forward in his seat, anger blazing across his face.

I let out a sad laugh. "According to Beast, Carter owed a lot of money after racking up hundreds of thousands of pounds in debt. The King paid those debts off in exchange for *me*. Beast found out and made another deal with the King. He'd kill Carter and Derby and the King would back off, leaving me to run Tales, providing he was able to stay a silent partner and Beast would keep his involvement in the whole debt exchange a secret."

"Fuck!" Hudson exclaims. "You're certain of this?"

"Positive. I had Beast's story checked out."

"You questioned the King?"

"Fuck, no. He thinks I'm still in the dark, and I'd like to keep it that way for the time being. Harris hooked me up with a hacker who pulled the information from The Crib Club's database in under thirty minutes."

"Harris, one of your mercenaries?"

"Yeah."

"Those men have a lot of connections."

"They do," I agree, refusing to elaborate further. There are some things Hudson doesn't need to know, and that includes just how many dangerous connections my soldiers really do have.

"Okay, so you've confirmed Beast's story. Aren't you concerned about what the King is going to make of his return?"

"The King is an arrogant narcissist. He also thinks I wouldn't dare take him on regardless of me finding out the truth, he's *that* certain of himself. As far as he's concerned, I've reaped the benefits of him being a silent partner, and I'd be a fool to cross him."

"Fucking prick," Hudson mutters in disgust.

"I'll allow the King to believe that I'm under his thumb until the perfect opportunity arises for me to exact my revenge. Right now, I'm benefitting from his connections, and despite wanting to put a bullet in his brain, I'm in this for the long haul. He'll get his comeuppance whether that's in a few months or years from now. I'll make certain of it."

"Got it," Hudson says, swiping a hand through his hair. "And how are you feeling about it all, knowing the real reason Beast did what he did, because that's fucking huge, Grim. It changes things, doesn't it?"

"You want the truth?" I ask, taking another sip of my wine.

"Of course I do. You're my best friend, you know you can trust me."

"I do trust you."

"Then talk to me," he urges, and I fall silent trying to unravel the knot in my stomach enough to give him some honesty.

"I feel weak," I admit eventually. "I feel angry, *relieved*. I feel guilty. But most of all I feel like that heartbroken girl he left behind two years ago, the one who refused to leave your spare room for days on end. When it comes to Beast, I'm not Grim; I'm Kate, and she's *never* stopped loving him."

"So what are you going to do about it?" he asks me.

"Honestly, I've no idea," I reply, but that's a lie.

A big fat lie.

I know what I want to do. I *want* to make Beast mine.

That doesn't mean I'll get what I want though, because even though Kate would take him back in a heartbeat, Grim doesn't have that luxury, and ultimately it's her that has to make a decision.

"I think you do," Hudson says, leaning across the table and taking my hand in his. "He's proven his loyalty to you, Grim. Should he have told you about Carter and the King's agreement? Yeah, he should've, but he did it out of love. He protected you. I'm not sure I wouldn't have done the same thing in his position."

"I know that now, but you can't ignore the fact that doing what he did took that decision away from me, that he left me alone for *two years*, Hud. If he really gave a shit about me, why not come back earlier, huh?"

"You've never been alone," Hudson says, looking affronted.

I sigh. "You know what I mean."

"He must have had his reasons," Hudson says, playing devil's advocate as he lets go of my hand and leans back in his seat, thoughtful.

I laugh bitterly. "Could it be that I've saved his fucking arse from a lengthy prison sentence?"

Hudson shakes his head. "I don't believe that. Beast has never struck me as a coward. You know that too, deep down."

"Then where has he been?"

"I think that's a question you need to ask him, don't you?"

"It's not as simple as that."

"Isn't it?"

"How would it look for me to just take him back? People might not know the real truth of what happened that night, but they do know he was Carter's second in command and that he fucked off the same night he *disappeared*. At best he was a coward for running out on me when I needed him the most, at worst he went into hiding because he killed Carter. Neither option does Beast any favours. I'll be seen as weak for taking him back into a position of trust, a traitor myself."

"Forgiveness isn't weak, Grim."

"Don't be a fool. You know as well as I do that in my world it is."

"Then get him to prove himself, to you, to the whole fucking criminal underworld if you must."

I chew on my lip, trying to think, trying to figure out what to do. Then I realise that I've already given Beast a way in. "I invited Beast to fight at Tales the night of my birthday."

"There you are then. He can prove himself in the cage, just like he did that night with Derby."

"Even if he wins, it still won't be enough."

"For who? For you or for everyone else."

I don't answer.

"It's a start though, right?" Hudson continues, standing as he gathers up the dishes.

"Maybe..." I reply, my voice trailing off as I help Hudson clear the table.

For the rest of the night we avoid the subject of Beast, choosing instead to watch my favourite movie, *Lock, Stock and Two Smoking Barrels*. Only I can't help but find myself wishing it was Beast with his arm around my shoulder and not my best friend. That need doesn't diminish as the night draws to a close and I head off home. In fact, it only gets more intense, especially when I climb into bed naked with my head filled with thoughts of Beast and my fingers whispering over my clit.

I JERK AWAKE, the sound of an incoming voice message on my phone making me groan as I reach for my bedside lamp, switching it on. Blinking back the bright light, I grab my phone as it buzzes again. I'd left it on silent whilst spending time with Hudson and by the time I got home it had run out of battery. Just before I fell asleep, I'd plugged it into charge and now it's lighting up with missed call notifications. Assuming the worst, I open up the voicemail and press play thinking it's either Dom or Mark and there's an issue with the club.

But it's neither.

It's Beast.

"Kate... Fuck, Grim. Would you answer, please. I just wanna talk."

Butterflies take flight in my stomach at the sound of his voice, and I shift in bed, sitting upright. He'd called when I was watching the movie with Hudson, right around the time I was thinking about how much I wished it was him I was relaxing on the couch with. The universe has a funny way of slapping you in the face with its backhanded humour.

"Fuck," I mutter, letting out a breath as I scroll to my missed calls.

There are five spread out over the course of the evening. I guess he really did want to talk.

Truthfully, there's a big part of me that's glad I had my phone switched off because I'm not ready to speak with Beast again just yet. I need to get my head together, and my heart under control before I do. I just feel way too vulnerable right now, and I don't like it.

This isn't the woman I've become. I can't be weak like this.

And yet, I can't seem to let go of my phone either.

Deciding that I need a drink, I get out of bed and grab my dressing gown, wrapping it around my naked body, then head to the kitchen and pour myself a large glass of white wine. A minute later Cleveland steps into the kitchen.

"Ma'am, I was just about to wake you. Beast turned up and is currently standing in your driveway. Want us to deal with that?" he asks, his hay-blonde hair falling into his brown eyes as he speaks. He looks like an angel, but like all my soldiers, he's far from angelic.

"Is that so?" I say, my pulse kicking up a notch. "Didn't George stop him at the gate?"

Cleveland raises a brow. "George sleeps on the job. You should fire his arse."

I smile then. "You think I don't know? He's nearing retirement, besides, I have you and Harris to protect me, right?

"Fair enough. So what do you want us to do about Beast?"

"Leave it. I'll deal with him."

"Yes, Ma'am." He nods then leaves the room.

Downing half the glass of wine, I stare at my phone resting on the kitchen island, pondering what to do next when a text message lights up the screen.

Do I read it? Do I go outside and confront Beast? Do I tell Cleveland I've changed my mind and ask him to escort Beast off the premises? Do I invite him in and forget about all the shit between us and do what I've dreamed of doing for years now?

Decisions. Decisions. Decisions.

When my phone beeps again, I snatch it up. "Fuck it!" I say, opening the text message.

Beast: I've left something for you on the porch.

I frown. Well, if that's not fucking creepy, I don't know what is. Clutching my phone in my hand, I scowl at it, watching the three little bubbles move as he types.

Beast: It's not a metal box filled with hearts. I swear.

A laugh bursts free from my lips, shocking me, but I shut down that warm feeling, refusing to allow myself to feel anything other than annoyance because it's three in the morning and I'm in no mood for games... Or *am I?*

Beast: Or a signed poster of that balding actor you like.

This time my laughter releases unrestrained, and that warm feeling I'm trying to repress seeps into my veins, momentarily softening all of the hard edges and painful memories. I feel them dissolving a little and I'm uncertain how to play this. I'm out of my depth here.

Beast: If I'm gonna be honest, I had considered doing a Milk Tray moment, and deliver you a box of chocolates through your bedroom window but decided against it. I'd rather keep my bollocks intact.

"Jesus Christ," I say, smothering another giggle because one, Grim does not fucking giggle, and two... I'm not a fucking besotted girl anymore.

Dragging in a deep breath, I blow it out roughly and stride over to the window that overlooks the gravel driveway. Other than my car there's nothing else parked outside. I narrow my eyes, refocusing as I peer into the darkness. My heartbeat kicks up a notch as I try to search for his familiar figure. Once again my phone beeps with another text message.

Beast: You really need to get better security. I don't think much of your guard.

Beast: And privacy glass. You never know who might be watching.

An irrational scattering of fear disperses down my spine because there's a chance that I could've read this all wrong, and Beast is back for vengeance. I did shoot him after all. Could this all be one big ploy to get his revenge, sweeten me up, tell me all the things I want to hear, then turn up at my house in the middle of the night, take out my security guards and murder me?

It's possible.

Then I remember Cleveland and Harris are sitting on my roof, and my shoulders relax.

Beast: You know I'd never fall asleep on the job. Your safety is my top priority. Always. You never have to fear me.

It's like he's read my thoughts, or maybe I haven't perfected my poker face as much as I'd thought. Flicking my eyes up, I search the edges of my driveway that's bordered by hedges on both sides, and see the tiny flicker of a flame that briefly illuminates Beast's face, followed by the deep red of a cigarette tip sizzling. My breath catches at that brief glimpse and my fingers hover over the keyboard, a snarky response on the tip of my tongue, or should I say, fingers. Should I respond?

Fuck it.

Me: You know standing in the dark staring at a lone woman in her house isn't convincing me otherwise. Turned to stalking now, have we?

Beast: It ain't stalking when I'm not bothering to hide myself.

Me: Tell that to the two men on my roof.

I grin, hoping that will shake him. If he thinks that George, a man pushing sixty and a retired gangster, is my only protection, he's in for a rude awakening. When I look back up, I see Beast shift in the darkness. He steps out of the shadows and into the moonlight that cuts across the driveway looking far too relaxed than he has any right to be. I watch as his gaze lifts to the roof, then as he raises his hand and salutes my men. He's so fucking certain of himself and I'm not sure whether that pisses me off or turns me on. Probably both in all honesty.

Eventually he drops his gaze back to me, and my breath catches. It's not that he's wearing a faded leather jacket over a black hoodie and slim fitting jeans that make him look sexy as fuck. It's not even the way he pulls in another drag of his cigarette before stubbing it out beneath his boot. It's the way he stares at me unabashedly, like I'm already his and this is just a game to pass the time before the real action begins.

"We're inevitable, you and me…"

He knows it. My sister knows it. Deep down I've always known it.

We stare at each other for long moments. Neither of us making any attempt to move or continue texting. I'm fully aware that my dressing gown has slipped open a little, and I'm showing off more skin than I'd intended and I can't help but wonder whether he sees how my nipples press against the thin satin material, or that the hem barely grazes mid-thigh. I think about pulling the material together and tightening the belt, but decide against it. Let him get his fill.

Beast: If I were a better man, I'd avert my gaze.

A minute passes as he stares, and I can't breathe knowing his eyes are on me. Fire licks beneath my skin as he strides across the gravel driveway towards me. He stops on the other side of the window, his chest heaving as he stares. I watch as his gaze travels slowly downwards, lingering on my breasts before tracking towards my bare feet and then back up again before he locks eyes with me. The lust, need and possessiveness billowing in his gaze has my breath hitching. His fingers move over the keypad of his phone as he types out another message barely glancing at the screen. A second later my phone beeps and I break his stare, reading the message.

Beast: Let me in.

My heart jolts. My throat tightens. It's a simple request, a demand actually, but it's layered with so much meaning. Yes, Beast is clearly here to talk, otherwise he would've left whatever it is on my porch and gone, but I also know he wants more. He doesn't just want inside my house, he wants inside my thoughts, my knickers, my heart.

And I'm just not ready for any of that yet.

Not because I'm still hurt. It's not even about my forgiveness, because the second he told me the truth I'd forgiven him about everything. It's all the other shit.

It's about the club, my reputation, the people who surround me, *us*. I'm a figurehead now, a powerful one, and there isn't one person out there who won't try and take what's mine if they thought for one second I'd gone soft.

Grim is tough, unyielding, unapologetic. She's her father's daughter.

She isn't someone who lets people into her heart, period.

But Kate, she's a whole other kettle of fish.

Chewing on the inside of my cheek, I lift my gaze to meet his.

"Let me in," he pleads, pressing his hand against the windowpane, his palm flat against the glass.

My clit throbs at the blatant need in his eyes, and I draw in a ragged breath, trying to think with my head and not my heart, or even worse still, my pussy.

For a long time I go back and forth, my heart battling my head until I finally make a decision. Looking down at my phone, I type out another message.

Me: Go home. I'll see you at Tales in a few nights.

Reading my message, he withdraws his hand and nods, then with one last look that guts me, turns on his heels and walks away. I watch him leave, still standing at the window long after he's disappeared in the dark. Some time later Cleveland enters the living room.

"Ma'am, he's left the grounds."

"I know," I reply. Gathering my dressing gown tighter around me, I turn to face Cleveland. In his hand he's holding a book. "What's that?"

"This is what Beast left for you. I thought you'd want it," he replies, striding across the room, handing it to me.

"Thanks," I say, taking the book from him and recognising it immediately. It's his mum's copy of Lady Chatterley's Lover.

"Didn't peg Beast for a reader," Cleveland remarks.

"He isn't. It belonged to someone else," I explain. "Not sure why he wants me to have it."

"Might have something to do with the letter inside."

I meet Clevelands gaze, narrowing my eyes at him. "You looked inside?"

"It fell out when I picked it up. Apologies, Ma'am."

"It's fine."

Silence descends between us as I stare at the envelope, my name written in neat cursive across the surface. A letter? Beast's a man of actions, not words. This is a surprise.

Cleveland clears his throat. "Will that be all?"

"Yeah," I reply, giving him a thin smile. "I'm going back to bed."

"Goodnight then."

"Goodnight," I respond, heading back to my bedroom, Beast's letter and his mother's book clutched against my chest.

Once I've climbed into bed I stare at the book, my fingers running over the well worn cover. The spine is cracked and creased, and some of the pages are torn. It has that distinct scent of mothballs and dust that all old books seem to have and I lift it to my nose, breathing in deeply. Pulling out the letter, I place it on the bed beside me, then open the book and begin to read.

Half an hour into reading, my phone beeps with a text message. I snatch it up thinking it's Beast, only to find a message pending from Christy. I immediately swipe to read.

Christy: Stop reading the book, and read his letter.

I gasp, then grin, replying immediately.

Me: You should be asleep.

Christy: Can't, I had to message you. Read his letter.

Me: You're a wonder, do you know that?

Christy: Stop stalling.

Me: And bossy.

She sends me a smiley face emoji followed by a devil's face emoji. Followed by another message.

Christy: Please read the letter. I won't be able to sleep if you don't.

Me: You're being manipulative.

I type, following it up with a smiley face so she knows I'm not being mean.

Christy: Well I've got twelve years to make up for. What use is it having an older sister if I can't twist her around my little finger?

Me: Ha! Funny. Well, I'm not easily manipulated.

Christy: True, but you do realise the best thing to do when you're scared is to face your fears head on.

Me: I'm NOT scared.

Christy: Liar.

"This kid," I mumble, chewing on the inside of my cheek as I pick up Beast's letter.

Christy: Better to just pull the bandaid off, right?

Me: Can you read people's minds too?

I type, shaking my head at how well she's able to get inside my head.

Christy: Not as well as I can see into the future.

"What the shit?" I exclaim, staring at my phone screen.

Me: You're kidding, right?

Christy: Of course I am... I can't read minds but I do want you to READ THE LETTER.

Me: Fine. GO TO SLEEP.

Christy: Night, Kate.

Me: Night, Christy. I'll call you tomorrow.

Christy: Okay.

Placing my phone on the dresser, I pick up Beast's letter, open it and start reading.

. . .

KATE,

I know you're Grim to everyone now, and I mean no disrespect calling you Kate, but I have to address this letter to the woman I hurt because it's her that I owe my complete honesty. After you've read this letter, know that it's both Kate and Grim I'll pledge my loyalty to, if you'll accept me that is.

For the past couple days I've been trying to figure out how to convince you that you can trust me, that you can rely on me, and today I remembered something my mum told me. I want to share that with you now.

Two days before she died my mum gave me a piece of advice that has stuck with me ever since. She told me that I should always be honest with the person I love, even if it hurts. At the time I didn't appreciate what she'd said. I was too fucked-up by the fact she was dying. I was filled with rage, Kate. Rage at my father for abandoning us and at the world for taking her from me. I vowed in that moment to never fall in love, because look what it did to my mum.

And so that's how I lived my life, without love. I was okay with that.

Until I met you.

If I'm being totally honest, I knew right from the moment that I threw you over my shoulder when we were training in the ring at Tales that you were it for me. Up until that point you were Carter's daughter, someone I liked, but had no interest in romantically.

But that changed the day we sparred in the ring and you took the piss out of my ride or die tattoo. It was like a flip had been switched on in my brain. I saw you clearly for the first time, and you stopped being my job and started becoming a beautiful, sassy-as-fuck temptation I couldn't ignore.

I tried too. You know that.

I did everything in my power to ignore my feelings because number one, a man like me doesn't deserve to feel jack-shit and number two, I was fucking scared.

Not of your dad, but of love.

But no matter what I did, I couldn't not feel.

When I finally admitted to myself what I already knew to be true, I was determined to do the right thing by you, by Carter.

Then I found out what he did.

I want to tell you the truth about how things played out the night I made a deal with the King, but talking about how it went down with that piece of shit isn't the kind of honesty my mum was talking about.

She was talking about love.

Being honest about my feelings.

So I'm going to be, right the fuck now.

You scare the fuck out of me. Not because you're a badass (you are) but because I never do feelings and all that shit. I don't open myself up to pain or heartache. I fuck and I walk, and I was happy with my lot in life.

Only denying my feelings for you made me un-fucking-happy.

So I'm gonna say again what you already know in your heart.

I love you.

I LOVE YOU.

There hasn't been a day since I left that I stopped loving you, and whether you choose to believe me or not, I've not been with anyone since I kissed you that night in my tattoo shop.

I don't want anyone else. I want you.

And I will remain celibate for the rest of my fucking days if I can't have you, blue balls or not, because no one will ever come close to how I feel about you.

No one.

You don't have to love me back.

You don't have to even like me. I just need you to know.

There isn't anyone else for me.

You're it.

You're the one.

If you want me to back the fuck off, I will.

If you want me to prove my words with actions, I'll do that too.

If you want me to leave and never come back, I'll go, but not because I don't love you, but because I do.

Tell me what you need and I'll do it.

I'll do anything, including finding an army worthy of you.

See, I have a confession to make: those men and women who walked into Tales and became your soldiers, I found them, I sent them. It took me two years to do it, but I was determined. That's why I was away for so long. Not because I didn't want to fight for you, or because I was fucking terrified you wouldn't want to see me (okay, maybe a little, ffs) I did it to protect you, Kate, so that even if you don't accept me back into your life, I will live a little easier knowing no harm will come to the only woman who makes my dick hard, my heart beat, and my soul at peace.

Forever yours,

Beast

. . .

I STARE at Beast's letter, his words blurring as tears form in my eyes and love swells in my heart. He didn't abandon me. He was sourcing the best mercenaries in the world and sending them to me. Fuck! I should never have doubted him.

Guilt swirls inside my chest, and I *hate* myself for thinking so poorly of him, for not seeing the bigger picture. It's not an excuse, but when you grow up in the environment I have, it's hard to see the good in people when all you're exposed to is the bad. I was blinkered, blinded by a disappointment that was unfounded.

I was a fool.

For the first time *ever*, I let the tears fall.

Not because I'm weak.

Not because I'm a bleeding heart.

Not because I'm an emotional *woman*.

But because I'm relieved, and I'm *scared*.

Loving someone should be the best thing to happen to any person, but loving Beast is dangerous. For us both.

I know that all too well.

CHAPTER SEVEN

Mutiny

BEAST

"Beast, look at you. You're fucking fucked!" Connall announces as he shoves open the door into the changing rooms that's set aside for the fighters of Tales, and nudges Joey out of the way, trying to get a good look at me.

"Thanks for the vote of confidence, mate," I retort, wincing as Joey tuts, continuing to dab the blood dripping from the cut to my brow. That last cunt I just knocked out managed to get in a pretty fucking lethal left hook. My head is pounding and my eye is rapidly swelling.

"Over the past few hours you've fought five men and won, but I'm telling you enough is enough," Connall says.

"No!" I growl.

"Have you seen the size of that fucker out there?" he persists.

"I don't give a fuck. I'm not backing down."

"Beast, will you listen to reason!"

Joey tuts, shaking his head. "Let me deal with his wound, Connall. Then he's going back out there and finishing this."

"You're not seriously encouraging him are you?" Connall asks, scowling at Joey who just gives him a stern look and applies some butterfly tape to temporarily hold the wound closed at my eyebrow.

"We all know he has to see this through. Now stop being such a fucking pussy, and give him the encouragement he needs to end this. Beast is the best of the best. Give him some fucking credit here."

"Shut up you old dick, Beast is my best mate, and I happen to give a shit about him. If I think this has gone too far, I'm going to fucking say so."

Joey drops the bloody rag in the bin beside his feet and rounds on Connall. "Now listen to me, and listen well," he says, jabbing his finger into Connall's chest. "Beast *needs* to do this. If you don't understand the reasoning behind that then you've never been a man in love."

"Fucking glad of that if this bullshit is anything to go by," Connall mutters, folding his arms across his chest like a petulant child. I would laugh if I knew it wouldn't fucking hurt.

"There's a lot at stake here," Joey says, grasping my shoulder and giving it a squeeze. He knows I've got to do this. He gets it.

"But that won't mean jack if he ends up a dead man," Connall counters. "Besides, she's not even here."

"Oh, she's here," I say, certain of that fact. Kate might not be in the crowd with the others, but I'll bet my aching bollocks she's watching from her office.

"Beast, come on man, if the truth wasn't good enough for her, what makes you think that winning this fight will change her mind?"

"It's complicated," I retort, refusing to acknowledge what stings far worse than these cuts and bruises. Had I wanted her to run into my arms the moment she found out what really happened? I'd be a fucking liar if I said no. Do I understand why she didn't? Yeah, I do. I've put her in an impossible position because in our world, the rules that apply to everyone else, don't apply to the likes of us.

I *have* to prove myself. There's no way around it.

"It's a test," he counters.

"Of course it fucking is!" I shout back, losing my cool. "But it's also a way in, and I'm taking it. You know the score, Connall. This is how we are. This is how it *has* to go down. I'm not a fucking pussy. She lays down the gauntlet and you bet your arse I'm picking up that challenge and owning it."

"Jesus, fuck. The things you do for that woman. The things you've done, Beast!"

"Shut the fuck up, Connall!" Joey snaps this time. "This isn't just about proving to Grim that Beast is someone who will fight for her or to those tossers out there that he's a force to be reckoned with. This is about Beast proving to *himself* that he's worthy of standing by her side."

"Of course he's fucking worthy!" Connall snaps back.

"I know that. You know that, and deep down Grim does too, but Beast can't be the man he needs to be for her until he lets go of his *own* baggage. So stop giving him grief and start giving him some encouragement!"

Connall scrapes a hand through his hair, glaring at Joey before turning his attention back to me. "Fuck, fine..." His voice trails off as he looks at me with concern and a brotherly kind of love. "You sure she's worth it?"

I try not to be offended by that question, and if it had come from anyone else my fist would've met their face for the sheer gall at asking, but I know Connall likes and respects Kate, he's just concerned for his best mate and I appreciate that.

"She's worth it. You know I'd die for that woman."

"That's what worries me," he replies solemnly.

"If anyone pulls that possessive, insane part out of me, it's her. I've *got* this," I say, ignoring the pain and grinning through it. "If I can't win her heart back with the truth, then I sure as fuck will make sure that I win my place by her side."

He nods, accepting that he isn't going to change my mind. "Alright... So, erm, *knock 'em dead*, before he knocks you dead."

"Fuck off, prick," I retort, pushing to my feet and rolling my shoulders to ease some of the tension. "I tell you something, those fuckers have gotten good since I ain't been fighting. That last cunt was a cunning bastard. Smart fighter too. I'm a little out of practice here."

"No, you ain't," Joey says. "You just need to remind yourself what you're doing this for. You need to prove to yourself that you're the only man for Grim, so go out there and end this. We all know that it's grit and determination that counts the most. You don't stop until it's done. Got it?!"

I straighten my spine, ignore the pain and nod. "Got it."

Sex Is On Fire

BEAST

THE MOTHERFUCKING CANVAS tips beneath my feet, but I stand my ground glaring at the arsehole who just won't fucking concede. Blood covers the floor and the crowd is going fucking nuts. The sound of their bloodlust echoing around the warehouse. Nothing's changed there then.

Feral cunts.

Don't get me wrong, my opponent is just as exhausted as I am, but he's also a stubborn prick. The allure of becoming one of Grim's soldiers is obviously a strong one. I don't blame him for wanting to stand by her side, but I *will* kill him if he doesn't concede soon.

Grim is *mine*.

She's been mine way before any of these pricks even gave her a second look, and she'll be mine long after her hairs gone grey and we're two old as fuck cronies who piss their pants and *still* only have eyes for each other.

"Come on then if you think you're tough enough," the arrogant, little—okay big—shithead has the demon-sized bollocks to say.

I don't even bother to respond with words, I just let the beast take over enough to end this fight.

Kate wanted to know if I'm still Beast. Tonight I'm certain I've proven that I am.

With a roar that's loud enough to be heard over the crowd, I charge the fucker, launching myself at him. Utilising every last drop of fucking rage, I bring down my elbow at that delicate spot where his neck meets his shoulder, breaking his collar bone in two from the impact. He goes down with a thud just like I knew he would, but I don't stop there, I bash the living shit out of him until he's unconscious and leaking blood on the canvas.

He ain't getting back up again any time soon.

As the red mist clears, and the sound of the crowd leaks back into my consciousness I stride over to the cage door and kick the fucker open, pushing roughly through the crowd who are gathering around me and slapping my back, welcoming me into the fold once again.

Not that I give a fuck if I have their approval, bunch of sheep. The only approval I need is Kate's and she ain't even in the room.

"Beast!" Connall shouts, shoving a few of the pricks who're getting in my way, out of the way. "You fucking did it! Let me get you a drink."

"I don't want a fucking drink!" I roar, all sense of control gone now. Kate wanted to see the beast and she's got her fucking wish. Now she's gonna have to deal with the consequences of that because my blood is boiling and my dick is rock fucking hard. "I want my woman!"

Connall smirks. "Then go get her, tiger."

I don't bother to respond, too riled up to do anything but stride to her office and kick down the fucking door. It slams against the wall as I make my entrance, consumed with the need to claim what's mine and damn it all to fuck.

With my chest heaving, covered head-to-toe in blood, I stare Kate down.

I'm pissed off.

And I'm fucking horny.

"I'm done waiting!"

"Congratulations," she says, calm as fuck as she regards me from behind her desk. Regal like the queen she is, she's wearing a simple black wraparound dress, her hair hanging loosely over her shoulders and her neck decorated in a long silver necklace. "You fought well."

Her gaze rakes over my body, making me harder still.

I'm so fucking hard for her.

"I imagine you could use a drink?" she offers, and it takes me a minute to notice one of her soldiers standing in the corner of the room pouring her a drink like he's comfortable doing so, like he's done it a thousand times before. He glances over at me and nods and I take in the blonde hair, dark eyes, and the calm measuring stare.

Cleveland.

I recognise him.

I recognise him because *I* was the one who sent him here. And it pisses me off that it isn't *me* standing by her side right now, doing the mundane shit for the woman I love. I want to be the one to serve her in *any* way she chooses.

"What the *fuck* is he doing in here?" I shout, rage fizzing in my blood. "Get the fuck out!"

He places the glass of bourbon on the desk in front of Kate, unphased, riling me up further.

"Ma'am?" he questions, not taking his eyes off me for one second. I bare my teeth at him, ready to fucking kill him. Pretty sure I'm capable of ripping his head off with my bare hands right about now, I'm so fired up.

"It's okay, Cleveland. I've got this," Kate says, picking up her glass of bourbon and taking a sip.

"Are you certain?"

Kate scowls, telling me that she isn't used to him questioning her decisions, but she doesn't call him out on it either, which also tells me she appreciates his concern and that they have a closer relationship than I'd anticipated. "I'm certain," Kate replies.

"I'll wait outside," he says before striding around the table and past me.

His expression is blank, respectful, and despite wanting to rip him a new one, I don't. I don't because deep down I know that it was him and the other mercenaries who've kept my girl safe whilst I've been gone.

The door clicks shut behind me and then it's just me and Kate, and the rest of the world ceases to fucking exist. A part of me, a really small part is telling me to calm the fuck down, to back the fuck up, but the rest of me doesn't want to. I'm fizzing with the need to act, the violence of tonight feeding the need to take what is mine, what will always be mine.

Even so, that small voice is enough to keep my feet glued to the spot, though it can't stop me from shaking with adrenaline and desire. It can't stop my dick from leaping at the way she shifts in her seat, her eyes tracking over every inch of me. It can't stop the fire in my blood setting alight to my skin. It can't stop this need I have to just fucking hold her in my arms and love her like I've wanted to do for so long now.

"Kate—"

"Grim," she counters.

"Goddamn it!" I shout.

I'll call her whatever the fuck she likes so long as she lets me back in her life. My fingers clench and unclench, my veins spiking with adrenaline and a whole host of other hormones that flood my system after almost five hours of fighting my way back to Kate's side. No, not five hours.

Two fucking years.

I'm beyond exhausted. I'm beyond frustrated. I'm at the point where this either ends with my dick buried deep inside of her, or my fucking heart giving out.

"Get in the shower. Clean yourself up," she demands, pointing to a door in the corner of her office I didn't notice the last time I was here.

"What?" I blink, fired up. "You're asking me to shower... right the fuck now?!"

"If you want to have a conversation with me, then I suggest you clean the blood off your body first."

The look in her eyes tells me she's not fucking around. I glance at my chest and the streaks of blood there, some of it mine, most of it not, and nod.

"Fuck, fine!" I snap, spinning on my heel and striding into her bathroom.

It takes me all of two point five seconds to rip off my shorts, step under the spray, scrub away all the blood with her shower gel then grab a towel and wrap it around my waist. I don't even bother to dry myself off because if she thinks that taking a shower was enough to cool me the fuck down, she's mistaken. Stepping back into her office, my dick making a tent out of the towel, I glare at her.

"What do you want?" Kate asks me, her arms resting on the desk in front of her, her gaze leisurely taking me in. If she notices my erection she says fuck all about it.

"What do I want?!" I shout back, unable to keep a lid on my emotions. Not fucking calm in the slightest.

"Yes, what do you *want*?" She rises from her seat, and there's a challenge in her gaze, one that wasn't there a few days ago, and it feels like an opening, one I'm going to take.

"I want you! Only you!" I grind out.

"You're two years too late," she says, letting out a sad laugh, one that fucks me over entirely.

"The fuck I am!" I retort angrily.

"Beast, it's complicated."

I shake my head. "The fuck it is."

"But—"

"You once told me that you didn't want a man who wasn't one thousand percent certain that it was you he wanted. I'm a million percent certain. I *always* fucking was. I came back for you and I ain't leaving until you understand that," I cut in, breathing heavily.

Something shifts in her stance, as though the breath she's been holding releases and acceptance fills her lungs instead. She knows as well as I do that there will never be anyone else. She's it for me and I'm the man for her.

"Do you understand?" I repeat.

She nods, the look she gives me telling me everything. The barrier she'd put up when I last saw her finally drops and right there in the depths of her gaze is yearning. She wants me as badly as I want her. "Yes, I understand."

"Thank fuck," I reply, then rush her like a man possessed.

One minute my arms are empty and the next they're filled with her.

With my woman.

My. Fucking. Woman.

"You own my fucking heart!" I grind out as her scent consumes my senses and I pull her flush against my damp skin, my fucking heart pounding and my dick rock hard against her stomach. "I will do whatever it takes to be by your side. Whatever you fucking need, I'll do it. I fought those fuckers to show you just how much you belong to *me*, how much I belong to *you*."

"Yes," she hisses, air rushing out of her chest as she reaches for me. "You've always been *mine*. You always will be."

Pretty sure my dick just bruised her belly the way it jolted at those words. If anyone owns me it's her, and I'm not mad about it, not in the fucking slightest. With a growl that sounds more animal than human, I bury my face in her hair, my lips pressing against the bare skin of her neck. She smells of everything a *real* man could ever want. She smells of lust and confidence, of femininity and strength, of power and womanhood.

She smells like *mine*.

My lips and tongue find the soft spot right below her ear, but I'm not gentle and I'm not soft. I bite and suck, drawing her skin into my mouth, marking her with a bruising kiss. My teeth scrape across her skin as I nip at her. I'm fucking feral, wanting to sink my teeth into her flesh and mount her like an animal.

She moans, gasping at the way I maul her, dragging me

closer, squeezing me tighter. It's as if both of us want to crawl under each other's skin. Holding each other isn't enough, we need to join together.

We need to fuck.

"I want in," I grind out, roughly pulling at the towel wrapped around my waist. It falls to the floor and I'm naked, grasping and tugging at her, squeezing her arse, grabbing her tits.

I'm fucking mindless, all hope of maintaining control gone now that I finally have her in my arms. Crushing her against my chest, I shove her dress off her shoulders so that I can taste more of her. My teeth drag across her skin, my lips and tongue trail sloppy kisses across her neck and shoulder.

More. More. Fucking more.

"Oh, fuck," she cries, her nails digging into my chest as she grasps my pecs, her neck arching, giving me more access as her body yields to mine. I suck on her, lap and lick, bruise and bite. Tasting her, teasing, getting her hot, getting me hot. "That feels... Oh, fuck that feels good."

"You and me, *this*," I say, flipping her around and hauling her back against my chest, my mouth pressed against her ear as my arm wraps around her waist and my fingers squeeze her hip, "Will only ever feel good from this point onwards. You hear me?"

"Yes," she breathes, conceding, yielding just a little as I rub my dick between the crack of her arse and wrap my hand around her throat, biting her ear lobe, licking it. All that stands between my dick and her beautiful pussy is the thin material of her dress and knickers.

"Off," I grunt, frustrated that she's still wearing clothes as I grasp her tit, trying to articulate what I want, but not finding the right words.

Instead I squeeze her breast, my fingers pushing down her bra and rolling her nipple as I continue to kiss and suck, bite and lick at her neck. She gives me better access, leaning her head to the side as she reaches up to grab the back of my head, her breath coming thick and fast as I fucking claim her with my mouth. I want to mount her, bend her over the desk and fuck her from behind. I want to sink my tongue into her wet heat, feel her pussy pulse around my fingers. I want to bury my cock in her mouth until she's fucking gagging and drooling around my length. I want her arse, that tight puckered hole making me forget my own name as I fuck her. I want her screaming my name, owning *me*, claiming me as she bucks up and down on top of my dick. I want to be on my knees for her, doing whatever the fuck she wants me to do.

I want it all.

My base instinct is to claim her in the most dirty, feral way possible, but at the moment I'm enjoying the way she writhes in my arms, moaning as I bring her pleasure from paying attention to a place on her body most fucking men ignore. One day soon, I'm going to kiss and lick every inch of her body until she's putty in my hands, then I'm going to fuck her slow and steady until nothing but the memory of *my* dick, and *my* love, is imprinted on her body, heart and soul.

Right now the beast in me needs to be satiated, and as much as this is about us finally claiming each other, it's also about the raw need to *fuck*.

It's been a long goddamn time.

"Touch me," she gasps, twisting her head to the side,

meeting my mouth with hers, kissing me deep, fucking me with her tongue as I yank up the skirt of her dress and find her knicker-covered pussy, the material soaked for me.

"So fucking wet. You're dripping for me, Princess," I say into her mouth, my fingers dipping beneath the waistband as I slide my index finger between her folds, feeling the hard nub of her clit and the piercing I've been desperate to play with ever since I found out she had one. Swirling my finger against her clit and gently tugging on the piercing, she cries out, her hips bucking as more wet, slippery heat greets me. I grind harder against her arse, releasing her mouth as I ravage her neck once more.

She rocks against my hand, moaning and whimpering, and I listen to the sounds she makes, the way her body moves, making a mental note of what she likes, following her lead. Then as her breathing becomes heavier, her moans louder, I pick up the pace, applying the perfect pressure to her clit until she's shuddering in my arms, her whole body shaking as she comes.

"Beast," she breathes, her chest heaving.

But I'm not done. Not even fucking close.

Twisting her back around, I look at her beautiful face. Her cheeks are flush, her pupils blown wide and with one hand I grasp the back of her head, then slide my cum-soaked fingers between her parted lips.

"Suck, Princess," I demand, watching her swallow my fingers, her mouth wet and warm.

She sucks, her tongue tasting, her cheeks hollowing out as she makes this humming sound that drives me fucking nuts as I withdraw my fingers, wishing it was my cock in her mouth. She grins, her cheeks blushing and her pupils blown wide.

"That was fun."

"If you think this is over, then you can think again."

"Wait there's more?" she sasses back.

"Fuck, look at you," I exclaim, so helplessly gone for her as she stares up at me, open and willing in this moment to forget the pain between us and forge a new path, one paved with fervent kisses, scorching passion and *love*. "So fucking beautiful. I can't wait to fuck your mouth with my dick."

"And they say romance is dead." She giggles and the sound is like pure gold.

"Do that again."

"Do what?"

"Laugh."

"Right now I'd rather moan..."

Her voice trails off and I yank her closer, slamming my mouth against hers and kissing her like a forest fire ripping through barren woods. It's a wild kiss, untethered by any previous restraints. It's raw and passionate and fucking everything I've ever dreamed off.

Carter isn't here to stop me.

And I've long since lost the power to stop myself.

So I kiss and kiss her, grasping her against me, rubbing my dripping cock against her belly like a fucking savage.

"I. Need. You," I grind out, fucking mindless.

I need friction, any friction until I can bury my cock inside of her. She yelps into my mouth, my grasp on her tit bruising, and I force myself to loosen my hold enough to pull back and speak.

"Fuck, fuck! I can't stop. I can't fucking stop!" I yell,

reaching for her again as I grasp her chin and twist her head to the side, licking and nipping at her jaw like a wild animal.

This isn't how I fuck, not the first time with a woman anyway, not with any woman period come to think of it. No one has got me this wound up, this *possessive*. I can't stop the ferocious need to impale her on my dick, to claim her, to fuck us both into oblivion.

"I. Can't. Fucking. Stop!" I pant between breaths.

"Don't stop. If you fucking stop, I promise I'll shoot you dead this time!" she snaps back, grasping my cheeks and slamming her lips against mine, forcing my lips apart with her tongue as she sits on the edge of her desk and wraps her legs around my arse, rubbing her hot cunt against my aching dick.

"Not now, not ever," I reply as everything about her consumes me. Her scent, her taste, her whimpers and moans, the way she grasps me back just as tightly as though she too can't get close enough.

I'm a fucking goner for her.

"Beast," she moans into my mouth, her hands pawing at my chest, her nails digging into my bruised skin as she kisses me with the same force, the same ferocity as I kiss her.

She matches my passion with her own.

We're teeth and tongue, lips and saliva.

We're frenzied and frantic.

Our kiss is messy and fucking hot. It stokes the fire within me to dangerous, billowing heights.

This is two years of pent-up sexual tension exploding like an atom bomb between us. This is pain and anguish, heartbreak and hate. This is longing and need, lust and passion.

This is *love*.

I don't care that my skin is bruised or that I can barely see out of one eye.

All I care about is this moment between us, right here and now.

"Beast!" she pleads, rubbing her hot, greedy pussy against my dick.

That need in her voice, the way it cracks with emotion, desperate for me as much as I'm desperate for her, is like a hit of cocaine straight to my fucking dick.

"I need to taste you," I say.

Hauling her to the edge of the desk, I reach behind her and swipe my hand across the surface, shoving everything to the floor, shattering the glass. The sound of it breaking alerts Cleveland, and the door opens, but I don't give a fuck. I'm already on my knees between Kate's legs, my fingers pulling her knickers to one side as I stare at the perfect swollen lips of her pussy.

"Ma'am?" he questions.

"Get the fuck out!" she demands before I can lift my gaze from her sweet, sweet cunt and tell him the same damn thing.

"Sure thing," he replies with a hint of a smile in his voice as he closes the door.

I don't wait a second longer. Lifting Kate's thighs over my shoulder, I grasp her hips and cup her arse, bringing her pussy to my mouth and lifting her up to my face. She falls back on the table, her elbows pressing into the hard wood as her head tips back and she moans.

Then I fuck her hole with my tongue.

Licking and lapping, my saliva mixing with her pleasure, I feast on her pussy.

Normally I spend a long time between a woman's legs,

bringing them to the edge then pulling back and starting all over again, because what I love almost as much as fucking is eating a woman out. You better believe that when I've calmed the fuck down and we get to do this again, I'm gonna take it nice and slow. But right now, slow isn't the name of the game. Making Kate come in my mouth within the next five minutes is.

So I do all the things I need to in order to get her off. I flick my tongue backwards and forwards over her clit until her body's shaking and her legs are trembling around my ears. Then as her orgasm crests, I wrap my lips around her clit and suck until she's screaming my damn name and suffocating me with her pussy.

"Oh fuck, oh fuck, oh fuck," she pants, holding me in place as she grinds against my face chasing her orgasm, shuddering and bucking with the power of it.

I lap at her like the greedy beast that I am, loving every second of her hot, wet pussy against my face. When her hands loosen, and her body softens, I rear upwards, my dick so fucking hard that I have to grasp the base and squeeze in order to temper my own orgasm that's desperate to fucking unleash itself.

"I knew you'd taste like my kind of drug," I rumble, swiping the back of my hand against my lips and chin.

She smiles up at me through heavy eyelids, her body relaxed, sated. "Is that so?"

Fuck I need inside of her.

"We're not done," I grind out, pulling at the belt of her wrap dress that's still stubbornly tied around her waist despite the top half hanging off her shoulders, and the bottom half hitched up over her hips.

"Damn right," she replies, smirking, as I press a kiss against her stomach and the underside of her ribcage, my tongue leaving wet trails across her skin.

"Are you taking contraception?" I ask, my love for her cutting through the thick fog of my lust enough to ask the question.

"Yes... I'm clean too," she adds, heat flashing her chest and neck pink.

The fact that she even needs to say that has me thinking murderous thoughts, but I push that feeling down. Now is not the time to be a jealous prick and demand to know who she's fucked before me. I'm just grateful I'm in her arms, that she's in mine.

"I haven't been with a woman since the moment I fell for you," I blurt out, wanting to remind Kate what I told her in my letter. Not because I want to earn brownie points or make her feel guilty for finding comfort in the arms of another man even though it *kills* me, but because I need her to understand that no one else would do.

No one.

She lifts her hand and cups my cheek, reminding me of the softness I remember so well. "I know, I read your letter," she murmurs, and some of the emotion she's forced below the surface rises in her gaze like the swell of the ocean.

"I could never betray you like that. I would *never* fuck another woman. You're it for me. Forever. Understand?"

She nods, drawing me back to her, kissing me roughly, tugging on the back of my neck, dragging me closer, making me mindless. "I do, I know that now."

"I want to make love to you, Kate. I *will* make love to you the right fucking way and soon, but right now I can't be gentle. I need to fuck," I blurt out, hoping she'll understand that there's a difference and that in this moment with the way I'm feeling, I can't hold back, that I don't want to.

"It's okay," she replies, kissing me deeply. "I need that too."

"Fuck, I just need to be inside you... but I'll stop. If you want me to stop, I'll stop," I say, forcing myself to speak the words. Forcing myself to look her in the eye so I can see for myself if she truly wants this. That I have her consent.

"I don't want you to be gentle. I want you to fuck me like you missed me, Beast. Show me how much you missed me. Make me come again," she demands, and I see the fire in her eyes. It matches my own as she grasps my dick in her hand and gently squeezes.

"Fuuuccckkkk!" I exclaim, and that's all I need to cut the final shred of restraint holding me back.

Pulling her bra down roughly, my mouth and hands are on her tits and I'm licking and sucking and squeezing her flesh whilst she slides her fist up and down my dick, moaning for me, pleasuring me whilst I pleasure her.

"Yesss," she hisses, her nails digging in my scalp as she releases me and falls back onto the desk, hauling me on top of her, kissing me deep. Her shoes drop to the floor as my dick slaps against the mound of her pussy, heavy and twitching. I feel her wetness against my shaft as she lifts her hips rubbing herself against my length wantonly, with abandon.

"Do it, Beast. Do it! I need you inside of me. *Please!*"

"Fuck, I love the way you beg for my cock," I say, reaching between us and grasping the waistband of her knickers. I pull, tearing one side then the other, my nostrils flaring at the thin pink lines left on her hips.

Chest heaving, her tits bare, her nipples tight, she bites down on her lip as I pull back just enough so that I can grasp my dick and rub it through her soft folds. I stare at her blush lips and the deep berry of her opening, all slick for me. The head of my dick is an angry purple, the barbell glistening with her arousal, with mine. I push my thumb over the slit of my dick, gathering precum and swiping it over her pussy lips, marking her on the outside, before I claim her on the inside.

"This pussy is mine now. Do you understand me?"

"Likewise. Any bitch comes near you and they're dead," she snarls, her possession doing crazy things to me.

"Only us from now on," I say.

"Only us," she agrees, rubbing her cunt against my dick and then pushing up onto her elbows. "Now will you please just fuck me, Beast."

"Believe me, not even a nuclear bomb going off could stop me now," I state, so fucking turned on as I nudge the head of my cock against her pierced clit, loving how fucking sexy it looks as I rub her with the head of my dick over and over again, teasing her, teasing myself until neither of us can take any more. The metal of our piercings clinking against each other is fucking music to my ears.

"Beast, *please*," she begs, her own breaths coming thick and fast, her stomach muscles contracting as she reaches down with one hand, spreading her pussy lips with her fingers so that I can guide the head of my cock into her glistening hole.

"Do you feel how hard I am for you? Only you do this to me. Only ever you," I say, gripping my cock, holding it at her entrance as we lock eyes.

"Take it," she murmurs, and it's the sexiest fucking thing

I've ever heard. The way she spreads herself and orders me to do what I've dreamed of doing for so fucking long.

"Fuck, yes," I reply, dipping the head of my dick into the tightness of her hole and seeing fucking stars. My head tips back and I groan, loving the way she spreads her legs wider, granting me entrance. "There's nowhere I'd rather be than buried balls deep inside of you."

She moans, her hand falling away as she braces herself on the desk, holding herself upright on her elbows. For a moment I'm blinded by feeling, my legs fucking shaking and streaks of white light spotting my vision as every single part of me hones in on the point where our bodies are joined and the feel of her pussy as it squeezes the head of my dick.

"You're so tight," I exclaim, breathless, mindless, hopelessly fucking in love with her as I try to control myself and not slam into her like the feral beast I am, because right at the back of my head there's a niggle, something I can't quite put my finger on, something important that I'm missing beneath the lust and the love. But that thought disappears as she grabs my arse, her nails drawing blood.

"Take it!" she orders.

I motherfucking take it.

I slam into her with one hard thrust, right up to the goddamn hilt. The force of my penetration pushing the desk across the concrete floor.

She screams, arching her neck as my dick hits her cervix and my fingers grip her hips.

It feels like heaven on fucking earth.

It feels like home.

Sliding my arm beneath her back, I grasp her to me, cradling her against my chest momentarily as she buries her teeth into my shoulder.

"This is what home is," I mutter, before pressing her back onto the desk and claiming the only woman I will ever love, fucking her rough, quick and hard.

Her breaths come hard and fast, her hands grasping my back, her legs wrapping around my hips as though she's hanging on for dear life. Perhaps she is, because I've never been more determined to obliterate every memory of every other man she's allowed into her bed than I am right now.

I pound into her, promising myself that after we've fucked I will love on her the right way, slowly, leisurely, for hours and hours and fucking hours.

But right now, I meet her energy with my own.

I'm desperate and greedy.

Fucking her with a frenzied kind on need.

My balls slap against her arse, my dick swells inside of her as we fuck. She's so tight, so fucking perfect and I don't hold back. I *can't* hold back.

And she's right there with me, returning my force in kind, lifting her hips to meet mine, carving her nails down my back, biting my skin and drawing blood until I'm half blind with sensation, with feeling, with emotion, as she screams out my name.

Right here on her desk, we fuck our feelings into life.

We drag out all of the anger and the pain, the frustration and the disappointment, the lust and the love, pulling it to the surface until her core is squeezing the cum out of my dick and we're a pile of sweaty, shaking limbs, sloppy kisses and battered hearts slowly knitting themselves back together again.

CHAPTER EIGHT

Secrets

GRIM

My heart is as bruised as my pussy.

But it's a good feeling, a *warm* feeling. Uncomfortable, yes, but also reassuring.

Beast just fucked the virginity *out* of me and spilled his love *into* me, and if I had any shred of doubt left about the way he feels for me, then that's been obliterated tonight.

In the cage, he fought with focus and a determination to win. The second I watched him step into the ring, I knew there'd be no doubt he'd be by my side at the end of it. Watching him tear his opponents to shreds was nothing short of erotic. I'd felt his anger and his rage, his passion and his need all the way over on the other side of the warehouse.

He fought them all for me.

He proved himself to every man and woman standing in the arena watching him fight that he is *still* a force to be reckoned with. That he will stop at nothing to be by my side. That if you fuck with him, with me, you'll end up like those men he just flattened.

If I said that didn't inflate my ego a little, I'd be a fucking liar.

But this *isn't* about my ego.

It's about him and me, about us.

Kate and Roger.

Grim and Beast.

Queen and... *King*.

Because if anyone has earned their place at my side, it's him.

"Beast?" I whisper, my fingers trailing down his spine as I shift beneath him.

We're still joined together, and I hiss, feeling the soreness between my legs despite how ready he made me, how completely he turned me on. I'm praying that there won't be any blood, but if there is, then so be it. He'll learn I'm a virgin and know that just like him, I couldn't bear to give myself to anyone whilst we've been apart.

"Princess," he murmurs, lifting his weight onto his forearms as he cups my head in his hands, swiping his thumb across my puffy, kiss-bruised lips. He gives me a rueful smile. "You okay?"

"I'm more than okay. You, on the other hand, look like you've done ten rounds in the ring with Tyson Fury," I say with a soft laugh as I reach up and press my fingers gently against his swollen eye.

He hisses, then grabs my wrist and kisses my palm. "Fury wouldn't last one round with me. I'd knock him clean out in the first five minutes."

"Is that so?" I tease.

"You know it, baby."

"*Baby?* That's new."

"You don't remember the last time I called you baby?" he asks, smirking.

"I remember," I admit, it wasn't long after I called him daddy.

"So you don't like it?"

"Well, if you're going to call me baby, how does Daddy sound?" I joke, biting down on another hiss of pain as his cock hardens and he rolls his hips.

"I'll answer to whatever the hell you want," he admits, dropping his lips to mine.

"Hmm, what about *honeybun?*"

"Sure. I'm sweet enough when I'm not annihilating wannabe hardmen in the cage," he chuckles. "Actually, I quite like *lambchop*," I mutter, pressing another smile-filled kiss against his lips.

"I'm sensing a theme here," he replies, kissing me back as he gently flexed his hips. "But if you're gonna go for a really good nickname that combines food *and* a compliment, I think *studmuffin* fits the bill."

"Funny," I reply, giving his arse a light slap as he pulls back and grins at me, wincing a little as he does so. His right eye is practically swollen shut now.

"You really need to get Joey to pack some ice on that, and I really need to show my face," I say, brushing his wet hair out of his swollen eye, wanting to remain in his arms, but knowing that I shouldn't.

"Later," he replies, rocking his hips with a smirk on his face and love in his eyes.

"Beast, I have a club to run," I repeat, feeling the warmth inside of me stir. I'm wet with our combined arousal from earlier.

"I don't give a fuck," he retorts, trailing his lips down my neck and running his tongue over my collarbone.

"Beast, seriously," I insist, grasping his face. "As much as I want to continue, I can't. I've got a club full of punters out there waiting on my appearance. Besides, I need to announce you officially as the winner and my newly acquired soldier."

"Newly acquired? I've never left your side even when I wasn't here."

"I know," I whisper, acknowledging everything he'd confessed in his letter. "And you have to understand that I have responsibilities now."

He smiles. "You know this whole badass businesswoman vibe you've got going on is killing me. I want to fuck you again," he confesses, pouting. It looks cute on him, but I resist the urge to indulge. Besides, my vagina really could do with a rest.

"I'm glad you like it," I laugh, gently easing him back.

"I do, so fucking much that my dick wants to permanently take up residence in your sweet, sweet pussy."

"Aren't you exhausted?" I ask with a laugh, trying to keep his attention on my face and not between my legs as he slowly pulls out of me. It doesn't work though, because we both stare at the spot where we're joined together.

"What's this?" he asks, his voice a little brittle sounding as he slowly withdraws.

"It's nothing," I say, my cheeks flushing with heat at the streaks of blood smearing his cock and my inner thighs.

"The fuck it is! Did my piercings hurt you? Was I too rough? Why didn't you say anything, Kate?" he reels off in quick succession, his face flooding with concern.

"It's not that." I shift on the desk, pushing upright and wrapping my dress around myself, tying it up and pulling the material over my bare legs. "You should get dressed. There are some clothes in that locker over there. Help yourself."

"You keep a spare set of *men's clothes* in your office?" he asks, thrown, blinking at me like I've suddenly grown two heads.

"Sometimes Hudson and his brothers train here, I keep their stuff in my office," I reply, pushing off the edge of the desk as Beast backs up, mouth agape. "Now, I really need to clean up. So if you wouldn't mind..."

I let my voice trail off, wincing at how I sound. I don't want him to go, not really, and I don't want to go out into the warehouse either but Kate's had her fun, and Grim has got to make an appearance.

"Just wait a minute. Shit!" he exclaims, running a hand through his hair and blocking my way as I try to move around the table. He's made no move to cover himself up and I drag my gaze upwards, refusing to feel any shame or embarrassment at my blood and our combined arousal drying on his half mast cock.

"We'll discuss this later."

"You're bloody right we'll be discussing the fact you've got the Freed brothers' shit in your office later, but right now I want to know why my dick is covered in your blood."

I tip my head to the side, taking my measure of him. "I would've thought that was obvious, Beast."

"Right now I'm gonna need you to spell this out for me, Princess," he counters, and the slight edge of anger in his voice has me feeling defensive all of a sudden.

"I'm a virgin, or at least I was up until a few minutes ago."

He stares at me for what seems like an eternity, so I adjust my dress and slide my feet back into my heels whilst he pulls his shit together.

"Oh fuck!" he exclaims, and I feel my cheeks heat, hating that they do.

Turning on my heel, I move past him and stride over to the bathroom. Right now he can deal with whatever shit's going through his head on his own. I need to clean up and then go outside and face the music.

Grabbing the flannel from the sink, I wet it, trying and failing to push away this weird sense of disappointment from my heart. I hadn't expected Beast to react quite the way he has. I thought fucking a virgin was every man's wet dream.

Guess I was wrong.

"Here, let me," Beast says as he steps into the bathroom.

"I can do it," I reply tightly, glancing at him in the mirror. He's still naked and something about the fact he's so comfortable in his skin makes me feel strangely uneasy in mine, especially given his dick is still streaked with my blood.

"Kate, let me," he insists, softer now as he grasps my wrist and gently takes the flannel from my hands. I keep my gaze fixed on the faucet, turning it off.

"You can't call me Kate out there," I remind him, if only to avoid the fucking elephant in the room.

"I won't. I'll stop calling you Kate from this moment on if it bothers you that much, but will you just look at me for a minute?" he asks, reaching for my elbow, his fingers grazing over my skin.

"I'm not ashamed," I reply, lifting my chin and meeting his gaze with a defiant look as I turn around. Maybe a little embarrassed, but not ashamed.

"Of course you shouldn't be ashamed. Fuck, Kate... *Grim*, that's not what this is."

"Then why are you acting so weird then? I thought all men liked fucking virgins or is it just you who's disgusted by my blood on your dick?"

"Disgusted? Jesus, fuck, you couldn't be further from the truth. I'm honoured, and I'm fucking angry at *myself* for assuming—"

"That I'd fucked other men," I finish for him.

He nods. "Yeah. Given the circumstances, I thought the promise we made to each other was broken after what happened."

"Did you break your promise to me?"

He shakes his head. "Never. There's been no one."

"Then the same applies to me."

"I thought you hated me," he says.

"I never hated you," I admit, bringing my hand up to the puckered scar just below his shoulder, touching it gently. "I'm so sorry..." My voice trails off as I stare at the scar.

"I'm not. You did what had to be done. You proved to the King that you're not to be fucked with. Your actions kept you safe all this time, but this isn't about that night. Right now I owe you an apology."

"You've already done that."

"No, I need to apologise for—"

"For fucking me?"

He sighs. "For fucking you the *way* I did. If I'd known, it would've been different. I would've been gentle."

I blow out a breath, relieved, heart-warmed. "I don't regret it."

"I hurt you."

"No, you didn't. You fucked me the way I wanted to be fucked. So don't you dare regret it, because I refuse to. It was *perfect*. Though I might need an ice pack for my lady garden," I joke.

"An ice pack? Jesus, you're not making me feel any better," he exclaims with a rueful smile, dropping to his knees before me.

"What are you doing now?"

"After care," he replies solemnly, then pushes up the skirt of my dress, his fist bunching up the material as he rests his forearm on my stomach and looks up at me. "Spread your legs, Princess."

The way he says it isn't sexual at all, but it sure as fuck makes my aching pussy think she's in for round two. The sheer fact that he's kneeling before me all busted up from his fights in the cage, and taking care of me says a lot about his heart. I've no doubt had he known I was still a virgin, he would've been as gentle as he promised, but it wouldn't have been the same. The fire, the passion, that absolute desperate way he fucked me, that's what I needed from him after two years apart.

"Your legs, Kate," he insists.

I spread them for him, feeling exposed. It's an intimate act, just as intimate as having sex and with as much emotion attached to it.

"You know I've dreamt about this moment for a long time," Beast says, cupping my pussy with the warm flannel and gently running it over my tender skin.

"What, being on your knees and washing my pussy?" I ask, a smile in my voice, my cheeks flushing at how gently he cleans me.

Softness, warmth, kindness. They're all things I've been lacking in my life, and to get them from a man like Beast, a man who cuts out human hearts and serves them up like a gift, is a little strange. Good, strange, but strange nevertheless.

"Yes, being on my knees and washing your pussy," he replies, dragging the flannel down my inner thigh and wiping the blood and cum staining me there. "I've also dreamt about fucking you until neither of us can see straight. I've dreamt about dropping on my knees and eating you out, and learning all the ways you like to be touched. I've dreamt about my cum spread across your thighs, your tits, your stomach, your tongue."

"That's quite a lot of dreaming," I reply, as he flashes me a toothy grin then kisses me gently right above my clit, then lower against my pussy lips. I let out a shuddering breath, my fingers finding their way into his thick, tousled hair.

"Tell me about it. At one point I honestly thought I might die of blue balls," he admits, letting his eyelids droop as I massage his scalp.

"It was the least you deserved for staying away for two years," I say, meaning it as a joke, but it comes out a little harsher than I'd intended.

"Kate," he begins, letting go of the hem of my dress and standing, dropping the dirty flannel into the sink behind me.

Turning around, I grab a fresh one, wetting it. "Your turn," I say, meeting his gaze in the mirror before twisting in his arms.

"You know why I was away so long," he murmurs, brushing a strand of hair behind my ear. His fingers follow the strand as he tugs on it gently before letting it go.

"That came out wrong. I just missed you," I admit, peering up at him.

"Believe me, it wasn't easy staying away, but I did what I believed was best for you."

"And I appreciate it," I say, pressing my hand against the tattoo over his heart. "Thank you."

"You're welcome," he replies, cupping my hand with his larger one, and squeezing gently. "Though I gotta say, the way you are with Cleveland is making me a little fucking crazy."

"The way I am with him?"

"Yeah, relaxed, comfortable. It's denting my ego a bit, Princess."

"He's a good guy, but there's nothing there," I say. "Besides, he's not interested in me."

"Why the fuck not?" Beast asks, affronted on my behalf.

I laugh, shaking my head. "I think he'd rather fuck you."

Beast shoulders relax and he smiles broadly. "Pretty sure most people do," he replies with a smirk.

"Pretty sure I'd gouge their eyes out," I reply with a raised brow.

"I know something that could poke a person's eye out," Beast replies, grinning as he drops his gaze to his growing erection. I laugh and it's a freeing kind of laugh, one I haven't experienced for a long, long time.

"You're such a dick."

"You're right, it *is* a big dick."

We both crack up then, but his laughter dies on his lips when I gently grasp his cock and begin to clean it. Fully aware of how turned on he is, I tease him, sliding the warm flannel up and down his cock in gentle, even strokes.

"Are you trying to kill me?" he croaks, swallowing hard as I drop the washcloth in the sink and keep my fingers wrapped around his cock.

"No..." I reply sweetly, manoeuvring his body so that his arse is pressed up against the vanity unit and I'm pressing butterfly kisses against his tattooed chest as I fist his cock, sliding my palm up and down his length.

"Liar, I definitely think you're trying to kill me." He groans as I drop to my knees and lick the tip of his dick. "Fuck. Me."

"As soon as my pussy's recovered, I intend to. Over and over and over again," I reply, looking up at him as I take the mushroom shaped head of his cock into my mouth and swirl my tongue around it. He stares down at me, his jaw slack, his hair falling into his eyes, and I hum around his length, loving how he tastes.

He's so masculine. So very, very *mine*.

"You're not the only one who's been dreaming," I say, then trace the thick vein on the underside of his cock with my tongue. "Every night I've made myself come thinking about you. About fucking you, taking you in my mouth just like this."

"Say that again," he mutters as I lick the tip of his dick, my tongue swirling around the piercing there.

"I've thought about sucking your cock, taking you deep..."

My voice trails off as I take the head of his cock in my mouth. He's big, we've already established that fact, and my jaw aches as I open as wide as I can to accommodate his girth.

"Fuck, fuck, fuck," he hisses.

The sound of his pleasure, and the way he grasps a fistful of my hair, rocking his hips into my mouth, does something to me. I feel powerful being the master of his pleasure, it's a massive turn on to know that I'm the one he's hard for, desperate for, in love with.

This big beast of a man is wholly and truly mine.

Picking up the pace, I suck him off in earnest, bobbing my head up and down his length, loving the feel of his piercings against my lips and forgetting for a moment that I have a club to run.

"Jesus, yes, just like that. Fuck me with that pretty mouth, Princess. Make me come," he groans, tightening his fist as he guides me down his length.

I gag, and he pulls back a little, allowing me to catch my breath. Then I grasp his hips and slide his cock deeper, taking him to the hilt.

"Fuuuuuckkk!" Beast's cock twitches in my mouth, the taste of his precum sliding down the back of my throat. "I'm gonna die, and it'll be fucking worth it."

If I didn't have his dick in my mouth, I'd be laughing.

"Baby, you're so fucking good at this," he murmurs, praising me as I pull back to the tip and repeat the action over and over again until his fingers grasp my hair painfully. He's close.

So I work him over, ignoring the ache in my jaw and bobbing up and down on his cock until he fists my hair with both hands and spills his cum in hot salty spurts against the back of my throat, his masculine taste filling my mouth as he comes.

"Look at me," he demands as soon as he's able to catch a breath.

I swallow his cum and tip my head back, eyes on him as I gently pull back, holding the head of his cock gently between my lips.

With his dick held in one hand, he slides his fist up and down his length, the last droplets of his cum decorating my tongue as he makes me a promise that I'll never forget.

"I want you to know that I will protect, honour and obey you until the day I motherfucking die. No man will be a better soldier than me, and no one, *no one* will love you as fiercely as I do," he says, hauling me upright and tugging me against his chest. "I love you. I fucking love you so damn much."

My heart swells and a flash of possession strikes my chest as his words echo the feelings in my own heart. Pushing back a little, I capture his gaze with mine. "And just so we're clear, you're *mine* just as much as I am yours, and I will kill anyone who tries to take you from me."

"Does that mean you love me back?" he asks me.

"Without a doubt," I say with a crooked grin before kissing him until we're both breathless and weak-kneed.

CHAPTER NINE

She's Always a Woman

BEAST

The air smells of cigarette smoke and danger as I follow Kate out into the main section of the warehouse wearing Bryce-fucking-Freed's clothing. Had Cleveland not knocked on the door a minute after Kate gave me the best blow job of my fucking life and told us trouble was brewing, I would've collected my own clothes from the fighters' changing room. As it is, I'm grateful that the fucker Bryce is as built as he is, because there was no way I was fitting into Hudson's fucking jeans and hoodie, the scrawny bastard.

Flanking Kate on her left, and with Cleveland on her right,

we head towards the bar at the back of the warehouse. The place is dimly lit and filled with criminals with chips on their shoulders and revenge in their blood. Ordinarily, it's unwise to mix crews like this, but Kate has three rules that any guest entering Tales must obey.

Number one: No weapons.

Number two: No drugs.

Number three: No fighting outside of the cage.

Anyone caught breaking those rules are shot dead on the spot. No exceptions.

The threat has worked so far. Though I'm getting the feeling that tonight that threat is gonna become someone's reality, and they'll be getting themselves a first class ticket straight to Hell courtesy of a bullet in their skull.

As we pass through the crowd, there are plenty of familiar faces and a fuck-load of new ones. Some catch my eye and nod respectfully, some look at me with interest, and the rest? Well, put it this way, if I weren't supporting my missus right now I'd be playing knock down ginger with their faces, the rude cunts.

No matter, I'm good at remembering people, and if any of the fuckers who're giving me the stink eye right now cross my path in the future and dare to disrespect me again, I'll be living up to my reputation.

"Who has an issue?" Kate asks, pulling my attention back to her as Cleveland leads us towards the bar on the far side of the warehouse.

"A guy named Fitzpatrick. He brought some men with him. Said he was an old family friend of your dad's. Dom and Harris have them cornered."

"I don't recognise the name," I say, trying to recall if Carter ever mentioned a Fitzpatrick.

"I do. He's been sniffing around since Carter's funeral. I kneecapped one of his men for disrespecting me at the graveside. Haven't seen him or any of his men since, but I am aware that he's been asking a lot of questions recently."

"Questions?" I ask, cricking my neck as I spot the group of troublemakers.

Dom's currently pointing a gun at some ugly, balding, fat prick's head. Just behind him, Harris is leaning against the bar casually cleaning his nails out with an eight-inch serrated blade. The guy is a gentleman with a deadly streak. Connall picked him up in Madrid. I'm pretty sure they've fucked.

"Yes, questions about what happened the night of my eighteenth birthday, your disappearance, that kind of thing."

"Right. So he's digging for information he's got no right to be digging for," I retort.

"Digging his grave more like," Kate points out, her voice taking on a dangerous edge, and fuck me if my cock doesn't appreciate it.

The way she holds herself, commanding respect and oozing power, gets me fired up like nothing else. Glancing over at her, I stifle a smile, because damn she's sexy with her bruised-kissed lips, stiletto heels, sex-tousled hair and deadly fucking smile.

"Stop staring," she hisses, a hint of amusement dancing around her eyes.

"Can't help it if my woman turns me the fuck on," I reply under my breath.

"Enough," she demands, as we approach Fitzpatrick who's

sneering at her as though she's nothing more than a piece of shit on his shoe. I roll my shoulders ready to kill the fucker. Kate briefly touches the back of my hand. "Let me handle this."

"You got it, boss," I reply, knowing that she'll have his bollocks just for that look alone.

Behind him his crew of five men regards us, weighing up their chances of surviving the night no doubt. There's only one of them who doesn't look like he's about to shit his pants all the way out of the warehouse. He's the one I've got my eye on. There's always one cocky cunt.

"This is no way to treat a family friend," Fitzpatrick has the gall to say as he points at Dom then eyes Cleveland and me in quick succession, his top lip curling over his nasty-arse yellowed teeth.

This guy must have some mega ego or a total lack of sense if he thinks he's gonna survive bringing trouble to Kate's door. He's not the first man to underestimate her, and he won't be the last. Her own dad was a prime example of that.

Kate keeps a smile fixed on her face, her shoulders relaxed as she waves at Dom to lower his gun. He does so instantly, though I see the caution in his stance. Behind him, Harris sheaths his knife and leans his elbows back on the bar. He's a good-looking fucker with an olive skin tone, deep blue eyes and a dusting of freckles across the bridge of his nose and cheeks.

"What can I do for you?" she asks calmly, motioning the bartender over. "Two glasses of Bourbon, straight, no ice."

"Yes, Ma'am," the bartender replies in her heavily accented voice. I watch as she flicks her gaze to Cleveland who gives her a slight dip of his head.

Unbeknownst to the punters, the curvy Italian with long brown hair and cupid-bow lips, is called Loretta, and is a mercenary on loan from one of Romeo Ricci's extended family members. She's cunning, smart, seductive and a skilled assassin. The perfect addition to Grim's team.

"I tell you what you can do for me," the wankstain replies, puffing out his chest and getting ballsy now that he thinks Kate has conceded to him with her politeness and offer of a drink.

He thinks she's trying to diffuse the situation because she's scared. He couldn't be more wrong.

"And that is?" she asks sweetly, playing up her feminine side so she can whoop him upside the head with her badass bitch streak.

Her self-assurance turns me the fuck on, and I find myself impatient for her to off the cunt so we can get out of here and spend some more quality time together in bed. Scratch that, anywhere the fuck she wants me.

"You can explain to me why this piece of shit is standing by your side and not fish food at the bottom of the Thames for offing *your* dad."

Kate doesn't react to his accusation, she simply takes the proffered drink from Loretta and downs it in one go. Swiping at the corner of her mouth with the pad of her thumb, she places the glass back onto the bar, then slides the second glass across the counter to Fitzpatrick. "Drink," she orders.

"I ain't here to drink," he snaps.

"I said, *drink*," she commands, her voice taking on a no-nonsense tone.

Fitzpatrick knocks back the alcohol, swiping his meaty hand

across his bloated face before slamming the glass back on the bar. "I'm here to put you straight."

"By putting me straight you mean telling me you *think* Beast murdered Carter?" she asks, giving me a measuring look.

If I didn't know any better, I'd be worried. But I do know Kate better, and I trust that she knows what she's doing. She's smart *and* ruthless.

"I know so."

"Oh yeah? And how's that?" she asks, folding her arms across her chest, waiting.

"I have my sources," he replies, looking me up and down like I'm already a dead man. The fucking idiot.

"Care to elaborate? Because if you're going to be accusing Beast, I need to know if your sources are as straight talking as you are or full of shit."

"I can't share my sources, you understand?" he replies, narrowing his eyes at her because he can't quite tell if she's just offended him or not.

Kate takes a while to respond, but when she does it's with a stunning smile that transforms her completely. The effect on Fitzpatrick is immediate. His shoulders relax and he grins, thinking he's got her on his side.

He hasn't.

Truthfully, I should be more concerned about where he's got his information from, but all I can think about is how he's leering down Kate's dress and licking his lips like he stands a fucking chance. I'm about ready to cut off his flaccid nob and feed it to him for the audacity, but Kate starts to speak and I'm respectful enough of her to not jump in when she's talking.

"Oh, I totally understand," she replies, with a flirty wink. "And that's why I think you should do the honours."

"Honours?" Fitzpatrick asks, frowning as he slowly drags his leery-arse, dirty-cunt-bastard gaze upwards.

"Offing Beast of course," she replies, jerking her chin at Loretta who bends down behind the bar and pulls out a Springfield XD handgun, passing it to her. "Given he's the one who killed my dad, *right?*"

"The fuck?! Grim, he's talking shit!" I exclaim, playing the game alongside my woman, because there's no fucking way she's about to let him shoot me. No fucking way.

"Quiet!" she demands, scowling at me before turning her attention back to Fitzpatrick.

"I knew you'd appreciate the truth," he says, taking the gun from Kate and pointing it at my head. Behind him his men start to laugh, the cocky, hairy scrotums.

"Go on boss, blow his brains out," the one who looks more likely to stay and fight says.

Fiztpatrick flicks the safety off and grins, but Kate reaches up and rests her hand on top of his.

"Not here, in the cage. Let's honour my father the right way, and send a message to the rest of the punters here, shall we?"

"It would be my pleasure," the fat prick says, pushing the gun into my chest.

I glare at him, un-fucking concerned. "Do that again, fuckface and I'll—"

"You'll what?" he goads, daring me to come for him so he can fire a bullet in my chest here and now. "You'll do fuck all because you ain't got no one, family or otherwise, to back you up."

I hack up some phlegm and spit it out at his feet. "And your family tree is a cactus, because everyone on it's a prick."

"Cleveland with me," Kate orders, amusement dancing in her gaze that she quickly shuts down. "Dom, Harris, make sure Fitzpatrick's friends have a glass of my *finest* bourbon." Then she's shoving me on the shoulder. "Walk."

I walk, mulling over why those men deserve any fucking bourbon, let alone her finest. Then it dawns on me, that phrase must be code for *off the cunts* or I'm not Roger-cut-your-heart-out Smith.

This woman. Fuck. Me.

Keeping my face neutral, or at least a little on the scowly side, I head towards the cage, keeping up the pretence. The whole way Fitzpatrick-cunt-waffle stabs me in the back with the butt of the gun every couple of steps. He's pissing me the fuck off, but still I play the part.

Around us the punters part like the Red Sea, all of them watching this play out with interest. You'd think the fucking arseholes would've had enough bloodshed for one evening. Fat chance. These bastards thrive on violence.

"Get in the cage," Grim orders.

I do as I'm told.

As soon as we've all piled in, Cleveland shuts the door to the cage, leaning against the exit. Then Fitzpatrick jerks his chin towards me. "Kneel."

I flick my gaze to Kate. She gives the smallest hint of a smile then says, "You heard him. *Kneel.*"

I drop to my knees, ignoring the cunt with the gun pointed at my head and keep my gaze fixed firmly on the woman I love.

She starts walking around the cage, addressing the crowd as she moves.

"Today Beast fought hard, reminding us all of his skills in the cage and earning his right to stand by my side as one of my soldiers, beating out stiff competition."

The crowd murmurs, scenting blood, but not certain how to react given she's just complimented me *and* I'm on my knees. Like me, they wait.

"However, Fitzpatrick here just brought something to my attention that needs resolving... *permanently.*"

Fitzpatrick laughs, the cunt's finger tightening on the trigger. Can't lie and say my heart rate didn't just kick up a notch, but I have faith in my woman to ensure I don't actually get shot in the head because, frankly, I need to spend the next month straight buried deep inside of her to make up for lost time and I ain't willing to die tonight for no man, let alone this fucking toad.

Kate makes a full circle of the cage, stopping beside Cleveland and says something under her breath. He nods and she takes his gun, flicking off the safety. Then strides towards me and presses the butt of her gun into the back of my head, addressing the crowd once more.

"Beast here killed Carter. Isn't that right, Fitzpatrick?"

"That's right, Grim," he agrees, his lip pulling up in a smirk.

The crowd draws in a collective breath, then I hear Fitzpatrick's men chanting from the other side of the warehouse. "Kill the cunt! Kill the cunt! Kill the cunt!"

"Before I pull the trigger," Kate says, her voice projecting around the warehouse thanks to the high ceilings and her need to be heard. "I want everyone to raise a glass to the man who told me the *truth*. To you and *only* you, I owe my loyalty, respect and appreciation. CHEERS!"

Fitzpatrick smiles, baring his yellowed teeth, but that smile drops a second later as four gunshots ring out around the warehouse in quick succession.

Bang.

Bang.

Bang.

BANG.

Dom takes out two of Fitzpatrick's men whilst Loretta kills two more. Blood and brain matter spurts out of the backs of their heads as they fall like dominos, leaving one man standing. He turns on his heel and runs.

He doesn't get far.

Harris's blade slices through the air and embeds itself in his spinal cord at the base of his skull, killing him instantly. The rest of the punters in attendance shift backwards away from the carnage, falling silent, understanding that if they make one false move, they're dead too. They don't need to look up to know that the rest of Kate's soldiers are watching from the metal walkway above us all, guns aimed and ready for her next order.

"WHAT THE FUCK!" Fitzpatrick shouts, his flabby jowls wobbling as his eyes widen in disbelief and shock. "You crazy bitch!"

"Not crazy, and not a *bitch*. Well, maybe a little," Kate replies, lifting the gun off the back of my head and stepping to my side. "Stand up, Beast."

I get to my feet, grinning at Fitzpatrick who looks like he's about to have a coronary.

"I'll fucking kill you myself!" he shouts, his finger pulling back the trigger. It clicks several times before he realises that the magazine is in fact empty.

"Surprise!" I goad, unable to help myself.

"No!" he shouts, pulling on the trigger as if the magazine will suddenly load with bullets and one will miraculously split my skull in two.

"You really didn't think that I'd give you a loaded gun, did you?" Kate asks him, rolling her eyes.

He looks from the useless hunk of metal in his hand up to Kate. "What the fuck is this?!"

Kate smirks. "This is me setting the record straight," she replies, then turns to the crowd and addresses them directly. "This is *my* club and tonight this man brought trouble to my door. You all know the rules of my club and Fitzpatrick fucking broke one trying to cause trouble with an accusation that is *false.*"

"Grim," I warn under my breath, seeing where she's going with this and not liking it.

She looks over her shoulder, glaring at me to shut the fuck up, and before I can stop her she squares her shoulders and says, "Beast is loyal. He's a trusted soldier, and a good man, if a little unhinged."

"Fucking cheek," I reply, a smile in my voice. She winks at me then, and my heart does a fucking summersault. Man, wait until I get her alone.

Fitzpatrick laughs hysterically, annoying the shit out of me. "Then if it wasn't him who the fuck was it?"

Kate sucks on her teeth, shooting a withering look at Fitzpatrick. "It was *me.* I killed Carter."

"What?!" Fitzpatrick splutters as the crowd begin to mutter

under their breath. I cast a quick gaze out into the warehouse, expecting someone to kick off. No one does. Just as well, because they'd be dead too.

"You heard me," she continues, raising her voice so the sound carries further. "I killed my dad because he betrayed *me*."

"You're a fucking liar! You're protecting him," Fitzpatrick accuses, pointing his pudgy finger at me. "You fucking whore!"

"Shut your goddamn mouth!" I snap, and in two paces I've got the dirty toad gripped by the throat and turning fucking puce. Grasping my wrists, he scrabbles on his tiptoes, struggling to break free, and when he gasps for breath I take the opportunity to grab his tongue and yank on it. "I'll fucking rip your tongue out for insulting Grim. Have some motherfucking respect."

"Put him down, Beast," Kate says firmly. "*I've* got this."

The protective part of me wants to ignore her order and rip this bastard's tongue clean out of his head. The respectful part obeys her request. "You're right, you do," I reply, acknowledging her handle of the situation and dropping the fucker. He falls like a sack of potatoes to the canvas, coughing and spluttering.

"Let me say this again so everyone can be clear. *I* killed Carter Davidson. It was my right as his flesh and blood to end his life for betraying me. The dirty bastard did something to *me* that is unforgivable, and he fucking paid for it," she says into the crowd. "What's more, there will be no retaliation. Not from the pigs and not from any of you motherfuckers in this warehouse. Anyone who tries to come for me or my business will be dealt with swiftly and permanently. No questions. Don't forget I know where every single one of you live, fuck and eat daily. I know who your friends are, your enemies, and your loved ones.

Fuck me over and find out exactly what I do to people who betray me. My father certainly found out the hard way."

My eyes widen and I can't help but grin at her ballsy attitude. Jesus fuck, I'm rock hard now. Just as well everyone's too intent on watching Fitzpatrick squirm to notice my boner.

Turning her attention back to Fitzpatrick, Grim narrows her eyes, her voice dripping with anger as she speaks. "Tonight you came into my club seeking violence," she says whilst pointing the gun at his dick. "Well now you've fucking got it. How's that going for you, huh?"

"Wait! I'm sorry. I didn't know. I thought your dad was a good man, an honourable man."

"He wasn't a good man. He was a liar, a fucking predator, and he hurt me. I did what I had to do. If you betray me, you die. I don't give a fuck who you are. Friend, foe, blood or otherwise."

"I understand. I apologise!" Fitzpatrick mumbles, shuffling back on his arse as she stalks him in her four inch stilettos, her shapely calves and long legs doing all sorts of things to my rapidly hardening cock. "Please don't kill me. We can work this out."

"You made a huge fucking mistake coming here tonight."

"I'm s—sorry," he stutters, his back hitting the cage wall as she stands over him. Fear strips him of his arrogance and turns him into a quivering crybaby. "It's none of my business. I'll keep my mouth shut. I swear on my kids' lives."

"Uh oh!" I say, smirking as Fitzpatrick realises a second too late that he's said the wrong thing to the wrong woman.

"You swear on your *kids'* lives?" she snarls, dropping to a crouch before him as she shoves the gun into his dick. He screeches and she gets in his face. "Don't fucking bring innocents into this, you piece of shit!"

"I just meant—"

"Shut the fuck up!" she hisses, lowering her voice. "I know men like you, my *dad* was just like you. Selling out your own kids if it meant saving your own fucking neck. Do not EVER mention your children again. You hear me?!"

"I won't! Sorry," he replies, holding his hands up and dropping his head in a move that proves he's all mouth and no fucking trousers.

"Good," she replies, leaning in close so no one can hear what she's about to say next. "Now tell me the name of the person who convinced you that Beast killed Carter, and I'll consider letting you live, and tell me *quietly*," she adds.

Fitzpatrick nods his head, his double-chin shaking like jello. "Rodriguez. It was Rodriguez Campo."

Of course it fucking was. I haven't seen that turd since that night at Tales. I knew he was a little two-faced, conniving prick when he worked for Carter. Not that it matters now because pretty soon he'll be a dead one.

"Is that so?" Grim rises, gun still pointed at Fitzpatrick's chest as she looks over her shoulder at me. "You hear that?"

"Yeah, I heard," I reply tightly.

We both know what this means. Either Rodriguez is on his own agenda or the King is using him to start trouble. Either way, it means we've got a fucking problem. Lifting her chin she looks out over the crowd, her gaze searching the warehouse.

"Let this be known that I won't tolerate anyone bringing trouble to my door. My club, *my* rules. No fucking exceptions. Pass that message on to whoever the fuck you want."

Then without even looking at Fitzpatrick she loads three bullets into his body, shooting off his dick, sinking a bullet in his heart and firing one right between his eyes.

Pretty sure I just came a little in Bryce Freed's jogging pants.

CHAPTER TEN

Mary Jane (All Night Long)

GRIM

"Did you find out where Rodriguez is hiding?" I ask, pacing back and forth in my kitchen a few days later.

Beast shakes his head, glancing over at Dom who's standing on the other side of the room, pretending to admire my recently purchased painting hanging on my wall when we all know he just likes the naked female sculpture sitting on the table beneath it. She's voluptuous with big tits, a round belly and wide hips, and exactly Dom's kind of woman. "We've got eyes and ears on the lookout. Don't worry, we'll find the little cunt."

"And what about the King?"

"Apparently, he's abroad on business," Dom replies, dragging his gaze away from the bronze sculpture and back to me.

"That's fucking convenient!" I shout, my nerves getting the better of me.

I'm not usually this reactive, but after killing Fitzpatrick and outing myself as the person who murdered my own dad, I'm feeling the goddamn pressure. I'm not scared of the King, and I certainly don't give a fuck if anyone else tries to come for me, I am, however, trying to gauge what move is coming next. This business is like a game of chess. I've made my move, now it's the King's turn to make his, because if Rodriguez is doing this on his own then I'm the fucking Queen of England.

"There are plenty of ways to skin a cat," Beast replies, reading me like a book.

I give him a brief dip of my head in acknowledgment. He's right, there is. "Yeah, I agree. Doesn't change the fact that by now *everyone* knows that I've confessed to killing Carter. News travels fast..." My voice trails off as I consider the repercussions of that.

"You know I would've taken the fall. I did kill him after all," Beast says, sighing heavily.

"And you know you'd have died for it," Dom says firmly, looking between us both. "Grim saved your arse. No one will come for her, not after what she implied. What's worse than a grass and a traitor? A fucking nonce."

"So what do we do now?" I ask.

"Sooner or later he'll make his next move," Beast says.

Dom chews on his nail. "And in the meantime?"

"We wait."

"Fucking fabulous," I reply just as Cleveland steps into the room, clearing his throat.

"Everything alright?" Beast asks, popping the cap off a bottle of beer that he's just grabbed from the fridge and passing it to me. I take a grateful swig, the cool liquid is just what I need to quench my sudden thirst and to take the edge off.

"Just wanted to let you know, Ma'am, that Loretta and I have done the rounds and the house is secure."

"Thanks, Cleveland."

He gives me a curt nod of his head then glances at Beast.

"Anything else?" Beast asks, filling the sudden, awkward silence.

"Are you going to need a lift home? It's my night off and I'm heading your way," Cleveland says without a hint of amusement or innuendo in his voice. Doesn't matter though, Dom seems to find it amusing, especially since Connall let it out of the bag that Cleveland swings both ways.

"No, Cleveland, I won't be needing a lift home," Beast says, glancing at me, the heat in his gaze undeniable. "But fuckface over there could do with one. Ain't that right, Dom?"

"And there's me thinking we were gonna spend some quality time together after you've been away so long," Dom responds with a wink before turning his attention back to Cleveland. "I could use a lift. Nancy will have my bollocks if I'm late for dinner anyway."

"No problem," Cleveland says with a curt nod, notably avoiding Beast's gaze this time.

Once Dom has said his goodbyes and leaves with Cleveland, I let out a quiet laugh. "He's smitten with you."

"Who Dom?" Beast asks, knowing full well who I'm talking about.

"Ha, ha! You know who I'm talking about. Cleveland."

"What can I say? I'm a hot commodity," he jokes with a wink.

"And entirely modest," I reply with a heavy dose of sarcasm.

"You ain't jealous?"

"Funnily enough, no. Should I be?" I ask, smiling at him from behind my bottle of beer.

"Nah, there's only one person who's got my sole attention, and it ain't that beefcake," Beast replies, snatching my bottle of beer and downing the rest of it in one long gulp.

"Is that so?" I ask, backing up as he pins me against the kitchen island with his hips and places the empty bottle of beer on the counter behind me.

"You know it, baby."

"Baby. You're using that a lot lately... *Daddy*," I murmur.

"Why the fuck does that turn me on so much?"

"I don't know. Daddy kink?" I reply, holding in a laugh.

"The only kink I have is a *you* kink. We've already established that," he replies, grabbing my hips and lifting me up, causing a light laugh to break free from my lips. I wrap my legs around his waist, my arms slung over his shoulders as I grin down at him.

"Is that so?"

"You know it!" he growls, pressing a kiss against my neck, his hands kneading my arse. But as he continues to kiss me, that momentary lightheartedness gives way to a rash of fear.

"Beast, we need to make a plan."

"Not right now we don't," he replies, perching my bottom

on the kitchen island so he can get a good look at me. He frowns. "Where's that smile gone?"

I blow out a breath, pushing back the flop of hair in his eyes as he stares at me. "I always knew what I was getting into, but some days it's just fucking hard."

"You're not alone. Not anymore. You've got me, and I will share the burden of your troubles from this moment on. But for now, just enjoy this. Enjoy us. Be selfish, Kate," he says, pressing a kiss against my mouth, his hands cupping my head as his tongue slides between my lips.

I want so badly to give in to his touch, to this tiny moment of joy, but that dark cloud that sits over me most days weighs heavy on me tonight. Being the *Queen of Tales,* as my soldiers now call me, is a burden on the best of days, and my proverbial crown is really no more than a ball and chain. Don't get me wrong, I have no regrets choosing this life, but I'm not infallible despite how I might portray myself to the world.

"Beast—" I begin, breaking our kiss.

"Don't," he says, shaking his head. "I know you're stressing out. I *get* it. But right now there's nothing more that can be done. We've got people searching for Rodriguez, and as soon as he's found we can deal with the cunt. Right now, you need a distraction, and I'm more than willing to give it to you. Let me."

"It's going to take *a lot* to distract me," I say, giving in to his logic, barely holding back a smile.

"Believe me, I'm up for the challenge."

"Hours and hours of distraction, in fact."

"Is that so?" he asks, smirking as his fingers slide beneath the waistband of my jeans and grab a hold of my thong, tugging on it. I feel the material tighten over my pussy, pressing against my clit.

"Uh huh," I murmur, my gaze honing in on his lips as I lean forward.

"Please tell me you've recovered from the other night," Beast says as I brush my lips against his. "Running around trying to locate that prick Rodriguez might've kept us all a little distracted these past couple days, but now that I've finally got you alone—"

"I've recovered," I interrupt breathily.

"Thank fuck, baby, because I'm gonna make love to you all night long."

"You got the stamina for that?" I tease, allowing myself to forget our troubles and just concentrate on the here and now because Beast's right, we've got to take our moments of bliss when we can, especially in our line of business.

"Princess, you've no idea," he replies, spinning on his feet and walking with me in his arms towards the fridge. I cling onto him as he uses both hands to gather items from the fridge and wedge them between us.

"What's this?" I ask, my stomach muscles contracting from the cold bottle of champagne pressed against it. He adds a punnet of strawberries, grinning at me.

"This is what I call a distraction," he banters, flashing me a dazzling smile that has my insides turning liquid and my clit throbbing

"You're thirsty?" I question.

"Baby, I'm always thirsty when I'm around you," he replies, striding towards the stairs, juggling me and the objects pressed between us as laughter bubbles up my throat.

Less than a minute later Beast places me delicately on the bed, and I unravel my legs from around his waist as he gathers up the items he collected from the fridge, placing them on the bedside table.

"Those are for later..." he smiles, backing away from me.

"Where are you going?"

"Nowhere," he says, closing the bedroom door and leaning up against it. "I just want a redo."

"A redo?" I ask, frowning.

He nods. "Of that night, when you touched yourself and I watched."

"You want me to touch myself so you can watch?" I repeat, my skin heating at the thought.

"Yeah, but this time. This time I ain't cockblocking myself. This time I'm joining in."

"Oh..."

"Yeah," he replies, jerking his chin. "As I recall, you were completely naked and spread out like a fucking feast."

"Was I?" I ask sweetly. "Funny, I don't remember."

"Kate, don't play with me," he growls, laughter in his eyes.

I grin, chewing on my bottom lip as I reach for my boot and unzip it, dropping it to the floor. I repeat the action with my other foot, removing my socks then stand, my toes sinking into the plush carpet.

Beast's gaze drops to my feet, and he licks his lips. "Pretty. I like the pink polish, it's very... girly."

"You sound surprised," I say, glad I had a pedicure recently given Beast is so appreciative.

"Not surprised, just turned on."

"By my feet?" I giggle, and the sound makes his gaze snap upwards.

"By everything about you."

"Everything?"

"*Everything.* There's not one thing about you I don't love. Fuck, you turn me on."

"I do?" I ask, acting coy, feeling anything but.

"Do I turn you on?" he asks me as he unbuckles his jeans and unzips his fly. A moment later his tattooed hand disappears beneath his boxers as he grips his cock.

"I'm not sure, let's see," I tease, unzipping my fly and sliding my fingers into my panties, feeling the slippery warmth there.

"Well?"

For a moment I don't answer, I simply meet his heady stare with one of my own as we both pleasure ourselves. My fingers slide easily through my folds, my clit throbbing as my index finger swirls over the sensitive nub. "Yes, you turn me on," I whisper silkily.

"Show me."

Pulling my fingers free, I hold up my hand and show him my glistening arousal. He licks his lips, a soft groan rising up his chest. "Suck your fingers for me, baby. Taste yourself."

I taste myself.

"Ah, yeah," he groans. "Wrap that plump mouth around your fingers and imagine it's my cock you're sucking. Can you taste me on your tongue, Princess?"

I let out a moan at the memory of sucking his dick, then pull my fingers free from my mouth, trailing the wetness down my chin and neck. "I want to taste you again," I admit, taking a step towards him, but he shakes his head.

"Not yet. Stay where you are."

"What do you want me to do now?" I ask, enjoying this game.

"I want you to strip, right the fuck now," he demands, his hand moving beneath his clothes as he strokes his cock watching my every move.

"You're being very demanding."

"I know what I want. *Strip*."

Keeping my eyes trained on him, I slowly undress, taking my time until I'm completely naked. My nipples pucker beneath his attention and my clit, she throbs, pulsing as he greedily drinks every inch of me in.

"Fucking beautiful," he says, his fist moving a little faster now.

"I want to see you too," I say, sitting back on the bed, resting against the headboard, goosebumps scattering over my skin from his attention. My legs drop open for him, my pussy lips spreading, giving him a clear view of my vagina.

It's drenched.

For him.

"You got it, baby," he replies roughly as he releases his cock and reaches up behind his head to pull off his t-shirt in that sexy way only men seem to be able to manage. With our eyes locked on each other, he kicks off his boots, removes his jeans and boxers and pulls off his socks. His cock bobs as he moves, thick and hard, the mushroom shaped head a deep angry red, a long thick vein running up the length.

"How's that?"

"Just perfect," I say, my breath becoming shallow as I allow my eyes to take in his broad shoulders, thick veiny arms, the sharp cut of his abs and his perfect v-muscle that points downwards to his impressive cock. Every inch of him is covered in tattoos that are stunning to look at and I take my time drinking in every single one. "You're beautiful."

He grins, swiping one hand through his thick, tousled hair whilst the other grips the base of his cock. "No one's ever called me beautiful. I'm just Beast to them."

"But you're a beautiful one, and you're mine."

"Yours," he agrees, the thick silver band at his wrist glinting in the low light of the room as he moves his fist slowly to the tip of his cock. "My heart belongs to you. My cock is yours. You got me, baby. Every fucking piece of me. Forever."

"Forever," I repeat, my mouth parting as his thick thumb rubs over his slit and the piercing there. He groans, his gaze falling from my face to my pussy as I slowly slide my fingers through my folds.

"I want to see you finger-fuck yourself. I want to see you come."

"Yes," I hiss, relishing in his attention, in the way he watches me, just as I watch him. What we're doing is so intimate, so erotic that everything is heightened. The way I feel right now is so different to how I felt when he fucked me on the table in my office.

That was raw, dirty, desperate. But this? This is fun, it's sexy, it's fulfilling a fantasy I've dreamed of over and over again for two years now.

"Talk to me, Princess. Tell me how much you want me," he says, his voice strained, gruff. I meet his gaze, knowing exactly what needs to be said.

"Do you know how many times I've fantasised about you?" I

ask, repeating the exact same words I spoke to him over two years ago in this very room.

"How many times?" he asks me, his gaze darkening as he fists his cock eagerly.

"So many times, Beast. I've touched myself like this hundreds of times imagining it was your thick fingers working me, your tongue tasting me, your cock—"

"Jesus fuck! How did I ever stay away from you?" he groans, his hips jerking as precum glistens on the tip of his dick.

"I've asked myself the same thing," I reply roughly, excitement rippling through my bloodstream.

My fingers work my pussy, rubbing my clit in a steady, circular motion as I continue with our reenactment of that night. I remember every second of it. How he'd looked at me, how he'd fought his desires and needs. I remember the pained look on his face and the feeling of heartbreak when he refused to act on what we both wanted. I remember never being more turned on in my life, except maybe now.

"I'm wet for you, Beast," I continue, the slippery feel of my pussy so fucking ready for him.

So, so wet.

"Say it," he orders, fisting his dick tighter, pumping his cock faster.

"Beast, I want you. I want *you* to make me come."

"Fuck, yes! Every fucking day for the rest of our lives," he exclaims, and in four strides he's across the room, grasping my ankles and yanking me to the edge of the bed.

I let out a squeal, laughing as he drags me towards him. Happiness and love bubble in my chest as lust and desire flare in my stomach. "You're such a caveman," I tease.

"A caveman? Woman, I'm a *beast* and I'm hungry," he replies, lifting my legs over his shoulders before lowering his mouth to my pussy and licking me from crack to clit, sending a bolt of pleasure straight down my spine and right to my curling toes.

"Oh fuck!" I'm already trembling in anticipation and he's barely done anything yet.

"Hold on tight, baby, because I'm gonna eat you out slowly until you don't know your name. Then I'm gonna make you come so hard you'll be begging me to stop," he promises, then lowers his mouth to my cunt and does exactly that.

CHAPTER ELEVEN

I Feel It Coming

BEAST

Fuck she tastes sweet.

My chin and cheeks are covered in Kate's arousal and I fucking love it.

This is where I belong, right here between her legs, giving head to the woman I love.

There's no bigger turn on than a woman coming all over your face because you know the right way to love on them, and believe me, this is just the start. I intend to love on Kate for hours and hours and fucking hours.

She needs to know that she's mine, and more importantly, that I'm hers.

I won't rest until she's passed out from orgasming, wrapped up in my arms and in a deep, restful sleep, because tonight isn't about me, it's about her. She needs to feel adored, worshipped, loved and I intend to show her just how much she means to me all motherfucking night long.

I ain't no *wham bam thank you ma'am.*

No sir.

My love language has always been physical touch and words of affirmation, or at least that's what I found out when I read one of those women magazines I picked up on my travels. Blew my fucking mind actually. The man who carves out the hearts of his enemies love language is basically affection, sex, and praise. Who'd have thought it?

Actually, it makes total fucking sense. I've always been a thoughtful lover, never a selfish one and being able to be that way with the woman I love...? Fucking bliss.

Grinning, I grip Kate's hips a little tighter and slide the flat of my tongue up her pussy, making sure to lick around and around her clit, dragging my teeth lightly over the sensitive flesh and tugging gently on her piercing before repeating the whole process over and over again. That steady build up of the same pressure seems to do the trick and Kate begins to writhe against my face mindlessly, her fingers grasping my head as she drags me closer and holds on tight.

"Fuck, fuck, fuck, fuck!" she cries, her whole body trembling as I keep up the steady pace.

"That's it, baby. Ride the wave. I got you," I say against her pussy whilst sliding two fingers inside of her. I reach for the soft spongy spot that when caressed the right way will give her an intense orgasm.

"Yes, like that. Oh fuck, like that Beast. Fuck me with your fingers and mouth just... like... that," she pants, her chest heaving.

Pretty sure my dick just punched a hole in the mattress at her words. Fuck, this woman makes me crazy with lust.

"Oh baby, I'm gonna make you come so hard. Do you hear me? I'm gonna love you until you can't take no more," I mutter against her mound, kissing, licking and laving my tongue over her clit whilst I gently rub her g-spot.

"Oh, oh, oh!" she replies, clamping her legs on either side of my head and curling her fingers into my hair, as she holds on tight.

Any moment now she's gonna come. Everything is slippery and wet, her cunt, my saliva mixing with her juices, my dick dripping with precum.

It's fucking glorious.

When I feel her inner walls tightening, I crook my finger, pressing firmer against her g-spot and suck on her clit, dragging out her orgasm, owning it and her in this moment of pure torturous bliss.

Bliss for Kate, fucking torture for me.

But good torture, the kind that gets rewarded with a pussy ready and willing to take a good fucking. There'll be no blood and no pain, just pure pleasure.

Beneath me Kate tenses, holding her breath as her whole body goes rigid, then she unravels screaming and jerking against my face as she comes. The sounds she makes are guttural, raw, and sensual as fuck. Music to my damn ears.

When her body relaxes and her hands slip from my hair, I

slowly withdraw my fingers from her cunt, her arousal glistening on her puffy, pink labia and engorged clit.

"You're such a good fucking girl," I praise, licking my fingers clean, then kissing her pussy and slowly climbing up her body, my cock dragging over the softness of her skin. I cage her in with my knees on either side of her hips and my forearms pressed against the mattress, palming her face. "Kate, look at me."

Her eyelids flicker open and I feel her fingertips brush gently up the side of my body, scattering goosebumps over my skin and sending electric currents straight to my dick. Fuck, just that slight touch from her has me almost coming.

"Is that how you treat all the women you take to bed?" she asks sleepily, still in a state of post orgasmic bliss. "Because I could get used to this."

"Yes, but it's only you that I want to take to bed for the rest of my life," I reply hoarsely.

She gives me the most beautiful smile in response and inside my chest, my heart swells. Whoever said loving someone was weak is a goddamn fool. Loving Kate, being loved by her, makes me feel like the most powerful man on the motherfucking planet.

"That sounds like a proposal. Are you proposing to me, Beast?" she mutters, sliding her hands over my chest and reaching for my face as she looks up at me. There's laughter in her eyes, but also a shred of hope.

Deep down this woman *wants* to marry me. That need to belong, though tentative, uncertain, is a powerful one.

"It's a promise. You're it for me," I reply. "And if that means you wanna stand in a church or a registry office and take my ring, I'll do that, without hesitation."

"Wait, you're serious?"

"Deadly."

"Beast, people like us don't marry."

"People in love you mean?"

"People who live the lives we do. Marrying you will only put a target on your head," she says, her fingertips brushing over my cheeks and jaw as she frowns. "You're already in danger because of me."

I scoff, shaking my head. "You don't think I have several targets on my head already? I'm not exactly Mr Popular. Besides, if Bonnie and Clyde can do it, I don't see why we can't."

"Bonnie and Clyde died violently, riddled with bullets. Bonnie was still holding a fucking sandwich, she had no idea it was coming," Kate points out.

I chuckle. "Okay, so maybe not a great example."

"Marriage is a dream, Beast. A fantasy. We *can't*."

Leaning closer, I cup her head, caging her in and brushing my lips against hers. "Truthfully, I don't need a piece of paper to tell me that I'm forever bound to you. I'm yours, you hear me, Kate. I'm yours."

"You're certain?"

"Never been more certain of anything in my life. Aren't you?"

"It's terrifying."

"What is?" I ask, dropping a kiss to her lips.

"Loving someone this much..."

Her voice trails off, and she looks away. I get the distinct impression she isn't just talking about me. "Kate, is there something you need to tell me?"

She sighs. "There is, but not right now, okay?"

"You ain't gonna break my heart and tell me you're in love with Dom too?" I ask, only half joking.

"Dom?" She gives me a half smile.

"Nancy says he's a catch..."

"He's perfect for her, but not for me. You don't need to worry, I won't break your heart," she replies, kissing me softly, gently.

Whatever it is that's troubling her, she clearly doesn't want to talk about it right now, and that's okay because we've got time to talk once she's been thoroughly fucked.

Our kisses turn from probing, searching, filled with love and happiness to passionate, demanding and motherfucking-toe-curling. Feeling her beneath me like this, so fucking needy for me as I am for her makes me want to tip my head back and bash my chest like a fucking ape. I want the whole world to know that from this second onward it's my dick she'll take to the hilt, my mouth she'll feel over every inch of her skin, my tongue licking her to orgasm and my motherfucking heart that belongs to her.

She writhes beneath me, pressing her hips upwards to meet mine and that slight adjustment has my dick finding the entrance to her pussy like a homing beacon finding its destination. The feel of her cunt wet and ready for me, fuck it makes my chest expand with another rush of love and lust.

"Baby, look at me," I say, gently biting her lip as I pull back a little. "I'm going to make love to you now, and I want you to look in my eyes the entire time. Okay?"

"Okay," she whispers, her skin flushing with heat as I palm

her cheeks and slowly slide my aching cock inch by inch inside her welcoming warmth.

"Fuck, you feel so good. So fucking tight. It's like you were made for me."

"A perfect fit," she agrees, her pupils widening and a breath releasing from her lips as I pull back to the tip and then slowly drive my cock back inside of her. She lets out a low moan, and the sound gets me high like nothing else.

"This, this is what home feels like," I say as her legs tighten around my arse and her core contracts, squeezing me tightly. It takes everything in me not to explode inside of her.

I let out a groan, wanting to shut my own eyes from the feel of her holding me so fucking tight, but I refuse to take my eyes off of hers. "Do that again and I'll be coming way too soon."

"I don't care, we've got the rest of our lives, right?" she replies, squeezing her inner muscles as I pull back and push inside her pussy over and over again.

"You're right, we do, but there's no way I'm coming before you do."

"I've already come," she replies, brushing her lips over mine as I keep up the steady pace.

"And you'll do it again, and again, and again. So be a good girl and drop your legs for me. Let me love you the best way I know how."

She smiles up at me, her head tipping back slightly as she unravels her legs from behind my arse, and drops her feet to the mattress, her knees bent and her thighs hugging mine. "Like this?"

"Just like that," I reply, pressing my mouth against hers and sliding my tongue between her parted lips as I draw back and slide in, draw back and slide in, over and over again.

My muscles tremble with the need to rut into her like I fucked her on the desk in her office, but I force myself to keep the pace, knowing it will give her a deeper, more fulfilling orgasm. I refuse to allow my own needs to overshadow hers. So I remain steady, fucking her slow and kissing her dirty just like I promised her I would.

This is what it means to connect. *This* is what making love is.

I would do anything for my girl, my perfect princess, my vicious queen, my goddamn heart.

I would carve open the chest of any cunt who tries to hurt her and smile whilst I do it. I will protect her with my life, fuck her with my whole heart and love her until I can't anymore.

"Beast," she breathes against my lips, her head turning to the side as she gasps for breath.

She's close, I can feel her tightening around me, her fingers digging into my shoulders as she holds on tight and kisses me with a desperate kind of need that only intensifies our connection. If I could melt into her, I would do it in a fucking heartbeat. Sliding my hands beneath her back and up her neck, I cup her head and pull back, needing to see her expression, but I don't change my pace, I don't rotate my hips. I fuck her steadily until her breaths quicken and her legs begin to tremble.

"Open your eyes, Kate. Let me see you."

Her eyelids flutter open and her mouth parts as she looks up at me, and I see it.

I see what I feel.

Love.

Intense, fucking life-changing, all-consuming love.

We have it, Kate and me. We have the kind of love my mum read about in her romance books. We have that connection, built on friendship, made strong through adversity. We ain't ever gonna be your typical couple in the real world where violence is the norm, but behind closed doors we can shed the skins we wear on a daily basis and just be ourselves with each other and that's all I fucking need.

"Look at you. I'm so fucking lucky," I say.

"Beast, I'm going to come," she whispers, and I see that love swimming in her eyes as she tips her head back, opens her mouth and comes silently, the overpowering orgasm conjured between us stealing her voice and the air from my lungs.

Seconds later, my balls tighten and a white hot heat expands outwards from the bottom of my spine as I spill my cum deep inside of her, silently promising to love this woman until death do us part.

"Fuck, I love you," I say when I can breath again.

Kate smiles, cupping my cheek. "Ditto," she whispers, staring right into the pit of my soul, whilst I find peace within hers.

"DID I FALL ASLEEP?" she murmurs an hour later as I shift on the bed beside her. Her naked body is soft, warm and relaxed wrapped up in my arms, her back to my chest.

"Yeah, I seem to have that effect on women," I chuckle, nuzzling her neck with my lips.

"So the rumours are true then," she says, grinning.

"Rumours?"

"That you put women to sleep with toe-curling orgasms?"

"What can I say? I'm a stud."

"A stud-*muffin*, you mean?" she replies laughing.

"Only for you," I confirm, just in case she needs to be reminded.

"Damn straight," she replies, stretching out beside me, then turning in my arms, her hip brushing against my cock that is still rock hard and has remained that way ever since pulling out of her.

"Does it hurt?" she asks, her palms smoothing up my chest as she runs her fingers over my nipples, tweaking them with a naughty look on her face.

"Does what hurt?"

"Your cock, being hard all the time," she replies, pressing her stomach against my aching dick and chewing on her lip as she tries to hide a smile.

"You've no idea," I chuckle, brushing my lips against hers as I roll her onto her back and reach for the bottle of champagne and punnet of strawberries on the bedside table. Sitting on my haunches between her spread legs, I place the punnet on the mattress beside her hip, then undo the metal clasp around the cork, removing it.

"Walking around with a hard-on has gotta be rough," she giggles, her fingers tracing over my abs, towards my dick which jerks for her attention.

"I can tell you it ain't no fun when you're in a church full of God-fearing people," I admit with a chuckle.

She gasps, watching me as I uncork the bottle of champagne. It fizzes and I capture some of the bubbles before they spill over the lip, swallowing them. "*You* were in a church?"

"Con and I were in Rome and he fancied a piece of Italian arse who happened to be pious. I was going along for the ride. Just call me *wingman extraordinaire*."

"And you got a hard-on... in a church? What the hell were you thinking about?"

"You."

"Me?" she laughs.

"Yep. I was thinking how hot it would be to fuck you over the altar right beneath the Virgin Mary," I reply with a smirk.

"Oh my God! So what did you do about it?"

"What any self-respecting man would do... I got on my knees and prayed to the Lord Almighty to save my godforsaken soul."

"And did it work?"

I shake my head, grinning as I place the bottle of champagne between her parted legs, resting it against her mound. She sucks in a sharp breath from the coolness, but doesn't try to move away. "No, it fucking didn't. I had to excuse myself and rub one out in the crypt they kept open for tourists."

"You jacked off in a crypt with *dead* people?"

"I was desperate. Besides it wasn't as if I could offend the fuckers," I argue, smirking.

She bursts out laughing and the sound does stupid things to my heart. "You really are going to Hell," she says.

"So long as I get to live this life with you, I don't much care what happens after," I reply.

Reaching for the punnet of strawberries, I take one out and lift it to my lips, taking a bite. Chewing, I lower the half eaten strawberry to her nipple, swirling it over the tip, teasing her with it. She gasps, and I move it across her chest, smearing a trail of juice across her skin as I tease her other nipple with it. Then I drag the strawberry downwards to her belly button, dipping it into the hole before lifting it to my lips and eating it.

The whole time she watches me with parted lips, her chest heaving as I lift the bottle of champagne to my lips, taking a deep pull. The bubbles burst in my mouth and I swallow them down. Ordinarily, I'm not a fan of champagne but I'm betting I'll be a fan once I drink it off her bare skin.

"Are you going to share?" she asks me, her fingers brushing over the tip of my cock.

"Of course, open up," I say, then take another mouthful before resting the bottle against the pillow beside her head.

Leaning over her, she looks up at me, a smile playing around her eyes as I let the champagne trickle from my lips and into her open mouth. She swallows the liquid, the tip of her tongue peeking out from between her lips as she licks them clean.

"More," she demands, so I repeat the process. Some of the liquid dribbles from her mouth and down her chin and neck. I lean down chasing the trail of liquid with my tongue. She hums beneath me. "That feels good."

"Does it now?"

"Uh huh," she nods, giving me a sexy smile.

Not needing any further encouragement, I grab the bottle of champagne, spilling some of the liquid over her tits. Then I lap it up, tasting strawberries and bubbles on my tongue as I suck on her skin. "Yeah, that's better," I mutter.

Kate moans, her fingers finding my hair once again as she tugs gently. "Do it again."

"You like that?" I ask.

"Yes," she whispers breathlessly.

"How about now?" I ask, tipping some more liquid into her belly button, her stomach contracts from the cold, but I soon warm her back up again as I tongue her hole, sucking the champagne from her skin and making sure I drink every last drop of liquid. "Does this feel good, baby?"

"Yes, it feels good," she replies, rolling her hips, her hand sliding towards her mound, but I grasp her wrist.

"No. I got you."

Sitting back on my heels, I press the lip of the champagne bottle against her clit then tip the bottle up and let the liquid dribble through her parted folds. She groans at the sensation and I smile, lowering my mouth to her pussy, tasting champagne and sex on my tongue. I keep pouring the liquid over her sex, bubbles popping over her delicate flesh as I lap it up, swirling my tongue through her folds, drinking Veuve Clicquot from her cunt. It's fucking decadent.

Pretty sure *this* is what getting drunk on pussy feels like.

It isn't long before all the champagne is gone and I pull back holding up the bottle. "It's empty, what are we gonna do now?"

"I don't know. Got any ideas?" she asks me, flicking her gaze to the bottle held in my hand, her cheeks flushing with heat.

"Do you trust me?" I ask, raising the bottle to my lips and sliding it into my mouth tonguing the neck.

"Is that a trick question?" she counters roughly, her breath hitching as I lower the bottle back to her pussy, running the lip of the neck through her folds. She sucks in a ragged breath, her fingers curling into the bed spread.

"Do you trust me, Princess?" I repeat, locking eyes with her.

She nods. "With my life."

"Good girl," I reply, then gently slide the neck of the champagne bottle into her hole. She shudders, jerking her hips, and I press my palm against her stomach. "Keep still, okay? Remember I'll never hurt you."

"Okay," she breathes out, then sucks in a ragged breath as I start to move the neck of the bottle in and out of her pussy, using it like a dildo.

"That's it. Relax into it, I've got you, baby," I say, laying the flat of my hand against her lower stomach and pressing the pad of my thumb against her clit.

Pretty soon she's moaning good, and my fucking cock bobs with every gentle thrust of the bottle into her sweet, sweety pussy, the neck slick with her arousal.

"Beast, this feels..."

"Good, baby?" I finish for her, watching her with awe and a heavy dose of lust as she unravels for me, trusting me implicitly. Trusting me with her body, with her pleasure, with her heart. My dick is rock hard watching her take the champagne bottle like a good fucking girl.

"Y-yes," she pants, her heels digging into the mattress as her thighs begin to shake. She's so fucking close. So close.

"Look at what I'm doing to you, Kate. Open your eyes and watch," I demand, my voice rough, my fucking dick leaking precum just watching her get off this way.

She opens her eyes, and pushes up onto her elbows, a sheen of sweat breaking out over her chest as she watches the neck of the bottle slide in and out of her pussy. "Oh God, oh my God," she exclaims, her tits wobbling as her body begins to shake with an oncoming orgasm.

CHAPTER TWELVE

Beautiful Scars

GRIM

"There's someone here to see you," Dom says, stepping into my office as I look up briefly from my desk.

"We're not open for another hour yet," I reply distractedly, my mind wandering to the past few days that I've spent with Beast making up for lost time. I *should* be more concerned about Rodriguez's whereabouts, or the fact the King has apparently disappeared off the face of the Earth, but I'm not. Even running through the club's accounts can't distract me from the memory of Beast's tongue on my clit and an empty bottle of Veuve Clicquot bringing me to orgasm.

"Grim, he's insistent. Mark can't get rid of him."

"Then tell him to shoot the fucker," I reply, glancing at my Excel spreadsheet opened up on my computer. "No one comes here and demands to see me. Who the fuck do they think they are anyway?"

"Mark's not gonna shoot him."

My head snaps up. "Why the fuck not? What do I pay him for?"

Dom pulls a face. "Because he's just a kid."

"What?"

"The person who wants to see you is just a kid. He might be tall for his age and wiry, but he ain't much older than thirteen I'd say."

"Why is there a teenage boy here to see me?" I ask, clicking on the icon that links to the CCTV unit on my computer.

"Your guess is as good as mine," Dom replies with a bemused shrug. "He won't say shit all unless it's to talk with Kate Davidson."

"Kate Davidson, eh?" I reply.

Clearly this kid doesn't have a clue about how things work around here. Lucky for him, I'm not in the business of having a kid beat up because he happened to have used the wrong name for me.

"He's persistent, I'll give him that, and a snarky little shit. Mark's close to giving him a hiding."

"Mark's the most patient man I know," I reply, which is precisely why he's the guy manning the gated entrance.

Takes a lot to piss him off, and he has this uncanny knack of chilling the most obnoxious criminal out should they start getting lary. Despite what I just said, I didn't hire him to kill every fucker because they're being arseholes. I hired him to calm them down, charm them. He's good at his job. So the fact this kid is pissing him off tells me a great deal.

I scan the screen, finding the camera that points to the front gate and double-click, enlarging it. Narrowing my eyes I take a look at the kid, seeing just a side profile. He's arguing with Mark who's leaning against the gate, but even I can tell his patience is wearing thin.

"What do you want to do?" Dom asks.

My gaze flicks back to the screen, and I see Beast walk into the frame. He looks huge, standing next to the lad. I watch how he assesses the situation quickly, a smile spreading across his face as Mark scowls. When he slaps his arm around the boy's shoulder and tips his head back and laughs, I know the kid's said something cutting aimed at Mark, who currently looks like he's about to murder him.

Time to step in.

"I guess you'd better invite him in. Beast just arrived with breakfast, he can accompany the kid inside. Let's see what he's got to say."

"Alright," Dom replies, pressing his phone against his ear and calling Mark as he wanders back into the warehouse.

Getting out of my seat, I follow him, needing to stretch my legs to help get rid of this restless energy I've been carrying around with me all morning despite my sexscapades with Beast. It's why I'm wearing my gym gear so that I can squeeze a workout in before the day gets started. Exercise always helps to focus my mind, and I need to be focused now more than ever.

"You good?" Dom asks me as he pockets his phone.

"Yeah, just a little restless. Figured I could work out this morning before we open up. You know how it is," I reply.

"What's this? Is the formidable Beast losing his game? I'm disappointed," Dom jokes with a smirk.

"Oy fuckface, I'll have you know I'm still a fucking stud-muffin, ain't that right, baby?" Beast asks from the other side of the caged reception area.

Dom snorts. "*Stud-muffin?*"

"Jealous that you're not as delectable?" Beast goads.

Dom snorts. "I'm telling you mate, I'm tasty as fuck."

"So who do we have here?" I ask, ignoring their banter so that I can focus on the kid standing next to Beast who has a scowl on his face that could rival mine right now. They might underestimate the lad, but I can already tell this one's a livewire. When you're one yourself it's easy to recognise that trait in someone else.

"I told you, a tasty fucking morsel," Beast repeats.

"Are you looking to get *fired?*" I joke back.

"Uh oh," Dom says, chuckling as he glances over at me. "Looks like your missus isn't in the best of moods this morning."

"I don't know why the fuck you're laughing," I reply, folding my arms across my chest. "Nancy said she was sick and tired of the same old moves. Looks like you need to up your game or risk losing the best thing that's ever happened to you because of *vanilla* sex..."

Dom's smile drops and his cheeks flush with heat. Looks like vanilla is actually his preferred choice of dessert given the way he's reacting. I hold in a laugh and give him my best resting bitch face.

It does the trick.

"Vanilla sex?! Is that what she said?" Dom replies, affronted.

"We're friends. We talk," I shrug, keeping this going. Truth is, whilst we are friends and we do talk, I would never break her trust and tell him what we actually discuss. She's only ever complimented him anyway, but he doesn't need to know that.

"If the shoe fits, mate," Beast adds, his eyes gleaming with amusement.

"Just wait till I strap her to the bed and fuck her into tomorrow," Dom mutters, storming over to the otherside of the warehouse and pushing the door open into the gym beyond.

Chuckling, I return my attention to Beast and the kid. Beast winks, a grin spreading across his face, the kid just stares at me like he's never laid eyes on a woman before, or maybe he's never witnessed three gangsters ribbing each other without one of them ending up dead.

Striding over to the cage, I rest my hand against the keypad, observing the boy. Dom was right, he's probably no more than thirteen even if he is almost my height. There's a softness to his features that haven't quite developed into a firm jaw and cut cheekbones, but there's a hardness in his eyes that only comes from living a tough life. Something about that pulls me up sharp and I remind myself that just because he's a kid doesn't mean he isn't dangerous. Maybe that says more about me and my upbringing than it does him. Either way, I'm cautious.

"If you've got any weapons on you, I suggest you put them over there," I say, pointing to the table. "You'll get them back when you leave."

"I ain't carrying. I'm not stupid," he replies, folding his arms across his chest and jutting his chin out.

"You've come to my club and given shit to one of my

soldiers, and expect me to believe that?" I reply, raising a sceptical brow.

"You better start talking lad, our breakfast is getting cold and if that's because you're bullshitting us then there'll be hell to pay," Beast adds, holding up the brown paper bag and wafting the smell of coffee and freshly cooked croissants around the space.

All we had for breakfast was a quickie in the shower, and whilst it was a very enjoyable, toe-curling session it hasn't fulfilled all my needs. I'm the type of person who gets *hangry*, hence sending Beast out to grab breakfast for us both. I can be a complete bitch if I don't eat. He knows that better than anyone.

"I told you, I ain't carrying," the boy repeats, but a flicker in his eyes tells me otherwise. The kid hasn't quite got his poker face perfected yet.

"Beast," I prompt, and without me needing to say anything further, he places the paper bag on the ground and strides over to the boy, pinning his arms behind his back before he's able to protest.

"What the shit?!" the boy snarls, baring his teeth at Beast who holds his wrists in one hand and pats him down with the other, finding a flick knife tucked into his sock.

"Not carrying? What's this then, kid?" Beast asks, flicking open the blade and shoving it under the boy's nose.

"What does it look like?" the boy snipes back, hiding his fear behind bravado.

For a moment I'm struck by the expression on his face. On the surface it looks like he really doesn't give a shit that Beast could cripple him for daring to bring a weapon and lying about it, but then I search a little deeper beneath the rebellious "I don't give a flying fuck" persona and see what he's trying to hide. Beast too, given the way he eases back just a little. The kids certainly dressed the part of obnoxious rebel with loose-fitting jogging pants, a t-shirt filled with holes and a black hoodie pulled up over his head. But it's the dark circles under his eyes, the hollow of his cheeks and the way he hunches his shoulders that really tell his story.

"Let him go, Beast," I say, sighing.

"The little toerag *lied*," Beast protests, eyeing me.

"I said let him go. It's not as if he can do any harm now, right?"

Beast nods. "It's your call."

"So do you want to tell me your name?" I ask the kid who takes a step away from Beast, absentmindedly rubbing at his wrists. I can't help but notice the bruises ringing them. There's no way those marks appeared just now.

That explains a lot.

"Ford."

"Ford what?" I ask.

"Just Ford," he replies, unwilling to give me his surname.

"Well, *Just Ford*, want to tell me why you came to my club with a flick knife?"

"Open up the door and I will," he replies.

Beast leans over and clips him around the back of the head. Lightly, I might add. "Have some respect and answer Grim."

Ford reaches up and rubs a hand over the back of his head, looking sheepish. "I want to learn how to fight, and I was told that this is the best place to do that."

Beast coughs back a laugh and I shake my head in amusement. "*You* want to learn how to fight?"

"Yeah." He nods, holding my gaze and ignoring Beast's laughter.

"Why?" I ask, my finger tapping against the keypad as Beast picks up the paper bag. This time it isn't my stomach that grumbles, but Ford's. I frown at that, noticing for the first time how loose his clothes hang from his frame.

"Just because," he shrugs, dropping his gaze and scuffing the toe of his boot against the dusty concrete.

"You want in my club, you need to tell me why," I insist, studying him.

He heaves out a sigh, stuffing his hands in his pockets to try and hide how much they're shaking. This kid wants to learn how to fight more than anything, and that in and of itself is concerning.

"Come on, kid. Out with it," Beast says, glancing at me before holding up the paper bag and handing it to him.

Ford takes it automatically, looking up at him from beneath his dirty blonde hair, hunger then shame flicking across his features. "What's this?"

Beast jerks his chin at the paper bag. "There's a coffee and a couple of chocolate croissants there if you want 'em."

"I'm not hungry," Ford replies, trying to push the paper bag back into Beast's hands.

"Yeah, and I'm not taking no for an answer," Beast replies, shoving it back at him as he meets my gaze. I nod. We both know we're letting this boy in, and I couldn't love the man any more at that moment. "If you want to learn how to fight you need to fuel up first. I ain't training nobody who's gonna faint in the first five minutes in the cage. Got it?"

"So you're gonna train me then?" he asks, and for the first time since meeting him, I see a little hope fill his gaze.

"Only if you tell me why you want to learn how to fight," I persist, my fingers hovering over the keypad.

Ford clutches the paper bag in his fingers and meets my gaze. "So that the next time my stepdad beats on me, I can kill the fucking prick."

"Then I guess you've come to the right place," I reply, tapping in the code and pulling open the door.

FORD EATS our breakfast but leaves the coffee stating that it tastes like shit, and for the next hour trains with us. By the time we've finished, we're all covered in a sheen of sweat and Ford is near collapse. I've got to hand it to him though, he's got the kind of grit you need in order to pass muster at Tales and has kept up despite his clear lack of nutrition. The kid needs to eat a good fucking meal, or ten.

"You might want to take a shower," Beast remarks, chucking Ford a towel from the stack piled up on the shelving unit next to the door of the changing room. "Here's some shower gel and shampoo. Go knock yourself out."

Ford catches the items, scowling as he swipes a hand through his sweat-slicked hair. "I don't need your charity."

"This ain't charity, mate, this is for my nose. You stink. Go shower before our members start to arrive or don't come back here again," Beast replies with a shrug.

"Fine, I'll take a fucking shower," Ford retorts, pushing open the door to the changing room and stomping off inside.

"What an ungrateful fuck," Beast grumbles, shaking his head. "You'd think I'd asked him to cut open a vein the way he just reacted."

I grab a towel from the stack and run it over my sweaty face, stifling a laugh. "So, what do you think?"

"I think the kid's got major issues and a shitload of baggage. Did you see those marks on his wrists?"

"I did, and what else...?"

"And I wanna know why he's *really* here."

"You don't believe his story?" I ask, grabbing a bottle of water from the fridge situated besides the shelving unit. We treat our members well, providing them with a supply of chilled water, fresh towels, toiletries and snacks. It's not all blood and violence at Tales. I like a little balance.

"Oh, that I do believe. It won't be long before that kid is beating the shit out of his stepdad. Pretty sure I'll be there to cheer him on when he does."

"But—" I persist.

"But there's more to it than that. He sought out you and this club for another reason and I wanna know why."

"Yeah, he's hiding something for sure," I reply, chucking the used towel in the washbag and side-stepping Beast so I can follow Ford into the changing room and question him some more.

"Where are you going?" Beast asks, gripping my arm and pulling me in for a kiss.

I relent, kissing him back until I hear the sound of people entering the gym and step out of his hold. Most members by now know that we're an item, but I refuse to give public displays of affection, not because I don't love Beast, but because I don't want to share what we have with any other fucker, and especially not the fuckers who choose to train at my gym.

"There's no time like the present. I want answers."

"But he's taking a shower."

I give Beast a scathing look. "I'm well aware. I'll wait in the changing room. Keep them out for a bit. I want this conversation in private."

"Fine, but if the little shit starts something just give me a shout."

"He's a kid. I've taken on men twice his age and size, and won."

"I know this, but he's also a kid who's clearly been beaten down in life, and those kids are the ones you need to watch out for."

"Are you talking from experience?" I ask, my voice softening as I look up at him.

"Yeah, I am," he admits.

"Beast..." I begin, then stop, remembering we're not alone.

"Go talk to him. I'll keep this lot out," he replies, then strides over to the two men who just entered and greets them both with a fist bump and a slap on the back.

Entering the changing room, I take a seat on the bench in the main locker area and wait for Ford to appear. When the shower switches off, I call out letting him know I'm here. The last thing I need is for the kid to walk out naked as the day he was born.

"What's this, checking to see if I've cleaned up to your standards?" he asks, glaring at me from across the room. Thankfully he's wearing his jogging pants.

"I wanted to talk, that's all," I reply, trying and failing not to notice the bruises covering his chest and arms. "That happen often?"

"Often enough," he shrugs, pressing his finger against a particularly nasty looking bruise on his abdomen. "I got this from my stepdad because I refused to steal money from one of the care workers in the childrens' home I live at."

"I see," I reply, at a loss of fucking words despite the anger coiling in my stomach. "So you don't live with your parents then?"

"Nah, been in care for the last few years, since I was ten."

"So how come this still happens?" I ask, gritting my jaw at the abuse scattered across his undernourished frame.

"My stepdad likes to *check up* on me every now and then."

"And that's allowed, is it?"

"Of course it ain't, social services talk all the talk but are generally fucking useless. They can't keep him from turning up at my school and waiting for me to come out or harassing me on the street."

"So that's why you need to learn how to protect yourself?"

"Exactly," he replies, his grey-green eyes flashing with hatred as his mind goes elsewhere for a moment.

"Ford?" I prompt after a minute of silence.

"And this one," he says, snapping back into the room and pointing to another bruise just above his right nipple, "Was because I called him a lazy cunt. Totally fucking worth it though." He smiles, but it doesn't reach his eyes.

"I bet..."

My voice trails off as I watch him rub the towel over his hair. I have this insane urge to give him a hug and tell him he doesn't need to worry anymore, that we'll look out for him. Fuck knows where this maternal feeling has sprung from, but there's something about the way he's so strong in his vulnerability that drags out my protective side. This kid's a fighter in every sense of the word.

"You ain't seen a kid beat up before, have you?" he asks, reading me well.

"I've seen a lot of violence in my life, but you're right, I haven't been exposed to violence against minors, at least not by their parents. I'm sorry."

"Why are *you* sorry? You didn't do this."

"I'm sorry that this happened to you."

"I don't want your pity. I just want to learn how to fight."

"I get that," I reply, understanding him completely. "You want to protect yourself."

"I want revenge," he bites out, anger blazing in his eyes as he fists his fingers.

"I get that too." Sighing heavily, I tuck a stray strand of hair behind my ear and frown. "How long has this been going on?"

"My stepdad beating me?"

"Yeah."

"As long as he's been with my mum."

"And what about your mum?"

Ford snorts, flicking his gaze away from mine. "She's worse," he whispers out. "They're both crack addicts. I don't ever remember my mum being normal."

"But it took the authorities ten years to get you out?" I ask, my gaze dropping back to his chest and the round puckered scars scattering his skin. Some look suspiciously like cigarette burns, and that anger inside of my chest ignites into an inferno.

"Like I said, social services are fucking useless."

The bitterness in his voice is hard to deny. I don't blame him for it, he's been failed miserably.

"Where did you hear about this place?" I ask, changing the subject.

"The street. People talk," he shrugs.

"And you just figured you'd show up here and barge your way in?"

"It worked didn't it?" he says, plonking down on the bench opposite me and giving me a wry smile.

"You're persistent, I'll give you that," I say, cocking my head to the side. "But membership starts at one hundred and fifty quid a month, off-peak. Think you can afford that?"

I know he can't, and he knows that *I* know he can't, but the way he straightens his spine and juts his jaw out tells me he's not willing to let money get in the way of what he wants. I admire him for that. He's tenacious.

"I'll earn my membership. I'll do whatever it takes. I just want to train, and get strong so that eventually when that cunt lifts a fist to me, he'll never be able to do it again."

"And your mum? Does she still hurt you too?"

Ford's shoulders drop, and his fingers lift to a spot on his right collar bone where two words are etched into his skin. Words I hadn't noticed until now.

Bad Boy.

"Not since she pinned me to the floor and let that bastard tattoo these words into my skin when I was ten years old."

"She did fucking what?!" I shout, jumping to my feet, ready to kill a bitch. I'm not sure why it's that revelation that has my rage suddenly bubbling over, but it does nevertheless. Aren't mothers supposed to want to protect their children, nurture them, *love* them?

Then I remember why Carter took me from my own mother at birth. She was a fucking headcase according to my dad, so I should know better. Being able to bear a child doesn't automatically make you a good mother just like being called dad doesn't make you a good father.

"Don't worry about it," Ford replies flippantly, pulling on his t-shirt.

He thinks I can't hear the pain in his voice just because he can plaster on a fake smile, but I do. I recognise the disappointment and sadness in him because over the years I've worn the same damn mask he's wearing right now. We are kindred spirits, him and me.

"So do we have a deal?" Ford asks, tying up his trainers and standing as he looks me dead in the eye.

I chew on the inside of my cheek, an old habit I thought I'd gotten rid of. "I'll tell you what. I'll give you a two week trial. You come here, have breakfast with me and Beast every morning at seven am sharp, then train for an hour, and in exchange you'll fess up to why you're really here at the end of those two weeks. After that, we'll figure something out."

"But I already told you why I'm here," he replies, folding his arms across his chest defensively and dropping his gaze.

I stride over to him, chucking my finger under his chin and forcing him to look at me. "And we both know it's only half the truth," I say, daring him to object. He keeps his mouth shut, but he doesn't deny it. "Two weeks. In that time you can decide whether you trust us enough to tell us the whole truth."

"Us?" Ford asks.

"Me and Beast. We come as a package. I keep no secrets from him," I say, but as soon as the words slip from my mouth I realise that's a lie.

"Everyone has secrets," Ford counters, a little too knowingly for my liking.

"That's the deal. Take it or leave it."

"I'll take it," Ford replies after a beat before striding from the changing room, leaving me pondering why I still haven't told Beast about Christy.

CHAPTER THIRTEEN

Enemy

BEAST

"Who's that?" I ask, leaning against the bar as a tribal-tattooed, weather-beaten, built like a brick shithouse of a man steps inside the cage to challenge Noah, a fighter from one of the clubs up North. It's Saturday night and the crowd is deafening, cheering and clapping and whistling as the two men face off.

"Malakai," Kate replies, taking a sip of her sparkling water as she watches the two men circle each other.

"What the fuck kind of name is that?" I ask as Dom rings the bell, indicating the fight can start.

"What, as opposed to Beast?" she asks, a smile in her voice as the punters cheer when this Malakai dude lands a right hook to Noah's cheek, knocking his head sideways and sending blood splattering across the canvas.

"You know what I mean. I've never heard of the fucker, and I tend to know all the good fighters out there."

"He's fairly new to the scene. Been around about six months. Whenever he's fighting the punters go wild. He hasn't lost a fight yet."

"Is that so?" I mutter, paying even more attention now as he dodges Noah's punches and lands a few well-placed ones of his own. It doesn't take a genius to work out this guy is one of the better fighters. He's light on his feet despite having a similar build to mine, powerful too given the punch he just landed has Noah staggering around the cage and shaking his head.

"He's earned the club a great deal of money. The punters love him, and because of that I offered him a regular spot, but he only comes in to fight when he's in need of cash. Last time he fought was a few weeks before you returned. According to Mark he's repairing his boat."

"His *boat*?" I question. "Why has he got a boat?"

"I'm guessing to sail on," Kate replies with a shrug.

"No shit," I mutter, narrowing my eyes at the guy who's just landed an uppercut and sent Noah sprawling against the wire. "Have you done checks on him?"

"Same checks I do on any of the fighters who join the club. He hasn't got a police record. No connections with any gangs or crime families. No family ties. He came up clean."

"Hmm," I reply, not convinced.

Kate angles her body towards mine. "What?" she asks, and for a moment I'm distracted by her fitted body top and light blue skinny jeans. She looks insanely hot tonight and I'm incredibly proud that this woman, no, this *queen,* is mine.

Forcing myself not to grab her and drag her back to her office for some alone time, I focus back on the fight unfolding in the ring. "So he just turned up at the club and wanted to fight?"

"Pretty much."

"With a clean record?"

"Yep." She frowns.

"And that doesn't ring any alarm bells? No one who ends up at this club is clean. No one."

"He's never given me any reason to question him. He fights, takes his cut of the winnings and we don't see him for weeks whilst he works on his boat."

"Right."

"It's docked in a boatyard in Putney," she explains.

"So you checked out his story?"

"What do you take me for? Of course I checked out his story. He uses his winnings to pay for the repairs on his boat. He doesn't mix with anyone. Not the punters, nor the other fighters. As far as I can tell he's a loner and likes it that way."

"Interesting," I muse, not convinced. "And he's been hanging around for six months, yeah?"

"About that, yes. Why?"

"When he's finished, I'd like to talk to him. Something doesn't sit right with me."

"Does that something have to do with the fact he's handsome?" she teases.

"He's old enough to be your dad. What is he like, forty or something?"

HEADS YOU LOSE   201

"Pretty sure he's just turned thirty," she chuckles. "But yes, he is *daddy* material, isn't he?"

I'm just about to remind her exactly who her *daddy* is when Dom appears to our left.

"You've got a visitor in your office," he says, eyes darting to the punters nearby. "Might want to go and have a chat."

"A visitor? It's almost midnight. Who wants to do business at this time of night? More to the point, what are you doing letting them into my office?" Kate asks, raising an unimpressed brow.

"It's about a car, a *ford* or something?" Dom says, giving us both a meaningful look.

"Ford you say?" Kate asks, glancing at me, concern slashing across her face.

Dom nods. "Yep."

"Something up with this punter's car?" I ask.

"Yeah, something like that. Best you go check it out for yourself. I'll cover the floor."

"Fuck, fine. So much for me getting to watch Malakai in action. He's definitely the best we've seen in the club for some time," Kate says, trying to make out that she's not itching to go and find out what's happened to her brother

"You make it sound like he's the best fighter you've ever seen," I say, keeping up with the act even though I sense some truth in her statement. Everyone knows *I'm* the best fighter, and therefore the best fucking entertainment, not this Malakai prick who's fighting style is very much like a man who has nothing to lose. Perhaps he doesn't.

Again. *Alarm bells.*

Anyone who fights like he doesn't give a shit about anyone

or anything is as dangerous as a woman who says they're *fine*, and any man with any shred of sense knows not to push a woman when those two words slip from her mouth. You may as well sign your own death warrant.

So, yeah, excuse me if I'm being fucking cautious.

"I don't think he's the best fighter I've ever seen. I'm merely stating he's a good one," Kate says, interrupting my thoughts. "We can discuss this more in my office after we've dealt with our visitor."

I nod, flicking my gaze to Dom. "Do me a favour, don't let Jack Sparrow leave before we've had a word."

He frowns. "Jack Sparrow?"

Kate rolls her eyes. "He means Malakai."

Dom smirks. "You've got it."

"WHAT THE SHIT?" I say the second we step into Kate's office and see Ford sporting a bruised and swollen eye, and a split lip. Blood is smeared across his chin and has crusted over a little on his lip. "Let me guess, courtesy of your stepdad?"

He nods, sinking lower into his seat, his hoodie dropping over his forehead as he tucks his chin to his chest. "Didn't know where else to go," he mumbles.

Kate meets my gaze. "The medicine cabinet in the bathroom has some iodine and cotton pads. Will you grab them for me?"

"Sure thing."

By the time I've returned with the items Kate is sitting opposite Ford, checking his face for other signs of injury. His hoodie is pushed back off his head and neither of them are speaking, but as she presses her fingertips gently against his face, I can see the concern in her eyes, *and* the rage. She's covering it well, but I can see how badly she wants to hurt the man who did this to him.

"Here," I say, handing the cotton wool and iodine to her.

She takes them from me and wordlessly unscrews the cap, pouring some of the liquid onto the cotton wool pad. "This is going to sting," she says, lifting it to his mouth and dabbing his lip.

He doesn't even flinch. That right there is a kid who's used to pain and covering up his reaction to it.

Silently she cleans him up. When she's satisfied he's as fixed up as she can get him, she drops the bloody cotton wool into the bin, screws that cap back onto the iodine and folds her hands in her lap.

"What happened?" she asks as I perch on the edge of the desk beside her.

"I snuck out of the children's home after curfew. Went to meet my mate Camden at the park. He's having a hard time with his mum and her new bloke, so we just hung out. I detoured on the way back..."

"Detoured?"

Ford nods, lifting his gaze to meet hers. "I just wanted to check how she was doing, I guess."

"Your mum?"

"Yeah. Except Trevor caught me standing outside the house and thought he'd *teach me a lesson*. He goes to the pub Saturday nights and comes home at about eleven. I forgot. He was raging drunk, and he's always been a mean drunk."

"Is that right?" I say, feeling my own blood boil for this kid who I barely know but has somehow worked his way beneath my skin.

He shrugs. "Should've known better."

"So you decided to come here?" Kate asks.

"Like I said, didn't have anywhere else to go. One of the other kids at the home must've realised I snuck out and locked the window I climbed out of so I couldn't get back into my room —the fucking dick. I would have slept under the arches by the river for the night but it was a bit sketchy, so I came here. Sorry about that. I'll just go." Ford moves to stand, but Kate grabs his hand.

He flinches at her touch and she quickly lets him go. "Sit down," she says gently. "It's all good."

Kate falls quiet for a moment as she tries to work out what to do. I can see her chewing on her cheek as she stares at Ford, a curious expression on her face.

"You hungry, kid? I can order some pizza," I offer, filling in the silence as I pull out my mobile phone.

"I ain't got no money," he says exactly at the same moment his stomach decides to rumble.

"Well you're in luck because I've got plenty," I reply with a grin. "Anything you like in particular? Got to say that Marco's pepperoni pizza is banging."

"Yeah, I could eat that," he replies, a small smile playing on his lips.

"Done," I reply, hitting the speed dial for the local pizza delivery.

Half an hour later we're sitting around Kate's desk tucking into pizza and watching Malakai fight Noah on the CCTV cameras. To be fair, they've both lasted longer than I'd anticipated and despite my doubts about the man, Malakai is definitely the better fighter, finally finishing off Noah with a lethal punch to the temple, knocking him out cold.

"He's really good," Ford remarks, swiping the back of his hand across his mouth, then wincing when he catches his split lip.

"Yeah, he's alright," I remark, chucking a piece of crust back into the box. "Though not as good as you could be with the right training."

"You think?"

"I know so," I reply, giving him a wink.

"Beast's right, you could be really good one day," Kate agrees, wiping her hand on a napkin.

"So you've changed your mind, and I can have a permanent membership here?" Ford asks, his eyes lighting up like it's Christmas morning.

Kate frowns. "Our deal still stands. Train with us for two weeks and then we'll talk. After that, I'll decide how we move forward."

"Two weeks, yeah?" I ask, looking between them.

"Yes. Ford trains with us every morning for two weeks, and at the end of that he tells us the real reason why he sought me out. If he doesn't, the deal's off."

"I already told you the reason. I want to learn how to fight," Ford mumbles, avoiding eye contact with the both of us.

Kate doesn't bother to argue with him. We all know the kid is keeping secrets, but he ain't about to tell us what that might be now. Maybe ever. Thing is, he'll learn soon enough that Kate is a woman of her word and will follow through on their deal no matter what. She might have a soft spot for the lad, but she won't tolerate lies or secrets. If he wants to remain a member of the club, he's going to have to fess up.

"You know you could just tell us now and get it over with. Much better to pull the plaster off quickly, right?" I remark.

Ford picks at the hole in his jeans, considering what I've said. When he finally looks back up, he opens his mouth to speak only to slam it shut again when there's a knock on the door.

"Looks like you were saved this time," I say, raising a brow at the kid.

He shrugs. "There ain't nothing to be saved from."

Kate eyes me then looks at Ford. "We'll pick back up this conversation another day, okay?"

Ford nods. "Yeah, cool. Whatever."

"Come in," Kate says, and the door swings open.

Dom steps inside followed by Malakai who doesn't even look like he's broken a sweat. He briefly glances at me, then Ford, before finally resting his gaze on Kate.

"You wanted to speak with me?"

"Actually, *I* wanted a word," I say.. "Thought I should introduce myself."

"No introduction needed. I know who you are, Beast," Malakai replies, and even though there's nothing disrespectful about his response, it feels that way.

"That's good, we can get right down to the nitty gritty then."

"Do you need me?" Dom asks, waiting for permission to leave.

"Actually, could you do me a favour and take Ford back to

your place?" Kate says. "He needs a place to sleep tonight and we're going to be a while yet."

Dom raises his brow, but he doesn't argue. Kate's the boss and what she wants, she gets. "Sure thing," he replies, motioning to Ford to follow him. "We got a spare room you can sleep in for the night and Nancy does a mean fry-up for breakfast. It'll be like staying in a hotel for the night."

"Sound good?" Kate questions.

Ford nods. "I guess so."

"Excellent. We'll see you in the morning at ten sharp. That should give you enough time to sleep, check in at your home, then eat and get your arse back here for training, yeah?" I add, only because I don't want to be up at the arsecrack of dawn on a Sunday morning, especially since I get the feeling this night ain't gonna end anytime soon.

Ford stands, his hands stuffed into his jean pockets. "Okay then."

"Come on lad, let's get moving. I got a woman to get home to," Dom says, jerking his chin to the open door, a friendly smile on his face.

He's a good man, one of the best, and despite Ford not knowing him all that well, he can sense it too. When you're a kid who's grown up in an abusive relationship with an adult you learn pretty quickly who you can trust and who you can't.

Ford moves across the room, giving Malakai a wide berth as he passes him by. When he reaches the door he turns to Kate and says, "Thanks... for everything."

"We look out for our members," she says before he disappears through the door, closing it behind him.

"No baby, God ain't the one fucking you with a champagne bottle, your beast is," I say roughly.

"Yes," she hisses, falling back onto the bed, her nipples hardening into points as she spreads her legs wider and squeezes her breasts. "Oh fuck, that's good. That's so fucking good."

"Touch yourself for me," I demand, removing my fingers from her clit and grabbing my aching dick. It throbs in my hand. I'm already on the edge, close to coming. So fucking close.

She nods, sliding her hand over her stomach and reaching for her engorged nub, rubbing tight little circles there, panting for me, losing herself to sensation as she pleasures herself and I gently fuck her with the champagne bottle.

"I'm so close," she cries, her finger moving faster over her clit as she nears the precipice.

"Come for me. Do it now!" I demand, gently sliding the bottle inside and twisting it inside of her, knowing the ridged lip of the bottle will massage her g-spot just right.

"Fuck, Beast," she exclaims, her heels digging into the bed, her head tipping back as she comes for a third time, screaming *my* motherfucking name as my cum spurts in thready ropes all over her belly and thighs.

"That kid's a member of Tales?" Malakai asks, a curious expression on his face.

"Take a seat, *Jack*," I say, jerking my chin to the chair Ford just vacated and ignoring his question.

"The name's Malakai," he replies.

"I know who you are," I say, throwing his words back at him. What can I say, I'm feeling a little petty tonight.

Malakai folds himself into the chair then says, "Respectfully, Grim, I'd like to get back to my boat, so if we could make this quick—"

"You'll go when she says it's time for you to go, fuckface, and not before."

Malakai raises his brows and shifts in his seat, but fortunately for him (and unfortunately for me) he doesn't act on his impulse to throw a punch and stays seated.

Fucking party pooper. I would've enjoyed a fight with the prick.

"Where did you learn how to fight?" I ask instead.

"Nowhere in particular. I've travelled a lot over the years and got in a few scrapes. I learnt how to protect myself, and picked up a few skills along the way."

"Travelled *where* exactly?" Kate asks.

"Everywhere. I don't stay in one place too long. This is the longest I've ever stuck around," he says with a shrug like it's no big deal, but I catch a flicker of something in his eye, pretty sure Kate does too given the way she uncrosses her legs, and shifts forward in her seat.

"Why's that?"

"Why's what?" he retorts, being facetious.

"Why don't you stay in one place for long," she repeats, not rising to the bait.

"Personal preference. I'm a wanderer by nature."

"I see," she replies.

"You don't strike me as a sailor. Interesting lifestyle for a man with an East End accent," I say, and for the first time since he stepped foot in this office, Malakai stiffens.

Fucking bingo.

He thought he'd hidden it well, and he has, but there's that slight twang that he hasn't quite rid himself of yet.

"I learnt how to sail when I was a kid," he says, refusing to acknowledge my observation. "Always preferred my own company anyway."

"Again, interesting lifestyle for an East End kid."

"I grew up on an island off the coast of Kent, surrounded by water. Not so unusual there, my friend."

"So you moved there from London?" I press.

"I *told* you I grew up on an island off the coast of Kent."

His response is a veiled warning not to dig any deeper. If he thinks I'm going to back off, he can think again. But for now I let that line of questioning go.

"And are you planning on moving along soon?" I ask, my fingers sliding over the gun holstered at my waist.

"The repairs on my boat are almost complete. I should be out of your hair in a few weeks," he replies, clocking my not so subtle threat before looking at Kate. "So if there's nothing else, I'd like my money now."

"Okay, let's cut the shit!" I say, pulling my gun free and aiming it at his head. He doesn't even flinch, which only serves to piss me off more. "Why don't you tell us both the real reason why you're here, and then we'll let Grim decide whether you live or die. How about that?"

"Well?" Kate says, folding her arms across her chest as she waits for an answer.

Malakai sighs, like we're the ones with the issue and not him.

"I'm here to gather information and report back to the King."

CHAPTER FOURTEEN

Confession

GRIM

"You're so fucking dead!" Beast exclaims, pressing the butt of the gun against Malakai's forehead.

"Wait!" I demand, resting my hand on Beast's forearm, my fucking heart beating out of my chest. I feel like a fool. How did I miss this? He came up clean. "I have questions, a lot of them. And he needs to be alive to answer them."

"And you'll get your answers. This is going to be so much fucking fun," Beast exclaims. "I'm going to enjoy getting Jack Sparrow to sing like a fucking canary."

"Jack Sparrow?" Malakai questions, looking about as tense as a cat warming in the sun. "Oh the boat. I get it."

"Shut the fuck up and listen," Beast continues. "I'm going to take you on a little trip into my basement, and you, *my friend*, are going to tell us every-fucking-thing whether you want to or not."

"No need for threats," Malakai says. "I'll tell you what you need to know."

"What?" Beast asks, frowning. "You're gonna rat on your boss?"

"I have no loyalties to him. Never have."

Beast drops his gun and steps back, narrowing his eyes at Malakai. "Words of a desperate man, right there."

Malakai shakes his head. "No, words of a *truthful* man. I don't owe my loyalty to the King."

"So what's the catch?" I ask, because no one betrays the King and gets away with it. I'm assuming this is all part of some bigger plan, one in which I get fucked over.

"No catch. The King and I are... How can I put this? *Old adversaries.* He thinks he owns me. I know he doesn't."

"If you're adversaries, why the fuck are you working for him then?" Beast points out.

"How we know each other is irrelevant."

"Not to us it isn't. Start talking," I warn.

"Or what? You'll kill me? If you haven't already worked it out, I don't fucking care whether I live or die. There isn't anything left in this world I care about apart from my boat, and inanimate objects don't really count. So you could shoot me now and I wouldn't try to stop you."

Beast snorts. "How does torture sound? Many men before you have said similar things but as soon as I start pulling out their toenails things change rapidly."

"Maybe so, but not me," he replies, looking Beast dead in the eye, and call it a sixth sense, gut instinct or maybe even a little bit of Christy rubbing off on me, but I believe him. He'll tell us what he wants us to know and take the rest to his grave.

"Let's go then," Beast says, jerking his gun, indicating for Malakai to get to his feet.

"No, it won't work," I say, not quite believing the words coming out of my mouth, but saying them anyway.

"What?" Beast frowns, staring at me like I've grown another head.

"He means what he says."

"And I'm very good at what I do. You *know* this," Beast reminds me. "I'll get him to talk."

Malakai looks between us. "I'll tell you everything you want to know *except* how I'm connected to the King. Take it or leave it, but if you leave it, I won't tell you a damn thing and I'll die before you get anything out of me."

Beast narrows his eyes at Malakai and leans in close. "You really don't fear pain or death, do you?"

"What gave me away?" Malakai asks with a soft laugh that's laced with sadness. It's disconcerting, and I can tell Beast is thrown by it as much as I am.

"I suppose you do fight like a man who has nothing to lose," Beast concedes.

Malakai nods, eying him. "I lost the only two people I cared about years ago. So, no, I don't have anything to lose and I plan on keeping it that way. Caring for someone, *loving* them," he says pointedly, looking between us, "Is a dangerous fucking game. Pretty sure you two know all about that. I heard what happened here the other night with Fitzpatrick. Word gets around quickly."

"Grim, and the way I feel about her, ain't a fucking game to me," Beast says, resting his steel-toed boot on the seat between Malakai's open legs. "I will protect her with my life and will end anyone who comes for her including the King. *Especially* that motherfucker."

"I can see that," Malakai acknowledges, "And because you're willing to do what many won't, I'll answer your questions."

"You lie, you die. Simple as that," Beast adds.

"Understood."

Reaching for my packet of cigarettes, I pull one out of the packet and light it. Dragging in a deep lungful, I blow out the smoke in one steady breath. "You're spying on me for the King. *Why?*" I ask.

"Because once I've fulfilled this last act of service, I can cut ties with him forever and live a solitary life on the ocean. "

Beast barks out a laugh. "No one cuts ties with the King."

"Says the man who's willing to do anything to help the woman he loves do exactly that, including gathering an army of mercenaries," Malakai points out.

"I suppose you fed that information back to the King."

"I shared my observations. Yes."

Beast reaches for his gun. "You're a cunt."

Malakai sighs. "Shoot me, don't shoot. I really don't give a shit. Like I said, I've long since past caring whether I live or die. You can end this now and be no better off, or you can listen to what I have to say."

"Let him speak," I say, feeling a heavy weight sink into my stomach.

"A few months back the King contacted me and asked me to report back on an investment he'd put money into. He wanted me to check on the business and, more importantly, the woman who runs it."

"Why didn't he just come and check the fucking books himself?" Beast asks. "Would've been a lot simpler."

To be fair, it's a valid question, because up until the point Beast walked back into my life, I had no idea about the original deal between the King and Carter. Yes, I might not have liked the King having such a large share in the club, but I had a get-out clause, raise two million and I could buy the fucker out. That's what I've been working on these past two years, until Beast returned and opened my eyes to the truth. Now I just want the bastard dead.

"The King trusts very few, and he sure as fuck doesn't trust a young woman who's managed to build an empire *and* an army," Malakai explains. "Why do you think he's stayed away?"

"He underestimated Grim, and now he's going to have to deal with the consequences of that," Beast says, a note of pride in his voice.

"Yes, it appears he did."

"So where is he?" I ask, more than ready to bring the fight to him. I'm done being a pawn in his fucking game. I want out.

"That I don't know," Malakai replies.

"What?" Beast asks, as confused as I am.

"I take instructions from him via the dark web. We communicate online. Nothing more than a brief instruction from him and a one word response from me. He could be anywhere in the world."

"Fuck!" Beast exclaims.

"So what changed?" I ask. "In the first year of business, the King checked in regularly. Granted, it was by telephone, but he made sure he knew what was happening at the club."

"As far as I can gather, the King was happy with how things were being run here. Your club was bringing in a good turnover and he was willing to wait and see how you'd evolve as a business owner and a person," Malakai says, eying Beast. "But then you started to surround yourself with an army of loyal soldiers, and the King started to get paranoid. That's when he sent me in to check things out."

"Of course he did," I say, taking another hit of my cigarette.

"Then Beast reappeared and the King realised that you'd gone from being a savvy business woman to an actual threat with a man who'd do anything for you standing by your side."

"Grim was always a fucking threat. He was just too arrogant to see it," Beast says.

"I'm assuming you know what he did?" I ask.

Malakai shakes his head. "I don't, actually, and I don't want to know what happened between you all. But I can tell you this, I'm not the only one who's been sent to dig around."

"Rodriguez?" Beast grunts.

"I don't know his name, but if you've already got your suspicions, then you're probably correct about the person's identity."

"Fucking perfect," Beast grunts, waiting for my reaction.

"I'm not afraid of the King or anyone he sends my way," I say, stubbing out my cigarette. "And honestly, I'm done being his bitch. Tales is mine. The profits of this club are mine. If he wants it, he'll have to fight me for it."

"Believe me. He'll fight you for it," Malakai warns.

"Then it's just as well we've built an army, right?" I shrug, never more grateful for Beast and what he's done for me than I am at this moment. Without him and his foresight, I might not be in such a strong position now.

"Exactly. You stand a better chance against him than most," Malakai says. "Which is why he's doing what he's doing. The King rarely gets his hands dirty if he can send in someone else to do the job for him."

"Like you?" I ask.

"My purpose was to gather information. Nothing more," he explains, getting to his feet.

"Where the fuck do you think you're going?" Beast asks, pulling out his gun. "You think we're just going to let you go? I think fucking not."

"Like I said, I have no loyalty to the King. I've told you everything I know."

"Which is *what* exactly? That you and the King go way back but you refuse to say how you know each other or that you've zero idea where the King is now. How about that insightful piece of information that the King wants Tales for himself, like we didn't already fucking know that, or perhaps it's the revelation that he sent someone else in to stir shit up," Beast says with more than a little sarcasm. "You've told us precisely jack-shit, *Jack Sparrow*."

Malakai shrugs. "Do what you want with the information. All I know is that after I take my share of the winnings tonight, I'll be close to clearing the final payment for my boat's repairs.

Once it's fixed up I can leave and never fucking return. The ocean is a big place to get lost in, and I intend on disappearing forever."

Beast laughs, shaking his head. "Have I not made myself clear? You're not leaving!"

"Lower the gun, Beast," I say.

"Grim, come on. Think about this."

"I have. Lower the gun."

Despite how badly he wants to shoot Malakai, Beast follows my instructions and lowers the gun.

"You're not seriously considering letting him go, are you?"

"That all depends," I reply, already knowing exactly what I'm going to do.

"On what?" Beast asks.

"On whether Malakai wants to watch his boat go up in flames or if he truly wants his freedom."

Malakai's head snaps around as he glares at me, but I say nothing as I pick up my phone and select the relevant number saved into the contacts, hitting the dial. Pressing the loud-speaker button I wait for an answer.

"Garsons Boatyard, how can I help?"

"Bill, this is Grim," I say, studying Malakai's face as I talk.

Like the King, he underestimated me. Everyone has a weakness, and whilst Malakai wasn't lying when he said he didn't care if he lived or died, I'm willing to bet he'd give a shit if I threatened the only thing in this world he loves, even if it is an inanimate object. That boat is his ticket to freedom and a life of solitude, which he craves more than anything. That's on the line right now.

"That boat you've been working on, the schooner owned by Malakai."

"Yes, I know the one."

"How long until the repairs are done?"

"Almost there, a month tops."

"What's left to pay?"

"Two grand."

"Consider it paid."

"Sorry what?" Bill says as Beast huffs out a breath and Malakai frowns.

"I'm paying off Malakai's bill. Get the boat fixed. You've got three weeks."

"It would've been cheaper to shoot him in the head," Beast grumbles as I hang up.

Ignoring his remark, I concentrate on Malakai. "Two grand to fix your boat. Thirty grand for you to find out where the King is hiding. You've got until your boat is fixed. If you fail, I'll burn your boat to the ground and let Beast do whatever the fuck he wants to you in the basement."

Malakai nods. "Consider it done."

"One last thing," I say as he strides towards the door.

"Yes?"

"The only people who were in this office before you arrived were me and Beast. That kid has nothing to do with any of this."

"What kid?" he replies, then pulls open the door and strides from the room.

CHAPTER FIFTEEN

O3' Bonnie & Clyde

BEAST

Wiping my sweaty hands down my blood-flecked overalls, I grab the serated knife from my trolley of torture instruments and pace about the basement, acting up the part of certified psycho. I mean, some people would say that it comes naturally to me, but seriously this batshit crazy persona I put on when torturing someone isn't really me at all. I'm actually a pretty laid back, well-adjusted guy who likes to kick back in the evening and watch soaps on the television then make love to his missus until she passes out from multiple orgasms.

Totally. Fucking. Normal.

"P—please," the prick stutters.

Stopping in my tracks, I stare at the man before me, secretly wishing it was Malakai and not Ford's stepdad, Trevor. Don't get me wrong, I'm not mad it's Trevor strapped to the seat in front of me, because he sure as fuck deserves to be here after what he's done to Ford over the years, it's just that torturing that arrogant fuck Malakai until he spills every last secret would be a lot more satisfying. I don't trust the fucker. Not one bit.

"*P—please*," Trevor repeats, close to shitting his pants, he's that scared. "I won't touch the kid again."

His whiny voice does nothing but agitate me further. Truth be told, I've tortured a lot of men over the years, but this fucker has got to be the worst. Crying, snotting and pissing all over himself like a motherfucking baby. I've seen more backbone on a jellyfish. Then again that's no great surprise, men like him are always fucking cowards.

"See, the thing I dislike more than snakes in the grass are people like you, *child beaters* who pick on the defenceless because they're too fucking cowardly to go toe-to-toe with someone their own age. You, dicksplash, represent all the things I fucking hate about humankind," I say, sliding the tip of the knife down his right cheek and opening up his skin like a hot knife through butter.

"Please no more," he begs, tears mixing with the blood and snot decorating his fuck-ugly face. He's as unattractive on the outside as he is on the inside with thinning mousy-brown hair, pockmarked skin, and yellowing teeth. The dude can't be more than five years older than me, but his addiction to crack sure as fuck makes him look twice his age.

"How many times did Ford have to beg you to stop before you listened, huh?" I ask, not bothering to wait for a response.

"From the state of his skin and the scars covering his body, I'm guessing a *lot* of fucking times."

"The kid was out of control. He needed discipline!" the cunt replies, earning him a punch to the jaw that snaps his head to the side so hard that I half expect it to go rolling off his shoulders.

"So you're telling me he needed you and his piece of shit mother to carve the words *Bad Boy* into his motherfucking skin because he was out of control at ten years old?"

"We were high that day—"

I pull back my fist and break his nose this time, and the scream that releases from his lips would make most people's skin crawl.

Not me.

Getting in his face, the serrated knife held against his throat this time, I bare my teeth at him, making sure I cut his skin deep enough to make it bleed. "He's just a fucking kid. You low-life, skank-arse, crater-faced piece of motherfucking shit."

"It w—wasn't just me," he stammers, dropping Ford's mum in it as I press the blade harder against his throat. I ain't surprised, he's the type of person to sell out his own mother to save his fucking neck.

"Oh, believe me. We know," I reply. "That bitch is on our shit list too, but Grim's dealing with her."

"G—grim?!"

His eyes widen as though he's only just realised who he's dealing with. He's clearly thick as shit as well as low-life, or maybe just fucking delusional. Then again I did knock him the fuck out before bringing him here so there is that.

"Yeah, *Grim*. You've heard of her, right?"

"What's she got to do with Ford?" he asks, swallowing hard, his Adam's apple slipping up and down beneath the blade. Not gonna lie, I love the fact that just the mention of my woman's name puts the fear of the Devil into this man. Her reputation precedes her, and that's fucking hot.

"Ford is a member of Grim's fight club."

"Since when?" he has the gall to ask, surprise making him stupid.

"Since none of your motherfucking business," I grind out, removing the knife from his throat then pressing the tip against his bare chest a few inches below his right nipple. "But I will tell you this, that kid has potential, and as such Grim has made it her business to keep him safe from the likes of you and that dirty bitch who calls herself his mother."

"She's not right in the head," he mumbles. "Fucking whore."

"THE FUCK?!" I roar.

"No! NO! I meant Ford's mum, *Mary*," he says quickly, the colour draining from his face. "*She's* not right in the head. She's also been fucking around on me, the dirty skank-arse whore."

"And I suppose you are right in the head, huh?" I scoff, pressing the blade deeper. A droplet of blood slips from beneath the blade, trailing down his skin. "Don't make me fucking laugh."

He looks down at the blade, snot and blood dripping from his nose and onto his piss-soaked jeans. "Look, I admit it. I was a cunt."

"Was?" I bark out a laugh.

"I *am* a cunt," he corrects himself. "But it's the drug's man. They make you fucking crazy. I love that boy."

"LOVE?!" I boom, the sound of my voice loud in this hot as

fuck basement. "You don't know the meaning of the word! Don't tell me you love that kid because we both know all you love is your next hit and the sounds of his screams when you beat him."

"I swear to you," he cries, eyes widening in pain as I bury the tip of the blade further, slicing through muscle this time. "I won't hurt him again."

"You're right, you won't," I reply, then shove the blade through the gap in his ribcage and pierce his motherfucking lungs, drowning him in his own blood. "And neither will she."

AFTER TAKING off my blood splattered coveralls that I wore to protect my clothes, and thoroughly scrubbing my hands clean, I head back upstairs into the main warehouse. To avoid walking through the gym, I take the longer route to Grim's office via the corridor that circles the building, passing Cleveland on my way.

He nods in greeting, sliding a finger beneath the stiff collar of his fitted blue shirt. It's got red edging around the pocket and cuffs, and reminds me of the uniform the employees of the local supermarket wear. I can't resist the urge to tease him just a little bit. Nothing like a bit of lighthearted ribbing after some good old bloody violence. It's all about the balance and shit.

"Clean up in aisle eight," I say, laughing at my own joke.

"Excuse me?" he asks, not getting it at all.

My smile drops. Cleveland's good at his job but he's stiffer than a priest's dick in a nunnery.

"I took care of things for Ford," I explain. "His stepdad is currently choking on his own blood in the basement, that is if he isn't already dead. I didn't bother to stick around to check. Can you call in the cleaners whilst I go chat with Grim? Make sure they come after closing hours."

He nods, pulling out his phone. "Consider it done."

"Good man." I grin, refraining from blurting out another joke that's on the tip of my tongue.

"Is that all?' he asks.

"Any news about Rodriguez?"

"Not yet... Don't worry we'll find him," he adds quickly.

"I ain't worried. That prick will get what's coming to him sooner or later."

"Indeed," Cleveland replies, as straight-faced as ever as he heads towards the basement and the carnage I've left behind there.

"Is it done?" Kate asks the second I step into her office.

"It's done," I confirm, striding over to the drinks cabinet and pouring us each a two-fingered shot of bourbon, passing her a glass.

"Thanks." She takes a sip, swirling the liquid as she stares at the screen on her computer.

"What're you looking at?" I ask, stepping behind her and peering over her shoulder.

On the screen is footage of Ford training with us both in the ring this morning just like he has every morning for the past week. He bounces on the balls of his feet like a natural, protecting his face and dodging Kate's jabs instinctively. Some people have to learn how to fight, and some are born to step into the ring. Ford is most definitely the latter.

"I've been watching our training sessions. He has a natural

talent. I've never seen anything like it. When he grows into his body, I think he'll be giving you a run for your money."

"Not a fucking chance," I reply with a dismissive snort. "The kid's good, but he's not *that* good."

"But he will be after you're done training him, right? You can't always hold the crown."

"I most certainly fucking can," I reply, perching on the edge of the desk watching Kate as she studies the boy.

"He looks up to you, you know," she remarks, sipping on her bourbon.

"And you've got a soft spot for the little fucker."

Kate laughs, leaning back in her chair as she meets my gaze. "I know you like him too. Don't pretend you don't care."

"Yeah, alright. He's a good kid beneath all the attitude," I admit begrudgingly.

"He's got fight, and I don't just mean his talent in the ring. He's like us."

"What, a little unhinged?" I say, only half-joking considering I just slid a twelve inch serrated blade into his stepdad's lungs not more than five minutes ago.

"I meant that he's had a rough start in life, but he won't let the actions of shitty parenting prevent him from getting what he wants, just like we haven't. I'm excluding your mum in this of course."

"Of course. Mum was a fucking angel. I wish you could've met her."

"Me too," she replies, frowning as she stares at the screen some more.

"What is it, Princess?" I ask, crooking my finger under her chin and urging her to look at me.

"There's something about him..." she says, chewing on the inside of her cheek.

"Like what?"

"I don't know. I can't put my finger on it."

"He comes from a broken home, he's tough, and perhaps a teensy bit unhinged, a bit like us. Maybe that's what you're picking up on," I say, palming her cheek and wanting to kiss the worry away.

"No. I mean, yeah he is, but it's more than that..." She looks back at the screen and takes another sip of her bourbon. Sighing she adds, "Don't mind me. Long fucking day."

"Then let's get out of here. Fancy something to eat at Sapori? It's been a while."

"Are you asking me out on a proper date this time?" she jokes, a smile lighting her eyes.

"I am," I agree, then putting on a posh accent, say, "Ma'am, would you do me the honour of accompanying me on a date to Sapori where I can wine and dine you, feed you morsels of delicious food then take you home for dessert?"

"Dessert at home? I'd prefer their almond semifreddo than a tub of ice cream from the freezer," she quips.

"That wasn't the kind of dessert I was talking about, but if you want we'll take the semifreddo to go. I'm sure Romeo won't mind."

"You think?" she grins, then her smile drops as she clicks off the CCTV and stares at an Excel spreadsheet filled with figures that make my brain ache just looking at it.

"Well that shit looks complicated."

"It is," she sighs, rubbing at her temples. "Honestly, I'd love to go to dinner with you but the club's opening for tonight's fight is in a few hours, and I still haven't gone through this month's accounts."

"So palm off the accounts to someone else."

"I could, but there's still a body to dispose of, and a deadbeat mother to deal with," she reminds me, her voice darkening.

"Well you don't need to sweat it about the body. Cleveland's calling the cleaners, and I can help you figure out the other shit."

"The other shit being Ford's mum, *Mary*."

"Yeah, have you got any plans in mind for her?" I ask, genuinely interested to know how she's going to handle the situation.

Whilst I have zero guilt killing his cunt of a stepdad and I despise his mum just as much, it ain't as cut and dry regarding her. I've no doubt that Ford hates his mother, how could he not after the abuse he's received at her hands, but I'm betting there's still love there, no matter how complicated it might be. If we go ahead and kill her, there's a possibility we'll lose him, and just like Kate said, I happen to like the little toerag. He's growing on me.

"I want to gut her for the things she's done to Ford," Kate says, pressing her mouth in a hard line and tapping her finger against her desk. "His whole body is covered in scars."

"And will you?"

"Will I what?" she asks absentmindedly.

"Gut her?"

She blows out a long breath. "Cutting someone open is normally your thing, isn't it?"

"Shoot her then?"

"Probably."

"Probably?" I question.

"I need to sort some things out first."

"You mean Malakai? You know how I feel about that. I don't trust him."

"I don't either, but he's the closest we're going to get to locating the King. Besides, that isn't my biggest concern right now."

"It's not?"

Kate shakes her head. "Ford's staying at the Pullen's Group Home for Boys on the other side of town. I was hoping to get him into the one closer to here. Make it easier on him to swing by the club. That and the fact that Pullen's has a reputation. Most of the kids who leave there are more damaged than when they went in."

"Yeah, so I've heard."

"I'm hoping Hudson can help with the move."

"Hudson? How is *he* going to help?" I ask snarkily. If I sound like a jealous prick, it's probably because I am one.

"Because he has contacts at the local authority."

"Since when?"

"Since you've been away. Hudson and his brothers haven't just been building a business, they've set up a charity specifically aimed at supporting kids in care."

"What exactly does the charity do?" I ask, trying to hide my motherfucking eye twitch because Hudson is proving to be a goodie two-shoes, pain in my arse. Don't get me wrong, I don't begrudge those kids' support, fuck knows they're deserving of it, but does Hudson really have to be such a good fucking guy?

"One that supports kids' emotional and psychological health, providing therapy, day trips out, that kind of thing."

I groan, not because I think it's a shit idea, but because Kate's gaze fills with pride and my little jealous heart wants to throttle Hudson for making her go all gooey-eyed. "How the fuck am I supposed to compete with that?"

"He's always going to be in my life, Beast," she replies, evading my question which only pisses me off more.

"Don't mean I got to like it," I grumble, folding my arms across my chest in a sulk. I know I'm acting like a petulant child, but I've started and now I can't seem to stop.

Kate squeezes my arm and gives me an indulgent smile. "If I've not already made it clear, I love *you*."

"Sounds like you love him too."

"I do."

"Fucking shitballs," I snap, really making a fucking fool of myself now. I'm not usually this insecure, and I'm pretty sure I deserve a good hiding if I don't reel my neck in soon, but I can't seem to help myself. Kate giggles then slams her mouth shut when I glare at her.

"You're jealous."

"I can't fucking help it."

The laughter in her eyes softens to love. "He's my best friend, Beast, but it isn't him that makes my knees weak. It's you."

"Me?" I ask, chewing on a smile as she shifts back in her seat and swivels her chair directly in front of me. Her black silk blouse opens a little at the neck with her movement, and I get a direct view of her pretty tits encased in black lace. My woman dresses well, and today she's wearing figure hugging leather trousers with heeled boots to match her shirt.

"Yes, you," she replies, placing the flat of her hands on my thighs, her thumbs stroking in circles and making my cock twitch.

"What else do I do to you that Hudson doesn't?"

"Are you fishing for compliments?"

"Might be." I shrug. "Got any more?"

"I've got plenty."

"Wanna enlighten me?"

She smiles, her hands smoothing up my thighs inch by torturous inch. "He doesn't make me laugh until my belly aches."

"Yeah, I'm fucking hilarious," I agree with a smirk.

"He doesn't cut out the hearts of my enemies and bring them to me as a gift," she continues, her fingers edging towards my cock.

"You actually liked that? I have to admit, I thought it was a turn off."

"I get a thrill out of reading Grimms' Fairy Tales, and grew up surrounded by violence. Is it really a surprise I'm into that? It's my kind of romantic," she admits with an unapologetic smile.

"Okay, noted. What else?"

"He didn't step in and save me from being given to that fucking creep the King."

"This is true," I agree, nodding my head.

"He didn't spend two years finding me an army."

I grin. "The slacker."

"Not to mention that Hudson sure as fuck doesn't distract me when I'm trying to work."

"And that's a good thing?"

"Believe me, my pussy thinks so," she replies, her neck and

cheeks flushing with heat even as she levels me with her best temptress stare. This woman, she's a fucking contradiction, and I'm here for it.

"Does it now?" I reply, widening my legs as she stands, stepping between them. My arms wrap around her back, and I give her a stupid grin. Fuck, she makes me feel like a lovesick teenager and just as fucking randy. My dick is constantly at half-mast, ready for action whenever she's around, but when she talks about her pussy like that... It's a lethal fucking weapon.

"It does."

"And what's your pussy thinking right now?"

Kate grins as I grab her leather-clad arse and pull her flush against my aching cock.

"It's not really doing much thinking... More like *throbbing*."

"Throbbing, eh?" I lick my lips, massaging her arse as she reaches between us and runs her hand over my dick. I let out an involuntary moan. "Looks like my dick is doing the same in sympathy... Anything else you want to add to the list of the things Hudson isn't and I am?"

"Yeah, all I need in this life is you," she says softly, pressing her lips against mine and giving me the sweetest kiss I've ever received in my life.

"Well shit, you sure know how to massage a man's ego," I say, unable to stop myself from fucking beaming.

"What's so amusing?"

"I'm just happy. Fucking ecstatic, actually."

"Happy?" she muses. "You just murdered someone."

"And? The fucker deserved to die. Besides, I wasn't talking about that, I was talking about *us*. Me and you. This."

"That *is* something to be happy about, isn't it?" she ponders before returning her lips to mine and kissing me slow and dirty until my dick nearly tears a hole in my jeans.

"You know we could sack off Sapori and Hudson-*goodie-two-shoes*-Freed, and just head home now," I say, punch-drunk on her kisses.

She shakes her head, her silver hooped earrings swinging. "No, this is important. Maybe Hudson can come to Sapori with us? Kill two birds with one stone."

I pull a face. "You're joking right? I'm not a third wheel, and this sure as fuck ain't a love triangle. Besides, Sapori is *our* place, let's not be tainting the memories we make there with that fucker."

"Love triangle, hmmm..."

"You better be pulling my leg, Princess, because I'm not averse to laying you over my lap and spanking that thought right out of you," I retort sharply.

"Is that a promise?" she asks, wiggling her eyebrows.

"You better believe it."

Pulling her in for a hug, I latch my teeth onto her neck like a fucking animal because I'm all about marking my territory, and I don't care how that makes me look. Besides, she likes it, and so long as she does I'll keep sucking on her skin and marking her up with my lips, tongue and teeth.

"You really are a beast," she groans, her nails burrowing into my back as I suck and nibble her flesh, refusing to let go until I've left a mark. It's been a long time since I gave someone a hickey, and I kind of fucking like it.

"Just in case you need reminding, I'm *not* into sharing. You. Are. Mine."

"Yours," she says, reaching for my cock and giving it a possessive squeeze. "And later on, your dick will be mine."

"Hell to the fucking *yes!*" I exclaim, my cock jerking in her hand at the thought. "Revenge, murder and sex all in one day, what more could a man ask for?"

"Indeed, but first we need to see Hudson, okay?"

"Okay, fucking fine," I sigh. "I suppose it's about time I thank the prick for watching over my woman."

"You might want to rephrase how you're going to do that. Not sure he'll appreciate being called a prick."

"Cunt then?" I offer.

Kate shoves me in the chest. "Behave!"

"Fine, I'll behave. This time," I say pulling her in for one last kiss before we head out of the office and go visit her *other* man who doesn't make her pussy flutter.

Thank fuck.

CHAPTER SIXTEEN

Tough Love

GRIM

"What in the mosquito bite is that on your neck?" Max asks with a smirk as Hudson ushers us both into their living room.

"Shut the fuck up, dicksplash," Beast grunts, shoving him as we walk past. "Have a little respect."

Max laughs, stumbling back into Bryce who's looking at us both in amusement. "I thought hickeys went out of fashion with flared jeans and gangster rap."

"And you can shut your trap, *man-child*. When did you grow all that facial hair, in the fucking womb?" Beast snaps.

Max bursts out laughing and Bryce smooths a palm over his

beard, "Mate, don't knock the beard, the girls love it. Don't they Grim?"

"I wouldn't know," I reply. "I'm a *woman,* and this woman prefers her men more beast than teddy bear. Know what I mean?"

Max and Hudson snigger and Beast gives me a panty-melting grin. "Hear that *Yogi Bear?* Grim ain't into cuddly toys."

Bryce shrugs, not in the least bit bothered. "Fair enough. To each their own and all that," he says before eying me with a cheeky smile, "But if you ever get bored of trying to tame the beast, this teddy bear is more than willing to comfort you."

"You're pushing your luck, fuckface," Beast growls, his smile dropping. I must admit, this possessive side of Beast is quite enjoyable to behold.

"Oh relax! I'm just playing with you," Bryce says with a roll of his eyes. "We all know Grim's off-limits. Besides, I ain't into stealing my brother's girl. On the other hand, if you're into sharing..."

"Not on your fucking life," Beast states, flopping down next to me on the sofa whilst Hudson gives Bryce a *shut the fuck up* look. "And we ain't brothers. I barely know you."

"Don't be like that, Grim is family so that makes you our brother. Right, Hud?" Bryce says, staring pointedly at Hudson.

"Right," Hudson replies with an easy smile. "Tea anyone?"

"Tea?" Beast scoffs. "A fucking teatotaller as well as a philanthropist. Fuck me, who are you? The patron saint of goody-two-shoesia."

"*Goody-two-shoesia?!*" Max repeats, barking out a laugh that Bryce quickly joins in with. "You bet your arse I'm using that one. Good one, Beast."

Hudson shakes his head in amusement. "I've got Scotch. Will that do?"

"Tea is fine," I cut in quickly. "We've got plans later."

"Coming right up," Hudson replies, heading into the kitchen just as Bryce leans forward in his seat and whispers conspiratorially under his breath to Beast.

"Mate, if you need a helping hand in the dick department," he says pointedly looking at Beast's crotch whilst wiggling his eyebrows, "I can get you a stash of those infamous little blue pills if you want. That'll keep you going even when you're half-cut."

"Number one, *Yogi*, I can handle my drink," Beast replies, reaching up and giving Bryce's beard a good yank. "And number two, unlike you, my dick doesn't need any help standing to attention."

"Oh for fuck's sake," I complain lightheartedly, "Would you two stop flirting with each other already?"

Max snorts. "Nothing like a good old bromance to warm the cockles of your heart, right Grim?"

"In all honesty, I'm about ten seconds away from shooting you all in the kneecap, so zip it!" I joke, actually rather enjoying their banter.

Max gives Bryce a wide-eyed look and Beast chuckles, pulling down his t-shirt and showing them his bullet scar. "Trust me when I say you do *not* want to piss my missus off. I've got the scars to prove what happens when you get on her wrong side."

"Jesus fuck," Max exclaims, poking at Beast's scar like a overstimulated toddler. "I thought Hudson was joking."

"When do I ever joke?" Hudson asks, returning with a tray of tea and biscuits and placing them on the coffee table.

"Good point," Max mutters, eying me a little more warily as Hudson takes a seat.

"You said you needed our help. What's going on, Grim?"

"Well..." I begin, and for the next five minutes explain about Ford showing up at Tales out of nowhere, telling them about his shady parents and the abuse he's suffered, and wanting to get him moved to a better home. Hudson is quiet for a moment after I finish, contemplating what I've said.

"Poor fucking kid," Bryce mutters, his face pale.

I don't know the full story of Bryce's past, but I do know his father was physically abusive and nearly killed him on one occasion, which led to him ending up in care. If anyone knows where Ford is coming from, it's him. Him *and* Beast.

"So, do you think you can help?" I press, taking a sip of my now lukewarm tea, my mouth suddenly dry. I don't know why helping Ford means so much to me, but it does.

"I can have a chat with my contact at the local authority, I'm sure she can pull some strings and get Ford transferred to our old home. The carers are good people. He'll do well there."

"Yeah, as far as social workers go, Charlotte's top class. Pretty too, ain't that right, Hud?" Bryce says with a cheeky wink.

Beast lifts his brows. "Oh it's like that, is it?"

"Charlotte's married and I'm not interested," Hudson answers. "But yes, I think she'll be able to help..." His voice trails off as he looks at me.

"What?" I ask, already knowing that I'm not going to like

what he's about to say next. We've known each other too long. I can read him like a book.

"Should you be getting this involved with the kid?" he asks.

"I couldn't turn him away."

Hudson locks me down with his piercing stare. "And that's admirable, but have you asked yourself *why*?"

"Because he came to me for help," I reply, a little agitated as to the direction his questioning is going.

"And you want to do that by letting him hang out at Tales?"

"What's the problem, afraid I'll take your thunder?" I bite back, feeling defensive. "You're not the only one on the planet who wants to do good things."

"I meant no disrespect. I'm just concerned for the kid. Tales has a reputation, and he's impressionable."

"What are you saying?" Beast complains, shifting forward in his seat and glaring at Hudson. "You think we're not good enough role models, or what?"

Hudson casts a glance at his brothers, who are shifting uncomfortably. I catch sight of Max running his finger across his throat as a warning, but they needn't worry about me. I love them all no matter how much they piss me off sometimes, and I respect their opinion, Hud's in particular. So as much as I hate the way this conversation is going, Hudson's got a valid point. I should be woman enough to realise that.

"It's okay," I sigh. "We're not exactly pillars of society, Beast."

"What's with this bullshit attitude?" Beast argues. "You're a *good* woman, and we're a great team. The guys at Tales will take care of him too."

Reaching for his thigh, I give it a gentle squeeze before

meeting his gaze. "You really think we're the best thing for Ford after what you did today?"

"Of course I fucking do, and I'd do it again in a mother-fucking heartbeat if it meant keeping that kid safe."

"What *did* you do today?" Hudson asks, then reading my expression holds his hand up. "Wait, forget it. I don't want to know."

"Yeah, it's better you don't. We wouldn't want to tarnish your squeaky-clean reputation," Beast snaps, clearly offended by Hudson's concerns.

"It isn't about my reputation. If it was I wouldn't have helped Grim out when she needed *you* the most," Hudson bites back.

When I think Beast is about to concede his point, he says, "Matter of fact, why the fuck are you still friends with Grim given you think she's such a bad fucking influence?"

"That's not what Hud is saying," Bryce pipes up, shifting forward in his seat.

I can tell he's preparing to step in if Beast and Hudson go toe-to-toe. That's what I like about their relationship; their bond is unbreakable, which is why I've always felt at ease in their company. Once the Freed brothers take you into their hearts, there's no escaping, and despite this tense-filled moment, I know they're affection for me extends to Beast if he'd only accept it.

"That's because I wasn't," Hudson says, holding Beast's angry stare. "I respect Grim. I care for her a great deal. I love her as a friend, and as a friend I'm going to be straight with her, *always*. Like I'll always be straight with you. This is the very definition of tough love."

"So be straight with us then," Beast demands, the tension in his shoulders releasing a little. I know he respects a man who's straight-up.

Hudson nods. "Firstly, and most importantly, I think I'll be able to get Ford transferred."

"Good, that's all I'm asking," I say, relief coursing through my veins.

"But I want you to be realistic about the kind of future you can give that kid," Hudson says, urging me to listen.

"Future? We're just helping him out right now," I say, refusing to meet Hudson's gaze because he knows there's more to it than that. "I'm not adopting him or anything."

"But you *are* becoming attached," he says, then sighs heavily. "Look, whether you like it or not, you're on the wrong side of the tracks. You're criminals. You hold illegal fights at Tales and have the local police chief in your pocket. From what you've told me, Ford has gone through enough turmoil in his short life. He needs stability, a safe place and probably a shit load of therapy."

"Boxing *is* therapeutic," Beast points out. "He'll learn how to take care of himself. It will build his self-esteem and confidence. Where's the fucking harm in that?"

"There's none because you're absolutely right, boxing does provide all of that, but can you honestly tell me that he won't eventually get sucked into your world? You're adults and you made a conscious choice to live the life you do."

"We wouldn't force him to do anything. What kind of people do you take us for?" Beast snaps.

"I know that, but I'm betting what Ford wants more than anything is a family, one that'll love him the way his parents should've and I can tell you, from experience, that he'll do anything to get that, including things he probably shouldn't. He deserves a stable home, safety, parents or carers who'll be around for the long haul without fear that they'll end up dead by the hands of their enemy or locked away for their crimes. Can you honestly say that you can provide him with that living the life you have?"

I grit my teeth, dropping my gaze to my lap, because every single person in this room knows that we can't, Beast included. What Hudson says cuts close to home, given I've thought the same things about Christy.

When I've finally got my shit together enough to meet Hudson's gaze, I say, "I appreciate your honesty. Once he's settled in his new home, we'll find him somewhere else he can train. I've a lot of contacts, and before you ask, plenty of them are above-board. In the meantime, we'll keep training him until we can get that in place."

"Grim, he'll be devastated," Beast says, swiping a hand through his hair, side-eying me.

"A little short-term pain is better than long-term heartbreak. Hudson's right, we can't guarantee him anything," I reply, getting to my feet. "Let me know when the move has been confirmed."

"Of course, I'll call you," Hudson agrees. "You're doing the right thing, Grim."

I nod. "Then why does it feel like I'm letting him down, that I'm losing someone special?"

It's a question I ask myself over and over again, and the answer to that question comes from the unlikeliest of places a little over a week later.

CHAPTER SEVENTEEN

Love Is A Bitch

BEAST

"Remind me again why we're here eating Chinese takeaway and not at Sapori's enjoying the fine dining experience with Romeo low-key flirting with you?" I ask, as we sit at the table nearest to the stage at Nine Lives, the strip club that Kate has revamped since I offed Carter.

"Because I wanted to be alone with you. *Just you...*" she replies, stabbing her fork into a king prawn and popping it into her mouth.

"We could've just gone back to your place," I say, leaning over and swiping at some sweet and sour sauce on the corner of her lips before licking it off my thumb.

"We're never really alone there either," she points out.

"You could just ask me to move in and then you won't need Cleveland and Harris acting as bodyguards because you'll have me there twenty-four seven, just as it should be."

"Bit presumptuous, don't you think? I might like my own space."

"You wound me," I joke, placing my hand over my heart.

"I don't mean to keep you waiting," she adds quickly. "I *am* serious about us. You know that, right?"

"Of course I do, and you gotta know that I'd move in with you in a heartbeat. It's not as though we've spent that many nights apart since I returned anyway. But, if you need a bit of time to make that step, then you've got it. Whatever you need."

"I appreciate that," she replies.

"Good. So getting back to the point at hand, why are we here exactly? Because in a couple hours this place is going to be heaving with punters."

"I'm well aware of the business hours, Beast." She smiles then, taking a swig on her bottle of beer.

"Shouldn't Matty and Nancy be here already?" I ask, peering over my shoulder towards the door that leads to the girl's changing room and Matty's office.

"Nope. I asked them to give us an hour alone. It's just us. No bodyguards. No punters. No kids or arsehole criminals to worry about. No trouble. Just us."

"Okay, you've got my attention. Come on Kate, spill. Why are we here?"

Kate chews on the inside of her cheek the way she's prone to doing when she's nervous. It's something that I've never seen her do in public since I've been back, and I know she hates that she does it, but I find it endearing. It reminds me that she's a woman with as many insecurities as the rest of the population and not just this badass queen who isn't afraid of anything. It makes me love and appreciate all aspects of her.

"Okay, so last week we reenacted that moment between us in my bedroom two years ago..."

"We did," I agree. "Though, I gotta say, we did embellish it a little."

She grins. "Thank fuck."

"Yeah, thank fuck. Junior was certainly pleased."

"Wait!" she says, wrinkling her nose, laughter in her eyes. "Please tell me you didn't just call your dick, Junior?"

"What would you rather I call it? *Moby Dick?*"

"Moby Dick?!" she splutters, choking on the mouthful of beer she's just swallowed.

"Yeah, why not? We both know that my cock is the biggest monster you've ever seen."

"The *only* one I've ever seen. It's not as if I've got anything to compare it to. For all I know you've got a weiner."

"A weiner?! The fuck I have, more like a Thor's hammer because this bad boy likes to grab and smash."

"Oh. My. God!" Kate says, flinging back her head and barking out a laugh, which sets me off too. "That's Hulk, you idiot."

"Who-the-fuck-ever," I reply, laughing with her.

I fucking love this woman.

"Wait, wait!" she says, holding up her hand and waving it in the air between us. "I have the *perfect* name for your cock."

The mischief in her eyes makes my dick leap. "Go on then, let me hear it."

"How about Rumple-*fore*-skin..." she says, laughing so hard tears roll down her cheeks.

"I don't know whether to be impressed by the fairy tale reference or fucking offended. Wasn't Rumplestiltskin a bearded dwarf?"

This only makes her laugh harder. "A bearded dwarf... I just can't," she chokes out.

"Kate, are you saying my cock's a dwarf?"

"If the shoe fits," she snorts, covering her mouth and nose with her hand and trying to stifle even more giggles.

I narrow my eyes on her. "You know, there ain't nothing wrong with a bit of rumple in your foreskin."

"Exactly," she snorts, swiping at her eyes. "That's what I meant. It's *perfect!*"

"You're perfect," I reply and for the next couple minutes we banter back and forth, laughter the best fucking medicine, because fuck knows she's had little to laugh about in her life so far. I've only been back a few weeks and I see how stressed she is daily. It ain't easy being the infamous Queen of Tales. She needs this. We both do.

Eventually, when our laughter subsides and we've come up with at least a dozen more cock nicknames between us, I say, "So, you were telling me the real reason why we're here tonight before talk of Rumple-*fore*-skin got in the way."

The smile slips from her eyes and is replaced with desire. I know that look. That look is me getting lucky.

"I want to dance for you again, that's why we're here."

"Dance for me...?" I point at my chest then flick my gaze to the pole on the stage, a wide grin spreading across my face like the fucking sun rising across the horizon.

"Yep." She shrugs, like she hasn't just made my whole fucking night, let alone year.

"Well, this I can get behind." I grin, swiping at my mouth with a napkin before leaning back in my chair, my fucking cock filling with blood in excitement.

"I thought you might," she licks her lips, giving me a naughty smile before pushing back her chair and standing. Pulling her phone from her pocket, she selects a track and sends it via bluetooth to the speaker system. A familiar tune starts to play.

"*Love Is A Bitch?*" I ask, biting on my knuckles as she saunters to the stage, her hips swaying from side to side. I might just come from the thought of her pussy sliding down that pole alone.

"Isn't it though?" she replies, and my heart ratchets up a notch as I watch her remove her clothes in a sexy striptease, doing so in time to the music until all she's wearing is her lace panties, bra and a seductive smile on her face.

"Jesus fuck, how did I get so damn lucky?" I mutter, completely and utterly mesmerised as she grasps the pole with both hands and struts around it in a wide circle on her tiptoes, her hips swaying with every step.

Fuck, her sass and sexiness is off the motherfucking charts, and whilst her body is pretty fucking perfect for me, I've never been a man who goes for looks alone. It's all about the confidence for me. I've always liked *women*, no matter their shape or size. Thick, thin, big tits, small tits, tall, short, tiger stripes or unblemished skin. It never mattered to me, what matters is how they feel about themselves, and right now Kate is feeling fucking phenomenal going by the way she dances around that pole like it's an extension of my cock.

My eyes trace over every inch of her skin as she sways her body, using the pole as her anchor whilst she undulates her hips, then opens her thighs and drops her arse to her heels, just like she did that first time I watched her dance. This time, she runs her fingers up her thigh and over her pussy, adding the tiniest bit of pressure before dragging her hand up her body and reaching above her head. Gripping the pole with both hands, she winks at me then pushes off her feet and flips her legs out in the splits before turning them in on herself like a fucking corkscrew.

My jaw nearly hits the floor, and as Kate shifts from one step to the next with ease, I grow impatient to touch her. Truth be known, it's taking all my willpower not to storm the stage and fuck her against the hardwood floor. The last time Kate danced for me, I was not in a position to do anything other than pretend she wasn't affecting me the exact same way she's affecting me now. All I could do was wrap my fingers around the back of my chair and hold on tight. At the very least, this time I can temper the urge to interrupt her show by unzipping my jeans and fisting my cock.

"Fuck!" I exclaim, as Kate throws some moves that defy gravity and that familiar tingle in the base of my spine makes itself known.

I've never come before just by looking at someone, but I can tell you I'm pretty fucking close to that now. The weight and heat of my cock, which is currently more Moby Dick than Rumple-*fore*-skin, can attest to that. Still I watch, stroking my dick as she kicks upwards, her feet near the ceiling. With one hand gripping the pole near the floor and the other grasping it between her legs she widens her legs into the splits, licking her lips in her upside-down position like a sexy fucking spider monkey. I damn near come then and there as my gaze hones in on her pussy and the thin strip of lace pulled taut between her legs.

As the music picks up speed, so does her movements and the rhythm of my fist around my cock. Righting herself, her feet touching the floor gently, she kicks out her right leg, wrapping it around the pole and slides around it in one smooth movement, her hair flying out behind her.

The way she moves is breathtaking. I wouldn't be able to look away even if her dad rose from the fucking dead and walked into the club right now.

As the music fades out, Kate stares at me, her chest heaving and a sheen of sweat covering her skin. She bites on her lip, her gaze dropping to my crotch then says, "What did you think?"

"What do I think? Princess, I've never been more jealous of a pole in my life, and right now Rumple-*fore*-skin wants you to come sit on his lap."

"I bet he does," she replies with a slow smile as she steps off the stage and walks towards me, her hips swaying from side to side like a goddamn pendulum.

When she reaches me her gaze drops to my crotch, "Is he feeling shy?"

"Fuck no!" I reply, kicking off my boots and shoving my jeans and boxers down over my hips, my cock springing free. Precum glistens on the tip and my fucking balls ache as Kate crouches before me, her fingertips curling around the waistband of my jeans and boxers.

"Good, because my pussy is more than ready to be smashed," she replies with a chuckle, yanking off my clothes, including my socks. "Who fucks with socks on anyway?"

"Not me, evidently."

Stepping between my legs, Kate leans over and kisses me. She's not slow or tentative, she *takes*, her tongue sliding between my lips as she claims me. Her kiss is possessive, filled with passion, heat and desire, and if kisses had the ability to end a man's life, right now I'd be knocking at Heaven's gates asking for absolution.

Reaching up I grasp her face in my palms, angling my head, my fingers curling into her hair. I need to kiss her more than I need to breathe. She consumes me.

Before I'm able to pull her onto my lap and take what belongs to me, Kate breaks our kiss and twists on her feet, facing the stage. Then, looking over her shoulder, she gives me a sexy smile and slowly removes her knickers, kicking them across the floor before saying, "I've always wanted to do this."

"Do wha—?" My question is cut short as she bends over before me, her slit glistening with arousal. Her ripe arse, peachy.

I gasp.

Yep, I fucking *gasp* at the sight.

"That is the sexiest thing I've seen in my fucking life," I grunt, squeezing my cock to temper the sudden rush of sensation. "Spread your legs a little, Princess. Let me get a good look at you."

Kate widens her stance, giving me a perfect view of both of her tight holes. "Like that?"

"Just like that," I groan, releasing my cock. It slaps against my abdomen, thick and heavy as I shift forward in my seat.

"Keep your hands flat on the ground, and try to hold steady because I'm about to give you the best orgasm of your life."

"Yes," she hisses as I reach between her legs, and with two fingers swipe upwards through her parted folds, spreading her juices all over her puckered hole, rimming it. Then I lower my mouth to her pussy and eat her the fuck out like the beast I am.

I'm not considerate in my approach like I was before. This is a man losing his motherfucking control. This is a man fucking starving and feasting on the woman he loves more than life itself.

I lick and lap, suck and bite, my tongue and lips gorging on her arousal, fucking high on it. I use two fingers to drive into her pussy, finger fucking her as she moans and whimpers, begging me to fuck her with my cock.

"Not yet, Princess. I'm gonna make you come before I fuck you," I reply, using her juices to lube her puckered arse. She gasps when I gently slide in a finger, but she doesn't pull away, and I don't stop fingering her, licking her, fucking her with my tongue.

Less than five minutes later, Kate's legs are trembling as she hurtles towards an orgasm, her knees buckling as she hits the floor. I follow her down on my hands and knees, refusing to let up, turned the fuck on as I bury my face in her pussy. My lips and chin are covered in her arousal but I don't ease off, I just grasp her hips tighter and lap at her like a fucking cat would a bowl of cream. When she screams out my name, her pussy pulsating around my tongue, I slide my arm around her waist and haul her onto my cock reverse cowgirl style, impaling her on my dick right here on the floor.

"Beast!" she screams, shivering and shaking and coming

long and hard as her core muscles squeeze my dick, fucking choking it.

I grit my teeth, willing myself not to come as I press my forehead between her shoulder blades and slam my eyelids shut, because damn I'm dancing on the precipice. I'm so fucking close.

Kate senses it too, her body so intune with mine. The minute her orgasm fades, I expect her to relax into me, but she doesn't. Instead she begins to ride my dick like a woman on a mission, fucking me hard and fast. She takes control, her arse slapping against my thighs as she takes me deep, the tip of my cock hitting her cervix with every downward stroke.

"Goddamn it!" I yell, my hands grasping her perfect tits as her equally perfect pussy fists my cock, and her thighs straddle mine.

I can't help but look down at the crack of her arse, a visual line to where our bodies join together. She's so fucking wet that her arousal slides down my cock and collects in the trimmed hair surrounding the base.

Seeing how wet I make her, how thick and hard she makes me, sets off an orgasm that rips through my body like a fucking hurricane, blinding me in a vortex of sensation and orgasmic bliss. Tipping my head back I roar, coming harder than I ever have in my life as she shatters around me, her own orgasm claiming her shortly after.

I should be fucking embarrassed for not lasting, but I'm not. I'm not because all I can think about is the way her tits feel in my hands, how perfectly my cock fits inside of her, and how fucking *happy* she makes me.

CHAPTER EIGHTEEN

Brave

GRIM

"He's a quick learner," Beast remarks as Ford takes off after our training session with a spring in his step and a belly full of food.

It's been almost two weeks since he barged his way into my club, and a week since Beast killed his stepdad. There's already a little more life and a little less jadedness behind his eyes, but that might have more to do with his new setup after his move into a better children's home a few days ago, and the support from Hudson's charity. Though these training sessions have been a great bonding experience, all of us have benefited from them. It's been a long time since I've felt part of a family, but everyday that's changing, and I'm becoming fiercely protective of it and the people I care about, including Ford. Which is making it all the more difficult to break the news that he's got to continue his training at another, more legit club. Frankly, I don't want him out of my sight, not when the King is still a huge threat and Malakai is no closer to locating him.

"He's got a mean left hook too," I say, wiping my face with a hand towel, and forcing myself not to think about the King.

"Yeah, he does. The power behind it is surprising given he's such a scrawny kid. He's gonna be lethal in a few years," Beast agrees, rubbing at his chin where Ford managed to sneak in a punch. "Might even best me."

"I told you," I say, watching Ford give Mark the finger as he exits the warehouse.

We both laugh.

"Why's that kid still such a little dick to me?" Mark grumbles as he strolls towards us both.

"You can't expect *everyone* to like you," Beast quips, ducking through the ropes and dropping to the floor.

"Why the fuck not? I'm a very likeable guy," he counters.

"Said no one ever," Dom adds, pausing from his bench press set and giving Mark a cheeky wink.

"I'll have you know I'm well loved, *prick*."

Beast chuckles, holding open the ropes so I can duck through them. "I'm not sure that's a flex. We ain't the Brady bunch, you know."

"A person can be likeable *and* a merciless killer," Mark complains, drawing a snort of laughter from Cleveland who has just entered the gym.

"Morning, Cleveland," I say, smiling as Beast gives me a light slap on the arse.

"A word Ma'am?" he asks, his tone and expression changing from amused to serious.

"Sure thing... *Beast*," I say, indicating for him to follow us as we head towards my office, the sound of Dom and Mark bickering following us out.

As soon as the door to my office is closed, Cleveland clears his throat. "We've located Rodriquez," he says, bringing out his phone and flipping through his messages until he finds what he's looking for.

"Where?" Beast asks.

"His credit card was used to book a stay at an Airbnb in a small village just outside of Cardiff this morning. We just got notification."

My fucking heart stills. "Cardiff, as in *Wales*?"

"Yes, Ma'am."

"Fuck!" I exclaim, grabbing my phone, car keys and bag from my desk.

"Grim, what is it?" Beast asks.

Ignoring his question, I focus on Cleveland. "I want hourly updates. If the prick takes a shit, I want to know about it."

Cleveland frowns, glancing at Beast in confusion. "We haven't got a man on him just yet, but Harris is on the way as we speak. Should be there in a few hours."

"Then we'd better get going too," I say, striding towards the door.

"They're on it, Grim," Beast says, clearly confused by my reaction to the news.

My gaze is sharp as I say, "We're going to Wales right the fuck now."

"We are?"

"Do you have a fucking problem with that?"

"Not in principle, no," he says as calm as I'm anxious, "But as Cleveland just said, Harris is on his way to pick up the prick. You don't need to travel all that way too. This is why you have *us*."

"Believe me, I do," I reply, striding towards the door and yanking it open.

"Grim, the guy's a trained assassin. He can handle that dick-head. Perks of being the boss means you don't have to get your hands dirty, not unless you want to, of course," he adds.

"Cleveland, Dom's in charge whilst we're gone," I bark out, unable to hide my agitation. Not at Beast, but from my need to get to my little sister as quickly as possible.

"Yes, Ma'am." Cleveland gives me a confused look, one that matches Beast's.

"Are you coming or not?" I demand, looking over my shoulder and glowering at Beast, my fuse shorter than it's been in some time. None of this is his fault and I realise I'm acting like a crazy bitch, but I don't have the bandwidth to explain myself right now and especially not in front of Cleveland. No matter how much I trust him, the less people who know about Christy, the better. "Beast?" I prompt when he doesn't answer right away.

"Of course I'm coming," he says, turning his attention back to Cleveland. "Call with updates. I want to know the second Harris has gotten hold of the cunt."

"Yes, Sir."

"Beast," he counters. "No need for formalities with me."

"Yes, *Beast*," Cleveland replies, and then we're gone.

"WANT to tell me what's going on?" Beast asks, as he breaks every traffic rule you could possibly break. Lucky for us both we haven't come across any police on the motorway, because the way I'm feeling I'd shoot any fucker who tries to stop me from getting to my sister.

"I'll explain when we get there," I bite out distractedly, gripping my phone as I send another round of texts. I've been firing off messages and calling Sandy and Frank's mobiles without success. I've also messaged Malakai, because if Rodriguez has made a move, then I'm pretty fucking positive the King will be behind it.

"Get where exactly? We're nowhere near Cardiff, Princess."

"Just follow the Sat Nav, okay? And fucking step on it."

"Kate? You've got to give me something to go on here," he replies, pressing down on the gas and weaving through the traffic. "I've been pushing one hundred for the last couple hours now. I know this isn't just about Rodriguez."

"I need to make sure she's okay," I reply, panicking now.

"Make sure *who's* okay?" he presses as we finally pass the sign for Betws-y-Coed.

"My sister."

"Wait, *what*? Your sister?" Beast suddenly swerves around an Audi TT, barely missing the bumper. My life would've flashed before my eyes had I not been so wrapped up in my own fear.

"Yes, her name's Christy. She's twelve," I reply tightly.

"Since when?" he asks, shocked.

"Since Carter's will was read and she was in it."

"Fuck," he exclaims.

"Yeah."

"Who's been taking care of her all this time?"

"You'll meet them soon enough."

"So she *is* okay then?"

"I don't know!" I shout, frustration and anxiety making me sharp. "No one's answering my fucking messages!"

"We're almost there, Kate," he says, trying to reassure me as he glances at the Sat Nav. He doesn't question why I haven't told him about her before now, he just tells me what I need to know at the moment, and I'm so grateful for that. "It says we're ten minutes out from our destination."

"If that cunt has hurt her..." My voice trails off as I contemplate that thought.

"Then we'll have our revenge," he states grimly.

"You're supposed to say she's going to be okay," I bite out.

"You know I can't promise you that."

"Yeah, I know," I retort tightly, the pain in my chest just from the prospect of losing her, excruciating.

For the remainder of the journey I sit and stew in my fear, silently going over all the ways I'll torture the bastard if he's hurt my little sister. It will be slow, agonising and I will make sure that he feels every single second of pain. Beast is smart enough not to question me further, and even though I realise there's so much more I need to fill him in on, I can't do that until I know she's safe.

Please, please be safe.

"We're here," I say a few minutes later as he pulls up outside of Sandy and Frank's cottage.

I'm out of the car and running up the garden path before

he's even unclipped his seatbelt. By the time he's joined me, I'm banging on the front door, hollering for Christy.

"They're not here, Kate," he says, grabbing my shoulders and gently pulling me away from the door.

"Then where the fuck are they?!" I shout, shrugging him off and peering through the front window.

"I don't know, but there doesn't seem to be any sign of a struggle," he says, taking in the neatly kept garden and pretty stone cottage. "Try to calm down. We'll find them."

"How?! I told them that no matter what they have to answer my calls and respond to my messages. She was supposed to be safe here!" I yell.

"*Kate?!*"

We both spin on our feet, and before I can fully comprehend Christy's outlandish outfit, she's running towards me and throwing herself into my arms, a ball of rainbow coloured tulle and sparkle. "Oh, thank fuck!" I exclaim, hugging her tightly and smothering her in kisses whilst she laughs in glee. Behind her Frank and Sandy look on in bewilderment.

"Kate? To what do we owe the pleasure?" Frank asks, eyeing Beast with a mixture of caution and surprise whilst Sandy stares at him with a hint of colour on her cheeks.

"Alright?" Beast says, winking at Sandy, the flirty bastard.

"Hello..." Sandy says, hesitating, her cheeks pinking up even more as she waits for one of us to fill in the gap.

"The name's Beas— *Roger*," he says quickly, giving me a wide-eyed stare.

Roger? If I wasn't so overwhelmed with relief I'd burst out laughing. Instead, I unravel myself from around Christy and take her hand in mine, grinning at her. "You look so pretty!"

"Well, it's nice to meet you, Roger," Sandy says, making conversation with Beast whilst I haul Christy back against my chest in another hug. "I'm Sandy and this is my husband Frank."

"What a lovely name for a lovely woman," Beast replies with a wink that has Sandy pressing her fingertips against her cheeks.

Seriously, is no one immune to his charms?

"And who do we have here?" he asks, turning his attention to Christy who's peering at him from around my body. There's a softness in his eyes that has my heart pitter-pattering.

"Christy," she says, giving him a little wave.

"Hey, sweet cheeks. You're a little beauty aren't you. Take after your sister, huh?"

"I can see why you're so in love with him," Christy says with a giggle.

"Yeah, he'll do," I joke.

"Well, maybe we should head on inside," Frank says, interrupting our sweet moment with a wide-eyed look and a jerk of his chin towards his neighbours house.

"Yes! Come on, come inside. I've got *cake!*" Christy exclaims, bouncing on her toes, her energy infectious.

"Cake? That sounds really good," I say, finally releasing the breath I've been holding ever since Cleveland told us the news about Rodriguez.

"Yep, Sandy bought it for me to celebrate my first dance show!"

"You were in a dance show? That's awesome!" I exclaim, my cheeks hurting from smiling so much. That might explain why I've had no answers from either Frank or Sandy. A heads up might've been nice, could've saved me a lot of fucking stress and Beast a four and a half hour drive.

"Yep! I was the rainbow!" Christy points out happily.

"I can see that," I say, my heart warming as I cast a glance at Sandy, who is watching our interaction with a mixture of confusion and concern. I don't blame her; my reaction to seeing Christy is enough to warn her that something is wrong. Then again, she needs to understand why it's so important they answer my damn calls. Perhaps this will be a lesson to all of us.

"I called you both several times. I left messages."

"You did?" Sandy exclaims, reaching into her handbag and pulling out her phone, pressing the button to turn it on. "Oh I'm so sorry! I turned it off and told Frank to do the same. I didn't want to interrupt the dance recital."

"I *really* needed to get hold of you," I say, my tone taking on an edge that I never thought I'd use in their presence.

"Kate," Beast warns, looking from me to Christy, who's frowning.

"I can see that," Sandy says as she switches on her phone and it begins to ping with all the missed calls and messages I sent.

I'm angry, but I know I need to keep a lid on it for Christy's sake. She doesn't need to see that side of me, the side where I take action with violence. Besides, no matter how high my stress levels have gotten, Frank and Sandy don't deserve that. It was an honest mistake, but one they won't be making again. They have to follow my rules if we're going to keep Christy out of harm's way.

"I thought that something had happened to Christy—" I begin but once again Frank shakes his head.

"Let's take this inside, shall we?" he says, looking pointedly at the twitching curtain of his neighbour's house. Lowering his voice he gives me a tight smile and talks through his teeth like a ventriloquist. "Mrs Parsons is a dear old lady but she just loves to gossip, and this village hasn't seen as much action since Jackie of number thirty-five had an affair with the vicar."

Beast chuckles. "Sounds like a good story."

"Oh, believe me, it is, but I'm guessing it's not as juicy as the one you've travelled all the way here to tell us about?" he asks, knowingly.

"You're right, we should go inside," I say as Christy skips happily up the garden path, pulling me along behind her.

CHAPTER NINETEEN

Don't you Worry Child

BEAST

"So *you're* the man that got my sister all in a tizzy," Christy says, eying me from across the kitchen table. "I can see why, you're just like a tattooed version of that actor Kate loves so much. I mean, apart from the small fact you have hair and he doesn't."

"Is that right? And who's this actor then?" I ask, knowing full well who it is.

"I dunno, some balding dude. Seriously, the way she goes on about him, you'd think it was him she was madly in love with and not you."

"Christy! I don't do anything of the sort" Kate exclaims, her cheeks heating as she cringes just a little.

"Alright, I'm exaggerating. She only mentions him *once* a week," Christy reveals, smirking.

"Liar," Kate mutters.

I roll my eyes. "Just once a week, eh?"

"That's right. You'll be happy to know that you get the most air time."

"I should fucking hope so!"

"Language!" Kate admonishes, holding in a laugh as Christy giggles behind her hand.

"I told you before, *fuck* is just another word in the English language. So don't mind me. Swear away."

"Right? Why does everyone get so hung up about it?" I reply, liking this kid already.

Kate smiles indulgently at the sparkling little rainbow even if she did just call her out. "We've talked about this before though. No swearing."

"Pshh!" Christy replies waving her hand at Kate. "You do it *all* the time!"

"That doesn't mean you should."

"I happen to agree with Kate," Sandy pitches in, handing us both a cup of coffee and Christy a glass of lemonade. "Just because someone does something, it doesn't mean it's okay for you to do that too, remember?"

"Yes, but that time was different. Darren was being a bully to Lucinda and I couldn't not punch him for making her cry. He hits her *all* the time," Christy points out with a look of disdain.

"Wait, you punched a kid for being a bully?" Kate asks, pride lighting her eyes.

"I did. He totally deserved it!"

I bark out a laugh, loving the kid's sassy and snarky personality. She might not look very much like Kate with her red hair and different coloured eyes, but she's similar in personality. They've certainly got the same moral compass, that's for sure.

"See, you agree with me, don't you, Roger?" Christy asks, staring at me pointedly.

"Maybe you should be listening to Sandy, eh? I think she's probably better at all this parenting shi—*stuff* than me."

"Good answer," Kate mutters under her breath.

"Well, *I* happen to think you did the right thing. That laddie has been asking for trouble for some time now. He shouldn't dish it out if he can't take it back," Frank says, snatching up a slice of cake and taking a bite.

"Frank!" Sandy admonishes.

"What, love?" he says around a mouthful of food. "You know I'm right."

"Well, what you or I think doesn't really matter. We have to teach Christy that there are better ways to deal with conflict than violence or we'd all be going around punching the first person to piss us off!"

"Sandy you said *piss!*" Christy says, the shock on her face telling me that Sandy really doesn't swear all that often, if at all. I don't think I've ever met two people who are genuinely as nice or as straight up as this couple. I'm not surprised Kate felt comfortable enough to leave her sister in their care. They're good people, anyone can see that, even a jaded fucker like me.

"Even the most conscientious person can slip up from time to time," Kate says, smiling warmly at Sandy who's acting like she's just killed a kitten and not uttered a swear word. Poor woman looks devastated.

"To be fair, as swear words go," I say, giving the old lady's hand a squeeze, "Piss is about as offensive as one of those YouTube videos of a dog on a skateboard."

"Well, when you put it like that..." Sandy says, chewing on a smile as her chest and neck flush pink. Either the old dear has got a hormonal problem or she's got the hots for me. What am I saying? *Of course* she's got the hots for me.

"See, the word piss is perfectly okay to use, isn't that right, *stud-muffin?*" Christy asks, immediately bursting into a fit of giggles at the look of shock on both mine and Kate's face.

I mean I'm all for them bonding after not knowing about each other for twelve years, but Kate telling her kid sister the pet names we have for each is going a bit far, surely?

"Jesus, Christy," Kate mumbles, her cheeks heating.

Even Frank and Sandy look like they've got secondhand embarrassment as they sip their tea and grimace behind their mugs. Although, to be fair, Frank looks more amused than embarrassed.

"What? It just slipped out." Christy chuckles.

"Well, I can confirm that I am indeed a *stud-muffin*. Did you know that we're actually a dying breed? There ain't many of us left. So consider this a rarity."

"Roger!" Kate exclaims, but I just wink at her and continue.

"I mean there are very few men in the world who can turn leftover horse meat into a light and fluffy muffin. It's a refined skill. Takes several years to master, I'll have you know," I say, making a joke out of the whole situation.

"That is *not* what stud-muffin means! I'm not an idiot."

"Maybe not kid," I say with a wink, "But I still stand by what I said. There really aren't many stud-muffins about. Frank should know, given he's clearly part of the elite group too. Ain't that right, Sandy?"

Christy snorts with laughter, setting off Frank and Sandy, and finally Kate. I follow shortly after, their mirth catching. Laughing like this is fucking cathartic and definitely needed. It's been way too stressful today.

"You're actually really funny," Christy eventually admits, her laughter giving way to seriousness as she stares at me with those peculiar eyes. "But you know, you can't lie to me. I'm good at seeing the truth."

"Is that so?" I say, loving her sass.

"Yep. I mean Kate didn't actually tell me anything about you being her stud-muffin," she says, stuffing a piece of choco-late cake into her mouth.

"Oh, Christ," Kate mutters.

"What, are you a mind reader or something?" I joke, my smile dropping when Kate pulls a face and Christy shrugs.

"Not a mind reader exactly," Christy retorts, taking a sip of her lemonade, eying me carefully.

Kate rests her hands on Christy's arm. "Not now, okay? We've got other things to talk about."

"What? Like why you turned up here today out of the blue?"

"Yeah, exactly." Kate nods.

"Hold on a second," I say, holding my hands up. "Can we just backtrack a little bit—"

"I tell you what, why don't you get out of your costume and into something a bit more comfy," Sandy intervenes. "You've been wearing it most of the day, love. All that scratchy material must be irritating your skin."

Christy frowns. "It's totally cool, you *can* tell him about me. I'm not embarrassed."

"Tell me about what?" I ask, fucking lost.

"And we're not embarrassed either," Frank says, lovingly. "But we'd really appreciate a moment to talk about why Kate and Roger are here today."

"Sure. Go ahead," she shrugs, still not moving.

"Christy, do you already know why we're here?" Kate asks, her question making my brain ache.

She looks at Kate and shakes her head. "No, I don't."

Relief passes over Kate's features. "Then I guess, this time, you weren't meant to know?"

Christy ponders Kate's logic—which, by the way, makes no sense to me—and then nods her head. "I suppose you're right. I'll go change, this dress *is* a bit itchy."

Frank gives Christy's nose a tweak. "Thanks, love."

"It's no bother. I know some people get weirded out about it all." She eyes me then, taking her measure of me in a way she hasn't done since we arrived. "But Roger's a good guy and I already know he'll be cool about it all. "

"Cool about what?" I ask, thoroughly fucking confused now.

"You're about to find out, *stud-muffin*," Christy says, snorting with laughter as she heads out of the kitchen and upstairs to change.

"Did I miss something?" I ask, looking between the three of them. Frank blows out a breath and Sandy gives me a guarded smile, but it's Kate's expression that concerns me the most. "What?"

"Let's take this moment to explain to Frank and Sandy why we turned up today," Kate says. "Then we'll get onto Christy."

"Sure thing," I say, patient enough to wait for the big reveal, or whatever this is, as Kate turns her attention to the couple.

"We came today because I had reason to believe someone was coming for Christy in retaliation to an incident that happened at my club a few weeks back."

Sandy gasps, and Frank looks at us both in shock. "Someone would hurt her to get at you?" he asks, his gaze darkening as he reaches for Sandy's hand and squeezes. Frank might be a nice man, but I recognise that look in his eyes. Like Kate, he'd do anything to protect his family.

"That's what I'd thought when I couldn't get a hold of you. So you understand that I didn't have any other choice but to come here."

"You must've been so worried," Sandy says, reaching for Kate's hand and giving it a pat.

"I was fucking terrified," she admits with a heavy sigh.

"We're sorry," Frank says earnestly. "We haven't had to deal with anything like this before. Christy was kept away from your world for so long because your father made sure no one knew about her."

"And that will remain the same. No one, apart from the four of us, will know we're related. Anyone who finds out will be dealt with accordingly," Kate says, reassuring them as much as herself.

"Dealt with? You mean...?" Sandy questions, her eyes widening as understanding dawns.

"I won't apologise for dealing with a threat to my family,"

Kate says. "I will do what I have to do in order to keep Christy safe. No question. You understand?"

Sandy's mouth pops open, then shuts again as she takes in what Kate has said.

Frank nods. "Yes, we understand."

"Good. I left Christy in your care because I truly believe she's safest here with you. I don't want her growing up in our world, but I'm not foolish enough to ignore the fact that anyone at any point could find out about her and use her to get to me," Kate explains, side-eyeing me.

"Which means," I continue on for Kate, "That you *must* follow Kate's rules. We need to be able to communicate with you at any point night or day, and vice versa."

"Of course, it won't happen again," Frank says, attempting to appease us.

"If you see anyone suspicious or out of the ordinary around the village or near your home you call us immediately," Kate says. "Don't second-guess yourself. Just call and we'll do the rest."

"Yes, absolutely," Sandy says, finally getting with the programme after her initial shock wore off.

"For now, we will station someone nearby who'll be able to get to you quickly should we feel she's in any danger, whilst we deal with the current issue," I say, glancing at Kate who nods her head in agreement.

"Good idea. We'll send you a photo of her, so you know who to look for if the worst was to happen," Kate adds.

"Her?" Frank grins. "Well then, that makes it all the more exciting."

"Yes, her. She'll keep to herself unless needed, no interaction otherwise," I point out.

"Oh darn it, this old boy could do with a little entertainment. What is this wonderful woman's name?"

"Loretta."

Frank grins. "Oh, nice name. Where's she from?"

"This old boy will get a pan on the back of his head if he carries on like he is," Sandy grumbles, making Kate smile and me snort with laughter. "Will she live in the village too?"

"No, I think that will draw too much attention. We'll make sure she's close by and that she won't ever approach you unless we've given her permission to do so. Think of her as a bodyguard you'll only ever get to meet if shit hits the fan. Which I hope is never," I add.

"So we carry on as normal?" Sandy inquires.

"Yes," Kate nods. "Do what you normally do, and we'll check in regularly. If you have any suspicions about anyone, trust your gut and call us. The rest we'll deal with."

"Will this be forever?" Frank asks, swiping a hand through his hair.

"For as long as I think it's necessary..." Kate responds vaguely, her voice trailing off as Christy enters the kitchen in a pair of pink heart print pyjamas and a wide grin.

"Have you told him yet? I'm getting bored waiting, and I thought maybe we could play a game of Twenty-one?"

"Nope," I say, pulling out the dining chair beside me and patting the seat. "Would you mind filling me in whilst Sandy grabs the deck of cards?"

"All right then. Are you ready to have your mind blown?" she asks, plonking down next to me.

"As I'll ever be. Hit me with it."

And so she does.

By the time Christy's finished regaling me of her *gift*—which is fucking debatable if you ask me—I'm shocked into silence. A left hook to the temple couldn't have stunned me more.

"It's okay to be scared," she says after a minute or so of me not responding. "Most people are scared of the things they don't understand."

"I'm not scared," I reply, snapping out of my trance. "I'm just... surprised, I guess."

And a little bit fucking terrified, but I won't ever admit to that. This is way too weird for my liking.

"It's hard to believe, I know," Kate says, chewing on the inside of her cheek as she reaches for Christy's hand and squeezes. "But Christy knew things about me, about *us* she couldn't possibly have known."

"Like the whole *stud-muffin* thing?" I say, trying to make light of what is a seriously fucking strange turn of events. I feel like I've stepped into an episode of Doctor Who and any minute now a dalek is going to come rolling into the room saying 'exterminate, exterminate,' or some such shit.

Christy giggles. "Yeah, like the *stud-muffin* thing."

I eye Kate who's cheeks start to flush and say, "You haven't seen us... you know..."

"Eww, no!"

"Oh, thank fuck!" I exclaim, letting go of the tension in my muscles.

"My thoughts precisely," Kate says, rubbing at her temples as she glances over at me.

"You know, this is the craziest thing I've ever heard."

"You think I'm crazy?" Christy asks, looking hurt.

"No, sweet cheeks, I don't think *you're* crazy. It's just that this stuff is out of the ordinary. I'm the kind of man who relies on what he can see with his own eyes and touch with own hands."

"And what about how you feel? What about that?" Christy asks, cocking her head to the side as she studies. "You feel love right?"

"Yes, of course."

"But you can't see love and you can't touch it."

"I touch Kate all the time," I joke.

"That's not the same," she points out. "Love is unexplainable. There's no formula or recipe. It just happens to us, and we accept it without question because we *feel* it."

"So you're saying that your gift is like love?" I ask, trying to understand.

"In a way, yeah. It's just as unexplainable but that doesn't make it any less true. I can't tell you why I am the way I am, all I can tell you is that it's real."

"You're a smart kid."

Christy grins, shrugging her shoulders.

"She's certainly very special," Kate says, leaning over and pressing a kiss against Christy's forehead.

"She is, but to be fair I thought Christy was special before I found out about her witchy gifts," I say, winking at the kid.

"She's not a witch!" Sandy snaps, and it's the first time her kindness makes way to a fierce protectiveness. I'm so taken aback that for a moment I can't form the words to speak.

"Shit! No, I didn't mean it as an offensive remark," I eventually say. "I think it's fucking cool. Sorry if it came out that way."

It's not a complete lie, I didn't mean to offend anyone and I do think it's cool even though I *am* still spooked by the whole thing. Imagine being able to see into the future. That shits gotta mess with your head, right? Then I look at Christy and she just seems like any normal twelve year old girl. Except she isn't normal. She's far from it.

"Apology accepted," Christy says.

"So are you able to tell me anything about my future?" I ask, curious now.

She shakes her head, her smile dropping. "No. I can't do that. It's dangerous."

"What do you mean?" I frown, and she sighs.

"I can't tell anyone anything specific."

"Why not?"

"Because..." she drops her head, her fingers twiddling with the hem of her pyjama top.

"Because she's afraid that bad things will happen if she does," Frank fills in, squeezing her shoulder gently. "So we never ask, and we accept what she feels comfortable telling us."

"I get it," I say, leaning back in my chair as Sandy hands Christy the cards and she takes them out of the pack, shuffling them. "Can't be easy to carry around all that knowledge though."

Christy's hand still as she looks up at me. "It depends."

"On what?"

"On what I see. It can be good too." She grins, then looking between Kate and me, says, "If I hadn't persuaded Kate to listen to what you had to say that day you turned up at the club, you probably wouldn't be sitting here now."

I sneak a look at Kate's who shrugs. "Probably would've got Mark to shoot you in all honesty."

Sandy gasps and Frank's eyes widen but Christy sniggers. "She's just joking, aren't you, Kate?"

"Yeah, once is enough," Kate retorts, grinning.

This time it's Christy's turn to look shocked, and then we all crack up, laughing at the irony. I guess that was something she hadn't seen in either of our futures, or rather, pasts.

An hour later we've all been drained of our spare cash as Christy plays cards like she's been hustling her whole life. Pity her dad wasn't half as smart as she was; if he had been, he might still be alive today. Then again if he was still alive, me and Kate might not be together, and I rather him dead with Kate in my arms and Christy in our lives than the alternative.

Part way through what must be our tenth game of Twenty-one, Kate's phone rings. I catch her eye, reading her expression. Neither of us have Christy's gift, but there's a pretty good fucking chance that's Cleveland with some news about Rodriguez.

"Excuse me for a moment," Kate says, pushing back her chair and striding from the room to take the call. She's gone less than a minute before returning with a grim look on her face.

"We need to go."

"Harris find what he was looking for?"

Kate shakes her head. "Yes and No."

"What do you mean?" I press, but she flicks her gaze at Christy and shakes her head. "We have to go now."

"I don't want you to," Christy says, her voice quiet as she places her cards on the table and rests her hands on her lap.

Kate crouches down beside her and grasps hold of her hands. "I know. I'm so sorry."

"I hate this," she cries, a little sob escaping her throat as she throws herself into Kate's arms, almost knocking her off her feet.

Kate pulls Christy tighter into her body. "We'll be back to visit soon."

"Not soon enough," she replies, clinging onto her for dear life. Eventually she pulls away, swiping at her tears until she's standing in front of me.

"Alright kid?" I ask, looking down at her, my fucking throat tight as she looks back up at me in a way that makes fear creep up my spine. I'm not afraid of her, but I am afraid of what she knows because whatever it is, it clearly ain't good.

"I told Kate this, and I'm going to tell you the same thing. Your story, yours and Kate's, it has a *happy* ending."

"That's a fucking relief," I say, my smile slipping from my face when her expression remains troubled.

"But it was never going to be a smooth path to get there. Epic love rarely is," she says, sounding more like a wise old woman than a twelve year old girl. "There will be a lot of obstacles, some the two of you will overcome together and some with the help of others. When it comes to those people, trust your gut because it already knows what your head and your heart have yet to discover."

"Christy, maybe you shouldn't say any more—" Kate says, but Christy cuts her off, taking Kate's hand in hers.

"Everything you do," she says, looking between us both, "Is

because you care about each other, about the people you love. I know that."

"Do what, kid?"

She shakes her head, tears welling in her eyes. "I *can't* say."

"It's okay. Don't sweat it. We'll figure shit out," I reply, even though I'm far from fucking calm as my heart pounds and my guts churn.

"Whatever it is you've seen, whatever it is that you know, none of that should be a burden for you," Kate adds. "I hate that it is, and if I could take that burden from you, I'd do it in a heartbeat."

"I know, and that's why no matter what I've seen, I *know* you're a good person," Christy says, her bottom lip wobbling as she tries so hard to hold in more tears threatening to fall.

Kate looks at me over Christy's head, her gaze filled with worry as my skin breaks out in fucking goosebumps. What else has this kid seen?

"Christy, I—" Kate begins, but what can she say? How can she respond to that?

"I'll still love you no matter what," Christy adds fiercely. Then sighing, she squeezes both our hands in hers. "Just have faith that everything will work out in the end, because it *will*."

And despite how fucking weird this whole thing is, her words hit home. I don't have to dig too deep to find out that I do have faith. I have faith in *this* kid's ability to see things no other fucker can, in my love for Kate, and in our story that's turning out to have way more twists and turns than any fairy tale Kate has ever read.

CHAPTER TWENTY

Loose ends

GRIM

"Ma'am, she's high and she's dangerous. I've taken the liberty of restraining her. She's in the basement," Cleveland says as he greets us both at the door of the club several hours later. It's been a long drive back from Wales. Tense, with stilted conversation and both of us stuck in our own heads.

"Thank you," I say tightly.

"Harris has already questioned the man using Rodriguez's credit card. According to the guy he got it from a *crack-whore*. His words, not mine."

"Ford's mum?" Beast questions, wanting to confirm what we already know to be true given the conversation I had at Sandy and Frank's house less than four hours ago. Turns out Mary sold Rodriguez's credit card to some punk in exchange for a hit.

"Yes."

"And Rodriguez?" I ask.

Cleveland shakes his head. "He's dead, Ma'am. It would appear she took a knife to him. Stabbed him several times."

"When?"

"From the state of his body, and rigour mortis, I'd say he's been dead at least 24 hours."

"Fucking hell," Beast exclaims, squeezing the bridge of his nose. He looks as tired as I feel.

"I took the liberty of removing his body from her flat. I've covered it up on a gurney in the basement. I assumed you wanted to see the body, check if it's him."

"You assumed right," I agree.

"Jesus fucking Christ." Beast swipes a hand through his hair. "How the fuck did they know each other?"

"I have no clue," I say, shaking my head. "But I want to know what she was doing with him, and more to the point, *why* she killed him?"

"I guess we're about to find out," Beast replies, and I feel a sense of impending doom skirting down my spine. I shiver involuntarily and Beast grasps my wrist. "You good?" he asks, sliding his hands up my arms and squeezing my shoulders.

"I don't know. None of this is making any sense."

"Yeah, you're right. It isn't," he agrees, a tightness around his jaw as he jerks his chin towards the open doorway. "Come on, let's get down there. The sooner we question her, the sooner we get some answers."

When we enter the basement, we see Ford's mum is

strapped to a wooden chair. Her hair is matted with dried blood and her skin and clothes are filthy with it. Wild eyes stare up at us as we enter the room, but there's no acknowledgement there, just a vacantness that's unnerving. She's grinding her jaw like a cow chewing grass, still high on whatever drug she's taken.

"She's off her tits," Beast remarks.

"No shit," I mumble, casting my gaze to the body laid out on the gurney in the corner of the room, covered in a white sheet.

Beast follows my gaze and strides over to the gurney, pulling back the sheet. I gag at the carnage. "Fuck me, she went crazy on his arse," Beast remarks. "She ain't just stabbed him a couple times, she's put so many holes in him his fucking intestines are hanging out of his stomach."

I swallow down bile rising up my throat at the ruin that is Rodriguez's chest and stomach, and turn my attention back to Mary who's as far from a fucking saint as you can get.

"Mary?" I say, taking a step slowly towards her. I know she's been restrained, but it doesn't hurt to be cautious. She's clearly psychotic, and when people get all in their head like that you'd be surprised how strong they can be. "Can you hear me, Mary?"

"Bastard. I won't have it. I won't have any of it," she hisses, her eyes snapping to my face, a little bit of lucidity registering before it's gone again and she's back to grinding her teeth. The sound is like nails on a chalkboard, and fuck does it makes my skin crawl.

"Careful, Kate," Beast warns, circling behind her and ducking down to check Cleveland's rope tying skills. "She's a loose cannon right now, and you're right in the line of fire."

"I'll be fine," I say, batting his concern away.

"She's well restrained. So, yes, you'll be fine because she ain't getting out of that. However—"

"Beast, now isn't the time for a lecture. Let's just get this done, okay?" I say, not wanting to get into a discussion about the rules of torturing someone. That's his bag. Not mine. Right now all I want are answers.

"Okay," he agrees, wisely choosing not to argue with me.

"Why did you kill Rodriguez?" I ask, pulling up a chair and sitting down in front of Mary.

Her head rolls on her shoulders and she mumbles, "My baby."

"What about your baby?" I ask, trying to get her to focus. "Did Rodriguez threaten him?

"My baby. My baby. My baby. My baby," she says, her dry and cracked lips trembling as she blinks at me, her bloodshot eyes hazy.

"Ford?" I question.

She drops her head, her chin pressing against her chest as she drools. Her hair is lank, and she's balding in patches. Her frame is thin, gaunt, and her skin is sallow. She's a wreck of a human being. Drug and alcohol addiction has ruined her mind and her body. When I think about Ford having to spend ten years of his life growing up under the care of this woman, my fucking heart breaks. That kid has some kind of superhuman strength surviving this woman and that cunt she brought into his life who's now nothing more than pig fodder.

"Mary, did Rodriguez threaten to hurt Ford?" I press.

Her head snaps up, her eyes hyperfocusing on me as she finally registers her son's name. "My baby!" she shouts, specks of blood and spittle flying from her mouth. I twist my head to the side, making a mental note to scrub myself clean once this is all over.

"We checked in on him, he's okay," I say, hoping that by reassuring her, she'll fight against the tide of her addiction and psychosis and stay lucid enough to answer some questions.

Not that she deserves to know he's okay, the bitch deserves to be rotting six feet underground for the abuse and cruelty she's inflicted on her son. But as much as I want to end her sorry life, I won't.

At least not yet.

Right now she has information, and I need that more than I want her dead.

"No! My baby! He took my baby!"

"Who did? What are you saying?"

"HIM! My baby!" she screams.

I gag at the smell of her stale breath and the metallic scent of blood that washes over me. This day can fucking do one. I'm over it already.

"Kate, she's too high right now. Let her sober up a bit. We'll question her later," Beast says, watching me, his arms folded across his chest. There's concern in his gaze, and I love him for it, but he needs to understand that I'm not weak. That I can and will do this.

"No, I want to know now."

"We don't need to rush. Christy's safe. Loretta has checked in and we've got time to figure this shit out."

"Christy's safe for *now*," I point out. "The King is still out there cooking something up. Rodriguez is dead so we can't question him, and somehow these two know each other enough for

Mary to kill him. I want to know *why*, and I'm not leaving here until I find out."

"Because she's an addict and he's her dealer," Beast says, as though that's the most logical explanation. It's not. It's the easiest.

"No way. Rodriguez would *never* get close to an addict like this. There's more to this story than meets the eye. You know that!" I reply stubbornly.

"Kate, just take a break. She's not going anywhere,"

"Look, it's been a long day. You can go. I'll take care of this."

Beast scoffs, pushing off from the counter he's leaning against. "Not happening. I'll stay until you get what you need, and then I'm taking you home and helping you put this long arse day behind you."

"Is that a promise?" I ask, giving him a small smile. The thought of being wrapped up in his arms is the only thing getting me through this day.

"It's a motherfucking guarantee."

An hour passes and I'm no closer to the truth.

"Kate, let me handle this," Beast says as I ask for the thousandth time what she knows.

"You're willing to torture a woman?" I ask, looking over at him.

It is not an accusation, but rather a sincere question. We both know that she's been cruel to Ford and doesn't deserve our sympathy, but I don't want to put Beast in a position where he feels any guilt. He's never tortured a woman before, and despite how despicable this woman is and all the terrible things she's done to her own flesh and blood, I have the feeling that it's a hard no for him but he'll do it for me anyway.

"Listen, I'm willing to do *whatever* it takes to protect the people I care about, Kate."

"Which is exactly why you shouldn't. I can't make you do this. I won't."

"You're not making me do anything," he says, grasping a knife from his trolley of torture instruments. He turns it over in his hands, looking at it for a moment. "Ford is a good kid. Christy deserves to be safe, and you need to know the truth so that we can face whatever the King has planned *together*."

"It will fuck you up," I say heavily.

"I'm already fucked-up, Princess."

"Beast—"

"No, Kate. I've got this."

"What about what Christy said? Maybe this is what she was talking about. She was troubled by it..."

"I hope to fuck this isn't what she was talking about because I don't want that sweet kid to see this kind of bad shit," Beast says, scrubbing his face, "But she was right about everything. I *will* do what it takes to protect you. Always."

"I know you would and that's the problem."

Ignoring me, Beast strides over to Mary, crouching before her. "I need you to listen very carefully, Mary. This is important," he says, lifting her chin so she looks at him. She blinks rapidly a few times and there's more lucidity in her gaze than when we first arrived. Perhaps the effect of whatever drug she's been taking is finally beginning to wear off.

"My baby," she whispers.

It's the same thing she's been saying over and over again for hours.

"We *want* to protect your baby," Beast says, stroking her cheek with his thumb.

He's gentle, soothing, and somehow that's worse than him being violent. I let out a shaky breath and grit my jaw.

"All we need you to do, Mary, is answer a few questions and we'll help you sort this out."

"I want my baby," she says, her lips wobbling, her eyes filling with tears.

"And you'll see your baby again soon. I promise," Beast lies, because we both know that no matter what, she's not leaving this basement alive. "I just need you to tell me why you killed Rodriguez? What happened?"

For a long time she just stares at Beast, then clarity filters across her face and I hold my breath waiting for her to respond, but just when I think she's about to tell us what we want to know, she closes her eyes and screams.

"I. Want. My. Baby!"

"Fuck!" Beast exclaims, dropping her chin and clutching a fistful of her hair in his hands. "If you don't fucking tell us what we want to know, you'll never see your baby again!"

"Wait!" I shout, just as he's pressing a knife to her neck.

"Kate, this is the only way," Beast says, but there's something in his eyes that tells me he wishes it wasn't.

"I have an idea. Just hold off, okay?" I ask him, pulling out my mobile phone and texting Cleveland.

Beast releases Mary from his hold and steps back, "So what's the deal?"

"She wants her baby. I'm fulfilling her wish," I say, hoping this is going to work.

"You're not seriously bringing Ford here?"

I shake my head. "No, but I am bringing her a baby."

Twenty minutes later, Cleveland enters the basement clutching a bag and sporting a confused look on his face. "I hope this is okay? It was difficult to find a doll at ten o'clock at night."

I take the bag from him and pull out one of those lifelike babies that are popular with kids right now. It's even wearing a yellow striped babygrow and has a matching blanket with yellow ducks embroidered along the hem. Its eyes are pressed shut and its rosebud mouth is relaxed in sleep. I bet it can fake pee as well.

"You think this is going to work?" Beast asks, eying the doll.

"I hope so," I say. "Where did you manage to get this?"

"It belongs to Casey's little girl,' Cleveland explains. "Best I could do at the last minute."

"Casey, as in one of the dancers at Nine Lives, right?" Beast asks.

"Yes. She was happy to help."

I wince, feeling guilty about taking a toy from a child. "Please tell Casey that I'll buy her little girl three brand new dolls to make up for taking this one off her hands."

"I will. Anything else, Ma'am?" Cleveland asks, flicking his gaze to Mary.

"Yes, get the cleaners ready. We'll need them here soon to clear up the mess. After that I want them to deal with her flat. Everything has to be destroyed. Understand?"

"Of course," he replies with a nod. "I'll make sure no traces are left behind."

"I appreciate it," I reply, waiting until Cleveland leaves the basement before showing Mary the doll. The moment her gaze falls on its sleeping form, a sob releases from her lips.

"My baby. Oh, my baby," she cries, tears spilling over her lashes and falling down her cheeks as she shifts in her seat, unable to reach out as her arms are still restrained behind her back."Please, let me hold my baby."

I glance at Beast. "Untie her."

"Kate?" he warns, giving me a look to tell me that he doesn't think that's a good idea.

"I said, untie her."

He does.

When her arms are free she reaches for the doll, and I hand it to her. She takes it gently, cupping its head in her dirty, blood-caked hands and bowing her head to drop a kiss against its cheek. "Thank you," she says softly, looking up at me, and it's the first time I see someone close to a human behind her eyes and not the addled gaze of an addict.

"You're welcome, Mary," I reply, sitting down on the chair in front of her.

She drops her gaze back to the doll, seemingly oblivious that it's not real and starts to rock her arms, humming a lullaby under her breath. Goosebumps erupt over my skin as a chill tracks down my spine.

Beast catches my gaze, "Kate?" he asks, so finely attuned to my feelings.

"I'm good," I say, shaking off this weird feeling. "Let's get this done."

It's been a long day. All I need to do is eat then sleep for a solid eight hours. At least, that's what I tell myself when Mary begins to sing in earnest and that weird feeling in my gut evolves into apprehension.

"*Hush little baby, don't say a word, mama's gonna buy you a mockingbird...*" Mary sings, a gentle smile pulling up her lips.

"Mary, I need to ask some questions," I begin, swallowing down my unease.

"Sure," she whispers, stroking the doll's cheek, humming under her breath.

"Why did you kill Rodriguez?"

"Rodriguez?" she asks, pulling the doll tighter against her chest as a panic flickers behind her eyes.

"Yes. Did he try to hurt you?"

"He wanted to hurt my baby," she scowls.

"Ford?"

"Ford?" She looks up at me then laughs coldly. "No. Not *him*. He's the devil's spawn."

"Jesus fucking Christ," Beast mutters under his breath, but Mary doesn't seem to hear Beast, let alone acknowledge that he's in the room.

"He wanted to hurt my baby!" she repeats.

"Why?" I press.

"I stabbed him, over and over and over again," she garbles. "I made sure he was good and dead. He'll never hurt my baby now. Never."

"Mary, listen, who are we talking about? *What* baby?" I press.

"She's such a beauty..." her voice trails off as she stares at the doll in her arms, a lone tear leaks from her eye and tracks down her nose, dripping onto the doll's face.

"*She?*" I glance up at Beast, confusion furrowing my brow. Ford never mentioned a younger sibling, and Cleveland didn't mention anything about anyone else being at her flat, let alone a baby.

"She was such a happy, *happy* baby. But she's gone now. She's gone," she wails, clutching the doll tighter. If it was a real baby, I'd be worried she was suffocating it right now.

"Man, this is fucked-up," Beast murmurs, watching this play out with a frown.

"Rodriguez tried to take your baby?" I ask, knowing that she's clearly still under the influence of drugs, despite seeming way more lucid than she has been so far tonight.

"Not him," she spits. "That bastard!"

"Who, the King?" I question, glancing up at Beast who is clearly just as confused as I am.

"No. *Carter.*"

Carter?

My heart stops beating. My lungs ice over.

The fucking world stops spinning.

"You had a baby with Carter?" I eventually manage to ask, my voice so soft it's a wonder she even hears my question.

"He took her from me!" Mary spits, her leg bouncing up and down in agitation.

"Please no..." I whisper out, my throat tightening as I think about how I might have another sibling out there that my dad hasn't told me about. "Carter *Davidson?*"

"Yes, you know him?" Mary asks me, her eyes narrowing as she looks up from the doll and really focuses on my face for the first time this evening. "*Wait...*" Her voice trails off and I wince at the look in her eyes. It's as though she's seen a ghost.

"Mary?" The way she's looking at me, the way she searches

my face makes every single alarm bell inside of me go off. "Mary, what is it?" I ask, my mouth dry, my voice hoarse.

This can't be my...

"Kitty Kat? Is that you?"

"Kitty Kat?" I question, shaking my head in a vain attempt to clear these intrusive thoughts. I don't like the way she's looking at me. I don't like the way this is going. I don't like any of it.

"Oh fuck!' Beast exclaims as my head snaps around to look at him.

"No!" I hold my hands up. "She can't be!" I hiss, refusing to believe it.

"It's you, isn't it?" Mary says, and I can see how she fights the effects of the drug she's taken as she stares at me.

"Kate, just go. Let me handle this."

"No!" I hold my hand up, stopping Beast in his tracks.

"Your *Ford's* mother, Mary, right?" I ask, like I don't know, because of course she is.

She nods, her eyes a little wild now as she waves her hand around, holding onto the doll with one arm. "He's my son but I don't love him. Not like I love my little Kitty Kat."

"Why don't you love him?" I ask, feeling sick, feeling like the whole fucking universe is falling down around me.

"His father was a bastard. A liar and a cheat. Ford is just like his father."

My heart thumps inside my chest "Carter is his dad?"

She throws her head back and laughs. "No, not him."

"But Kitty Kat, *she's* his daughter?" I press, forcing myself to switch off my emotions, to remain cold, detached.

"Yes. He took her. My darling girl. She was such a good

baby. Happy." Mary smiles then, and beneath the blood and the grime and the years of drug abuse I can see the shadow of the woman she once was, the woman my dad might've been attracted to once upon a time. "She slept so well, and when she woke up all she did was smile and laugh."

"You loved her?" I whisper as Beast steps beside me and rests his hand on my shoulder in a silent show of support.

"Yes, with my whole heart."

"But you don't love your son?"

She snarls, her lip curling up, her cruelty revealing itself. "He was sickly. He would cry! He would never shut the fuck up!" she screeches, her grasp on the doll tighter now.

"What happened to your daughter?"

"I told you. He took her from me."

"Carter Davidson?" I repeat, needing to be sure. Hoping she'll say another name. Any fucking name.

"Yes. He fucked me, got me pregnant, then when he found out about her, he came to my flat and he stole her from me."

"Why didn't you try to stop him?" I ask, feeling nauseous.

She laughs bitterly. "No one stops Carter Davidson. He's to blame for all of this. For everything!" she shouts, her gentleness replaced with anger as she flings the doll out of her hands.

I catch it, hugging it to my chest, my protective instincts forcing my arms to hold it tight. It's fucking ridiculous. I know it's a doll, but I feel the need to protect it from her nethertheless.

"Kate, let me finish this," Beast says, grasping my shoulder in his hand, giving me another reassuring squeeze. I register his touch, but I don't feel it.

"No. It's okay," I say, knowing it isn't. Knowing that this is a truth I don't want to believe, that I refuse to believe. This woman can't be my mother. She fucking *can't*.

"Did the King put you up to this?" I ask, anger rushing like fire through my veins. "Is that why you killed Rodriguez because you didn't get what you wanted out of the deal, huh?"

"No. I killed him because he wanted to hurt *my baby*."

"Your baby is all grown up now!" I spit and she flinches, shaking her head.

"No. No. She's only been gone a few months. My little Kitty Kat. My girl. My Katie."

Bile burns the back of my throat and I swallow it down, but I can't hide the fact my hands are shaking and I can't hide the tears that are spilling over my lashes for this empty shell of a woman, for that little girl she loved, for Ford who has never filled the void, and for me.

I swipe them away angrily, hating myself for fucking crying for this woman, this monster.

"Rodriguez said he would kill my baby. Said he had people who could hurt her," she whines, hugging herself as she rocks her body. "I had to do it. I had to protect her."

"Tell me what he said exactly. Word for word. It's important," I press, grasping her thin shoulders and shaking her so much that her teeth clack together.

"He said he would hurt my baby."

"Your baby?" I point to the doll that Beast is holding in his arms. "That baby, Kitty Kat? Did he say *her* name, specifically?" She frowns, her mouth opening and closing like a fish out of water as she tries to remember. "Mary. *Think*."

"Yes he said that he would kill Kate if I didn't do what he asked."

"And what was that?"

"He wanted me to *lie*," she says, grasping at me now.

"Lie about what?" I press, losing my patience. Feeling sick.

She rocks back and forth, her eyes glazing over then refocusing as she tries to remember. It's like watching a pair of curtains being opened, allowing the fresh air and light in, only to have the window slammed shut and the curtains snatched closed again. She's here one minute, then gone the next. Focussed then lost.

"Mary! What did Rodriguez want you to lie about?"

"The police," she stutters, the curtains opening a little, her conscious thoughts becoming clear.

"What about the police?" I press, taking her blood-encrusted hand in mine, squeezing it, trying to keep her in the room and not lose her to her mind again.

"He wanted me to tell the police..."

"Mary!" I snap as her eyes glaze over. "Mary!"

This time I shake her roughly. I'm tempted to slap her. I have this sudden urge to hurt her like she hurt Ford, but I refrain, forcing myself to calm down. Her gaze limps up to meet mine, her pupils dilating as she focuses on my face.

"He wanted me to say that I witnessed a man called Beast murder her father. If I didn't he would kill my baby." She sobs now, her tears mingling with the dried droplets of blood on her face and neck. Her shoulders drop and she hunches over on her seat as she rocks backwards and forwards.

"I said no. I said no, no, no!"

My fingers curl into her arms in a bruising grip. "What happened then?"

"He said he would kill my baby. So instead, I killed him. I. Killed. Him."

She laughs then. No, she cackles, and the sound is like something out of a horror movie.

"You killed him," I repeat, knowing that she did it for me, or at least the baby that was taken from her because somehow, some way, she's separated her realities, living in the past and still thinking about the baby Carter took and not the woman she grew into right under her nose. Carter never kept me secret, he didn't change my name, she could have approached me at any time. Then again, I know Carter. He would've threatened her life. There's no doubt.

It's just another sin to add to his long, long list.

"I just wanted to hold my baby one last time. Just one last time," Mary continues, lost now as she stares blindly off into the distance. A life of drug abuse, psychosis, heartbreak and a poisonous heart ruining her mind and her ability to grasp a hold of what is real and what isn't. Part of me hopes that the child she remembers wasn't me, but I know she's telling the truth. I know in my gut that this woman before me is my mother, and I hate it.

I fucking hate it.

"Mary, listen to me," I say motioning for Beast to give me the doll.

He hands it to me and I squeeze her arm. She looks up, her deep brown eyes flashing with something close to recognition, but then she's gone again. Handing her the doll, I stand, pushing the chair backwards as I stare at her.

"Can I ask you something?" I say.

"Yes," she whispers, smiling down at the sleeping doll, her fingers stroking over its cheeks.

"If Rodriguez threatened Ford's life, your *son's* life instead of Kitty Kat's, what would you have done?"

Her gaze lifts, the almost trancelike state she's been wearing for most of her time down here making way for a sudden, lucid coldness that makes my stomach twist in knots and dread creep up my spine.

"I'd tell him to go right ahead and kill the little fucker, and if he didn't then I would because that little shit ain't worth the air he breathes."

"That's what I thought," I say, then pull out my gun that's holstered at my waist, aim it right between her eyes and squeeze the trigger.

CHAPTER TWENTY-ONE

As

BEAST

"Kate, can I come in?" I ask, rapping my knuckles against the bathroom door. She's been in there for over half an hour, and whilst I've respected her need for privacy, my gut is telling me that now isn't the time for her to be alone. What she found out tonight... Christ, I don't even know how to digest that information, so fuck knows how she's coping right now.

"Kate?"

When she doesn't answer, I push open the door and step inside the bathroom. Steam rises from the bathtub, misting up the mirror, the air thick with the scent of lavender. Sunken up to her neck, Kate is staring off into space, completely oblivious to my presence. She's clearly in shock, and right now what she needs more than anything is for someone who loves her to fucking hold her close. Killing someone is never easy, but killing your own mother, a woman who you've never previously met and who has a vicious darkness in her soul, that's gonna hurt.

It's gonna hurt bad.

Stripping off, I sit on the edge of the bath and rest my hand against her shoulder, my fingers sliding over her silky skin as I caress her gently. "Kate? Can I join you?"

My touch seems to register in her brain and without uttering a word she looks up at me, nodding. Shifting forward in the water, she makes room for me behind her so I can slide my legs either side of her hips, the water splashing a little over the lipped edge of the bath as we make ourselves comfortable. Fortunately the bath is large enough for my bulky frame as well as Kate's slim one. She fits perfectly between my legs, and despite it not being the right moment, my dick hardens at the feel of her pressing against it.

"Beast…" she murmurs, allowing me to ease her back against my chest.

"I know, baby. I know," I say, understanding what she needs instinctively as I wrap my arms around her in a hug.

She's the toughest woman I know, but she's not infallible, and beneath the toughness she's honed so well over the last couple of years is a woman who feels deeply, who hurts, and who protects the people she loves fiercely.

"He's my brother, and I just blew his mum's brains out… *Our* mum," she adds quietly.

"She would've killed him eventually. You heard what she

said. You saw what she was capable of," I say, trying to ease her guilt.

"She was an addict," Kate argues.

"Maybe so, but her addiction can't be used as an excuse for her cruelty towards Ford. She was abusive, callous. We've both seen the scars on that kid's body, the tattoo they inflicted on him when he was just ten years old."

"I know that. I know she was a monster..." Her voice trails off as she twists in my arms and presses her cheek against my chest. I feel how my heart thumps harder at the way she melts against me and a wave of fierce love takes my breath momentarily.

"But?" I say gently.

"But she was also Ford's mother."

"And yours."

"And mine," she agrees. "But only by blood. Not in any way that counts."

"Do you think that's why Ford sought you out, because he knew somehow?" I ask.

"Yeah, yeah I do..." She falls silent for a moment, and then with a note of panic in her voice, suddenly asks, "Who have you got watching him?"

"Dom and Harris."

"Good. I want around the clock eyes on Ford until we deal with the King and this threat."

"Already done," I say, and she relaxes a little in my arms.

For a while she remains thoughtful as she rests back against my chest, then eventually she shifts position, turning a little to face me. "How am I supposed to tell Ford that I killed his mum, that I killed her because she was a monster who wanted him dead?"

"I don't know," I say, reaching for her, tucking a wet tendril of hair behind her ear. "Maybe you don't, maybe this is something we keep to ourselves. We'll figure out a story, one that won't tear that kid to pieces."

"Fuck," she utters, looking even more lost. "He's my brother and I'm already lying to him."

"To protect him. You'll do it to protect him. Just like Christy said."

She nods, her fingers absentmindedly tracing the tattoos on my chest, and my heart stutters.

Fuck I need her. I want to wipe away the bad and give her something good.

"Yeah... But I can't protect Christy from the truth," she continues, forcing me to concentrate, to ignore my throbbing cock. "She saw this happening."

"You don't know exactly what she saw, Kate."

"Enough. She saw *enough*. Tell me, Beast, how the fuck am I supposed to look her in the eye again?"

"She loves you anyway. You heard what she said. She understands."

"She's twelve, how can she possibly understand?"

"Because that kid has experienced more than most adults have in their lifetime," I say, cupping her cheek and gently urging her to look at me. "You did the right thing."

"I could've got Mary into rehab or something."

I shake my head. "Then what? So she gets off the drugs, that doesn't change the fact she's an abuser. It doesn't change the fact she beat Ford, cut him and burnt him with cigarettes. She wished him dead. Addict or not, I saw the intent in her eyes just as clearly as you did. That kid is better off without her."

"Logically, I know that. I do."

"As much as I fucking hate your dad, he did the right thing taking you from her, and you did the *only* thing you could in the circumstances. Hear me?"

She nods, and whilst I know she does hear me, I also know she won't ever let go of the guilt because like it or not, Kate isn't like the rest of us. She can't compartmentalise the bad shit, lock it away and forget about it. Despite everything, she feels.

She always has.

Her dad saw it as a weakness. I see it as her biggest strength.

Tell me what's more fierce than a woman protecting her family?

Nothing is. Absolutely nothing.

Resting back against my chest, Kate is content to just lie in my arms, and as much as my dick is eager to soothe her the only way it knows how, I don't try to initiate anything more intimate. That's not what she needs right now. What she needs is someone to be there for her when she's feeling vulnerable. She needs someone she can be herself with, her *true* self with, and I want to be the man. I will be that man. Every fucking day for the rest of my life.

Picking up the bodywash resting on the ledge beside the bath, I pour some in my hands and slowly rub it over her shoulders and arms, the scent of blossom and honey lifting into the air as I soap up her skin. She sighs a little, relaxing as I wash her, but as much as my dirty fucking mind wants to I don't grasp her tits. I keep things purely soothing, not sexual.

"Beast, what if I'm like them?" she confesses after a while.

"Like your parents?"

"Yes, what if I end up like them. Cruel, sadistic, *evil*."

"It's not possible," I say with conviction, pressing a kiss to the top of her head.

"You're wrong," she protests. "I shot Fitzpatrick without a second thought. I kneecapped one of his men at my dad's funeral and had another man beaten to within an inch of his life for calling me by my real name. Less than an hour ago I blew my mother's brains out whilst she was holding a doll that she thought was *me*... I shot you, didn't I? How can you say I'm not like them?"

"Because of this, right now. You feel remorse."

"No, you don't understand. I don't regret any of it. Not even shooting you," she admits quietly. "I'm sorry I hurt you, but I'd do it again in that situation because if I hadn't, I probably wouldn't be here now."

"You had to do it. I understand that," I say, and I do. I really fucking do. "Just like you had to kneecap that prick for disrespecting you at your dad's funeral, and shoot Fitzpatrick for calling you out in front of everyone."

"But they were selfish acts, I was protecting myself."

"Protecting yourself isn't selfish. It's *smart*. It's a fucking necessity in this life, Kate."

"That still doesn't change the fact I'm capable of murder, of violence."

"Maybe so, but you never kill for the sake of killing. You don't get a thrill out of it. It hurts you even if there isn't any regret. There are so many people in this life who think nothing of killing someone, and there are many more that enjoy it."

She presses her hand over my heart, fitting it perfectly

within the tattoo. "You told me once that you were numb to killing people."

"I am, and that's a fuck ton better than getting kicks out of it," I say pointedly. "We do this because we have to. You had to kill Mary to protect your brother, just like I had to kill your father to protect you."

"Except you're skirting the truth, Beast, because it's convenient for you to do so."

"What truth?"

"You cut out the hearts of my enemy, and I liked that you did that for me. That you cared enough to show me those men were dead. That you proved your loyalty."

"You liked the meaning behind it, not the act itself."

"Maybe so, but that's still twisted. That's still fucked-up. I've always been drawn to the darker side of life. I grew up on Grimms' Fairy Tales, surrounded by violence for fuck's sake."

"The difference is you don't beat on children and get a kick out of it. You wouldn't dream of selling your own kid to a creepy cunt to pay off your debts. You took in Ford before you even knew he was your brother. You love Christy fiercely. You're *not* them."

"I don't know..."

"Well, I do. You're *not* like them," I insist.

"Perhaps I should've listened to you," she says after a while. "You gave me the chance to choose. Maybe I should've walked away when I had the opportunity."

"It's never too late. You could do that now, Kate."

"I can't do that. I don't want to do that. I've fought too hard to get where I am. I refuse to back down."

"But if you did ever want to, I'd come with you, you know

that right?" I reply, pressing a kiss to the top of her head, hugging her close. "I'd follow you into the fires of Hell if you asked me to."

"You'd do that for me?" she asks, twisting in my arms, searching my face.

"I'd do anything for you. *Anything* you understand?" I say, sliding my hands into the wet tendrils of her hair and cupping the back of her head.

"Anything?" she whispers, her vulnerability fucking killing me.

"Yes."

"Then love me until I have no other thought in my head but you," she begs, her fingernails digging into my skin as she turns to face me fully, the water sloshing as she moves. "Love me until all I feel is you. Make me forget. Just fucking love me, Beast."

"I already do. I already fucking do," I say fiercely, tugging her towards me and kissing her hard. My tongue slips past her lips as she climbs onto my lap, clawing at me as though she doesn't ever want to let go.

I don't want her to.

I don't want to be anywhere but here with her, holding her close, loving her fierce, fucking her blind.

"Let me take care of you," I mutter against her mouth as I shift in the bath, hauling her against my chest, a fierce protectiveness lighting up something primal inside of me.

We've fucked and we've made love, but this feels different.

This is more.

This is the moment when all bets are off.

This is the moment when every layer is stripped away.

This is when two bleeding hearts collide.

"Hurt me with your love, make me feel how much you want me. After so much death, I need to feel alive, Beast," she replies, her legs wrapping around my waist, her pussy grinding against the hard shaft of my dick as she licks her way back into my mouth and fucks me with her tongue.

It's too much. It's not nearly enough.

Clasping her against my chest, I rise up out of the water like fucking Poseidon out of the ocean. She clings to me, her slippery body wrapped around mine as I step out of the bath. Fuck knows how I don't slip, but the moment my feet hit the cool tile of the bathroom floor, I push on her hips, urging her to stand.

She pulls away from me, breathless, flushed, her chest heaving. My balls tighten and my dick hardens painfully as I watch the droplets of water slide over her skin, jealous of the way they get to be so close to her.

"I want to fuck you hard, Princess," I grind out, any sentimental words lost beneath the haze of lust.

"Then fuck me hard, Beast. Fuck me so hard that all I feel is you buried deep inside of me. Fuck me until I pass out, then wake me up with your dick slamming into me. Fuck this feeling out of my chest, *please*," she begs, tears welling in her eyes at the pain she's been trying so hard to deny.

Grasping her hips, I spin her around and press my dick against the crack of her arse. Then I slide my palm up over her stomach, between her breasts until I reach her neck, pressing my lips to her ear.

"Don't ever doubt yourself. Don't doubt your decisions. Don't doubt who you are or what you need to do to survive. This is an ugly fucking world, Kate, and to me you're the brightest fucking light amidst the chaos. Now be a good girl and bend over so I can fuck you into next week and show you just how much I love you."

She drops forward, her fingers grasping the edge of the bath, her wet, tangled hair sticking to her back as I grasp the base of my dick and line it up with her pussy.

"You're a queen and the ruler of my heart, and I'm going to fuck you until neither of us can stand," I say, slamming into her with one hard thrust.

Her head flies back, her neck straining, her mouth open in a scream as she grips the bath and I imprint my body onto hers.

There's no slow build, not this time.

With one hand grasping her hip, I reach forward and fist her hair, fucking her like a man possessed. My cock thickens and lengthens with every thrust, with every gasp, with every pant and cry of pleasure that releases from her lips.

She bears down on me, meeting my thrusts with her own as we both work ourselves up into a frenzy of heat, passion and lust. Pulling tighter on her hair, I force her head back and to the side so I can watch her face as she takes me deep. Her skin is flushed, her mouth parted and her eyes at half mast as I pound into her, wanting to get deeper, needing to fill her up. Skin slaps against skin as the room echoes with our combined pleasure, and my balls draw up tight to my body, ready to fucking explode and fill her with my cum.

"What if I'm like her," she cries, her fear and doubt suddenly bubbling to the surface trying its best to tarnish this moment.

"You're *nothing* like her," I argue, slamming into her, wanting to rid her of those ugly thoughts. "You are the exact opposite of that woman."

"But—" she cries, moving to pull away, running from my words and my conviction.

She's still scared that she's fucked-up like her parents. She needs to know that she isn't. She needs to know that I believe in her heart, that she isn't weak for caring or loving or feeling pain and grief. That she's the strongest, bravest, most fucking courageous woman I know.

So I release her hair, and slide one arm around her chest, hauling her back up against me, my dick sliding out from inside of her as I twist her in my arms and pick her up, pressing her against the tiled wall instead.

"You're. Not. Her," I repeat, keeping my gaze fixed on hers.

"You can't know that!" she cries grasping at me, her nails digging into my shoulders as she leans her head back against the wall and squeezes her eyes shut.

"Look at me!" I demand, my dick fucking hating me right now for not sliding into her pussy that's hovering just above its slick head.

"I do. I know that if you ever wanted a baby, you will love that kid with every atom of your being. I fucking know it," I reply, having this viceral need to fuck, to reproduce. Even though right now that isn't a possibility, since she's on the pill, I would put a baby in her belly the second she asked me to.

"You can't know that."

"Listen to me, Kate. I saw how you were with Christy, how much you love her and want to protect her. I saw the way you were with Ford, how fucking crushed you were to witness his pain. You aren't cruel. You give a fuck about the people you love. You. Are. Not. Her."

Slowly Kate opens her eyes, her fingers uncurling from my

skin as she smoothes her palms over my shoulders and up my neck to cup my face. For a long time we stare at each other, our ragged breaths falling in sync with one another, but I can see her thoughts receding to a bad place and I won't let them.

Fuck that.

"Maybe you'll never want kids, and that's okay, but don't close yourself off from having children of your own because you believe you're like your parents, because you're *not*. Whatever you choose, I need you to know that I will be there by your side. Either way, kid or no kid, I'll love you. You hear me? You are loved."

She nods, something shifting in her eyes, a release of sorts. "And if I ever choose to have a child, it'd be you and only you I'd want to have it with," she replies before slamming her mouth against mine and kissing me deeply.

That thought does something feral to me, and I thrust my hips upwards, slamming into her once again. Then with her pressed against the wall, and my body supporting her weight, I fuck her with abandon.

I fuck her with a blind need.

I fuck her with a soul-deep love.

I fuck her with possession and passion, knowing all the while that she's the one with all the power.

That. She. Owns. Me.

She owns every inch of my body.

She owns every motherfucking beat of my heart.

She owns my soul.

"Fuck, Kate. Fuck, fuck, fuck!" I pant, and unable to help myself, I bite her shoulder, latching on as I reach beneath her arse and palm her pussy, feeling my cock sliding into her body.

It's so fucking base, this need. Raw, this feeling. Fucking crazy, this love.

I cup our joined flesh, my fingers sliding through her slick folds, circling her other untouched hole.

"Yes. Oh fuck, yes!" she cries, her core tightening around my dick as I slide a finger inside of her.

She's close, so fucking close. I am too.

I'm mindless as I ram into her, bucking, fucking, slamming my dick deep, deep inside of her until sensation drags down my spine, sending white hot heat straight to my cock.

"You're my beating heart, Kate. My fucking life," I say breathlessly, earnestly.

Then I let go, my cock pumping her full of cum as she screams out her orgasm, her whole body jerking and shaking as she comes too.

CHAPTER TWENTY-TWO

Brother

GRIM

"Take a seat, Ford," I say, pointing to the sofa the following day.

Ford eyes the pristine white sectional and then looks down at his dirty jeans and mud encrusted boots. "Should I take my shoes off first?"

"Whatever makes you feel comfortable, kid," Beast says as he pours us both a cup of percolated coffee and adds them to a tray with a glass of orange juice for Ford. There's also a pile of freshly baked croissants Beast brought this morning especially for the occasion.

Ford unties his boots then places them neatly on the tiled floor beside the kitchen island. He hesitates for a moment, chewing on the inside of his cheek in a way that makes my heart squeeze.

He's my brother.

And the more I look at him, the more I see the likeness. His eyes might be a different colour to mine, but the shape is the same. We share the same high cheekbones and regal nose too. Then there's that strength he holds inside of him, that rigid determination to survive. We both have that. It's ingrained into his very being because of the life he's lived and the trauma he's suffered, and because of that there's caution too. It's as though at any point, at any given time, he believes that someone's going to turn on him and he'll have to fight or run. Isn't it funny how, when you notice the same traits in someone else, it brings up your own personal trauma?

We're very alike in many ways.

"Sit down, we ain't gonna bite," Beast says, jerking his chin towards the sofa as he passes by with the tray of drinks and croissants, and places it on the coffee table.

"Sure, whatever you say," Ford mumbles under his breath as he takes a seat.

He's guarded, and I don't blame him.

"Here," Beast says, handing him the glass of orange juice and nudging the plate of croissants towards him.

Ford takes a sip of the orange juice. "I've already had breakfast."

"Well, if you've got room for one of these croissants there's plenty to go around. Best croissants in the whole of London. They melt like butter on your tongue."

"Thanks," Ford replies tightly, frowning as he looks between the two of us. "So you wanna tell me why I'm here, coz it ain't every day you get invited back to the Queen of Tales crib and get offered breakfast?"

"Straight to the point. I like it," Beast says, smiling. He picks up his coffee and takes a sip, eying me. I guess it's now or never. Fuck, why am I so damn nervous to tell him that I know he's my brother?

Probably because you murdered his mother, an intrusive voice reminds me.

Ford places the orange juice on the table. I can't help but notice that his hands are shaking, though he hides his nerves by tucking his hands beneath his legs. Meeting Ford's gaze I swallow down the nausea and just come out with it.

"I know who you are, Ford."

"What do you mean?" he replies, looking like a deer caught in headlights, a shadow of guilt tracking across his features.

"I know you're my brother."

"I—" he begins, and then it's just sheer panic as he drops his head, hiding from me, from the truth. As his chin hits his chest, and his dirty blonde hair covers his face in a shroud, he mumbles, "I'm sorry."

"For what?" I ask gently, wanting to reach for his hand, but knowing that for him, physical touch is going to be difficult, maybe even impossible.

"For not telling you. For being... *me*," he says, swiping roughly at his face, still refusing to look up.

I look over at Beast, feeling a little helpless in this situation. When I met Christy for the first time it was different, she smashed the barrier of physical touch between us when she threw herself into my arms. But for Ford physical touch is going to be hard given the cruelty he's had to endure in his short life.

He's like a beaten down dog just waiting for someone else to hurt him, ready to snap, snarl and bite. So as much as I want to hug him. I won't. At least not yet.

"First of all, I'm not angry that you didn't say anything," I say, shifting closer to him so that I can reach out and press my fingers lightly against his arm, if only to get him to look up. He stiffens, but he still refuses to look at me. "Secondly, there's nothing wrong with you. Nothing, you hear me?"

He nods, still staring at his lap.

"Chin up, mate. You ain't got to fear us. You're a good kid," Beast says, and I can hear the crack in his voice which he covers up with a cough.

Ford must have heard it too, because it's that glimpse of emotion that makes him look up. Beast isn't one for showing his emotions outside of when he's alone with me, at least not the ones that other people would look down upon. So to hear his voice crack with emotion is quite something.

"I'm really sorry," Ford says earnestly.

"For what, for protecting yourself? Don't ever be sorry for that," I say, drawing my hand away.

"You don't hate me?" he asks, swallowing hard, and I know he's doing everything in his power not to cry. This kid, he breaks my heart.

"No. You're my brother. How could I hate you?" I say fiercely.

"My mum does. She hates me, but she loves you," he replies tightly, the tendons in his arms stiffening as his fingers curl into fists.

"That doesn't matter to me."

"Not to you maybe, you don't even know her."

I swallow hard. "You're a *good* kid."

"You don't know me. Not really," he says, hugging himself.

"I know you've endured great cruelty by her hands," I say, forcing myself to speak through the emotion I feel. "I know you've survived a difficult life. I know you've got a strength very few people can say they have. I know you're determined. I know you're an exceptional fighter—"

"Yeah, then why are you palming me off to another fight club?" he asks, and the hurt in his voice is like a knife through my heart. I didn't even realise he knew.

"That was *before* I knew who you were. We didn't think, given your circumstances, that we were the best people for you to hang out with."

"Why, don't you think I can handle it?" he asks, swallowing down his hurt. "I'm not an idiot. I know who you are. What you're about."

"It was never about you handling anything, kid," Beast says, cutting in for me because fuck if my voice has dried up in my throat with the agony I feel for him.

"Then what?"

"Being my brother puts a target on your head," I admit.

"I don't care. I'll learn how to fight with the best. I'll be able to protect myself and I won't tell anyone you're my sister. *Please*, don't send me away."

"It isn't just that. We're not exactly the best role models," I say weakly.

"And you think my mum and stepdad are any better? At least you don't want to beat the shit out of me on a regular basis. Well, at least not outside of the ring," he adds, attempting a joke that really isn't fucking funny.

"No, kid. Kate and I don't think your parents were any better. In fact we think they were mothefucking cunts," Beast says darkly.

Ford stiffens. "Wait, *were*?"

"What?" Beast replies, trying to act calm but I see the panic in his eyes. He's let the proverbial cat out of the bag and Ford isn't the type of kid to miss the meaning behind Beast's specific choice of words.

"You said, *were*," he points out, looking between us both now.

"Kid, I just meant—"

"No!" I hold my hand up, forcing Beast to stop mid lie. We owe him the truth. *I* owe him that at least. Maybe yesterday I was willing to lie under the guise of keeping more bad shit out of his life, but in the long run the truth always comes out and it'll hurt him even more then. It's better to do this now no matter how fucking hard it is.

"Kate," he warns, but I shake my head, focusing back on Ford.

"What?" Ford whispers, fear rearing its head.

"They're dead," I say, ripping the fucking plaster off.

He flinches. "What?!"

"Last night. House fire," Beast cuts in quickly, giving me a look.

"I don't understand?"

"It was a house fire—"

"No, it *wasn't*," I say, glaring at Beast, cutting him off.

Ford looks between us, confusion written across his face. "But Beast just said..."

"It wasn't a house fire," I repeat.

"I don't understand."

"Beast killed your stepdad a week ago. I killed Mary last night."

He stares at me, eyes wide, the blood draining from his face as he tries to comprehend what I've just said. "You're lying!"

"It's the truth. We did it to protect you."

"No!" he shouts, shooting to his feet. He looks between us with utter horror as he rounds the sofa and backs away towards the kitchen.

"Beast killed Trevor because he was cruel to you," I continue, needing to purge it all, wanting to start our future with a clean slate. "I killed Mary because she stabbed a man to death in a craze because she hurt you time and time again. She was unstable, Ford. *Dangerous*."

"Fuck, Kate," Beast says, running a hand through his hair.

"He needs to know the truth about what happened, and he needs to understand the truth of who we are if he wants to be a part of our lives," I say to Beast, needing him to understand. I won't base our relationship with Ford on a lie.

"You want me to be a part of your life after this?" Ford asks, confusion, shock and fear making him shake violently.

"You sought me out knowing who I was, and I don't just mean your half-sister. You *knew* my reputation. You understood what you were walking into."

"But I didn't—"

"Want us to kill them for hurting you," I finish for him. "Maybe not consciously, but you knew of my reputation, and heard what I'm capable of. Why did you seek me out, Ford?"

"What do you mean, *why*? Because I wanted to meet my sister. I wanted to meet the person my mum loved more than she ever loved me. Look how that turned out for her," he spits, the tears he was holding back, streaming down his face now.

"I'm sorry she treated you the way she did. I'm sorry she wasn't the mother you needed. You didn't deserve that life, and I couldn't let her live knowing what she did to you," I say, stepping towards him.

He backs up into the kitchen counter, shaking his head. "Don't come any closer. Don't!"

"You came to me because you knew exactly who I was," I press, forcing him to face the ugly truth. "You wanted protection as much as anything else."

"I wanted to learn how to *fight!*" he shouts, swiping at his face.

"You wanted to learn how to fight so that the next time your stepdad beat on you, you could kill him. That's what you said, Ford," Beast reminds him, glancing over at me. "You wanted him dead, and neither of us blame you for it. I'd have wanted the same thing too."

I ignore the look of concern in Beast's gaze. He thinks Ford will rat on us. I know he won't. He's in shock, granted, but Ford won't talk and I know that because I see the relief behind the shock and the pain, even though he's denying that right now.

"I never asked you to do this! I never asked you to kill them!" he shouts.

"We did what we had to do, and we did it to protect you, kid," Beast continues, taking a step closer to him.

"But my *mum...*" he says, pain making way for more tears as his knees buckle. "She's dead. She's dead. SHE'S DEAD!"

Beast reaches him just before I do and hauls him into his arms, hugging him close. I hesitate, watching as my brother, a boy who's only ever known cruelty and abuse, collapses into Beast's strong arms and cries for a mum who couldn't love him. Ford has lived a life of trauma at the hands of the one person in the whole world who should've loved him the most. No child should ever have to go through that. Not ever.

And seeing him hurt so badly guts me. I want to rage at the world for being so fucking cruel. I want to shoot her all over again for hurting him. I want to resurrect my dad for never telling me about my siblings, for not allowing me to be in their lives when they needed me the most, then kill him with my *own* hands.

Things could've been so different for all of us if he had just told me.

Christy needn't have gone through what she did on her own. Ford could've lived a very different life if my dad had been a better man.

What if my dad hadn't taken me from her arms as a baby, could Mary have loved me the right way? Did the pain and loss of losing me twist her mind into this evil, cruel woman, or was she always going to be that way? If she had kept me around and still had Ford, would she have treated him any differently? And if not, could I have protected him from her abuse?

There are so many questions I have, and no answers. All I know is that he's my brother, he deserved better, and I killed her for what she did to him, what she *wanted* to do. I will live with that decision, that choice, and only *I* will bear the weight of it.

This isn't on him. It's on me.

"She's gone. She's gone. My mum is gone!" he wails, but beneath the sadness there's relief. I see it in the way his shoulders relax, his body telling a truth that his brain isn't able to catch up with yet.

"It's alright, kid. We got you," Beast says, and those six words seem to unlock something inside of him, something Ford's kept chained up his whole life.

He purges it now with a scream that is deafening, fucking heartbreaking. Neither of us are immune to his pain. Not me, and certainly not Beast who wraps his arms tighter around Ford's frame and fucking cries with him.

My Beast, my protector, my lover, my best friend and my heart, cries with Ford. He's not ashamed. He's not telling Ford to pull his shit together. He's not accusing him of being weak. He's not belittling Ford's feelings, or his own. He's just holding him, comforting him, crying with him, *for* him.

"Come here, Kate," Beast says, noticing me hugging myself as I watch them both.

"He needs a moment," I say, wanting so much to go to them, but knowing that Ford may never get over what I did. Maybe he never truly believed that my protection would come in the form of murder, but he needed someone to step in on his behalf, and I was the only one who could have done that for him.

I don't regret it.

I'm glad she's dead.

I'm glad she can't hurt him anymore.

Eventually his tears subside and his sobs quieten. When he steps out of Beast's arms he looks almost embarrassed, but Beast just squeezes his shoulder and gives him a warm smile.

"Ain't nothing wrong with tears, mate. You gotta get it out one way or another."

Ford nods, using the sleeves of his holey sweater to clean the snot off his face.

Beast's nose wrinkles. "You ain't gonna be pulling anyone with snot halfway up your sleeve. Rule number one, always keep yourself looking sharp," he says.

It's so out of left field, given the conversation we're having, that Ford lets out a nervous laugh.

"Like you?" he asks, raising his brows at Beast's outfit.

He's wearing a pair of joggers and a well worn t-shirt that has seen better days. To be fair, he didn't get a chance to go home and grab a change of clothes after helping Cleveland and the cleaners shift the bodies, so he only had what he'd left here previously.

"I've already got the girl," he shrugs, winking at me.

"Yeah," Ford says, finally resting his gaze on me. "My sister."

He's conflicted, uncertain, unsure. Scared in all honesty, and I don't blame him for any of that. I don't even know what to say, but I know that I have to say something. So the truth it is.

"It was quick."

"How?"

"A bullet to the brain."

He swallows hard, tucking his hands into his pockets. "Why?" he asks, his voice tight as he holds back the tears.

"Because she hurt you."

"So you hurt her back?"

"She was dangerous, Ford. She killed a man."

"Like Beast killed Trevor?" he says, eying him warily like he wasn't just wrapped up in his arms.

"He was a cunt and he hurt you," Beast says shrugging. "He got what he deserved."

"And the man my mum killed, was he a cunt too?"

"Yes," I admit.

"So what's the difference? Why does Beast get to live and my mum gets to die? They both killed people."

"Because Beast did what he did to protect you. *I* did what I did to protect you. I won't apologise for that."

"And mum, why did she kill that man?" he asks.

"That ain't important," Beast says.

"It is to me," he counters.

I sigh. "She killed him because she thought he was going to kill me."

"And you repaid her by putting a bullet in her brain?" His skin pales further and he gags. "I'm going to be sick."

Ford turns on his heel and runs towards the kitchen, hurling up the contents of his stomach into the rubbish bin. He chokes and sputters, heaving as he clutches his stomach.

"Here, take this," I say, offering him a bottle of water from the fridge when he wipes the back of his hand over his mouth. He snatches it from me, swallowing the whole lot before dumping the empty bottle into the bin.

"She was my mum. She was *your* mum," he accuses, stabbing his finger in the air between us. "She barely even knew I existed after I was taken into care, and before that she was so hung up on you that all I became was an inconvenience, a nuisance, someone to hate because she couldn't have *you* to love. Did you know that she kept a photo of you in her wallet? I asked her once who the baby was and do you know what she did?"

"No, what?" I ask.

"She beat me with her belt. Told me that's what *bad boys* get for asking questions they have no business knowing the answers to."

"I'm sorry."

"You're sorry! You're *sorry*! You weren't there when I needed you!" he yells, his face red with anger, with pain and disappointment. "You weren't there to stop her. You weren't there for her to love so she didn't have to hate *me* so much!"

"That's not her fault, kid," Beast coaxes.

"I KNOW THAT!" he shouts. "But it *is* her fault that she's dead. Mum might've loved me if she'd had you back in her life. She might've loved me if I was the one who brought you back to her!"

"Is that why you came to me?" I say, hurting even more now that I understand the real reason he sought me out.

Fuck, that hurts, not because I need him to want me, but because he truly believed that his mum would love him if he was the one to find me. The thing is, I *know* it wouldn't have made a difference with how she felt about and treated him. How unutterably cruel was that woman to make him believe that he was so unloveable? "I thought if I could give her you, she'd love me for it," he admits.

"How did you find out about Kate?" Beast asks for me, understanding that right now I'm too fucking overwhelmed to ask that question myself.

Swiping the back of his hand over his face, Ford roughly wipes away his tears that started falling again. "I dug around in her personal stuff one day a few weeks ago when she was out of it on drugs. I just had this feeling she was hiding something important. So imagine my surprise when I found a birth certificate with your name on it, *Kate Davidson, daughter of Carter Davidson.* Everyone knows who he is. He's practically a celebrity around here. *Was* a celebrity," Ford says, correcting himself. "So I came to find you. I was going to tell you who I was. I was going to introduce you to mum."

"It wouldn't have made a difference," I say softly, getting what he was trying to do and feeling so fucking bad for him. "She wanted to hurt you, Ford. I couldn't risk that. I wouldn't be able to live with myself if I let her go and she finished what she started."

"What do you mean, she wanted to hurt me? Apart from me breaking into her flat, I haven't seen her in months."

"This isn't going to be easy to hear," I say, trying to prepare him, hating that he needs to know the extent of her loathing towards him, but knowing it's the only way he might truly understand my actions, so that he might begin to heal.

"Do you honestly think that anything you've said today has been easy to hear?" he questions angrily.

"No, but this *will* hurt, and I'm sorry for it," I say, reaching for him. He takes a step back.

"Just say it!"

"Your mum didn't just want to hurt you. She made it clear that if Rodriguez—the man who came after me—wanted to kill you, she wouldn't have stood in his way."

"W—what?" he stutters.

"I'm so sorry," I say, not wanting to repeat it again. Once was hard enough.

"She wanted me dead?" he whispers, and that truth, that painful, hurtful truth forces his shoulders to drop and more tears to fall.

He sobs quietly, wrapping his arms around himself as he slides down the kitchen cabinet and rests his forehead against his knees, and this time I don't hesitate. This time I slide down onto the floor beside him and wrap my arm around his shoulders, pulling him into my side. He doesn't flinch away, instead he leans into my side and lets me hold him.

"You're not to blame. Not for her actions. Not for her terrible thoughts. Not for her hatred or evil heart. You're not to blame for her death or her decisions in life, Ford. You were a child who needed a mother to love him. She couldn't give that to you and I'm so, so sorry you had to endure what you have. I'm sorry I didn't know about you. I'm sorry that I didn't step in earlier," I say, forcing the words out through the tightness in my voice. "I want to give you a family, Ford. I truly don't want you to go to another fight club. I want you to train with us. I want you to get stronger. I want you to be in our lives, but I'll also understand if you choose to walk away. You never have to fear me or Beast... we will protect you. Always."

My voice trails off as I meet Beast's gaze, and then we wait. I'm not sure how long Ford remains crying silently in my arms, but by the time his sobs have quietened, his body is limp from fatigue and he snores quietly.

"Should I wake him up?" Beast asks. "I could drive him back home."

"No. I don't want him alone right now. Will you take him up to the spare room? Let him sleep for a bit. It's early anyway. In the meantime I'll call Hudson. I'm going to tell him that I don't want Ford training anywhere else but my club."

"You reckon Hudson is gonna be cool with that given the lecture he gave us both?" Beast asks.

"I love and respect Hudson, but this is non-negotiable. Ford is *my* brother. We'll bring him into the fold at Tales and keep training him. I can keep a better eye on him there anyway."

"Aren't you worried someone might target him?"

"Who, aside from the King?" I ask.

"Stupid question," he admits.

"Look, of course I am, but it's too late now. Even if the King kept that important piece of information of Ford being my half-brother to himself, he's already connected to us, to *me*. I won't announce to the world our relationship but I won't leave him for the sharks either. I'll make sure he's taken care of—"

"*We'll* make sure he's taken care of," Beast cuts in. "Your family is my family, Kate."

"Yes," I nod, agreeing with him, loving him even more for it. "We won't abandon him. The doors of our club will always be open to him, and he will have our protection from this moment on."

"And the King?"

"Better be afraid, because I'm coming for him."

CHAPTER TWENTY-THREE

Enemy Fire

BEAST

The early morning air has a bite to it as we get out of the car and head into Garsons Boatyard. Murky river water laps at the dock and the smell of wood and oil greets us as we step into the main office area that's tucked right beside the yard where a huge boat is docked.

"Is that his?" I ask.

I'm no sailor, and I haven't once stepped foot on a boat, but even a man like me can appreciate this boat's beauty. It's sleek, white, with silver edging, and the sails are cream. Dark oak lines the deck, and the same varnished wood holds up the sail.

"Apparently so," Kate replies, jerking her chin towards

Malakai who walks down the gangplank from the deck towards us. He's dressed in worn jeans, a faded t-shirt full of holes, scuffed-up trainers and looks like he hasn't slept in a few days. Not surprising given he's failed to locate the King and we're here to turn his boat into ash.

"Good morning," he says, greeting us. He's as cool as a fucking cucumber despite his appearance that suggests otherwise. Either this fucker has taken lessons in keeping a lid on his emotions or he's got some news for us.

"Is it?" I ask. "Because from our point of view the only way this morning is going to look any better is if you've found out where the King is hiding."

Malakai nods. "Then I guess it's going to look better."

"Start talking," Kate says, getting straight to the point.

"Not out in the open. Follow me," Malakai replies, walking back the way he came and climbing up the gangplank leading onto the deck of his boat.

I glance over at Kate, noticing the dark circles ringing her eyes. She barely slept last night, tossing and turning, going over her decision with regards to Ford. After she reluctantly dropped him off back at the children's home yesterday evening, Kate and I spent the evening talking to Hudson trying to figure out the best way to protect the kid. Kate wants him to live with her, but Hudson convinced her that for now he'd be safer at the children's home given it has twenty-four hour security and every single person who passes through its doors is vetted beforehand. Kate had argued the toss, but stealing a kid from the custody of the local authority probably isn't the wisest move, given she put a bullet in his mum's brain and I killed his stepfather.

"Watch your step, I've spent the morning waxing the deck.

It's a bit slippery," Malakai warns as we step onto the beauti-fully polished wood.

Taking my hand Kate steps onto the boat, which is even more impressive seeing it up close and personal. A great deal of care and attention has gone into refurbishing it, and a part of me is impressed by the sheer fact a man like Malakai has the skills to both maintain *and* sail such a huge boat.

"It's beautiful," Kate says, her fingers trailing along the rail.

"She is," Malakai agrees.

"She?" I ask, following Malakai as he steps down into the cabin.

"All boats are females."

"Why?" I find myself asking, nothing like a bit of chit-chat to lull a man into a false sense of security before we ruin his fucking life.

"No one knows for certain," he replies. "But historically sailors and the captains of ships were predominately men who used to decorate the bowsprit of a sailing vessel with images of the women they left behind. Add to that the protective female figure of a mother or goddess and the boat ends up being humanised in the same way."

"Right," I reply, pulling a face as I glance over at Kate. "You learn something new every day."

"I can see why you're so attached," Kate says, taking a seat at the small table built into the cabin. Like the deck, the cabin is beautifully maintained. The same polished wood lines the walls with silver, white, and blue accents. It's as sexy as any car I've driven, that's for damn sure, and I can certainly see why this boat is a 'she' with all its curves and natural beauty. But as much as I appreciate it, we ain't here to ogle a boat. We're here to set it alight if Malakai hasn't got the information that we came for.

It's in all of our best interests that he has.

Sliding onto the seat beside Kate, I study Malakai's expression as he opens up his laptop and searches for something on the screen. Right now he isn't giving anything away, and as much as it pisses me off, I've got to admire how he's holding his shit together.

"This has been my home for a few years now," Malakai says, almost as an afterthought. "I'd like to keep it that way."

"And she can continue to be your home, providing you tell me where the King is hiding," Kate says, reaching into her pocket and pulling out a lighter. She rests it on the table between us, using it as a symbol of what will happen if we don't get what we came here for.

"It hasn't been easy. The King doesn't want to be found."

"Not my problem," Kate says, picking up the lighter and striking the flint wheel. A small flame lights up, flickering in the breeze that's coming through the open window to our left.

"You're right, it isn't," Malakai responds, his gaze focussing on the lighter Kate is purposefully striking on and off. "It's been mine."

The look in his eyes right now is the first sign of any real fear I've seen since we've met, and I can't help but admire Kate's instincts about Malakai. He might not care if he lives or dies, but knowing that this boat could be turned to ash has fired a rocket up his arse better than any amount of torture I could threaten him with.

"Show us what you've got then," I say, tapping my fingers on the table, refocusing his attention on the task at hand.

"Bear with me. It'll take a minute or two," he says, tapping on the keyboard before turning the laptop around so we can all see the screen.

"What's this gobbledygook?" I ask, watching a bunch of random green letters and numbers move across the black screen at an impossible speed. Even if it was slow enough to read, I wouldn't be able to make heads nor tails of what I was seeing.

"This is code."

"Code?" Kate questions, frowning.

"Whenever the King and I talk, our conversation is scrambled behind a series of complicated code. Think of it like a brick wall that prevents anyone on the other side of it from seeing what the wall is protecting."

"Okay, so we're looking at a brick wall right now," Kate says.

"Exactly. My conversations with the King are protected by this code. Every time the King wants to contact me, I'm sent a seven digit number that will carve a path through the brick wall —the code—allowing me to converse with him. The number I'm given has a time limit. If I don't enter it within two minutes of receiving the number I remain locked out and I have to wait for a new combination to let me in."

"Clever," I remark.

Kate frowns. "So how does this tell us where the King is hiding?"

"It doesn't."

"So what's the fucking point of showing us this then?" I ask.

"Last night I was sent a seven digit number indicating that the King wanted to speak with me. During that conversation he told me that he'd found out some information about you, Grim. Well, actually, more specifically about your half-brother."

She stiffens beside me, and though this isn't a surprise, hearing Malakai confirm what we already know to be true is sobering as fuck.

"And what did he say exactly?" Kate asks carefully.

"He instructed me to take the boy to him tonight at midnight. I'm assuming your brother was that kid you had in your office the night of my last fight."

"You fucking cunt!" I exclaim, reaching for my gun and pulling it free.

"Wait!" Malakai holds his hands up. "Let me finish."

"Then fucking speak!" I demand, ready to shoot his fucking brains out.

"Do you honestly think I would be sitting here now telling you this if I planned on doing what he asked?"

"Beast, he's got a point," Kate says, resting her hand on my arm.

"I have no interest in hurting that kid," Malakai adds. "I was telling the truth when I said I have no loyalty to the King. In fact, I'll go as far as telling you that I hate him. This is my chance to finally be free of him, once and for all."

"You want him dead?" Kate asks, cocking her head to the side as she stares at Malakai.

"I want my freedom, and his death is the only way I'm going to get it."

"Then tell us where he is so you get to keep your boat and have your freedom."

"On one condition," Malakai says, closing the lid of his laptop and looking between us both.

"You really think that you're in a position to barter with us?" I threaten, keeping the gun pointed at his head.

"You burn my boat, I can assure you that I'll take this information with me to the grave, but if you let me sail out of here right now, I will send you the address of the location he'll be at as soon as I hit open water."

"You expect us to trust you? How do we know you're not going to fuck off without telling us a damn thing?"

"You don't, but I give you my word that I will tell you where the King is as long as you let me go. I have no issue with either of you. I'm just a man who wants to live out the rest of his days on the ocean. That's it. That's all," Malakai says, resting his hands on the table as he waits.

"My head is telling me not to trust you, but my gut...?" Kate says, her voice trailing off as she heaves out a sigh. I know she's running through all of our options and coming up with the same result as me, which is that we're out of options.

"Your gut...?" Malakai prompts.

"There aren't many people I believe in, but someone special once told me to trust my gut because it already knows what my head and my heart are yet to discover. On this occasion, I'm taking their advice."

"So you agree to my terms?"

"Give me your phone," Kate says, holding her hand out. Malakai drops it onto her palm and watches as Kate punches in her telephone number before handing it back to him. "It's because of that person I'm letting you sail out of here."

Malakai meets her gaze and nods. "Thank you."

"You can thank me when the King is dead."

"Fair enough."

"And Malakai..." Kate leans across the table and grips his arm, whilst giving him a look that could slay a fucking army.

"Yes?"

"If I'm wrong and this is a trap, not only will I kill the King, I will spend the rest of my days hunting you down, and when I find you I will set this boat alight with you inside of it."

He nods, something close to respect lighting up his eyes. "I wouldn't expect anything less."

CHAPTER TWENTY-FOUR

Wild Blood

GRIM

"This is definitely the address?" Beast asks quietly as we crouch behind a partially collapsed brick wall and look up at the back entrance to the abandoned warehouse just outside of Reading. It's pitch black, the only light coming from the moon and the smattering of stars not already hidden by the rain clouds above us.

"Yes. Malakai was very specific with his instructions."

"I hope you're right about him," Beast says, pulling down his balaclava so that only his eyes and mouth are visible as his gaze skirts over the building, clocking the boarded-up windows and heavy metal doors. "It's a perfect place to ambush a couple of gangsters."

"Which is why I brought Cleveland and Harris along. I'm not stupid, Beast," I reply, my voice clipped, strained. "If this isn't over in fifteen minutes they'll come after us."

"Hey," he says, reaching for me, his gloved hand gripping mine. "I never said you were. I trust your instincts."

"I appreciate that," I say, hoping to fuck I'm not leading us both to our deaths. Just thinking about how much I could lose tonight if this all goes wrong makes me want to reconsider, but equally with Beast by my side I know I can do anything. The King is right to be scared of a man who gathered an army from around the world and a woman who gained their loyalty and built a business from the ground up. Together we're a force to be reckoned with. "Thank you."

"For what?"

"For being there for me even when I didn't realise you were. For being here now. For loving me..."

Beast reaches up and cups my face. "Don't do that. Don't you dare say goodbye."

"I need you to know that I appreciate you, that I *love* you."

"You can tell me that when this is over and you're fucking me like the queen you are."

"Beast—" I begin, but he cuts me off.

"No, show me the woman who was strong enough to shoot the man she loved to prove to the world she shouldn't be fucked with. Show me the woman who commands respect from the criminals who were foolish enough to underestimate her. Show me the woman who'll do anything to protect the ones she loves," he demands, clutching my face in his palms, forcing me to meet his gaze. "Where's she at, huh?"

Gritting my teeth and forcing every last dark thought out of my head, I nod. "She's still here. *I'm still here.*"

"Good because tonight the King dies. That's the only way this story ends."

"Yes," I nod, allowing his words to sink in, to fuel my determination. I didn't get this far by being a meek bitch, and I'm not about to start now. Tonight the Queen of Tales is going to claim her throne once and for all. "Let's get this done."

"That's my queen." Beast grins, pressing a hard kiss against my lips before he pulls the black cloth bag from his jacket pocket and places it over my head, covering up my face and hair. "You good?"

"I'm good. You think this will work?" I ask, turning away from him so that he can tie my wrists behind my back. Our plan is simple, Beast is about the same height and build as Malakai and I'm not much bigger than Ford. With my baggy clothing, and my head covered I can easily pass myself off as a teenage boy. When Beast hands me over to the King, that's when I strike.

"Providing the King's still as arrogant as he's always been, this will work. You've got to remember, he believes no one would ever have the balls to betray him, let alone walk into the vipers den like we are about to now. Doing this should get you close enough to kill the fucker," Beast says, tying a loose knot around my wrists just to give the illusion that I'm bound. "I want to apologise in advance if I'm rough, we have to make this look real."

"I know," I reply, flexing my fingers, the heel of my hand

pressing against the base of the seven inch knife hidden up my sleeve. First chance I get, I'm driving it directly into the King's heart.

"Are you ready?"

"Yeah, I'm ready."

With his palm resting between my shoulder blades, Beast guides me across the asphalt and towards the metal door that has been left partially open. As we step inside, I hear the low murmur of male voices talking and peer through the bag covering my head, trying to make out the shadowy figures at the other end of the building.

"Malakai, it's been a long, *long* time," a familiar voice says.

Just like Malakai had promised, the King is here. My gut instincts were right, Malakai was telling the truth. Now we just have to pray that this isn't a trap.

Beast shoves me forward with a grunt of acknowledgement. Although the King is unlikely to recognise Beast's voice, we agreed that he should keep his answers brief in order to avoid giving himself away too soon.

"And I see you've delivered my package. Excellent," the King continues, unconcerned that *Malakai* is less than chatty. I don't need to be able to see his face to know he's smirking, I can hear the arrogance in his voice all the same. "Any problems on the way here?"

"No," comes Beast's gruff reply as he shoves me forward, his gun pressed into my back as he acts the part just like we'd planned. "Move!"

I stumble forward, barely able to see where I'm going and that's when I trip over something laying across the floor. Without my hands to break my fall I go down hard, my knees cracking against the concrete, sending a jolt of pain up my spine. I muffle my cry, forcing myself to swallow the pain. *Fuck, that hurt!*

Tears well up in my eyes, and I blink them away, forcing myself to move as Beast grabs my upper arm and hauls me upright, whispering an apology under his breath as the King and whoever he's brought with him laugh at my expense.

"Careful, we don't want to break the kid, *yet*," the King says as I limp towards him.

Beast relaxes his grip then squeezes twice in quick succession, indicating that the King has the company of just two more men. Either the King really does trust Malakai, or he's a fool.

I'm going with the latter.

"Grim's reaction is going to be priceless when she realises I have her brother," he continues with a laugh. "That bitch might think she has the bollocks to go toe-to-toe with me, but she's going to learn very quickly that she's just another cunt that needs to be taught a lesson. She's been a useful tool, but now that Tales is the best fight club in Europe, I've no further use for her. The only position of importance she'll have from this moment, is on her knees sucking my dick. Mark my words, she'll fall in line."

"Yeah, boss," one of the men with him agrees. "She'd look good on her knees."

Beast's grip tightens, and subconsciously or not, he draws me closer to his side, stalling for a moment. I can feel the way his body vibrates with anger, and I pray he doesn't break character before it's time. He just needs to focus on the outcome we need and not lose his cool to a few incendiary words. Despite the King's opinion of me, I'm a big girl with very thick skin. His words don't upset me, they *fuel* me.

"Bring him to me!" the King snaps, forcing Beast to act.

In a few more strides, Beast releases me from his grip and shoves me into the King's chest.

Three things happen at once.

The King pulls the bag from off my head.

Beast pulls out his gun and shoots the King's men right between the eyes.

And I pull out the knife tucked up my sleeve and drive it into the King's heart.

There's no hesitation.

No second-guessing.

Just action.

"The only cunt that needs to be taught a lesson is you," I say as the King's eyes widen with shock and I push all my weight against the handle of the blade driving it deeper into his chest.

Blood gurgles up and out of his throat and he doesn't even have the time to comprehend what's happened before the light in his eyes flickers out and he crumples to the floor in a heap.

Standing over his body, my chest heaving, I reach down and grip the handle, pulling the blade free.

It's over.

The King's dead.

CHAPTER TWENTY-FIVE

Struggle, Succeed, Rewind, Repeat

GRIM - A MONTH LATER

"Shit!" I exclaim, gritting my teeth as Beast presses the needle into my skin, filling in the outline of the rose tattoo with colour. He's already completed the section on my neck and décolletage, now he's working on my upper arm. There are two more roses to fill and then it's done.

"Nearly there," he says, briefly glancing up at me before focussing back on his artwork.

Two weeks ago we were in this exact same position as he outlined my tattoo, now we're back to finish it off.

"I think you're enjoying this," I grumble, pressing my eyes shut at the bite of pain, whilst waiting for the rush of endorphins to kick in. A lot of people enjoy getting a tattoo, and are addicted to the pain, I can see why.

"By *this* you mean getting to tattoo the woman I love with my artwork? Of course I'm enjoying it. Biggest buzz of my life so far."

"Is that so?" I ask as he grins mercilessly.

"Just relax into the pain, I promise that once you embrace it, this whole experience will be a thousand times better."

"I know what'll make me feel a thousand times better and it's not that needle digging into my flesh," I joke, biting on my lip as a sexy smile spreads across his face.

God, I love this man.

"I guess I could use a break," he says, resting the tattoo gun on the metal trolley desk next to him.

"*You* could use a break? See, I knew you loved torturing me. I bet you've been hard this whole time watching me squirm."

"Hard as granite," he admits as I swing my legs over the side of the recliner, and he positions himself between them, his hands sliding up my thighs beneath the skirt of my dress. "Those little whimpers and gasps you've been making turn me the fuck on, but you know that already, don't you?"

"Really, I had no idea?" I hold in a smile.

"Funny."

"You love seeing me writhe beneath you, don't you?"

"Fucking love it," he agrees.

"So, how are you going to make it up to me?" I ask, letting that smile spread across my face as his fingers reach my core and he realises I'm not wearing any knickers.

"Oh fuck, Kate! Are you trying to kill me?" he groans,

pressing the palm of his hands against my upper thighs and urging me to widen my legs. Of course I oblige.

"Just a bit everyday. What do the French call it? *La petite mort?*"

"Little death," he mutters. "Those French know what they're talking about because I'm in heaven every time I touch you, let alone come inside of you."

"Same," I whisper, pulling up my skirt and revealing my already slick pussy.

His gaze drops to my core as his thumbs gently pull apart my outer lips. "And there's me thinking you weren't enjoying getting tattooed. You're wet, Kate."

"I wasn't enjoying it," I lie.

"Your body tells me otherwise," he replies, dropping a delicate kiss to my mound as his thumb swirls over my clit. "I will never get tired of tasting you."

"I'll never get tired of you tasting me either," I reply, gasping as he swirls his tongue around my clit then lower to my hole.

"Then we're both in luck," he chuckles, sliding his hands over my thighs and around my arse as he pulls me towards the edge of the recliner. "Lean back and put your legs over my shoulder."

"Shouldn't we lock the door?" I ask, following his instructions and feeling the sting of my tattoo as I adjust my position.

Beast raises a brow, kissing my inner thigh. "Trent and Casper know not to enter before knocking."

"Shame," I say with a giggle.

"Don't even joke. I told you before, I'm not sharing you with anyone. *Ever.* Got it?" he says, nipping my clit gently.

"Fuck!" I exclaim, the pain and the pleasure sending bolts of electricity up and down my spine.

"Behave, Kate, or I'll make sure you die a little death over and over again for the next fucking hour."

"Hey," I protest. "I never said I wanted you to share me, but someone watching could be fun?"

"Absolutely not!" he shoots back. "I practically want to throttle the motherfuckers just glancing your way on a normal day, I do not want to be responsible for their deaths."

"Just mine then?" I counter huskily as he lowers his mouth to my pussy and licks me from arse to clit sending my eyes rolling into the back of my head.

"Never, there's only ever going to be pleasure for my queen."

"Says the man who's trying to kill me right now," I exclaim as he works his magic, and as much as I like to tease Beast, I know that I'd never want to share him either. Not ever.

"Shh, baby, let me show you just how much I love you," he says, and pretty soon I've forgotten about the sting of my tattoo as he plunges his tongue inside of me until I'm shuddering and jerking in my very own *la petite mort*.

Another hour later and my tattoo is complete and I stare at it in the mirror with Beast standing behind me.

"Do you like it?"

"Like it? I love it? I love you," I say, turning around to face him, letting out a small laugh. "We made it, didn't we?"

"You sound surprised?"

"I am a little to be honest."

"I'm not. I always had faith in you, in us. That hasn't changed and that will *never* change no matter what is thrown our way. Besides, a little dicky bird told us we will get our happily ever after."

"That's right, she did, didn't she?"

He cups my face in his hands, studying me with silent appraisal. "There's something I've been meaning to ask." He draws in a breath, watching me closely.

"What is it?"

"Will you—"

Right at that moment, my phone buzzes, vibrating across the desk with an incoming call. "Shit, sorry," I say. "I should probably take that."

"No, it's cool. It can wait," Beast replies, tucking his hands in his pocket as he steps aside.

I reach for my phone and press the answer button, lifting my phone to my ear and wait.

"Grim?"

"Malakai?" I reply, frowning as I look over at Beast.

"What does that fucker want?" he grumbles, folding his arms across his chest as he glares at the phone in my hand like Malakai could climb out of it any moment now and ruin his day.

The line crackles and I swear I can hear thunder rumbling in the background. "What is it?" I ask, my gut churning suddenly.

"It wasn't—" Malakai begins, but what sounds like a loud crack of thunder comes through the line, preventing me from hearing the rest of his sentence.

"Shit, Malakai, I can't hear you properly," I say, punching the loudspeaker button and resting the phone on the table so that Beast can listen as well.

"I said it wasn't him!" he shouts, and the churning in my gut feels just like the stormy sea that Malakai is evidently sailing on right now.

"What wasn't him?" Beast bites out, stepping closer to the phone as if that will help make this conversation any clearer.

"The man you killed. It wasn't the King!" he shouts, and for a moment all I hear is white noise, or maybe that's just the sudden rush of blood to my head.

"The fuck?!" Beast exclaims, picking up the phone and shouting into it. "You'd better be fucking joking or I'm gonna reach into this phone and strangle your bastard neck!"

"Listen, I'm heading into a squall and the call might cut out at any moment, but I wanted to tell you as soon as I found out. You need to watch your back. This isn't over."

"What are you saying exactly?" I ask.

"The man you killed wasn't the King. It wasn't him," he repeats, louder this time.

"Yes it was. I should know, I stabbed a seven inch knife into his fucking chest!" I reply, shaking my head in disbelief.

"That *wasn't* him—"

"You're making zero fucking sense, arsewipe!" Beast cuts in, losing his cool.

"Tell me this, was the man you stabbed the same man your father did business with?"

"*Yes*," I confirm. "Beast and I met him in person. The man I killed was the man who called himself the King, the same man we all ate dinner with, and who watched Beast kill my dad!"

"Then he's had you fooled this whole time. The man you thought was the King wasn't the *real* King. He was his second in command. I should've known it wouldn't have been that easy to kill him," Malakai says, the line crackling with the storm, whilst my insides churn with its own cyclone.

"How do you know? You didn't see the body. You said your-self you haven't talked in person for years and that you only communicate via the fucking internet. How. Do. You. Know?" Beast repeats.

"Last night I spoke to someone who knows the King as well as I do... *Fuck!*" Malakai yells suddenly, and for a moment all we can hear is static.

"Is this really happening?" I ask, looking at Beast in disbelief.

"I don't know. I don't fucking know."

"Are you still there?" Malakai says through the speaker half a minute later.

"Of course we are!" Beast asserts. "Explain. Now!"

"The person who talked to the King, go a long way back."

"And who is this person exactly?" I ask.

"His brother."

Beast runs a hand through his hair. "The King has a brother?"

"Two," Malakai says.

"And his brother told you about this conversation because...?"

"Because we're family. Because the King is my cousin. Because not only do I want him dead, so do his brothers."

"You're his cousin? *Jesus.*"

"Yes," Malakai confirms. "The King is alive and well, and he isn't happy that he was outsmarted by a *girl*. His words, not mine."

Snatching up the phone, I squeeze it tightly in my hand. "Alive and well, *where?*"

"We don't know. He's very good at hiding," Malakai says.

"No shit!" Beast yells.

"I'm sorry to be the bearer of bad news. But this isn't over. Not for you and not for me."

"Not over for you? You're in the middle of the fucking ocean. It's not as if he can get to you. Fucking convenient if you ask me!" Beast snaps. "We never should've trusted you."

"If I'd have known he was using someone to act as him, I would've told you. I wasn't lying when I said I wanted him dead. That hasn't changed."

"Then it looks like you owe us a debt," Kate says, glancing at me briefly before she straightens her spine and grits her teeth. "I'm going to call that in one day."

"You have my word that the second you do, I'll be there."

"And what do you suggest we do now?" Beast asks. "Because I don't know about you, Kate, I don't fancy waiting for the first bullet to be fired, do you?"

"I know him. He won't act. At least not yet. You've surprised him, and he's wary now. He won't take you on unless he knows he can win. Sit tight. Keep your eyes and ears open and keep building your army. I will call you with any news as soon as I get it. We'll find him, *eventually.*"

And with that the line goes dead and I'm left staring at the phone, unable to speak...

Fall In Line

GRIM - TEN YEARS LATER

"That's where you end it? Where's the rest?" Pen asks me as she places my diary on the coffee table and watches me apply the last touches to my makeup. I can't believe this day has finally come, and I'm able to share it with the most important people in my life without fear of some bastard gangster trying to ruin it for us.

"Rest! Rest!" Iris repeats, clambering up on Pen's lap as they both wait for me to respond.

My best friend and my daughter have always had an incredible bond, which was strengthened when I had to leave Iris in the care of Pen and her partners for a couple of weeks four months ago. Beast, Ford and his friend Camden accompanied me to a remote castle in Scotland with every intention of rescuing Christy from her kidnappers. Well, I say rescue... Because as it turned out, my little sister didn't need rescuing. She's a Davidson after all.

She's a bad bitch just like all of the women in this room.

My gaze falls to Iris as she babbles happily on Pen's lap. At the time, I hated leaving her, but I also knew that she was in safe hands. It didn't do her any harm, she's the happiest, most well-rounded almost two year old in the world and that has as much to do with her extended family as it does me and Beast.

"Well?" Pen insists.

"I guess I didn't feel the need to write down my feelings, not when I had Beast to share them with," I say with a shrug, brushing on a layer of blush to my cheeks. "To be honest things got kind of insane for a few years, and I didn't really have time to keep it up. Besides, a lot of the stuff that happened after that point in my life wasn't really my story, not in quite the same way anyway."

"But the King?" Pen asks, planting a kiss on the top of Iris's head. "You never did tell me exactly what happened to him..."

"Don't worry, he got his comeuppance," Asia says, stepping out of the bathroom in her fitted, black Versace dress, long purple hair and glammed up to the hilt. She looks incredible, and I'm proud to call her family. A queen in her own right, especially given the strength and courage she showed to keep her own family safe, including my brother, Ford. "We made sure of it."

Pen frowns. "We?"

"Yes. Me, Camden, Ford, Sonny, Eastern, the Freed brothers. Grim too and my old principal of Oceanside Academy, the reform school where I met my guys. Malakai too actually. Is he here by the way?" Asia asks.

"Couldn't make it. Connie is heavily pregnant and he didn't want to make her travel all this way when she's so close to giving birth."

"Fair enough. I'm glad they're happy," Asia says.

"Yeah, me too."

"Wow, okay. I think as soon as Grim and Beast are back from Paris, we need another girl's weekend because I want your whole story, Asia. It sounds like it's a good one."

"Not quite the fairy tale like Grim's," Asia says, winking at me.

"Oh I don't know. It seems like we've all managed to get our own happily ever after," Pen says as Iris clambers off her lap and leaps into Asia's arms.

"I guess you're right," Asia agrees, hauling Iris onto her hip and kissing her on the nose.

"You know I saw *that* coming too," Christy calls out from the bathroom where she's putting on some lip gloss.

"What?" Pen, Asia and I all ask simultaneously.

"Asia's happy ever after. Though at the time I had zero idea who you or Ford were, given Kate was still in her *I'm going to keep my siblings a secret* phase."

"I did it to—"

"*Keep us safe,*" Christy finishes for me with an indulgent smile. "I know. We know, and we love you for it," she says, stepping out of the bathroom in her pale green Vivienne Westwood dress.

Apart from a touch of mascara she's not wearing any other

makeup, and her birthmark is proudly on display. She stopped covering it up when her men, Jakub, Leon and Konrad, otherwise known as The Masks, said they loved her all the more for it. They might've had a rocky start, and some days I still have the urge to shoot them in the nuts for what they put her through in the beginning of their relationship, but they've come a long way, and they make her happy so I have to respect that.

"You know I'm still pissed at you for not warning me that the pipe was going to burst at the club last week," Pen says, changing the subject. "You could've saved me thousands of pounds in repairs. The place is still a bloody wreck. I'm not sure when I'm going to get it up and running again."

"Sorry about that, I don't get to choose what I see, and burst pipes aren't usually something the universe deems important enough to show me."

"Not unless we're talking about *the* stud-muffin's burst pipe, right?" Asia snorts, and I glare at her whilst Pen and Christy crack up with laughter.

"Did you *have* to bring that up today of all days?!" I groan.

"Oh come on, it's funny," Asia protests.

"I'm still not over it," I say, scowling at my sister, my cheeks heating. Even though she's an adult now, I still can't get over the fact that she had a vision of one of the most intimate scenes between me and Beast when she was just a child, and then *lied* to me about it for years.

Urgh. Not cool.

"Listen, it's not as if I saw you fucking," Christy says, cackling. "It was just a brief moment in time."

"Christy, we were *naked* when we were having that conversation," I protest, feeling all kinds of icky.

"If it makes you feel any better it was only Beast's arse that I saw," she replies with a shrug.

"Oh my god! You poor thing," Asia snorts, and a moment later we're all laughing again, interrupted only by a tap on the door.

"Are you ready?" a familiar voice asks through the thick wood.

Asia opens the door, the love of her life standing on the other side of it, or one of them at least. Unlike me, Asia is in a relationship with four men, one of them my little brother. In fact, I'm the only one of the four of us girls that is with just one man. Not sure how they manage to juggle all that testosterone in all honesty. Beast is a handful all on his own. His big dick energy is more than enough for me, more to the point his *moby dick* is the only dick for me.

"You look beautiful," Ford says, grasping Asia's cheek and smacking a kiss against her ruby-red lips, before he places another kiss on Iris's head.

"Mwah. Mwah. Mwah," she babbles, delighted to see her uncle Ford.

"Are you ready, Grim?" Ford asks, stepping into the room. "You look amazing by the way, Beast is going to have a heart attack when he finally sees you. Seriously, the guy's a mess. Dax, Xeno and Hudson have been trying to calm him down."

"Is it working?" I ask, my heart squeezing at the thought.

"Nope." Ford laughs, taking Iris's chubby hand and kissing it. "Your daddy is going to need a stiff drink or five."

"Daddy! Poo. Poo." Iris yells, squirming in Asia's arms.

Ford barks out a laugh. "Yep, Daddy's shitting a brick."

"Stop that!" Asia admonishes. "We don't need her first full sentence to be full of swear words!"

"Oops. Will you be punishing me for it later?" Ford asks, a gleam in his eyes that I don't need to see ever again, thanks very much.

"Behave," Asia says, tutting. "Grim is traumatised enough as it is."

Christy snorts. "Grim traumatised? *I* was the one who witnessed the whole dick conversation and the crack of Beast's arse!"

"Wait what?!" Ford asks, his eyes widening with disbelief. "You need to fill me in!"

"Not a chance in Hell!" I exclaim, cringing a little inside.

"Oh come on, this is way too juicy to let go!" Ford snorts with laughter. "Just wait until I tell the lads."

"Don't you dare!" Asia warns.

"Aren't we late?" I ask, gathering up the skirt of my dress and trying to change the subject. I mean, this is supposed to be the most magical day of my life, I do not want to relive the fact my baby sister saw me and Beast in a vision in post coital bliss, thank you very much.

"Oh shi—! Sugarplums," Asia exclaims looking at her watch and ignoring Ford's smirk. "Would you like me to take Iris through now?"

"Please, I'd just like a minute with Ford and Christy if that's okay?" I ask, looking from Asia to Pen, who smiles as she stands, her gold A-line Gucci dress floating around her ankles like a wisp of a cloud around the top of a mountain. It's the perfect dress for her, and she looks incredible in it. Her Breakers are going to lose their mind when they see her.

"Sure thing," Pen says, pulling me in for a quick hug before she leaves the room with Asia and Iris.

"So," Ford says, stepping into the room.

"So," Christy repeats, taking one of his hands and one of mine. I reach for Ford's other hand and we stand in a little circle just looking at one another.

"You okay? Nervous?" Ford asks, his dirty blonde hair styled off his face, making him look especially handsome. Long gone is the lost little boy who was jaded by life. Asia has been good for him. Sonny, Eastern and Camden too. They've got an incredible bond, one that many can only dream of ever experiencing in their lifetime. I'm so happy they found each other.

"I'm not nervous at all. I'm *happy*," I say, a laugh bubbling up my throat. "Though admittedly there were times that I never thought this day would come. But I always had faith. Mainly because a little girl once told me that I'd get my happily ever after."

Christy smiles, her eyes welling with happy tears. "You deserve it. You both do. Look what you've done for me and Ford. For Asia and Pen. You and Beast, you're good people like I always knew you were."

"And you're my family," I reply, swallowing back the lump in my throat. "Come here," I say, folding my arms around my little brother and baby sister, thankful that they got their happily ever afters too.

Beast of Burden

BEAST

THE MUSIC BEGINS to play and I have to admit, I feel like I'm about to lose my guts out of my arsehole and ruin this banging Ted Baker suit. Thing is, everyone thinks I'm nervous because I'm about to marry the love of my life.

I'm not.

I'm nervous because somehow I got talked into doing a performance right here at Tales on my motherfucking wedding day by those arsehole Breakers who call themselves my friends.

Fuckwads.

We've been practising for weeks. Whenever Kate thought I was training at the gym with the other fighters at the club, I was secretly meeting with the lads, and going over this bastard routine.

I mean, what the *fuck* was I thinking?

How the hell did I let Dax persuade me to do this elaborate number where the Breakers are spinning on their knees down the fucking aisle and I've got these complicated dance steps.

Even Hudson and his brothers, as well as Ford and his bros, are joining in.

I mean seriously, I'm a fucking cage fighter not Micheal-bloody-Flately.

"Ah fuck! I'm gonna be sick," I say to Connall who just slaps me on the back and grins.

"Mate, you wanted to be the ultimate romantic. This shit is legendary. You'll be getting guaranteed blowjobs for the rest of your days if you pull this off."

"Fuck off, you're not even taking part!"

"Can't, sprained my ankle training with you in the gym," he replies, smirking.

"How fucking convenient!" I gripe.

"Fuck!" I exclaim, looking up at Dax who gives me a wink and then steps out of the row of seats just as Pen, Asia and Christy enter the warehouse.

Behind them, Kate and Ford follow and for a moment my heart stops fucking beating.

Fuck me, she's a vision.

Next to me Connall whistles, but I barely register him as my eyes lock with Kate's and she gives me the most dazzling smile before her attention is taken by Dax who steps out into the aisle and starts twirling on his right foot like one of those spinning top toys. The bastard makes dancing look effortless.

Pen gasps, this is as much of a surprise for her as it is for Asia and Grim. Even Christy looks shocked and we all know that barely anything gets past her. But the surprise doesn't stop there and they all look on in amazement as Eastern, Sonny, Camden, York and Zayn step out of their seats dotted around the space and start dancing the routine that Xeno has been teaching us all for the past few weeks. Of course the guests love it and start cheering and whistling. A few get to their feet as well, joining in just for the hell of it. Beside me Connall snorts with laughter, he knows as well as I that I can't fucking dance.

"Oh mate, you better pull this off or you're going to look like a right tit," Connall whispers as Xeno leaps off a seat halfway down the aisle and somersaults in the air, landing on the floor in front of his girlfriend, Pen. He reaches up and presses a kiss against her hand then looks over his shoulder at me and nods.

Fuck. Fuck. Fuck.

Back to the panicking.

Fortunately for me, Kate is distracted as Hudson, Bryce and Max all stand next, throwing off their suit jackets before stepping into the aisle and joining in on the dance too.

If you've watched the movie Dirty Dancing, then their moves ain't far off that sequence at the end of the movie when Johnny lifts Baby into the air. Throw in a bit of hip-hop, and a couple Bachata steps and this is the torture I've been inflicted with.

"To be fucking fair, *I'd* give you all a lifetime of blowjobs after this," Connall mutters, barking out a laugh as I elbow him in the stomach.

"Shut the fuck up," I mutter under my breath, sweat sliding down my temple as it nears my cue. I'm so sick with nerves that for a moment I don't really take in the full vision that is my soon to be wife until our eyes meet, and just like that the music fades, and with it my fear.

"Wow," she mouths, tears in her eyes as she looks at me.

"You look beautiful," I mouth back, then draw in a deep breath as I step from the raised platform we're standing on, down onto the aisle to join my friends as the verse of the song, *Beast of Burden* begins to play.

Throwing out my arm, I spin on my feet just like Dax taught me. Then I cross one foot in front of the other, duck down and click my fingers as I dance up the aisle, singing along to the song as I move.

Flipping up the lapel of my jacket, the guys all give me space to move between them, then fall into step behind me, copying my moves.

We dance up the aisle. Mostly I hit my cues, and sometimes

I fuck it up, but none of that matters when all I see is the biggest, most beautiful smile on my woman's face. Spinning on my heel, swaying my hips, clicking my fingers, I dance up the aisle towards the only woman I will ever love. Fuck, she takes my breath away in her figure-hugging cream lace dress that hugs her tits, waist and arse, falling to the floor in a swathe of fabric.

Reaching her, my fucking heart pounding in my mother-fucking chest, I drop to my knees and grasp her hand, pressing a kiss to her hand.

"This is... This is *crazy*," she laughs as all of our guests get to their feet, cheering and clapping.

"Crazy bad, or crazy good?" I ask, looking up at her, my chest heaving from the effort.

"Crazy good," she laughs, beaming at me as I rise to my feet.

"Thank fuck, I thought you might decide you didn't want to marry me after you saw me dance."

Ford slaps me on the back, winking. "Not a chance, mate. That was smooth," he says, then gives me her hand, his smile wobbling a little now. "Love her for the rest of your days for me, yeah?"

"Always have, always will," I reply, fucking choking on the lump in my throat.

"And you take care of him, he's a goodun," Ford adds, kissing Kate on the cheek.

"Always," she agrees, smiling through her tears as she hugs her brother.

Stepping back, Asia moves forward, Iris wriggling in her arms as she reaches for us both.

"Daddy!"

I take her from Asia and press a kiss against her curly hair. "Hey, sweetheart. You look so pretty."

"Mummy!" she exclaims.

"Mummy too. She looks good enough to eat," I say, laughing through the fucking emotion. "Fuck, I love you both so much."

"We love you too," Kate replies, taking my hand. "Shall we do this then?"

"Nothing's gonna stop me," I reply, taking her hand in mine and leading her back down the aisle, Iris in my arms as we walk towards the Vicar who's waiting patiently for us.

A few minutes later, Kate has said her vows and now it's time for me to say mine. Pulling out the folded piece of paper from my jacket pocket, I take a deep breath, casting my gaze over the words I know by heart. Words I wrote down that same night I tattooed her hand print onto my chest and asked her to be patient, to wait for me.

Taking a deep breath, I hand her the piece of paper and recite the words from memory.

"You and me, we're two sides of the same coin. You're the Kate to my Roger, the Princess to my Beast, the Queen to my King. You're my beating heart, my soulmate, my *every* happy memory. You're the heroine of *my* story, Kate. Your heart, your courage, your strength, your beauty and badassery, your beautiful fucking pussy—sorry Vicar," I say, laughing sheepishly as our guests join in. "I never believed in love, or happily ever after until I met you. But I do now. *I do now*. You were made for me, Kate, as I was made for you. Two people who never believed it would be possible to love in this crazy, violent fucking world have found our happily ever after. We found it in each other, and I want you to know that I will love you until my very last breath."

"Until our last breath," she agrees, stepping into my arms and sealing our vow with a kiss.

And that's exactly what we do.

Through the trials and the tribulations.

The laughter and the tears.

The fucking and the fighting.

The good and the bad times.

Through loss and sorrow, happiness and joy.

We love each other until our very last breath.

The End.

AUTHOR NOTE

Well, there we have it. Grim and Beast's love story is complete. I hope you enjoyed reading their love story as much as I enjoyed finally bringing it to life!

Like I mentioned in the Foreword, Grim and Beast are well known characters and appear as cameos in other series of mine. Please refer to the Foreword for more information about the recommended reading order, and which characters cameos in each series.

But back to Grim and Beast. These two characters have been the thread that ties many of my series together. They've always been there in the background begging for me to write their story. In fact, my readers have also been doing the same for some time now, so I was happy to finally give them their happily ever after.

If you're new to my books and have joined this world by reading Grim & Beast's duet, then welcome, thank you for taking a chance on my books! I hope this duet has encouraged you to pick up some of my other series. You've got a whole universe to discover!

To all my readers who've been with me for some time. Thank you. Thank you for reading my books, thank you for wanting Grim & Beast's story. Thank you for having my back and supporting me. Thank you for making my dreams come true!

This book is truly for you. I wrote it with you in mind. If this duet was Grim and Beast's love letter to their daughter, Iris. Then their story is my love letter to you all.

Much love,

Bea xoxo

ABOUT BEA PAIGE

Bea Paige lives a very secretive life in London...

She likes red wine and Haribo sweets (preferably together) and occasionally swings around poles when the mood takes her.

Bea loves to write about love and all the different facets of such a powerful emotion. When she's not writing about love and passion, you'll find her reading about it and ugly crying.

Bea is always writing, and new ideas seem to appear at the most unlikely time, like in the shower or when driving her car.

She has lots more books planned, so be sure to subscribe to her newsletter: beapaige.co.uk/newsletter-sign-up

ALSO BY BEA PAIGE

The Deana-dhe Duet (dark reverse harem)

1 Debts & Diamonds

2 Curses & Cures

Grim & Beast's Duet (M/F second-chance, bodyguard romance)

#1 Tales You Win

#2 Heads You Lose

Their Obsession Duet (dark reverse harem)

#1 The Dancer and The Masks

#2 The Masks and The Dancer

Academy of Stardom

(friends-to-enemies-lovers reverse harem)

#1 Freestyle

#2 Lyrical

3 Breakers

4 Finale

Academy of Misfits

(bully/academy reverse harem)

#1 Delinquent

#2 Reject

#3 Family

#4 Academy of Misfits box set

Finding Their Muse

(dark contemporary reverse harem)

#1 Steps

#2 Strokes

#3 Strings

#4 Symphony

#5 Finding Their Muse box set

The Brothers Freed Series

(contemporary reverse harem)

#1 Avalanche of Desire

#2 Storm of Seduction

#3 Dawn of Love

#4 Brothers Freed Boxset

Contemporary Standalone

Beyond the Horizon

For all up to date book releases please visit

www.beapaige.co.uk

Lightning Source UK Ltd.
Milton Keynes UK
UKHW020040110123
415109UK00015B/814